LOVE LIFE

ZERUYA SHALEV, poet and novelist, was raised on a kibbutz in Israel and now lives in Jerusalem. She has a Master's degree in biblical studies and is chief literary editor of an Israeli publishing house. *Love Life* is her first work of fiction to be translated into English; it is also translated into eight other languages.

DALYA BILU is a well-known translator of Hebrew literature and has been awarded a number of prizes for her work including The Israel Culture and Education Ministry Prize for Translation, and the *Times Literary Supplement* and Jewish Book Council Award for Hebrew–English Translation.

LOVE LIFE

Zeruya Shalev

Translated from the Hebrew by
Dalya Bilu

CANONGATE

First published in the UK in English in 2001
by Canongate Books Ltd,
14 High Street, Edinburgh EH1 1TE.
First published in Israel in 1997 by Keter.

10 9 8 7 6 5 4 3 2 1

The publishers gratefully acknowledge general
subsidy from the Scottish Arts Council towards
the Canongate International series.

British Library Cataloguing-in-Publication Data
A catalogue record for this book is available on
request from the British Library

ISBN 1 84195 184 6

Typeset by Palimpsest Book Production Limited,
Polmont, Stirlingshire
Printed and bound in Great Britain by
Creative Print & Design Wales, Ebbw Vale

www.canongate.net

1

He's not my father and not my mother so why does he open the door of their house to me, filling the narrow space with his body, squeezing the door handle, and I begin to retreat, I must have made a mistake, but the decorated plate insists that it is their house, at least it was their house, and in a weak voice I ask, what's happened to my parents, and he opens his big, grey mouth wide, nothing's happened to them, Ya'ara, my name flutters in his mouth like a fish in a net, and I burst inside, my arm brushing against his cold, smooth arm, cross the empty living room, and open the closed door of their bedroom.

As if caught red-handed, they jerk their faces towards me, and I see that she's lying in bed, her head wrapped in a flowered kitchen towel, her hand holding her forehead as if to keep it from falling, and my father is sitting on the edge of the bed, a glass of water swaying in his hand, moving rhythmically from side to side, and on the floor between his feet a nervous little puddle has already formed. What's wrong, I ask, and she says, I don't feel well, and my father says, only two minutes ago she was feeling fine, and she complains, you see, he never believes me. What did the doctor say, I ask, and my father says, what doctor, she's as healthy as an ox, I wish I was as healthy as she is, and I insist, but you called a doctor, didn't you? He opened the door to me, didn't he?

That's no doctor, my father laughs, that's my friend Aryeh Even, don't you remember Aryeh? And my mother says, why should she remember him, she wasn't even born when he left the country, and my father stands up, I'd better go to him, it's not nice to leave him by himself. He seems to be doing okay, I say, he acts as if the place belongs to him, and my mother begins to cough, her eyes redden, and he thrusts the glass of water, which is already almost empty, at her impatiently and she wheezes, stay with me, Shlomo, I don't feel well, but he's already at the door, Ya'ara will stay with you, he says, stepping into the transparent puddle, what are children for?

Angrily she drinks the rest of the water and shakes the wet towel off her head, and her sparse hair sticks up in sad wisps like a hedgehog and when she tries to make it lie flat on her scalp I think of the braid she used to have, the magnificent braid that accompanied her everywhere, as full of life as a kitten, and I say to her, why did you cut it off, it was like amputating a leg, would you have cut off your leg so easily? And she says, it didn't suit me any more, after everything else had changed, and she sat up in bed, looking nervously at her watch, how long is he going to stay here, I'm tired of lying in bed in the middle of the day.

You're not really sick at all, I say in surprise, and she giggles, of course not, I just can't stand that character, and I say immediately, neither can I, because the touch of his arm on mine stings like an insect bite, and I even check to see if the arm has swollen or turned red, and then I ask why.

It's a long story, she says, your father admires him, they studied together, thirty years ago, he was his best friend, but I always thought that Aryeh was only playing with him, exploiting him even, I don't think he's capable of feeling at all. Take now, for instance, for years we haven't heard from him and suddenly he turns up because he needs your father to fix something up for his wife.

But you said he didn't live here, I found myself defending him, but she went on angrily, that's right, they've been living in France, they've only just come back, but if you want to keep in touch you can, from there too, and her face shrunk to a point of concentrated insult, a triangle covered with wrinkles and age spots, but at the same time childish, with the eyes narrowed in suspicion, dusty as windows that haven't been cleaned for years, guarding the beautiful straight nose, which I have inherited, and below it pale lips set in bitterness which gradually emptied, as if they were being sucked in from inside.

What was he doing in France, I asked, and she said sourly, the same as he does everywhere else, in other words nothing. Your father's sure he was there on some sort of security job, something high-up and secret, but in my opinion he was simply living on his rich wife's money, a guttersnipe who married money and now he's come back to show off the airs and graces he picked up in Europe, and I saw that her eyes were fixed on the mirror on the opposite wall, watching the words coming out of her mouth, dirty, venomous, and again I thought, who knows what she's capable of saying about me, and I felt suffocated next to her and said, I have to go, and she exclaimed, not yet, trying to keep me with her like she tried to keep him, stay with me until he goes, and I asked, why, and she shrugged her shoulders in a childish gesture, I don't know.

A sharp smell of French cigarettes rises from the living room, where my father, who never allows smoking in his presence, sits shrinking on the sofa, shrouded in the heavy smoke, while on his favourite soft armchair the guest sits at his ease, complacent and relaxed, observing my entry into the room. You remember Ya'ara, my father wheedles, almost pleads, and the guest says, I remember her as a baby, I would never have recognized her, and he rises to his feet with surprising agility and holds out his beautiful hand with its long, dark fingers, and asks with a mocking smile, do you always expect the worst? And he explains to my father, when she saw me at the door she looked at me as if I'd murdered the pair of you and she was the next in line, and I say that's right, and my hand falls from his, heavy and surprised like the hand of someone who has just fainted, because he suddenly dropped it, before I was ready, and he sits down in the armchair again, his sombre grey eyes scanning my face, and I try to hide my face with my hair, sit down opposite him and say to my father, I'm in a hurry, Yonny's waiting for me at home. How is your mother feeling, the guest asks, and his voice is deep and provocative, and I say, not so good, and a crooked smile escapes me, as always when I'm lying, and my father looks at me with his eyes twinkling, you know that we studied together when we were young, he says, younger than you are now, we even lived together for a while, but the guest's eyes don't twinkle back at him, as if he's much less enthusiastic about those memories, but my father perseveres, wait a minute, he springs up from the sofa, I have to show you a picture of us, the past, as always, affecting him with enormous, almost insulting, excitement.

From the next room come echoes of his search, drawers opening, books thrown to the floor, covering up the silence between us, an oppressive, unpleasant silence, and the guest lights another cigarette, he doesn't even try to make conversation, he observes me with his arrogant look, provocative and at the same time indifferent, his presence fills the room, and I try to look back at him brightly, but my eyes stay low, not daring to climb up the open buttons of his short shirt, exposing a smooth brown chest, and they stray to his feet, to his highly polished, almost ridiculous, pointed shoes, and the big, black carrier bag between them, with the words 'The Left Bank, Parisian Clothes', printed in gold letters, and I swallow a snigger, the dandyism rising from the bag confuses me, how does it fit in with the coarse purposeful face, and the snigger sticks in my throat and I cough in embarrassment, searching for something to say, and in the end I say, he won't find it, he never finds anything.

He won't find it because I've got it, the guest confirms in a whisper, and at that moment there's the sound of a thud and a curse, and my father limps into the room, holding the drawer that fell onto his foot, where can it be, where can that picture be, he mutters, and the guest looks at him mockingly, leave it, Shlomo, it's not important, and I feel angry, why doesn't he tell him that he's got it, and why don't I tell him, and how does he know that I won't tell? Like a pair of crooks we watch him rummaging desperately through the drawer, until I can't stand it any more and I get up, Yonny's waiting for me at home, I repeat, like a magic formula, the magic formula which will rescue me. That's a shame, says my father regretfully, I wanted to show you how we were, and the guest says, she doesn't need it, and you don't need it either, and I say, that's right, even though I would actually like to see the blunt dark face in its youth, and my father accompanies me to the door limping and whispers, she isn't really sick, is she? And I say, of course she is, she's really sick, you should call a doctor.

The steps at the entrance to the building were covered with slippery leaves which had already begun to rot, and I stepped carefully on their quiet ferment, holding fast to the cold railing, only yesterday it blazed in my hand, and today the heat wave was over and the sky was even drizzling a little, a half-hearted autumn drizzle, and I reached the main street at the hour when the drivers are beginning to put on their lights, and all the cars look the same, and all the people resemble each other, and I mingled with them, the evening blackens us all, my mother imprisoned in her bedroom, and my father veiled in the smoke of the friend of his youth, and Yonny waiting for me at home, blinking with tiredness in front of the computer, and Shira who lives not far from here, right here in this alley, in fact I'm already standing opposite her building, and I'm tempted to see if she's at home. I feel as if there's a lot to tell her, even though we already spoke at lunch-time, at the university, and I ring the bell but there's no reply, and nevertheless I persevere, maybe she's in the shower or the toilet, and I go round to the back of the building and knock on the closed shutter, until I hear a wail and Shira's cat Tulya jumps out of the kitchen window, he's tired of being alone in the house all day, and I stroke him until he purrs, lifts his grey tail, and the stroking calms me a little, and him too, and he lies down at my feet, appearing to be asleep, but no, his erect tail accompanies me as I leave the building and advance down the dark alley, where the single street lamp flickers and dies.

Tulya, go away, I say to the cat, Shira will be back soon, but he insists on accompanying me, like an over-zealous host, and I think of how my father is now accompanying his guest, clinging to him like a sweet memory, and it seems to me that they are crossing the street opposite me, my father with short, hurried steps, his delicate limbs swallowed up in the darkness, and next to him the guest, with bold steps, his bronze face firm and resolute, his silver hair shining in the night like a reflector, and I run towards them with the wailing cat behind me, and

I kick out in his direction, Tulya scram, go home, and I cross
the street after them, and suddenly there's a screech of brakes, a
faint thud, a car door opens and someone shouts, who does the
cat belong to? Who does the cat belong to? And another voice
says, it doesn't matter now.

I run away, not daring to look back, seeing my father and
the guest walking arm-in-arm in front of me, my father's head
rubbing against his broad shoulder, but no, it isn't them, when
I run past them I see that it's a couple, a man and a woman no
longer young, but their love is apparently still young, and I rush
down the busy road to our building, my sweat pouring like the
cat's blood, which follows me down the slope in an aggressive
stream, and I know that it will flow and flow and stop only
when it reaches our door.

What happened, Moley, Yonny asks, his face warm, his soft
paunch wrapped in an apron, and I see that the table is laid
for supper, the knives and forks waiting politely on the red
tablecloth, and instead of being glad I'm annoyed, don't call me
that, how many times do I have to tell you that I'm sick of you
calling me that, and his eyes open wide with hurt feelings and he
says, but it was you who started with those names, and I say, so
what, I also stopped it and you didn't, only yesterday you called
me that in front of other people, and they all thought we were
idiots. What do I care what they think, he mutters, I care what we
think, and I say, when will you get it into your head that there's
no we, there's me and there's you, and each of us is entitled to
his own thoughts, and he insists, but you used to like it when
I called you that, and I snap, okay, so I've changed, why can't
you change too, and he says, I'll change at my own pace, you
can't dictate to me, and he snatches up his plate resentfully and
sits down facing the television, and I looked at the table which
had abruptly changed its nature, suddenly turned into a table
for one, and I thought how sad it was to be alone, how could
Shira stand it, and then I remembered her cat, plump pampered
Tulya, soft and furry as a cushion, and I said, I'm not hungry,
and I went to the bedroom and lay down on the bed and thought
what were we going to do now without our sweet little names,

he wouldn't call me Moley any more and I wouldn't call him Ratty, so how were we going to talk to each other?

I heard the phone ringing and his soft voice coaxing the receiver, and then he came into the room and said, Shira's on the phone, and I said, tell her I'm sleeping, and he said, but she needs you, and handed me the sobbing receiver. Tulya's disappeared, she wept, and the neighbours said that a cat was run over here earlier and I'm afraid that it was him, and I whispered, calm down, it must have been another cat, Tulya never strays far from home, and she cried, I have a feeling that it was him, he always waits for me in the evening, and I said, but Tulya hardly ever leaves the house, and she said, I left the kitchen window open, because there was still a *hamseen* this morning, I didn't think he would go out, why should he have gone out, what did he lack at home?

He's probably hiding under the bed or something, I said, you know what cats are like, they appear and disappear as the fancy takes them, go to sleep now and tomorrow he'll wake you up in the morning, and she whispered, I wish, and she began to cry again, he was my baby, I'm lost without him, you have to come and help me look for him, and I said, but Shira, I've just come home and I haven't got the strength to move, let's give it one more day, but she insisted, I have to find him now, and in the end I agreed.

At the door he asked, what about the food I prepared, his eyes disappointed above his chewing mouth. A bit of tomato slipped out with the words and hung trembling on his chin, and I said, I have to help Shira look for her cat, and he said, you always complain that I don't prepare food and when I do you don't eat it. What can I do, I flared up, if you had told her I was sleeping I wouldn't have to go out now, believe me I'd prefer to stay at home, and he went on chewing steadily, as if he was chewing over what I said, turning the words over in his mouth, staring at the television, and I gave him a farewell look and left, whenever I parted from him I was sure that I would never see him again, that it was the last time, and instead of all the hundreds of times I was proven wrong shaking this certainty, they only reinforced it, they only increased the fear that this time it would happen.

Shira was sitting in the kitchen, her head on the dirty table, her hair mingling with the crumbs. I was so afraid of this, she wept, and in the end it's even more terrible than I imagined, and I said, wait before you begin to mourn, let's look for him first, and I started crawling round the flat, looking for him under the beds, inside the cupboards, and calling like an idiot, Tulya, Tulya, as if the harder I tried to find him the less guilty I would be, because of course I should have taken him home, or at least removed him from the road, and I went on crawling stubbornly, fuzzy curls of dust covering me as if had dressed up as a sheep, cursing the moment when I had decided to drop in on her, why hadn't I gone straight home, what did I have to tell her that was so urgent, until my knees hurt and I said, enough, let's go and look outside.

When we went outside she clung to me, her tiny body rigid, and whispered, thank you for coming with me, I don't know what I would do without you, her words fixing the guilt to me like sharp nails, and we walked up and down the little streets next to the main road calling, Tulya, Tulya, and every time a cat jumped out of a dustbin she grabbed my hand in suspense and then let it go in disappointment, and in the end we had no option but to approach the main road, and she said, you look, I can't, and I searched between the fast, cold lights, pair after pair of malevolent eyes, and I couldn't see anything, so quickly had they removed the big, pampered, trusting body with the long whiskers hiding an imaginary but absolutely palpable smile.

This shows me how lonely I am, she said when we sat down on a bench next to the building, you're lucky not to be alone, and I felt uncomfortable, as always when the subject came up, because she had known Yonny before me, and it had always seemed to me that she was in love with him, and now I had taken not only him from her but also the cat. Now I could no longer say to her in a joke, you take Yonny and give me the cat, as I would sometimes say when Tulya fawned on me, reminding me of all the cats I had loved in my life, I had always got along better with cats than with men, but Yonny wouldn't let me keep a cat because in his opinion it never ended well, and now it seemed that he was right, but what does end well? I felt so bad it was hard for me to breathe, and then the upstairs neighbour came out with the garbage, and Shira asked her, have you seen Tulya, and the neighbour said I think I saw him an hour or two ago, following a tall girl with long curly hair, and her hands trying to sketch the height of the girl and the length of her curls freeze in front of me, and I think in dismay why didn't I change my clothes, or tie my hair back, and Shira looks at me and the neighbour looks at me, and I say, no, not me, I wasn't here today, I was at my parents' place, I stayed because there was somebody there with a frightening face, and the neighbour says, in any case someone who looked like you was hanging around here and the cat followed her in the direction of the main road. I heard that a cat was run over here earlier, Shira mumbled, and the neighbour said, I don't know anything about that, and she went into the building, leaving me alone with her, and I said, Shira, I swear, I would have told you, and she cut me off in a cold voice, I don't care what happened, I just want my cat. He'll come back, I pleaded, you'll see that by tomorrow morning he'll be back, and she said, I'm tired, Ya'ara, I want to sleep, and again her voice broke, how will I sleep without him, I'm used to sleeping with him, his purring calms me, and I said, then I'll sleep with you, and purr like a cat, and she said, stop it, that's enough, you have to go back to Yonny, she always made a point of considering him, showing her love in indirect ways, and I said, Yonny will manage, I'll stay with you, but she said, no, no, and I heard the heavy, uneasy doubt in her voice, I have to face it by myself, and I whispered in a small voice, there's still a chance that he'll come back, and she said, you know he won't.

On the way home I thought, I'll always deny it, nobody but me knows, and if I deny it for long enough the truth will be defeated by the lie, and I won't know myself what really happened, and I thought about the anxiety which had seized me on the slippery steps, how it sometimes precedes the event, and I tried to remember what had been so threatening about that face, and I couldn't remember the face but only the fear, and as always at moments like these I thought with relief of dear, sweet Yonny, now we would begin the evening from the beginning again, and I would eat the food he had prepared, I wouldn't leave anything on my plate, but from outside I saw that the apartment was dark, even the television was off, and only the telephone was awake, ringing insistently, and I picked it up, afraid that it was Shira again, but it was my mother.

He's still here, she whispered angrily, I'm telling you that Daddy's doing it to me on purpose, I know he is, he wants to see who'll break down first, I'm dying of hunger and I'm shut up here because of him, and I said, so go out to the kitchen for a minute, what's the problem, and she said, but I don't want to see him. So close your eyes and you won't see him, I suggested, and she shouted, but he'll see me, don't you understand? I don't want him to see me, and I said, don't worry, Mother, he won't stay forever, and I went into the dark bedroom. Yonny lay there breathing quietly with his eyes closed and I put my hand on his brow and whispered, Good night, Ratty.

2

Where did I see those letters, square, decorated, like letters in an ancient *Torah* scroll, with all those crowns, and gold too, gold on black, filling my eyes when I stare out of the window. The bus stops at the bus stop, opens its jaws, and I stare at the huge, disturbing sign, until the letters run into each other, THE LEFT BANK, they scream at me, PARIS FASHIONS, and I get up quickly, try to push my way to the exit, as if I've forgotten something particularly precious there, something that can't wait.

From close up you can hardly see the sign, it's so big and high, and only its gold shines with a sweet promise like winter sunshine, and I bask in its glow, draw closer to the big, new display window, only a month ago they were selling building materials here and now these clothes, which had peeped at me, enticing and mysterious, from his carrier bag, between his pointed shoes, and now they're completely exposed, proudly on display. Especially that burgundy dress, short and tight with long sleeves, which looks so great on the mannequin in the window, underlining her pointed plastic breasts with their erect nipples, and her slender shapely legs, and I stand there opposite her, sadly listing the differences between us, and beyond her widely parted legs I see his narrow buttocks neatly packed into the black corduroy trousers which he tries on in front of the mirror, stepping backwards and forwards, backwards and forwards, and I could hardly see his face, it was hidden behind the mannequin's slender back, but I could guess its gratified expression. What's he doing there all the time, I wondered, who does he think he is, sucking up to the mirror like an aging model, and then a void gaped between the mannequin's legs and someone standing at the entrance to the shop said to me, you can try it on, we've got it in all the colours, and I stammered, I want it in that colour, and the shop assistant said glumly, it's a shame to take it out of the window for nothing, let's see how it fits you first, and I insisted, I only want to try that one on, determined to see the mannequin in its humiliation, and went into the shop after her.

He had already emerged from the narrow changing cubicle, wearing brown trousers this time, advancing on the mirror with a savage step, while I, without thinking, seeking shelter, as if a hard rain was coming down inside the shop, slipped into the changing cubicle which was now empty of him, but not of his pungent smell, treading on the black trousers he had just taken off, sniffing the old trousers hanging on the hook, rummaging in the pockets, what does he need so many keys for, and the shop assistant asks, where's the girl who wanted the dress in the window, and in a husky voice I answer, here, and hold out my hand. She hangs the dress on my hand, and I quickly get undressed, mixing my clothes with his, but instead of trying on the dress I put on the trousers he had taken off, and they feel cool and exciting, as if his smooth skin is stuck to them, and I hear footsteps approaching and the shop assistant says, it's occupied, someone's trying on here, and his deep voice says, but I'm trying on here. I'm sorry, she says, the cubicle will be free in a minute, and I can hear him explaining something in French, and through the gap between the narrow doors I see him in the brown trousers, and an elegant girl waves a brown shirt at him, coaxing him in soft French, and he begins undressing in front of the mirror, apparently all the cubicles are occupied, exposing a full young chest which is almost the same colour as the shirt, and swelling like a peacock in the new clothes, he lights a cigarette for himself and one for the girl next to him, and I see that she is smoking it in a long holder which goes brilliantly with her hairdo, a neat red bob, and with her tailored jacket. In hesitant Hebrew she asks the shop assistant about the dress that was in the window, the burgundy one, and the shop assistant answers, someone's trying it on, but we have it in other colours. I hear the girl insisting she wants that one, and the shop assistant shouts at the closed doors, what are you doing in there, there are customers waiting for the cubicle, and the dress too, and I pipe up immediately, I'm taking it, revelling in the disappointed exclamations of the girl with the cigarette holder, and then I quickly took off his trousers and put on the clothes I was wearing before, but before I had time to close the zipper I heard an angry cry, hurry up, what's going on here, and the doors swung violently into the cubicle, pushing me to the wall.

Korman's daughter, he said.

With one hand I held the dress, and with the other I tried to pull up the zipper, in which a few pubic hairs had been painfully caught, while my bare feet trampled his trousers and opposite me I saw buttons opening one after the other until he took off the shirt, releasing a pungent smell from his smooth armpits, a dense smell of pine resin, and his thick lips pouting thirstily, and his wide, dark tongue appeasing them, running over them to and fro. His eyes regarded me with painful concentration, sombre as smouldering coals, and without taking his eyes off me he opened the zipper of his trousers and let them slide down his long, boyish legs, exposing tight black underpants with a bulge in the middle, while I tried to avert my gaze, as if I had accidentally seen my father in his underpants, but he wouldn't let me, with one hand he turned my face towards him, and then lowered it, exactly like someone manipulating a mannequin in a shop window, and then he took my hand and placed it on the hot bulge. I felt the black underpants filling with life, as if the trunk of an elephant was coiled up there, eager to stretch out and trumpet, and my hand tightened round it, and I put the other one there too, wriggling out of my clothes, and he didn't touch me but his eyes were as heavy on me as hands, sending a shuddering current through me, pushing me down, to crush his trousers lying on the floor with my knees and to press my cheek against the tense silent struggle going on there between the skin and the fabric. And then I heard the girl with the cigarette holder saying, *alors*, Ari, and he placed a warning finger on his lips and pulled me up, pressing my hands hard against his underpants, and then he hastily put on his old trousers, nearly zipping them up with my hands inside them, covered his smooth bare chest with his shirt, and escaped from the cubicle, dragging a pile of clothes behind him, and I got dressed quickly, looking for the dress in the empty cubicle, he must have taken it with him by mistake, and rushed out without even tying my laces.

They were already standing next to the cash register, he tall and erect, arranging his grey hair on his skull, and she attractive and elegant in short pants and a fashionable jacket, not beautiful but polished, the kind of polish more impressive than beauty, whispering something in his ear, rummaging in the pile of clothes and extracting my dress, and I hurry up to them, tripping over my open laces, there were so many mirrors it was hard to tell them from their reflections, and in my confusion I bump into one of the mirrors instead of his living body still pulsing in my hands. That's my dress, I say, out of breath, excuse me, that's my dress, and the cashier looks at me suspiciously, and I call the shop assistant to be my witness, and luckily for me she says, yes, she tried it on first, and only then he deigns to raise his head from his wallet and say in surprise, Ya'ara, what are you doing here? And to explain to his French friend, *la fille de mon ami*, but he doesn't bother to introduce her, and he asks with exaggerated friendliness, how's your mother? I hope she's recovered, and I say, yes, she's fine now, and see the concentration vanish from his face to be replaced by a mocking self-satisfaction. I have some credit with you, he explains to the cashier, I'm returning some things I bought here last week, and she examines the receipts and says, ID number and telephone number please, and he dictates the numbers to her, slowly and loudly, and repeats the telephone number, and I repeat it to myself, moving my lips soundlessly. When they leave with the huge, black, plastic carrier bag, even bigger than the previous one, he gives me a friendly wave and says, give them my best at home, and then he adds as if he's just remembered something, tell your father that I'm still waiting for his answer, and I say, all right, watching them recede, his hand guiding her arm, leading her firmly, their backsides moving in a uniform rhythm which takes them further away from me, and the cashier tells me the price of the dress and I hardly take it in, my head is full of his telephone number, and she repeats the price and I mumble, how come it's so expensive, I didn't know it was so expensive, putting the dress down on the counter and taking a step backwards as if it's about to explode, and the shop assistant advances towards me with a threatening step, instantly shedding her geniality, what do you think you're doing, we lost a customer because of you, you can't not take it now. I didn't pay attention to the price, I stammer, I have to ask my husband, I only mentioned him in order to reassure myself, to conjure up his solid presence, so that they would know I wasn't alone, that I wasn't as lost as I seemed now, and the shop assistant snatches the dress up angrily, next time check the price first, she says, and I say, you're right, I'm sorry, sorrowfully seeing my beautiful velvety dress which I didn't even get to try on being pulled over the head of the expectant mannequin again, and then I'm standing opposite the display window once more, exactly as I was half an hour ago, contemplating the perfect compatibility between them, the absolute triumph of the mannequin, and I think, nothing's happened, you can carry on as if you never went into that shop at all, everything's the way it was before, nothing's happened, but deep inside my hands I feel a jolt, as if the order of my fingers has been changed in a painful operation.

Shamefacedly I beat a retreat, the dress waving at me like a red sheet, provocative and disturbing, and I walk backwards, afraid to turn my back, in order not to expose it to the vindictive stabs of the two women in the shop. It seems to me that the mannequin raises her hand in farewell, and I blink at her apologetically and bump into a crowd of people walking close together, and they're so close together that I can't extricate myself from them, rank after rank like walls, and I have no alternative but to be swept along with them until I find an opening, and gradually it becomes almost enjoyable, this togetherness. I notice that they're wearing brown clothes on which big leaves in autumn colours are hanging, swaying with every step they take, until they suddenly stop, in the middle of the astonished mall, and raise their hands to the sky like trees, and I ask a woman standing next to me, what are you doing, and she says, we're celebrating the autumn, and they murmur quiet benedictions, and beat drums, and then silence falls and all at once they rip the leaves off their clothes and trample them savagely, stamping and kicking, and I ask the woman, what's this, and she says, we're celebrating our liberation from the leaves, we're casting off all our parasites and returning to our purity, like the trees, just trunks and branches. Her radiant face hypnotizes me, her hair is completely white but her face is young and full of enthusiasm, and then she begins humming with the rest of them a bitter-sweet tune, and I try to escape from the circle, to mingle with the ordinary people, some of them sneering, scram, loonies, go back to the loony bin where you belong, but others looking at them with the anguished expression people wear when they come across pure spirituality, and I wonder, I always thought the trees were sorry to part from their leaves, like parents from their children, but perhaps parents are happy to part from their children too, husbands from their wives, perhaps every parting is a release, a purification, a shedding of gross matter, and I like the idea of there being less sorrow in the world than I thought there was. Encouraged by the good news I walk up the mall, and then I realize that my happiness was premature, it's not that there's less sorrow, the amount of sorrow stays the same, they just changed the circumstances, with them partings are joyful and meetings are sad, like the old riddle about ups and downs, which is always confusing for a moment, and I hoped that I would bump into them again so that I could ask them what they did in the spring, did they mourn when everything was blooming, but I didn't want to dawdle there because I had a reception hour at the university, and it was really unpleasant to be late, and when I looked at my watch to see how late I was in danger of being, I saw that my reception hour had begun fifteen minutes ago.

In a panic I went into a café at the top of the mall and phoned the teaching assistants' room, and luckily Netta answered in her nasal voice which I never thought I would be glad to hear, and I said to her, do me a favour, Netta, take my place today and I'll make it up to you, and she drawled, that's exactly what

I'm doing, and I asked her, did a lot of students come? And she said, I've already spoken to two and there are a few more outside, they need help with the introductory course, where are you? And I said, in town, I got off the bus on the way because I wanted to try on a dress and I didn't notice the time. I hope you enjoyed it, she said, and I said in embarrassment, no, in the end I didn't buy it, it was too expensive, and Netta laughed, I could imagine her shaking her dense brown curls which moved without stopping like insects with a lot of legs, and I thanked her for covering for me, but I couldn't ignore the note of triumph in her voice, it was impossible to deny the close competition that had been going on between us for the past two years for a place in the department, any slip-up on my part was a point in her favour, even if nobody else knew about it, it was enough that we knew.

There was no point in going to the university now, and I sat down at an outside table, the strange procession had disappeared but the strangeness remained, and I looked at the faded trees surrounded by high fences, as if they were plotting to escape, and at the old buildings which had been renovated only on the upper storeys, but who looks so high up, and at eye-level there were run-down old shops selling military accessories, insignia, uniforms, surplus flags, and on the striped tiles living people march to and fro, moving their arms and legs in unison, as if the rhythm had been agreed in advance, and among the marchers a swarthy child scurries, trying to sell peacock feathers, huge brightly coloured eyes swaying over narrow quills, but nobody buys. And I asked myself if all these people milling about here had ever felt what I had felt only a few moments before, it was like swallowing fire, I had always wanted to know what it was like to swallow fire, what you feel a moment before thrusting the burning brand into your mouth, what you feel when it's inside, threatening to destroy the delicate tissues, and now I knew, but what to do with this knowledge, where to take it? And I thought of his member coiled inside his underpants, and of the girl with the precise haircut, who could she be, and I hoped that she was his daughter but I didn't really believe it, and she was too young to be his wife, and where did they go with the full carrier bag and the full underpants, why didn't they take me with them, because I had lost something there, in the little changing cubicle, I had lost an asset I didn't even know I possessed, the ignorance of what it feels like to swallow fire, and with this knowledge came a terrible dreariness, because anything less would never excite me again.

All at once I felt weak, a sudden sinking of my limbs, and I put my head on the little round table, warmed by the autumn sun, like a faithful pillow, and I tried to remind myself of my life plan, of the thesis I had to hand in by the end of the year, the baby we would have after the thesis, the apartment we would buy after the baby, and in the meantime the suppers cooked once by him and once by me, the meeting with the head of the department, who admired me, who thought I had a future, the dresses I would try on in narrow changing cubicles, with or without a mirror, but everything looked dusty, as if a desert wind had come and covered the world in a thin, grey layer of sand. And I remembered that it had happened to me once before, a fall like this, not with such intensity but like a hint, a warning, when a few years ago, soon after my army service, I had fallen in love with someone who lived next to a bakery, and on the only night I was with him the bed was full of the smell of fresh bread, but in the end I didn't see him again, and it seemed to me that all the freshness of my life had remained in his bed because he lived next to a bakery and he had a smell of bread from the sheets. I had a hard time for a while, but quite soon I met Yonny and tried to forget him, but when I smelled fresh bread I would think about him, and now the smell of the bread mingles in my nostrils with the taste of the fire, burning inside my head, and Aryeh Even's coal eyes shoot bullets all around me, and I am full of dread, he has the walk of a hunter, the look of a hunter, and I see him coming up the mall and my body is slung over his shoulder with terrible ease, flesh and fur. I swallow a scream and begin to run, like animals in the forest when they hear a shot, and only on the main road do I feel safe, among all the cars, and already I am close to my parents' house and the ferment of the rotting leaves on the pavement deafens my ears and I go up to their apartment, only a week ago he stood behind this door, as if he lived there, but now my mother stands there instead.

Go away, I feel like saying to her, this isn't your place any more it's his, his, and she says in surprise, you're not at the university, and I say, I'm on my way there, I just forgot to take a coat, and it's getting cold, and she runs to the closet and takes out an old checked jacket and glances suspiciously out of the window at the fine morning, you're sure you won't be too hot? And I say no, it's cold outside, and she shrugs her shoulders and offers me coffee, and I sit down with her in the kitchen and say casually, I met your friend Aryeh Even in town, with his daughter, and she corrects me, Daddy's friend, and immediately explains, he hasn't got a daughter, he hasn't got any children. Disappointed I try again, then it must have been his wife, what does his wife look like? An aging French coquette, my mother declares triumphantly, I haven't seen her for years, but some things are inevitable. Not even trying to hide her satisfaction at the fact that there is a certain moment in life when both she, who always resolutely neglected her appearance, and pampered Frenchwomen reach the same irreversible point.

Why haven't they got any children? I asked, his flagrant maleness writhing between my fingers, and my mother said, problems, why should it interest you?

Problems with him or problems with her? I persevered, and she said, with him, what difference does it make to you? I haven't got time for coffee now, I say as I take my revenge on her, my reception hour is due to begin, and I took the jacket and emerged into the day which was getting hotter, flushed with the certainty that she wasn't his daughter or his wife, she must be his mistress, the intimacy between them was frank and obvious, and I went home, seeing the buildings growing older and greyer as our house came closer, whereas the people seemed to grow newer, young mothers dragging a pram with one hand and a wailing toddler with the other, and I thought of his sterility, hollow and concave and piercing as a moon, the fuller he was the hollower it was, laughing at him, teasing him, what use was that arrogant penis in his black underpants if it couldn't perform the function for which it was intended, and when I got home I went straight to bed, as if I were ill, but there too I couldn't calm down, a bleak sense of loss covering the little windows like curtains, and I stared at them, listening to the greedy little animal gnawing at my insides, and I said to myself, wait, wait, but I didn't know for what, for my next reception hour? For the washing I had hung out this morning to dry? For the temperatures to go down? For the shortest day of the year? For the longest day of the year? And when I couldn't wait any longer I picked up the phone and dialled the numbers rampaging in my head.

I had almost given up, falling back into bed, when he answered, after at least ten rings, a strange, affected hello, presumably Parisian, his voice heavy and dull, and I asked, did I wake you up? And he said no, and breathed heavily, as if I had disturbed him at something else, and I bit my tongue and said, this is Ya'ara, and he said, I know, and was silent. I just wanted to tell you that I gave my father your message, I stammered, and he said, good, thank you, and was silent again, and I didn't know what else to say, all I knew was that I couldn't let him hang up, so I said simply, don't hang up, and he asked, why, and I said, I don't know, and he asked, what do you want, and I said, to see you, and he insisted, but why, and again I said, I don't know, and he laughed, there are too many things that you don't know, and I joined in his laughter with a sense of relief, but he stopped me short in an official tone, I'm busy now, and I said, so when you're free, and he was silent for a moment, as if considering, all right, be here in half an hour, and he stated the name of the street and the number of the house as if he were ordering a taxi.

Immediately I regretted not having bought that dress, because nothing in my wardrobe could compete with the cigarette holder's short yellow pants and matching honey-coloured jacket, and in the end I put on a pair of tight trousers and a black knit blouse, and a gilt band on my hair, and with a black pencil I emphasized the blue of my eyes, and was quite pleased, and I saw that the taxi-driver was pleased too, the minute I got in he

asked, married? And I said, yes, of course, and he sighed as if his
heart was broken, but recovered and asked, for how long? And
I said, ages, nearly five years. So it's time for something new,
he cheered up, and I said, but I love my husband, a declaration
which was received with a certain forgiving tolerance in the
interior of the taxi, and I felt ridiculous, making declarations
in these circumstances, but I had to hear the words next to me,
and he whispered, his mouth giving off a bad smell, you can love
two people, and he pointed at his heart which had just ostensibly
been broken, the heart's a big place. Mine's very small, I said,
and he laughed, you think it's small, you'd be amazed how it
can stretch, did you think the only thing that got bigger was a
cock? I was already disgusted by this conversation so I started
looking out of the window, at the widening streets, and next to
a small, well-tended building at the end of the street he stopped,
his hand resting on his heart again, in farewell.

A thick creeper covered the building like fur, and when I
approached I saw dozens of bees buzzing merrily within the
dense foliage. It's a sign, I said to myself, it's a sign that you
should leave, because I've always had the feeling that I'm one
of those people who die from a bee sting, after all you don't
know things like that in advance, only when it's too late, and I
began to retreat, turning my back to the building, but the sight
of the world, the sight of the world without that building, was
so familiar and dull, pale apartment houses with little urban
gardens that use up too much water, trees whose names I always
forget, rooms that are dirtied and cleaned by turn, mail boxes
that are filled and emptied, all that vast enterprise, which no bee
sting would stop, seemed so gloomy and hopeless to me without
that well-tended building with the creeper covering it all over
like fur, swarming with dozens of bees, that I turned towards
it again and walked boldly into the stairwell.

He took his time, he was in no hurry to give me shelter, and
only after I had rung twice did the door open, and he led me
silently into the big, well furnished living room, whose walls
were covered with paintings and whose floor was covered with
carpets, until it seemed to me that the floor was a reflection of

the walls, or vice versa. He was wearing his new brown trousers and new shirt, but their newness just emphasized his antiqueness, and he suddenly looked old, older than my father, the deep lines on his cheeks and forehead looked like scars, and his hair was actually more white than silver, more sparse than dense, and there were black clouds under his eyes. People in their homes resemble who they really are, and it's only outside that a kind of light is shed on them, I thought in relief, sitting down on the pale sofa, suddenly calm in the face of the old age which had pounced on him with unsheathed claws, as if he would soon die of cardiac arrest right here in front of me and stop bothering me. Shamelessly I stared expectantly at his left shirt pocket, behind which his tired heart was presumably beating with the last vestiges of its strength. All kinds of inner organs crowded in front of me, hidden behind his pocket, red-blue, reminiscent of sexual organs on the inside, repulsive and attractive, the kind of thing I had seen years before, tagging behind my mother at old-fashioned butcher shops. I would tug at her sleeve, Mother, let's go, but along with the nausea I would feel rising inside me a painful longing, obscure and sad, at the sight of the cutting boards laden with the small, concrete leftovers of life.

Rivetted by the rising and falling pocket I tried to coordinate the rhythm of my breathing with his, to check how serious his condition was, perhaps even to catch his last breath, like catching a wave, but the pocket suddenly reared up, and he was standing over me, what would you like to drink, Ya'ara, and I, haughtily, announced, I'm not thirsty, feeling a sudden, joyful liberation, no, I wasn't thirsty or hungry, I didn't need anything from him, and I couldn't care less who the girl with the cigarette holder was, or what they did when they left the shop, what was he to me? Home, I had to go home, to Yonny and to the thesis I had to present at the end of the year.

3

Just one more time, I promised myself, one time that will wipe out the first, transform humiliation into victory, how can I live with the memory of my hands raised at the door, clinging to the cold metal hooks, after all, there's no difference between cheating once or twice, both sins will be imprisoned later in the same cage, and if I've already done it, at least let me have a sweet memory instead of a bitter, choking one. This is what I would repeat to myself when I marked the introductory course exercises, as I vacillated opposite the books in the library, opposite Yonny's round face, opposite his soft back at night.

Let's leave it like this, he said when, trembling with excitement, I finally called him. What's like this, I asked, and he said, like this, as it is, and I said, but I have to see you, and he said, believe me, Ya'ara, it's better to leave it like this.

What's like this – walking round all day with one thought in my head, clinging to my brain and not letting go, sometimes needling and sometimes knocking, sometimes wheedling and sometimes begging and for a brief moment hiding, and I breathe a sigh of relief but then it suddenly pounces with the force of a fierce wind, like the winter winds which have suddenly blown up, wet, hungry, flinging open the little windows, breathing mockingly down the back of my neck, and Yonny says, but once you loved the winter, and I snap back, so now I hate it, what's the matter, aren't I allowed to change, do I have to stay the same from the age of twenty until I die, and his eyes say, but once you loved me, me, me.

How to see him again. It seems to me that only if I see him again will I free myself of him, and I frequent all the chance meeting spots, peering into the boutique in town, where the mannequin is now wearing a thick wool coat, climbing my parents' stairs again and again, charging with beating heart into the dim living room, how he sat there at his ease in the big armchair, naturally assuming the role of host to my timid, shrinking father, filling the room with smoke, how simple it had been to see him by accident, without effort, without planning, and now it seems fantastic, hopeless, he will never climb the wet steps, never strut to and fro opposite the gleaming mirror, smugly examining his backside.

Then there was a night when I thought that everything could be resolved and I was almost happy. I realized that the person who had to act here was my father, I wasn't asking for continuous, strenuous effort, but a single, decisive act, to cut short his life, in other words, to die. If he died Aryeh was sure to come to the funeral and I would cry on his shoulder, cling to him as if he were my new father, and he wouldn't be able to refuse me. The question was what my father would say about it, everything now depended on his good will. Tomorrow morning I would stand before him and say, Daddy, the moment of truth has come, how much is my happiness worth to you? And perhaps I would say, Daddy, it's become clear to me that at this stage of my life, under these circumstances, your death will help me far more than the continuation of your life, and you can console yourself with the thought that there are worse situations than this, some of my girlfriends are so far gone that even the death of their parents couldn't save them, imagine how lost they are.

He was already about sixty years old, my father, and I had no idea how precious his life was to him, how tightly he clung to it, if at all. He spoke a great deal about the past, interminably in fact, but very little about the future. He had no special plans for the future, as far as I knew, and even if he had, plans were made to be cancelled.

What makes sense at night seems absurd by day, and perhaps the opposite too. When I stood before his delicate, worried face I was already prepared to compromise on a fatal illness, pretended of course, which would propel his friends into frequent visits. I would be touching in the role of the devoted daughter, with the entire family leaning on her shoulders, and when he came, he would surely come in the end, I would say to him, Daddy asked about you, Daddy wanted to see you, and he would be dismayed by the time that had passed. Am I too late, he would ask in alarm, and I would reassure him, no, not yet.

What's with that friend of yours, Aryeh Even? I asked him, and he said, he's fine, I spoke to him yesterday. Why don't you invite him and his wife to dinner, I suggested, and I immediately heard my mother yelling from the kitchen, that's all I need, that pompous ass.

Mind what you say about my best friend, my father flared up.

If he's such a good friend of yours where has he been all these years? Why didn't he keep in touch? She rushed out of the kitchen, confronting him with a sour face.

You and your petty calculations, he yelled, I don't keep accounts with my friends.

Because you're naïve, at best, not to say an idiot.

And they didn't even notice when I left, sucked into their rotten old ritual, and I began to walk, learning the route detail by detail, how many steps exactly between me and him, how many traffic lights, how many grocery shops, how many butchers, how many pharmacies, how many pedestrian crossings, and in my head there began to emerge a map of distance, of everyday urban reality, and at the same time a different world, completely new. I had never seen the grocery shops like this before, full of meaning and power, mystery and passion, the pedestrian crossings painted in phosphorescent stripes, the traffic lights spitting fire, and my steps, I had never known what it was to step with feet pursuing each other like beasts of prey, and I felt a great wonder, almost a miracle, as if I were a statue beginning to move.

Only outside his door did I stop, opposite the clear, rectangular name-plate, approximately opposite the place where my forehead had been on the other side, it seemed to me that I had felt the screws stabbing me then, and I thought how my moans had been absorbed into the close-grained wood and now they were part of it, and perhaps his wife had heard them rising from it and they tickled her ears, and I didn't even know if I was jealous of her or sorry for her. How easily she was betrayed, true, but on the other hand how easy it was for her to see him, all over the house, she didn't have to stand mortified outside the door and think up excuses.

But I didn't need an excuse either, because he looked pleasant and almost glad to see me, and he said, I owe you coffee, right? And I agreed as enthusiastically as if he had offered me the nectar of the gods. I don't like owing a debt, he said and immediately went into the kitchen, and I crept after him into the magnificent, dazzling room, how did this kitchen produce so much light from the weak winter sun, and his movements were full of gaiety, and I wondered, if he was really pleased to see me why did he try to keep me away, why did he say, let's leave it like this, as if he wanted to test my resolution, the power of my will, and now that I had passed the test, he was as pleased as a teacher with an outstanding pupil, almost proud. He gave me coffee in a blue cup, which was also steeped in sunlight, and yawned, I'm dead on my feet, I only got back from abroad early this morning. Really? I exclaimed. Where did you go? And he said, France, mainly, and I asked, on holiday? He laughed, some holiday, I was working, and I remembered my mother saying that he was involved in secret security business, and I asked, what work? Manual work, he said, laughing, and a little brain work too, and he pointed at his big head covered with wet grey hair, he must have just emerged from the shower, and yawned again. There was something exaggerated about these yawns, demonstrative, and it seemed to me that he was making it all up, because it embarrassed him to be caught lazing at home in the morning, sleeping late, and I remembered my father saying that he had spoken to him yesterday, so I couldn't resist asking, have you heard from my father? And he said, no, actually I haven't heard a thing, I'll have to phone him today to find out if he has an answer for me, and I thought, what's going on here, one of them is lying. I tried to guess which of them had the stronger motive, Aryeh wanted to prove he had been abroad, and my father wanted to annoy my mother, to show her that they were in touch, and the question was which of them to believe, and as if to strengthen his version he took a box of chocolates out of the cupboard, straight from the duty free, and made a big fuss of unwrapping it. So how was it, I asked, and he said, difficult, and pulled a grave, important face, and again I asked myself why he looked less attractive in his home than in my head, he looks like a tame tiger as he sits down opposite me, smiling a polite, hospitable smile, sipping the coffee he has made for himself with enjoyment, ah, it's good, he sighs, I can't remember him displaying so much enjoyment when we fucked, then he lights a cigarette and the smoke begins to dance around us, and my tension dissolves in the light of his surprising friendliness. I lick the bitter chocolate and examine him cautiously, because there's no closeness here yet, no intimacy, his body is completely alien to me, mysterious, even when he's friendly there's no intimacy, as if nothing has happened, absolutely nothing, and it seems as if nothing will happen either, ever, I'll never feel his presence invading me with that thrilling and unpleasant masterfulness, why deny it, pleasant it wasn't.

So what have you got to say for yourself, he said, and I said in embarrassment, nothing really, what have I got in common with him, what have I got to say to a complete stranger, I don't even know how to begin, and he asked, how has it been these past few weeks? And I thought of the slow, tormented, anxious days, with the pangs of humiliation, with the tramplings of regret, with the squeaks of lust, suddenly it seems to me like a nightmare, continuous and meaningless, like a disease which you're ashamed of when you recover from it, and I said, difficult, in exactly the same tone as he had described his trip, and I even tried to pull the same grave, important face. Why, what's so difficult, he asked, absolutely innocent, as if he had nothing to do with it, but all the time I felt that his questions were leading somewhere, they weren't accidental, just as his satisfaction at the door wasn't accidental, and I said, you know why, and he said, I have no idea, and I whispered, because I wanted you. Me? He smiled in demonstrative surprise, really? And I said, yes, you, and I repeated again, it was difficult for me, because I didn't really know how to describe it, it sounded so absurd in the gleaming kitchen, and he asked, but why, and I whispered, ashamed of the banal words, because I love you, and he smiled again like a teacher who has finally succeeded in getting the right answer out of a pupil, and asked, why? What do you love about me? And I had the uneasy feeling that this was the point towards which the whole conversation had been leading.

What did I love about him? I didn't even know him, what could I already love about him, and nevertheless, once I'd said it I had to stand behind what I'd said, and so I postponed my answer, and the longer I postponed it the more embarrassing it became, and I sensed that he was waiting in suspense, and in the end I stammered, I don't know, there's nothing clear that I love about you, but nevertheless I know that I love you.

So how can you love me, he sounded disappointed, almost aggressive, in that case it's just an empty declaration.

Not at all, I felt I was getting in over my head, I'm simply not well enough acquainted with you, but love sometimes precedes acquaintanceship with a kind of inner knowledge, and for a moment I knew that I was simply mouthing slogans, because it wasn't love, how could it be love, and then he said, as if in revenge for the inadequate answer, I have to go. No, don't go, I blurted out hysterically, as if my world would collapse again if he left now, and he sat up straight, full of importance, and said, look, Ya'ara, you're not careful enough, and just as you make unconsidered declarations you're liable to take unconsidered actions, actions you haven't got the mental strength to back up. Real life demands difficult decisions which you aren't capable of confronting, so for the time being you should remain with the life you've got. Listen to me, you mustn't let every obstacle disrupt the right flow. I almost choked with the desire to prove mental strength and resolution, and I asked, but how can you tell which is the obstacle and which is the right flow? And he said, I think you know, I think everyone who makes a mistake knows in advance that he's going to make a mistake, he simply can't stop himself. The surprise is perhaps a reaction to the size of the mistake, not the fact of its existence.

But this responsible speech did not prevent his brown hand, with its long fingers, from coming to rest on my knee, and I stroked finger after finger, I didn't dare to touch them all at once, and I even pushed them up, under my skirt, and they stopped there, not where I wanted them, but close, so close that I felt that at any minute it would come, and I was so excited I couldn't finish my coffee, all I could think of was the long fingers hesitating at the door to my body.

But then he suddenly pulled his hand away as if he had been stung and looked demonstratively at his watch, a huge, black watch without numbers, with transparent hands, and it was impossible to tell what the time was, only that nothing good was going to happen now, and he stood up quickly, I have to go, I'm already late, but I couldn't let go, all I could think of was how to keep him there, and in the end I said, I have to go to the toilet, and he showed me impatiently where it was, and I sat on the closed lid and thought about how to stop him leaving, how to gain control over him, and then I washed my hands opposite the mirror and suddenly I saw a straight, fine red hair in the basin, and I examined it closely until I had no doubt as to whose head this hair came from. Before my eyes, as if reflected in the mirror in front of me, I saw the precise, polished haircut, and I looked round apprehensively, as if the mysterious niece was about to jump out of the bathtub and pounce on me, and indeed, on the side of the tub I discovered another one, curly this time, a darker, pubic hair, and I thought, what's going on here, does she live here? With him and his wife? And for a moment I felt reassured, apparently she really was a member of the family, but something still looked suspicious to me, and in order to express my protest I pulled a hair from my head and laid it next to her hair in the basin, and since I didn't want to leave the curly hair by itself either, I laid one of my own, surprisingly similar, next to it on the side of the bathtub.

When I emerged he looked more relaxed, and he said, they called to put off the meeting, I have a few more minutes, and I was sorry that I had wasted precious minutes in the bathroom, but I was a little surprised, because I hadn't heard the phone ring, and I sat down next to the blue cup, the coffee was already stone cold, and his official face oppressed me, and I thought what do I do next, what do I do, and then he asked, so what, in fact, do you want? And with a sense of oppression I said, what do you want? Don't you have a will of your own? And he said, I have a will of my own, but there's no balance between us, you're so hungry and I'm so full. I immediately dropped the nibbled chocolate in my hand, trying to contradict him, but I knew that he was right, I felt the hunger piercing me from inside, that was the word, hunger, not desire, which is a more fastidious word, because when you're famished you eat anything, and then he looked at his hands, examining the manicured nails, and I too looked at his hands and wondered how to bring them back to me, and I heard him say in an official tone, I won't go to bed with you today, Ya'ara, and I, in my embarrassment, asked, why, and he said, because I've already been to bed with one woman today, in a stern, serious voice, as if he was announcing, I've already eaten red meat once today and twice is against doctor's orders. So what, I asked, and he said, I don't go to bed with two women in one day, it's my rule, and all the time I hoped that he was joking, that in a minute he would burst into pleasant, uninhibited laughter, but this didn't happen, and in the end I was so tense that I began to laugh myself, not exactly pleasant, uninhibited laughter, and he asked what's so funny, and I said, nothing really, and I tried to calm down, because nothing was funny, on the contrary, and I said, so what then, I have to catch you earlier in the morning, the early bird catches the worm, or make an appointment in advance, or what? He recoiled slightly from my mockery and said coldly, let's leave it at that, I only wanted to spare you unpleasantness, but I apparently couldn't do without the unpleasantness and I was overcome with ambition to break this rule of his, and I said, there's always an exception, and he said, yes, so I hear, and looked at me with dead eyes, and I tried to imagine his face burning as he made love to her, to the girl with the cigarette holder, she could be both his wife's niece and his lover, there was no contradiction, or perhaps he was the same with her as he was with me, dead and cold, and then he said, I'm free tomorrow morning, casually, and went up to the coat rack and took a black coat and wrapped himself in it carefully, as if he were wrapping a precious object. I fell on the bone and asked what time, and he said, I'll be free at about nine, and opened the door, signalling me to follow him, and I thought, what will I do until tomorrow at nine?

But the time actually passed quickly, Shira was busy, or said she was in order to avoid me, so I began to clean the house, I put on music and danced with the broom, hugging its stiff back, and I felt festive, because at last I had something to wait for, and I was afraid to think of what would happen afterwards, say tomorrow at twelve, or this time tomorrow, so I concentrated on cleaning, and when Yonny came home he looked round happily and suspiciously, unable to believe his good fortune, and I was glad and proud to see his happiness at the evidence that I was functioning again.

You look as if you've been cured of an illness, he said, and I said, yes, that's how I feel, and he hugged me, I was in such despair, Moley, I didn't know what was happening to you, and he immediately withdrew, afraid I would be angry, and I snuggled up to him, I feel much better, Ratty, I'm sorry if I hurt you, and he said, apologize to yourself, not to me, because first of all you hurt yourself. You're right, I said, and I remembered how hard I had tried to love him at the beginning, how I had thought of him with the dedication of a mourner reflecting constantly on her dead, not allowing herself to think of anything happy, and now it was coming back to me, the love for him, like a cat coming home after disappearing, exuding the daunting smell of the wide world, not sure of its welcome, and I received it with joyful surprise, how right that taxi driver was, it is possible to love two men at once, it's even easier to love two, because it creates a balance in the soul, two loves complement each other, and it's less frightening, how come I didn't think of it before, and in my excitement at what's in store for me tomorrow it seems to me that Yonny too excites me, and I sit down on his lap and kiss the root of his neck, let's go out for a bit, I'm sick of staying at home all the time. Now that the house is so clean it would be a pity to go out, he laughs, but I tug at his hand, don't worry, it won't get dirty again before we come back, and we walk up the main street, right at the intersection a new café has opened, and next to Shira's lane, exactly where I had heard the faint, heart-breaking thud, I say to him, let's invite her to come with us, and he isn't enthusiastic, but he doesn't object, and she opens the door with a glum expression, no, she really doesn't feel like going out, it's chilly outside and she's got a cold, and by the way she says to me, I thought you were sick because I saw Netta today in the cafeteria and she said that you hadn't showed up for your reception hour again, and I hit myself on the head, how could I have forgotten that it was Wednesday today, what was happening to me, suddenly nothing existed apart from him, and I was going to lose the appointment, a post only became available in the department once every few years, and in the end Netta would get it and not me. It seems to me that Shira enjoys seeing me pressured, perhaps it's her small revenge, ever since that evening she hasn't wished me well, and I can't resist asking, has Tulya come back? And she says, not yet, and Yonny says in his soothing voice, he must be on heat, cats always disappear during the rutting season and then they come back, and Shira protests, but it's not the rutting season now, and I say, actually it is, I saw a lot of cats on heat round here, I can feel it in the air, and Shira shrugs her shoulders indifferently and says, I can't feel a thing, and leans against the open door, you're letting in the cold, make up your minds if you're coming in or going out, and I say, we're going, and Yonny coaxes her, why don't you come with us, and I feel annoyed because he's got no character, first he didn't want her to come and now suddenly he wants her, but Shira has got character and she says, no, definitely not, some other time.

By the time we returned to the main road a feeling of oppression had settled on me, and I found it difficult to reconstruct my previous happiness, happiness isn't the word, but wholeness, it was a rare feeling of wholeness stemming precisely from the contradiction which had appeared in my life, the contradiction between my love for Yonny and my attraction to this old man, and instead of feeling torn I felt that the tears inside me were being mended, but Shira's grim look had undermined me all over again, and also the thought of the reception hour I had forgotten, and Yonny apparently sensed that the moment of grace was fading and he became anxious, drumming his thick fingers on the round café table and swinging his foot briskly and nervously to and fro. We ordered onion soup and I tried to relax and retrieve the wholeness, which was impossible to retrieve, because it was basically untenable, because an inner contradiction was busy undermining it all the time, and I decided that tomorrow would be the last time, and then I would start work on my thesis, and I asked Yonny again what had happened between him and Shira, and he said nothing, and I insisted, so why does she always look at you with such yearning, and he said, I don't know, nothing happened, really, we are friends, like brother and sister. Suddenly my stomach contracted in sorrow, because we too, it seemed, had become like that, brother and sister, and it was so hard to break, and only fleetingly, by virtue of the excitement aroused in me by a gloomy old man, did I succeed in feeling excited by him, too, and I took his hand and put it on my knees, exactly where that smooth brown hand had crept before, and tried to push it under my skirt, and he went on drumming nervously with his fingers, and my skirt rose and fell as if little grasshoppers were jumping there, and he stopped only when the soup arrived, withdrew his hand, grabbed hold of the spoon with an expression of relief, and fell avidly on the soup.

The music was loud and it was hard to talk, so we ate in silence, dunking the bread in the pungent soup, and I thought, it was like receiving a gift, my happiness when we first met, but how quickly it became oppressive, because the gift didn't suit, and by the time I found out it was too late to change, I knew that I wouldn't get another one, not ever. I tried to ask him what was new at work, and he said that they were working on a new programme that had made a good impression, and there was a good chance they would be able to distribute it, he worked in his father's computer company, and then he asked the waiter to turn down the volume of the music, because we could hardly hear each other talk, and the waiter said, okay, no problem, but he didn't turn it down, perhaps even the opposite, and then Yonny asked again and the waiter pretended that it was the first time and said again, okay, no problem, and again he didn't turn it down. Yonny sighed in resignation, he always preferred to avoid confrontation, to suffer in silence as long as he could, and I said, let's leave, but our demonstration made no impression, two youngsters immediately appeared and took our places, and on the way home we walked hand in hand, the sky was thick and cloudy, tickling the tops of our heads like a wedding canopy held by four short, tired people.

Perhaps this was why I thought of him that night, when I couldn't fall asleep, of my short, tired father, and I had a dim memory of how once he was tall and then he shrank, as if he had been cut in two, half remained with us and other half he kept for himself, and I tried to imagine him against the background of the low hills of our neighbourhood, where we had lived in our first life, hills that were too low, unambitious, that was why he had seemed tall then and now he was short, and not because then I was a child and now I was an adult, I had never succeeded in dividing my life into childhood and adulthood, I was no less a child now than I was then, but into a first life and a second life which had no connection between them, and in each of which I was both a child and an adult. And perhaps he hadn't been cut only into two, but into three or even four, and this was apparently what you had to do to get through life safely, to divide yourself into a number of parts, and the more I thought of my father the harder it was for me to fall asleep, and I felt pity for him churning inside me, ancient and inexplicable, and I remembered something I had once read in a newspaper about a student who was working as a call-girl in some hotel and suddenly her father turned up as a client, and again I asked myself, who was more to be pitied, her or him, and I remembered that Yonny had said, both of them, but I wasn't appeased, I had to know, which of them more, which of them should I bestow my

pity on, and since the paper said she was a student I suspected all
the girls who had studied with me, I even suspected Netta for a
while, until I found out that she didn't have a father. Once more
I tried to think of what it was like then, before I was born, in
that sweet past of his, which was so perfect, so inspiring, only
the past interested him, his childhood landscapes, the friends of
his youth, his first studies, the rented flats, there was no way of
competing with this arrogant past, and I, unfortunately for me,
couldn't be part of it, only of this grey, disappointing present,
and I thought that perhaps tomorrow at nine, or at five past
nine, I would ask Aryeh Even about this past, about the tall, vivid
past of my short, tired father, but it didn't work out, because on
the elegant sofa in his living room, on the stiff narrow towel he
spread severely beneath my buttocks, marking the limits of my
freedom of movement, I forgot all about it, and it was only a
few weeks later, on the way to Jaffa, that I remembered.

4

In the mirror above the basin in his bathroom, where I deliberately laid two long, thick hairs, I looked pale, almost anaemic, but here, among the racks in the shop, I am radiant, my cheeks are flushed and my eyes burning, alight with excitement, because this is my revenge on him, on his mechanical movements, his few, cold words, more than talking to me he coughed into my throat, a charred smoker's cough, hopeless and automatic.

Luckily the previous saleswoman isn't here, her place has been taken by a flustered young girl, and I rummage among the racks of dresses, if it's there it will be a sign, and it really is there, my wine-coloured dress, once so desired and now unwanted, and I take it to the narrow changing cubicle, my whole body full of intense excitement, just like this morning, but the minute I saw his indifferent face my excitement evaporated, slinking into hiding like a kicked animal, and now it emerges again, when it's alone with me it isn't frightened.

The resinous smell of his body rises from me when I undress, his expensive aftershave, the strange, repellent odour of his barren semen, and all the smells are covered by the beautiful, velvety dress, and I sense its beauty even though there's no mirror in this tiny cubicle which once held both of us, me and him. Longingly I think of his concentrated, painful gaze, not like the cold, formal one that opened the door to me today, what was it here that pained him, perhaps precisely the closeness of the girl with the red hair, the hair I was corresponding with so faithfully. Over the dress I put on my blue sweater and wide jeans, which swallow everything, and a stab of suspense and pleasure pierces me as I emerge from the cubicle, and instead of leaving at once I delay the release, wander round the shop,

rummage in the racks, exactly as I used to do then, in the first
life, after the baby died, and I would wander with my mother
round the depressing streets of the little town. How can I console
you, Mother, I would ask her, and she would look at me with
eyes demented by grief, not saying a word, and once we passed
a display window with an embroidered, feminine dress, the kind
she liked, and I said, perhaps the dress will console you, Mother,
and I went into the shop, she sat on a bench outside and waited
for me and I put the dress on under my clothes like now, I was
about ten years old but very tall, and I hung around the shop for
a while on purpose, to feel the suspense, and when I came out I
gave her my hand and we began to run, laughing like lunatics, the
sleeves of the dress peeping out of my coat, and I asked, does this
console you, Mother, and she didn't say yes but she didn't say
no, and that evening she wore it in my honour and we walked
round the neighbourhood arm in arm. Ever since then, whenever
I saw that she was sad I would bring her surprises, coming home
flushed with excitement and emptying my bag on the bed in my
room simply in order to see her laugh, simply in order to laugh
with her and to feel something of the sharpness of life, and I
try to remember when it stopped, perhaps when I saw that it
no longer made her laugh, and the things piled up in my room,
clothes, jewellery, books, and she grew fat and repulsive and
only wore disgusting clothes, and threw away all her jewellery,
and it no longer gave me a thrill either, it had become too easy,
but now, years later, it gives me a thrill again, and when I walk
out of the shop, smiling at the new saleswoman, at the tensest
moment on the threshold, I say to myself, I deserve it, I deserve
it, the frustration vanishes and gives way to a sense of triumph,
small, private and secret, which to me symbolizes the victory
yet to come, his love which is yet to come, and the stolen dress
hugs me in a supportive, maternal embrace, protecting me like
armour in my new war.

   And on that morning, a few weeks later, when he called and
invited me to go with him to Jaffa, I knew that it was the
beginning of the victory. Actually he didn't really invite me,
he only said, in his way, as if to himself, I'm going to Jaffa,

I'm driving down alone. I was so surprised to hear his voice over the phone, I didn't even know he had my number, and in my delight I even teased him a little and asked, why don't you go with the cigarette holder? That's what I called all his girlfriends, although I didn't even know if they existed, he never said anything, except sometimes: I'm busy, or I was busy, or I'll be busy, in a vague and provocative tone, as if there were a herd of women grazing next to his house.

All the cigarette holders are busy today, he retorted, you're the last on the list.

Perhaps I'm busy too? I said, and he sniggered, perhaps.

I really was busy. I had a class in the morning, and afterwards a meeting with the head of the department, to discuss the subject of my thesis. He insisted on believing in me, this senile old man, on pushing me ahead, he always had time for me and for my vague plans, Shira claimed that he was in love with me and I denied it, but I knew that he felt something special for me, and that like all feelings it wouldn't last for ever, and I shouldn't push my luck. Nevertheless I phoned and left a message with the department secretary to say that I was ill, and for Yonny I left an unclear note, hoping to get back before he returned, or rather not to come back at all, to remain in Jaffa in a rented room, in the role of a mistress, to gaze at the sea and make love, and at night to eat fish and drink white wine, and I sent a parting look round the little flat which we had painted a yellowish shade by mistake, and everyone had consoled us with the promise that it would fade, but time had only made it darker. Strange how little I had become attached to this place, for years it had been my address but not my home, apparently I only had one home, my first home, in the first life, and now I would have only one man, and I would want only one thing of him. But when I got dressed, in my wine-coloured autumn dress, in spite of the cold, with shiny stockings and boots, I thought fearfully of what we would talk about, I had never been with him for more than a hurried hour or two, usually in the middle of the day, with one eye on the dark stain of his watch, and suddenly this whole day, like a cream cake before the knife has touched it, tempting but harmful. Of course I could always listen to him, his conceited loquaciousness didn't demand too much of me, but if he kept quiet what would I say, what did I have to say to him except that I loved him, and without even knowing why.

And then I thought, this is the opportunity I've been waiting for, it seems to me I've been waiting for it for years, to talk about my father, about the young father I never knew, and suddenly I felt close to Aryeh, we weren't complete strangers after all, we had a common acquaintance whom we both knew well, but not from the same years, which made it more interesting, and he could always come to our rescue.

Tell me about my father, I said as soon as I got into the car, even before I fastened the seat belt, afraid of a single moment of silence coming between us, afraid that he would regret inviting me, of all people, to share one whole day of his unique life with him. Again the oppressiveness of that hidden competition, so hidden that I didn't even know who I was competing with, his wife? The girl with the cigarette holder? It was already beginning to seem like a competition with all the women in the world, so oppressive it was and so unspecific.

About your father? He was surprised, stuck a cigarette between his fleshy, grey-brown lips: I think you know him better than me.

Yes, I almost apologized, ostensibly I do, but you never really know your parents, it's all pretence, you, for example, would never dare show your child your real face.

But then I remembered that he had no children and I fell silent, and crouched down in my seat because we were just passing Yonny's office, and pretended to be looking for something in my bag, and in the meantime I tried to think of another subject, now that the first one had been dismissed so quickly.

He was brilliant, I heard him say, as if to himself, everyone said he had a brilliant future in store for him, but his illness screwed up his life.

At precisely that moment I straightened up and my eyes encountered a red tree-top, in the middle of winter in the middle of town, like a mysterious bonfire, and I thought that

I must have misunderstood his last words and I said, illness? What illness?

And he said, a little alarmed, his cigarette disappearing into his mouth, the smoke mingling with his grey lips, what, didn't they tell you about it? And I said, about what? I don't know what you're talking about, and he whispered, I'm sorry, I seem to have made a mistake.

And I almost shouted, tell me, if you've already begun then go on, what illness, of the body, of the mind?

But he had already turned on the radio, looking sullenly for a station, coasting easily down the descent from the city.

At least tell me if it's hereditary, I tried, and he only said, don't worry, don't worry, and in the end he said, forget it, I was only joking.

And I pressed my forehead to the cold window, looking at the long yellow snake of the verge of the road stubbornly pursuing us. What could it be, there were never any doctors in our house, maybe once in a while but nothing out of the ordinary, he had never had any operations, hospitalizations, only 'flu and sore throats like everybody else, there were hardly even any medicines in the house, so what could it be?

And then I remembered that day, right in the middle of the first life, when the mad dog devoured the kitten our cat had just given birth to and I thought that there was something wrong with my father. It was addicted to cats, that dog, but it always took care to leave some remnant, so that people in the neighbourhood would know that something had once existed and was no more, not just wipe it off the face of the earth, and then my father found the chewed-up kitten on the front steps of the house and he turned completely red, I had never seen him like that before, and he picked the kitten up by the ear, apparently it still had an ear, and ran with it to the neighbours, the owners of the dog, and put it down on their dining table, they were in the middle of eating their lunch and there was a wonderful smell in the kitchen, I think he even put it on the neighbour's plate, between the schnitzel and the peas, and he began to cry.

I ran after him stunned, in the wake of the blood and the

sobs, he was always so quiet and mild, afraid of what people would say, always silencing my mother, who was much more vociferous than he was, and suddenly this total indifference to public opinion. And he didn't even like cats, he never stroked them, only demanded that we wash our hands, and now the entire neighbourhood saw him going crazy because of a kitten he hardly knew.

Cautiously I ran after him, hiding behind the bushes, afraid that he would see me, that he would turn the mass of his rage on me, and I saw him come out of there, wrapped in the smells of their kitchen, thin and stooped, bend down next to the acacia tree and vomit, vomit and cry.

Then too I didn't go up to him. I felt a strange satisfaction in seeing him suffering so openly, I had always sensed the presence of some suffering in him, inward and muffled and inarticulate, so inward that there was no way of relating to it, of helping him, and suddenly all this sorrow was outside, like a coat put on inside-out, with the lining and the seams showing, suddenly everything was exposed to the dark winter sunlight, and I believed that now that it was all coming out, I would have a different father, a happy father, because all the quantities of suffering he had contained within him would come out and be absorbed into the earth. I waited there for him to finish and stagger home, red and stinking. Expectantly I followed him all day, to see what had changed in him, but he hardly emerged from his room, he didn't even want to have supper with us. That night I couldn't fall asleep because of his sobbing, all night long I heard him whimper, as if it were him who had swallowed the kitten and now it was wailing inside him. Early in the morning the suspicion began to grown on me, where was it, the chewed-up kitten? Had he left it there, on the neighbour's heaped plate, between the schnitzel and the peas, or had he really swallowed it in his derangement, completing in his madness the madness of the dog, and that was why he had vomited next to the tree, and I felt so deeply disappointed that I nearly cried, because that newborn kitten had been mine, and for a moment it had seemed to me that my father was fighting for my sake, fighting my war, and only at daybreak did I realize that it was apparently a different war, private and secret, which I would never understand.

In the morning I went there, to the great acacia tree, and I crawled among the stones and the mud, trying to find the remains of the kitten which had been expelled from my father's throat. The earth was soft, because it had rained in the night, and it was hard to identify the exact place, there were soft, moist twigs there, which looked like the tails of many kittens, and I arranged them in a row, trying to sort them out, and suddenly it began to rain hard again and I ran home, and when I wanted to go out again my mother put her hand on my forehead and said that I was burning up, that she had suspected something from the moment I got up in the morning, and she put me to bed, and in a moment the whole bed was full of vomit, and in the middle of all this I knew that I wasn't going to have a new father, that any change would only be for the worse.

Was it perhaps connected to cats, his illness? I asked Aryeh, and this question sounded so silly to me, and apparently to him too, because he gripped the steering wheel hard, with the same unpleasant forcefulness as he held me, and asked, what illness, and I knew that I wouldn't get anything more out of him.

So what was I going to talk to him about? I should be charming, amusing, attractive, and all I want to do is sleep, pity I'm not just some hitchhiker, everything would be much simpler between us then, open and natural. Why don't we pretend that I'm your hitchhiker, I suggest hesitantly, and he agrees enthusiastically, he even insists on stopping and letting me off so he can pick me up a minute later, in the most convincing way. We have to really believe it, he says as I get out of the car, watch him rapidly reverse and stop at the nearby gas station. What's to prevent him from driving past me without stopping? How little faith I have in him. In a minute I might be a real hitchhiker, but somebody else's.

I was almost surprised when he stopped, with a broad smile which shone through the washed window. I opened the door and he said, I'm going to Jaffa, and you?

Jaffa too, I said and got into the sharply resinous smell of the car and examined the driver suspiciously, mindful of the fact that every trip like this could be the last, and he sensed my look and said, you have nothing to fear, a rapist I'm not.

So what are you? I asked, perhaps the truth might come out by accident, and he laughed, a travelling salesman, that's what I am. I looked at his dark profile, and suddenly he looked to me like an Indian, with his brown skin and silver-grey hair and high cheekbones, a wise old Indian, and I imagined him with a turban on his head and I laughed, what did I have to do with him, and he looked slightly embarrassed and asked, and you?

I'm Avishag, I said, I'm from a kibbutz in the south. There was an Avishag from a kibbutz in the army with me, she was my room-mate and she always fell asleep without any problems while I tossed and turned till morning, cursing my spiteful sleeplessness, envying her wearily, despairingly, wishing I was her.

Avishag, he said enthusiastically, obviously preferring my new identity, what have you got on under your panty hose?

Panties, I said, what did you think?

That's what I thought, he said, disappointed, you know, Avishag, I lived for a long time in Paris, you know what I discovered there?

I haven't a clue, I said coldly, my new name protected me from him.

I discovered that the women in Paris don't wear anything under their panty hose, he said, and believe me, it's worth their while. Take them off, Avishag, you'll see that you don't need them.

And it'll be worth my while, I sniggered, and he resumed his usual supercilious tone and said, don't do it for me, do it for yourself, you'll feel closer to your body like that, I'm telling you.

Actually I wasn't particularly keen on coming closer to my body, but to his, and not really to his body, but to something more inward which for lack of an alternative I called body, which sorrowfully I called body, long fingers and smooth dark skin and shapely lips and eyes which suddenly came to life, looking alternately at the wide flat road and at my legs, unable to hide their expectation.

Then I began to get undressed in the car, to pull off my boots and afterwards my panty hose, wriggling so as not to tear them, like a huge spider with several long legs getting tangled up in each other, and I removed the superfluous accessory, and put everything back on again and waved the panties at him, and he smiled a satisfied smile and pushed them into his trouser pocket as if they were a handkerchief, and they were still peeping out of it when we got out of the car and began to walk. Deliberately I didn't ask where we were going, if this was an adventure then let it be one to the end, and I knew that he was waiting for me to ask so that he could resent it, because he wanted me to trust him completely, unconditionally, so I said to myself, today we're practising trust and living without panties, as if living without panties was some lofty goal, an advanced stage on the way to womanhood, or rather mistresshood. I imagined how people would ask me what I did and I would say: I'm a mistress, with a pride that would take them aback.

I thought that we would go to art galleries or to look at the sea, but he turned quickly into a narrow alley and climbed an old staircase, my panties peeping out of his pocket, and knocked on some door, and after a few minutes the door opened and a sleepy man stood on the threshold, beaming with joy.

Aryeh, he said in a high-pitched voice, wonderful to see you, I didn't think you would come, and then he looked at me and he seemed embarrassed but pleased, and Aryeh said, this is Avishag, a kibbutznik from the south, my hitchhiker.

I felt quite comfortable with my borrowed identity, and I wondered what the real Avishag would say now, presumably she wouldn't have landed up here in the first place, anyone who slept so well at night didn't find herself in a dump like this by day. It was a real dump, but at the same time it wasn't a conventional apartment, there was only one big room with a double bed in the corner, a table made of a round copper tray and a little fridge, a kind of student's flat, but the person who

lived there looked more like a pensioner than a student. They
must have seen my surprise, because Aryeh suddenly said, this
is where Shaul cheats on his wife, and it seemed to me that he
glanced at the bed, and Shaul laughed in embarrassment and
denied it like some virgin, no, no, nonsense, this is where I rest,
have some time to myself between one trial and the next, and
I looked at him suspiciously, why was he on trial all the time,
what had he done, and then I thought, maybe he's a lawyer,
even a judge, which seemed unlikely because there was nothing
in the least magisterial about him, but his shy, modest presence
reassured me a little. Strange that both of them are called men,
I thought, they look like a completely different species, why are
there only two possibilities for all of us, either men or women,
like tea or coffee, when reality is so much more complex, and I
was glad that he wasn't like Aryeh and I smiled at him gratefully.
He asked what we would like to drink and I hesitated between
tea and coffee, but he began to list brands of beer, whisky and
brandy, and recommended an excellent cognac he had brought
from Hungary, he had returned only last week, and he had
brought back excellent salami too, and he had passed through
Paris and collected a few cheeses as well, he spoke as if Europe
was one big supermarket where you walked round filling up your
trolley with goodies, and in a moment the treasures of Europe
were laid out on the low, dirty, oriental table, and next to them
the bottle of recommended cognac, and we sat round the table
and Aryeh poured a glass for me and then for himself, and then
he cut slices of salami and put them into my mouth with an
intimate gesture, and the sharpness of the salami mingled with
the sharpness of the cognac and gave me a feeling of life, real
life. And then they started to talk about Paris and I didn't really
listen to the names of restaurants, wines, women, streets slipping
past my ears, I had only spent three days in Paris and I didn't
have much to contribute to the conversation, only that I'd had
a terrible migraine there and lain prostrate in the hotel with
my eyes closed, and what I remembered most were the patterns
of the flowers on the wallpaper and the pink bedspread, but I
enjoyed listening to their relaxed chatter, they were apparently

old friends, and I felt comfortable sitting between them, I was specially glad of the presence of Shaul, who as it were guarded me against Aryeh, and it seemed to me that Aryeh too saw me in a new light now, through the eyes of his friend.

From time to time Aryeh would light me a cigarette or push a piece of salami into my mouth or fill my glass with cognac, and I would chew and swallow without thinking, enjoying the role of a baby whose decisions were taken for her. When I got up to pee I felt pleasantly giddy, and on the toilet my eyes closed for a moment, but when they opened I was glad to find myself there, in this surprisingly spacious lavatory, as if it were intended to accommodate cripples in wheelchairs, and when I emerged Shaul asked, are you all right, Avishag? We were worried about you, and I thought what simple solutions there were for complicated problems, you could invent a new name even on a temporary basis and be a different person. When I passed Aryeh's armchair he stroked my leg under my dress and felt the top of my thigh as if to ascertain that my panties had not escaped his pocket and returned to their natural place, and then he said, come and sit on my lap, and I sat on his lap and he went on stroking me under my dress with one hand and with the other he went on feeding me, pushing his fingers into my mouth until I began to chew his hands, I could hardly distinguish between his fingers and the slices of salami, they too were sharp and salty, and in the end I actually preferred them, because I could no longer swallow, I was so full, so I simply held his hand as if it were a sandwich and chewed it on all sides, and he went on talking to Shaul, who seemed to be losing his concentration, most of the time he stared at me and the movements of my mouth and in the end he got up and stood next to us and I heard his breathing and he touched my face, my nose and eyes, and then he too began to push his fingers into my mouth, and Aryeh removed his own hand and made room for him, and in the meantime he lit himself another cigarette, and Shaul groped inside my mouth like a dentist and his hands were soft and I felt as if they were about to melt in my mouth and I was a little disgusted, and he apparently sensed my disgust and went back to his chair looking somewhat snubbed, and Aryeh laughed and said to him or to both of us, it's all right, it's all right.

And so my mouth emptied all at once, and I felt an urge to do something with it so I put my head on Aryeh's shoulder and began to kiss his neck and his ear and the edge of his cheek, where the smell of the aftershave is strongest, and I looked at his ear, it was the first time I had paid any attention to his ear, which was actually quite ordinary, but suddenly seemed to me miraculous, small in relation to his face, almost pink, and for a moment I thought that deep inside it there was a tiny hearing aid, pink and round as a cherry, and I poked my finger in to touch it but I couldn't find anything, and all the time Aryeh went on talking in his husky voice, without panting or showing any signs of excitement, but I sensed a tension in his body which hadn't been there before.

So that's what you're really like, I thought, I always wanted to see him on fire, he was always cold and denying with me, just like a machine, and now he was a little different, his hands moved over me with less indifference, tense and supple. Suddenly it began to rain, a serious cloudburst followed by thunder and lightning, and the little flat looked like Noah's ark, dark and dilapidated, and they fell silent, letting the thunder speak, and Shaul looked at me, he had a question in his eyes, perhaps he was wondering what a girl like me was doing inside the ear of a pathetic old man or something like that, and for a moment I too felt a certain doubt, but Aryeh, who apparently sensed the retreat, began to peel off my panty hose, and then he stood up and pulled me to my feet, the panty hose stretched tight around my knees, and said, come to bed, you'll be more comfortable in bed, and I said, but what about Shaul, and Aryeh said, it won't bother Shaul, right, Shaul? He said this in a loud, emphatic voice, like a kindergarten teacher, and Shaul said in his high, squeaky voice, no, it's okay, I'll just lie here and watch, as if he was doing us a favour, and Aryeh pulled down his trousers as he advanced on the bed, for a moment we looked like two toddlers running to the lavatory, with their bums exposed and their trousers round their ankles, and he lay down on his back and waited for me to kick off my boots and panty hose and sit on top of him, it was clear that this was what he wanted, and I tried to sit with my back straight and to move gracefully, like an actress, because I could sense Shaul's eyes on me all the time, I had never had an audience before, and I knew that it imposed an obligation.

My ambition increased from one minute to the next, I wanted to astonish my audience with my performance, so I stretched and arched my back until my hands touched the end of the bed and I almost expected applause but instead I heard panting and the sound of undressing, and I saw that the shadowy figure in the armchair was growing white, his fair skin was exposed as his clothes came off, he was almost phosphorescent, but suddenly I couldn't see anything because Aryeh turned over and covered me completely, and now it was his turn to impress with his performance, his pelvis moved energetically, and I began to moan, not only with pleasure, actually he was beginning to hurt me and I was getting fed up too, but I felt an obligation to supply the sound as well, so that it wouldn't be a silent movie, and my moans goaded him to even greater heights, and he said, you love it, you love it, like some sort of mantra, and I felt an urge to suddenly say no, and ruin everything. And then the bed sank a little as if something heavy had fallen on it, and Aryeh withdrew abruptly, and I felt Shaul's soft hands caressing me and all the time I searched for Aryeh's body and held onto it, I didn't want to remain alone with Shaul and I was prepared to accept him only as a kind of extension of Aryeh, and I felt him rubbing against me, and his soft white penis groping in confusion like a blind man's stick, and Aryeh held me tight as if he was afraid I would run away, and he said, it's all right, it's all right, and his voice sounded so clear and convincing that I repeated the words to myself and Shaul said, you're beautiful, you're beautiful, and I was glad that Aryeh heard, and he tried again and again to enter me and failed, apparently Aryeh's blatant virility put him off his stroke, and when he gave up I felt great relief, and I didn't mind him stroking me, licking me all over my body, as long as Aryeh was holding me tight. And then they brought the bottle to bed and we drank, passing it from hand to hand like in the game

'truth or dare', and the sweet, sharp feeling came back to me and
I thought that perhaps having been born was worth it after all,
and Aryeh put his penis back into me and I leant against Shaul
and we both swayed under the assault of Aryeh's strong thrusts,
until I heard them both come, almost at the same time, as if they
were the perfect couple, and I felt Shaul's semen on my back and
Aryeh's on my front, like a juicy bone licked on all sides by dogs
or cats and I remembered the dog which had devoured the kitten
and my father's mysterious illness and my meeting with the head
of the department and Yonny and I began to cry and all the time
the sentence echoed in my head: what's done can't be undone,
what's done can't be undone.

They took no notice, both of them fell asleep, Aryeh into the
tense, alert sleep with which I was already familiar, and Shaul
into the heavy sleep of the no longer young or healthy, and
I went and sat on the lavatory, peeing and crying, and then
I stood up and looked in the mirror, and apart from the red
eyes I looked the same, and this reassured me somewhat, if I
looked the same apparently nothing had happened, and I took
a shower in the old shower, in almost cold water, and I said to
myself, it's all right, it's all right.

When I came out Aryeh was already dressed, and his face had
resumed its remote, dignified, official expression again, a kind of
Indian authority, and this too reassured me, with a face like that
a person knew what he was doing, and my anxiety dissolved, and
he lit another cigarette and made coffee, and Shaul too woke up,
and we sat round the table again, Shaul and I naked and Aryeh
dressed, and Aryeh asked, aren't you cold, Ya'ara, and I said I
wasn't, and Shaul was surprised, why Ya'ara, I thought her name
was Avishag, and Aryeh sniggered and said that my name was
really Ya'ara, and Shaul said, it's a pretty name, isn't Korman's
daughter called Ya'ara too, and Aryeh said, she is Korman's
daughter, I forgot that you know him, and Shaul said, what
do you mean know him, the three of us studied together, and
Aryeh said, right, I forgot, and I was ashamed of being naked
and I began to collect my clothes, and I was especially ashamed
of bending down and turning my bare backside to them, but my

clothes were on the floor, and I attempted a grotesque kind of crouch and found myself flat on the floor.

I heard them talking about the old days and about my father, how they used to copy from him, and how he would argue with the lecturers while they went out on dates, and how all the lecturers were afraid of him, and how he dropped everything because of the war, and here they suddenly fell silent. I felt nauseous and my head ached, so I lay down on the bed, and Aryeh asked with a laugh, you want another round? And I didn't feel like answering, especially since Shaul answered for me, leave her alone, let her rest, and I saw the question on his face deepening, his uneasiness at the fact that he had almost fucked Korman's daughter, or watched her fucking, and I was afraid that he would tell my father, that he would send him an anonymous letter and tell him that his daughter was screwing old men instead of working on her thesis, and I tried to concentrate on my thesis, to go through the list of subjects in my head and finally choose one, and suddenly I fainted.

I saw them standing over me, like anxious parents, Aryeh the father and Shaul the mother, wetting my face and throat with a wet towel. I felt as if I had woken from a long, sweet sleep, the sweetest there was, my head ached slightly, as in the aftermath of great pain, and the overall feeling was one of sudden, extreme recovery, of radical, almost revolutionary change. I smiled at them and saw their faces softening, and Aryeh said, you fainted for a few minutes but don't worry, and he brought me a glass of water, and Shaul began to tell a story of how the same thing had happened to him once in the middle of a trial, and I realized that he really was a judge, and I thought it was hilarious that I had almost gone to bed with a judge, and I said to myself, it must be okay if a judge approved it, and Aryeh looked at his blank watch and said, we have to go, Ya'ara, and at the door Shaul kissed me and said, give my regards to your father, and Aryeh held my elbow and led me to the car, without us even having seen the sea, and in the car I asked, where are my panties, and he put his hand in his pocket and brought it out empty and said, I must have left them there, and I said resentfully, but I liked them, they were the prettiest panties I had, and Aryeh said, we're not going back now for panties, another time, and I knew that there wouldn't be another time, and I felt incomplete without them, as if I had set out whole and returned damaged, and the whole trip seemed to me like a malevolent plot to rob me of my prettiest panties.

I kept quiet and looked out of the window, I decided not to make an effort this time and to let him think of what to talk about, but he apparently had no intention of exerting himself, he was satisfied with himself and the steering wheel and the songs on the radio, and it was only after about half an hour that he remembered me and asked, was that your first time like that? And I said yes, and yours?

He laughed his smug laugh, certainly not, don't forget I was in Paris in the hottest years, I tried everything, everything, that's why it's hard for me now.

Hard for you? I was surprised.

Yes, everything bores me now. I know you think it's aimed against you, but you're wrong. It's a general boredom which is hard to dispel. It needs sharper and sharper stimulations all the time, until they too stop working. As you see, an ordinary fuck, man on woman, in out, seems about as exciting to me as gymnastics in front of the television.

That may be technically correct, I tried to recite, but what about feelings? That's what's supposed to make the difference, if a woman interests you then fucking her will interest you, no? It's like a conversation, no?

What makes you think I'm interested in conversation? he said sullenly. What I said about sex goes for conversation too. The stimulation has to be sharper every time. And feelings? I don't know what they are any more. With the years human beings become more bestial, or infantile, what counts is needs.

I felt a sudden despair, total, terminal despair, as if I had swallowed poison and could no longer be saved even though I bitterly regretted it, as if nothing could help me. I was destroying my life and he was being destroyed by boredom, and then he put his beautiful hand on my leg, in an attempt at appropriation, and said, you know, when I saw you like that with Shaul, it was the first time I really saw you, the first time I was attracted to you. His admiration of you affected me.

But this only increased my despair and I said, so what's going to happen, and he said, nothing, why does anything have to happen, and I said, but I love you.

And again he asked, why, what do you love about me?

As always I began to squirm, put off by his need to hear how wonderful he was in my eyes, especially since it was far from true, I thought he was egocentric, inconsiderate, childish, arrogant, and insensitive, but I couldn't even hint at all this. So what do you love about me, he asked again, I'd really be interested to know.

At last something interests you, I said sulkily, I love the colour of your skin and your voice and your walk and the way you light a cigarette, and I knew that he would be disappointed by this meagre and random list but he smiled contemptuously and said, if such little things give rise to such great love in you, what will you do when you meet a really impressive man? And I said if only that kind of relation existed between the greatness of the love and the qualities of the beloved, but that's not the way it works, and I thought of Yonny and his excellent qualities, and Aryeh looked perturbed, he hadn't received the fix he required, because if my love wasn't connected to his virtues, it didn't flatter him or testify to his superiority, and it was apparently hard for him to waive the right to be loved for the right reasons, and he said, I think that you simply don't understand me yet, you're so obsessed by what you get or don't get from me that you can't see me as I am, independently of you, and I said, right.

I looked at the black clouds advancing in our direction, heavy and low, as if there was a heavenly highway above our heads, and it seemed to me that the borders were about to be blurred, either we would rise up, or they would come down and collide with us, and outside the light faded even though it was still early and a hard rain began falling again and shook the car. I leaned against the door and looked outside and thought that this was what I should do now, open the door and jump out, just as I was, without a coat, without panties, and end it, because there was no other way of ending it. I covered my eyes and looked at him through my fingers, like you look at a frightening scene in a movie when you're not prepared to miss it completely, and he looked to me like an enormous grey caterpillar, with his bulging eyes and thick lips and pink ears, all his dark flesh, which seemed slightly overcooked, and suddenly he smiled to himself, a rich smile, and I thought, what are you smiling about, don't you know that I'm getting out, and I was so delighted by the rhyme that I made up a tune to it, and I hummed it quietly to myself and cheered up slightly. You can always die, I said to myself, let's give life another chance. Now you can see him as he is, it's a good thing you went with him because now the picture's getting clearer, thirsty for compliments and ego-boosts just as you're thirsty for love, but what can you do, that's life, when you're thirsty you stay thirsty, nobody gives you a thing. So why bother in the first place, let some other girl bore him, why does it have to be you, you've got more exciting things to do with yourself, but here I became somewhat stuck, because nothing seemed more exciting to me, and I thought about the moment when my mouth was full of fatty Hungarian salami and twenty fingers.

I went on looking at him with my eyes covered, that was the way I saw him most accurately, amputated and incomplete between my fingers, with me in absolute control of the picture, and I said to myself, okay, let's say you love him, let's erase the him and remain with the love, love's a good thing, right? Every child knows that love's a good thing, so let's simply give it to somebody else. Let's say you make a cake for someone, and he's not interested in your cake, what will you do? Give it to somebody else, so do me a favour, take your love and pass it on to you know who, the person who's got the same address and telephone number as you have. And then I began to think about him hard, about Yonny, I tried to think of every detail separately, because he was strong on details, about his brown eyes, with the long lashes, and the orange-coloured, almost feminine lips, and the brown curls I liked to tousle on his head at the beginning, about his whole cameo-shaped face, but then

I saw him swaying from side to side, like the windscreen wipers which were working energetically, and I didn't understand why, and when I understood a scream escaped into my hands because I saw him hanging, I knew that I would come home and see him swaying in the bathroom, his lashes lying on his pale cheeks, having that very moment kicked the chair out from under him. Someone had told him about me and Aryeh, and he couldn't go on living with my lie and he couldn't leave me either, just as I couldn't leave Aryeh. Or perhaps he could, perhaps at this very moment he was packing, or writing me a letter, I trusted you, he would write, and you deceived me, you besmirched our love. I never held you on a tight rein, I never burdened you with questions, I gave you freedom in the hope that you would do only good with it, and I asked only one thing, that when you no longer wanted me, you would tell me. I always told you that as far as I was concerned you were a free agent, that I had no control over your body or your mind, and I didn't want you to stay with me out of constraint either. I wanted you to choose me freely every day anew, and to be honest enough to tell me if you had chosen someone else.

If only it was so simple, I would say to him, you think that's the way it works? Yes, no, black, white? And what if I chose someone who didn't choose me?

Then too, you have to take me out of the picture, he would say, the results don't matter, even if you wanted somebody else for a single minute, and I would persevere, but what if I'm not sure yet, what if I change my mind, and he would say, with his clear, rigid thinking, impatient of contradictions, I told you, the results don't matter.

I've lost him, either way I've lost him, because of you I've lost him, and I want to tear Aryeh's self-satisfied face to pieces, to grab the wheel and throw him out, into the pouring rain, but he grips the wheel firmly as if to say, forget about it, honey, I'm in control here. You can dream about seeing me tomorrow, I think, you can dream about seeing me the day after tomorrow, in two weeks' time, in two months, in two years, I'm going now to rescue what's left of my life, if anything's left, and I say, Yonny, wait, don't kick away the chair, not from under you and not from under me, give me a chance, and the rain comes down harder, Aryeh curses under his breath, and I'm afraid we'll never get back, there'll be an accident, he'll have a stroke, and I'll never be able to make amends, and then I take an oath that if everything is okay, if we get home safely and if Yonny stays with me, I'll never see Aryeh again and instead I'll have a baby with Yonny and occupy myself exclusively with him and the child all my life until I die.

Are you looking for something, he asked me as we entered the city, driving along the same streets as this morning only in the opposite direction, and I said, yes, there was a tree here with a red crest that I wanted to see, and he asked, why, and I said, because if I find it it will be a sign and if I don't find it it will also be a sign, and he said, so then it makes no difference, and he remarked that he too had seen something red here this morning, but it was a tiled roof. Again I lowered my head as we neared the computer services office, hoping that Yonny was still there, putting his tame computer animals through their paces. At the top of our street the car stopped, and I protested, it's a little further on, and he said, I know, but this is what's called the safety limit, I don't want you to get into trouble. He said this importantly, as if he were instructing master spies, at least, and I tried to join the act and said to myself, keep cool, act like a professional, and I gave him a penetrating look, because I knew I would never see him again, I tried to learn his face by heart so that I would be able to understand it one day, like solving a riddle. He kept a tight grip on the wheel, and I thought that if he let go of it and touched me it would be a sign, and also if he didn't it would be a sign, and he let go of the wheel but only in order to scratch his nose, and then to light a cigarette, and I had more or less finished looking and so I said goodbye coolly and got out, and when the car drove off I wondered if I should have said thank you, and I also remembered that I had forgotten to examine his eyebrows, if they were still black or going grey like his hair, and now I would have to go through life without knowing what colour his eyebrows were.

Next to the house my heart began to beat faster in fear but I said to myself, keep cool, keep cool, no one would suspect you of anything so terrible, at the most he'll think you were wandering round town buying clothes, he would never believe that you went all the way to Jaffa to get a fuck and a half, even if you tell him he won't believe it, that's the good thing about the truth, that it's unbelievable. And at the door I said, do me a favour Yonny, don't be at home, for your own sake don't be, what do you need it for, and he wasn't.

The flat was dark and warm, they had apparently turned the central heating on early, in honour of the stormy weather, and I stroked the boiling radiators as if they were faithful pets, only the heat had preceded me and it was on my side, it would keep its mouth shut. The sink was full, but it had been full this morning too, I didn't get the impression that any ominous new plate had been added, and with a feeling of relief I took off my clothes and pushed them into the wardrobe, took a quick shower, soaping all the contaminated places, put on my pyjamas and got into bed. The best thing would be to pretend to be sleeping, that way I would both gain time and be able to check out the atmosphere when he arrived, and so I lay in the dark room, celebrating my narrow escape, but the relief soon gave way to anxiety, because it was already six or seven o'clock and Yonny hadn't come home, hadn't called, and nobody else called either, and I began to feel afraid that I had missed some unique opportunity today, some train that passes once in a lifetime, and everybody had climbed on except me.

I imagined them celebrating something far from me, Yonny and my parents and the head of the department and all the students who had been looking for me today, and Shira too, lusting after him in her own shy, indirect way, and then I decided to phone her, she always knew what was happening, even if nothing was happening, and I dialled her number in the dark, and she was actually nice to me, and I asked her if she had heard from Yonny, because I hadn't managed to talk to him, and she said, 5786543, which was his number at the office, and she wasn't nice any longer, and she said, excuse me, Ya'ara, I've got people here, and I was sure that the celebration was taking place at her house, all the people in my life were sitting in her living room now and planning the future without me.

I tried to test my memory of Aryeh's face, which seemed to me to be always shrouded in smoke, even when he wasn't smoking he was surrounded by smoke blurring his features, as if he were saying, what do the details matter, and behind the smoke his stylized face, with its blatant combination of authority and license, as if he were above good and evil, moral and immoral, conventional and unconventional, and with a kind of rage I thought, who put him there, so high, and I said, he did, and then, you did, in other words, I did.

And then I began testing myself on other things, to calm down and pass the time, and I tried to reconstruct my first house, for instance, to remember if it had stucco on the walls, and I decided that at first it didn't and later it did, and I decided that that house looked exactly like a house should look, or like people think a house should look, in other words, a caricature of a house. It even had a tiled roof, if I'm not mistaken. Why should I be mistaken, it was my house for almost twenty years, I should know it better than anything, but sometimes precisely the most familiar things remain unknown, as if everyday familiarity does away with the need to pay attention to detail. Like the story my mother liked telling me about my Aunt Tirza, who on the day of her divorce from her husband, after thirty years of marriage, wanted to be nice to him and make him a cup of coffee in the morning, and she asked him how much sugar he wanted in his coffee and he said that for thirty years he had been taking saccharine.

Not an age to divorce, fifty, she would sigh, just as twenty isn't an age to marry, but one mistake apparently leads to another, and then she would give me a threatening look, as if to say, be careful the same thing doesn't happen to you. She didn't appreciate her husband, he was too good for her, and she apparently wanted to suffer a bit, she didn't want to end her life without her share of suffering, and she got what she wanted, with compound interest.

She was tall and slender, Aunt Tirza, handsome and cold, and I could never imagine her really suffering, she always looked so bored and indifferent, as if even suffering bored her to death, and her husband, Uncle Alex, really looked like a beetle next to her, short and black and laborious, and I could understand why he got on her nerves, but he soon found a young woman who thought he was wonderful, and he actually became wonderful. Sometimes he would come round on Saturdays to show her off, and I would be amazed at the change, suddenly he looked like a man, with self-confidence and a sense of humour, and Aunt Tirza too would be amazed behind the bedroom door, where she would hide on these Saturdays. My mother would always inform her of these visits in advance, even though Alex was her brother she preferred Tirza, and she would invite her over to peek, and every time it happened my father would declare angrily that this was the last time, that he wasn't prepared to be a party to such trickery and deception. My job was to smuggle coffee and leftover refreshments in to Aunt Tirza, and to empty her ashtrays, and once Uncle Alex saw me carrying a full ashtray and he said suspiciously, what's this, Ya'ari, are you smoking already, as if it was obvious that one day I would fill ashtrays and it was only a question of time, and I said no, I'm just cleaning up, and he said, good, good, but he looked worried and afterwards he said to my mother that I was growing beautiful, but it wasn't a good beauty. Why not good, my mother leapt to my defence, and he said, a beauty like her aunt's, which remains inside the person and nobody enjoys it, including the person herself. All this Tirza would hear, and she would light cigarette after cigarette, and when the happy couple left she would come out of the bedroom drained and red-eyed, stinking of cigarettes, and begin talking about the new woman, how she dressed like a tart, which was how she sounded too, and how it shamed her to be replaced by someone like that, and she would never forgive Alex for it, and my mother would say, but Tirza, don't forget it was you who wanted the divorce, he would never have left you, even though he knew about all your affairs, and here they would begin to whisper, and in the evening she would wash her face, which was still smooth and handsome at the age of fifty, and take her departure with a sigh of relief, like someone emerging from a sauna, having suffered to the limits of her endurance in the belief that it was good for her.

You're nothing but a sadist, my father would say to my mother later that night, in the bedroom which still reeked of cigarettes, why do you feed her information all the time, why do you invite her to torture herself here, you're simply jealous because she's a successful lawyer and you never made anything of yourself. Under the guise of loyalty you're tormenting her, don't think I can't see what you're up to.

I never made anything of myself? my mother would flare up. And why didn't I make anything of myself? Because all my life I took care of you!

Took care of me! That's a good one! What's there to take care of? No, you simply preferred to waste your life on nonsense!

Bringing up your children is nonsense? Looking after everyone is nonsense?

Who exactly is everyone? he would rage. You looked after yourself. We saw what happened when you had a baby who really needed you!

How dare you, she would scream, what's so great about what you did with your life? Buried in the laboratory all day like a rat! If you'd finished your studies and not dropped out in the middle, you might have been able to save the baby and we wouldn't have had to depend on the backward doctors in that backward hospital! And then the bedroom door would slam behind my mother, carrying a blanket and a pillow, and she would lie down on the living room sofa, where she would soon fall asleep, like someone with a clear conscience, and I would come and peek at her, trying to find in her wrinkled face a sign of the truth. The truth? That wasn't the question. The question was always who to feel sorry for, and I would go from bed to bed, examine him in his sleep, her in her sleep, wondering which of them to feel sorry for, bearing my bundle of pity like a dose of medicine which was only enough to save one person, and not knowing which of them to give it to. Sometimes I would fall asleep on the floor halfway between them, and in the morning I would see their eyes gazing at my face, full of the demands of all the years they had tried to give birth to me, almost as many years as I had lived, and in the end I let them down, I had failed to justify their efforts, I had not brought them salvation, and salvation was the oppressive burden of my pity, which I didn't know who to give to and in the end I gave it to myself, and in the secret of their hearts they knew it, and treated me as if I had done them a grave injustice, behind my back they held quick trials in kangaroo courts, heaping me with innumerable little guilts which accumulated, especially at night, into one ancient guilt looking for a bed to sleep in.

Sometimes he would hiss, she's going to be like Tirza, I can see it, which for him was a serious curse, even though they seemed to get on well together, they always found plenty to talk about, and it seemed that it wasn't Tirza herself he hated but some part of her, which he regarded as female treachery, arrogance, cruelty, a kind of essence of Tirzaness which did not fill the real, concrete Tirza but only became apparent when an attempt was made to define it.

And my mother would say, nonsense, Ya'ara is so warm and Tirza is so cold, and my father would say in a hurt voice, maybe she's warm to you, not to me.

What kind of warmth exactly do you want from her? she would pounce. What warmth do you give to entitle you to such expectations?

And then the light went on in the next room, without my having heard the door opening, and I saw Yonny taking off his coat, remaining in short pants and a short-sleeved shirt, and my heart was wrung. He looked so young, especially in his white tennis clothes, young and angelic and sweet, and I felt a kind of pride looking at him from the darkness, as if he were my child and I was amazed at how well he had learned to walk, and to take off his coat by himself, and to switch on the light, he could do everything already, my clever little boy, everything, and then he advanced toward me, quietly, so as not to wake me up, and stood in the bedroom doorway and tried to gaze into the absolute darkness. I could see him so clearly and he couldn't see me, he didn't even know for certain if I was there, and he didn't dare come closer to check, I saw the handsome features under the brown curls, and once more I wondered, as I had the first time I saw him, why these handsome features didn't add up to a handsome face.

Moley? he whispered, and I pretended to stretch and rub my eyes and I said, quickly, before he could ask, yes, I fell asleep, I was worried about you, I forgot that it was your day for tennis, and I was overwhelmed with joyful relief that nothing had gone wrong, that his voice was as gentle as always, but then he said, I phoned you at work, they said you hadn't turned up, and I said to myself, keep cool, keep cool, and I murmured, yes, I didn't feel well and I stayed at home, and he said in his gentle voice, which suddenly sounded cruel and frightening to me, but I came home before, to change, and you weren't here, and for a moment I wanted to tell him everything, to start crying and tell him what a dump I had landed up in, and that he should look after me and not let me leave the house, but I repeated to myself, keep cool, you can always confess later, in the meantime try to get out of it with a clean record, and I said, I just popped out to the chemist to get some aspirin. Good, he said, my head's splitting, I really need an aspirin, and he suddenly switched on the light, and I closed my eyes against the sudden light and mumbled, they must be in my bag, and he brought me my bag as if he were bringing me a baby to feed, and said, I don't like looking in your bag, you know I respect your privacy, and I pretended to be looking for the aspirin and in the end I said, it's not here, maybe in the kitchen, and maybe I had such a headache that I left at the chemist's by mistake, and I prayed that he wouldn't volunteer to go and get it, and luckily for me the rain began to come down in a deluge, and I said to him, come to bed, I'll take your headache away.

He sat down on the edge of the bed but suddenly he stood up as if he had remembered something that was bothering him, I have to shower first, I'm stinking with sweat, but I couldn't smell anything and I was a little surprised, because I usually had to remind him to bathe, and I began to suspect that he hadn't come from tennis at all, perhaps he was stinking from some woman, and straight away I thought of Shira, and of her voice when she said, I've got people here. How was the game, I asked him, and he said, the same as usual, and began to get undressed, and I asked, who did you play with today, and he said, I've got a steady partner, have you forgotten? And I said, remind me who it is, and he said, Aryeh, and it seemed to me that he was hiding a satanic smile under his angelic lips, and I said, Aryeh, who's that? How old is he? And he said, my age, maybe a little older, don't you remember him? We ran into him in the supermarket a couple of weeks ago.

He turned his soft, fair back to me and went to the shower and I said to myself, take it easy, take it easy, don't panic for nothing, and I didn't know what put me into more of a panic, the thought that he gone to wash off the smell of another woman, or the thought that he wanted to avoid me because he knew I was lying. How come this other guy's name was Aryeh, it sounded like too much of a coincidence to me, he must have made it up to hint that he knew everything. When I heard him beginning to hum in the shower I ran to the living room and rummaged in his briefcase until I found his dairy with the phone numbers and I looked under A and there was no Aryeh there and then I looked through the entire alphabet and I didn't find him attached to any surname either, and then Yonny called out, Ya'ari, towel please, and I put the diary back into the briefcase and went into the steamy bathroom with a towel.

This has always seemed to me the height of intimacy, the most significant advantage of living with someone, the possibility of shouting from the bathroom, towel, and knowing that this shout will rouse someone from his bed, or chair, or his prying in your phone book, and lead him to the cupboard and from there to you, all thanks to a single word.

I stood there and watched him drying himself, his body soft as dough, the rubbing leaving marks and dents on his skin, and again it seemed to me that he was smiling, so I hummed the tune I had made up in the car to myself, and went back to bed. Only time would clarify the situation, I decided, but in the meantime let's see if he comes to bed. If he does, it is a sign that he hasn't been with any other woman, but then I remembered that I had come from another man and nevertheless I was prepared to go to bed with him in order to scotch the suspicion, so what was to prevent him from making exactly the same calculation, and I saw that all these signs did nothing but confuse the issue, worrying about them was exhausting and frustrating, and I would be better off if I resigned myself to the fact that we could never know the whole truth about each other, not even the half of it, and I thought that the same thoughts were probably running through his head right now, because he didn't know either, and this made me laugh and afterwards it made me sad.

He came into the room and asked if I was hungry, and I said, ravenous, and immediately regretted it, because if I wasn't feeling well presumably I wouldn't have an appetite, and I thought that I was failing all the tests he set me, but he began cutting up vegetables in the kitchen, in a steady, even rhythm, and the movements of the knife did not suggest any particular agitation or uncertainty on his part.

I joined him in the kitchen, took some eggs out of the fridge and made an omelette, and as I was frying it I embraced him and told him that I loved him, and I really felt it, and he smiled and said, I know, and suddenly his complacency irritated me, and I said, how do you know, maybe I'm just saying it, and I saw that he didn't suspect anything, and I felt a momentary relief, but afterwards I regretted it, because suspicion, especially mutual suspicion, made us equal, and now we were unequal again, like a mother and child, and his trust burdened me once more with the guilt which for a moment had lightened. I felt it churning in the pit of my stomach, the guilt, and I lost my appetite, so I turned the omelette which I had almost burned over and said, I'm feeling sick again, I'm going back to bed.

I lay in the dark and listened to him chewing, thoroughly and energetically, cutting himself a slice of bread and dipping it in the salad dressing, I identified every single sound, and afterwards the wiping of his mouth with the napkin, and after that the dishes being thrown into the sink, joining their fellows from the day before, just as he joined me in bed, with a weary sigh.

And then he began to stroke me, and I forgot what this was supposed to be a sign of and tried to concentrate on what I should do now, if I said I didn't feel like it, it wouldn't be unusual but it might be suspicious, as if I had had enough sex for one day, and if I showed enthusiasm it would be suspicious in its unusualness, as if I were covering up for something, and I didn't know how to untangle this knot, so I decided on limited cooperation and remained indifferent but didn't remove his hands, which suddenly reminded me of Shaul's hands, and for a moment I caught his look, which was baffled and lost, as if he didn't know what to do now with the assembled parts of my body, or of his. I felt so sorry for him, I was literally flooded with pity, it flowed from me like a river, I even felt its wetness between my legs, and I tried to turn myself on, as if I were with Aryeh, or as if both Shaul and Aryeh were watching me and I had to live up to the occasion, I tried to move more and to caress him, but the life had already gone out of him, he lay there next to me like a dead man, with his eyes open, and I forgot what I was supposed to do, every movement seemed ridiculous to me, so I simply stroked his curls and rumpled them, and kissed his forehead and his eyes, I had always felt more comfortable with his face than with his body, and afterwards I lay beside him and we held hands and laced our fingers, naked but sexless, like children growing up together on a kibbutz, indifferent to each other's nudity, and we listened to the rain.

I was afraid that he would want to talk, but luckily for me he fell asleep, I heard his quiet breathing, even in his sleep he was so polite, until I didn't hear it any more and I was sure that this was it, now it had really happened, cot death. A suitable death for him, even though it happened to three-month old babies, and I touched his curls, I didn't dare touch his face, and said all kinds of silly things to myself, such as let's see how his curls grow cold, and thought about how they would take me to the police station and say I was a murderer, because I didn't really want to go to bed with him, and they would all point their fingers at me and chant, she's a murderer, she didn't wriggle her bum, and I would say, it wasn't me, it was cot death, the death of angels, and they would say, don't make us laugh, cot death at the age of thirty? And suddenly I would see Shaul there in a black judge's robe, and I would run up to him and say, you remember me, Shaul, I'm Ya'ara, Korman's daughter, you have to get me out of here, and he would say, Korman? You're lying, Korman hasn't got a daughter, and I would shout, don't you remember me? For complete strangers we were unusually intimate, even my father who changed my diapers doesn't know me as well as you do. And then I would begin to take off my clothes, to remind him, even though I didn't pin any hopes on it, what was so special about my naked body that it would remain etched on anybody's memory, and when I stand before him naked, trying to reconstruct the movements I had made then, on his bed, movements from a pornographic movie, he begins to remember, feels me reluctantly with his white fingers and says, yes, could be, I remember something, but you're from some kibbutz in the south, aren't you? And I say, no, that was a joke between me and Aryeh, and he blinks suspiciously, and in the end he says, look, even if I wanted to get you out of here I couldn't, don't you see that I'm here as a prisoner, not a judge, and he holds out his hands to me and I see that they're cuffed, and everybody starts laughing and singing, when she wants to she gives it a go, she waggles her backside to and fro. I get dressed quickly and all the time I'm looking for Aryeh, he has to be there just like us, even with chains on his legs, because he's the most dangerous, but I can't see him anywhere, and Shaul says, don't waste your time looking for him, he doesn't hang around places like this, he doesn't like places like this, and then I'll say, but I don't like them either, and he'll say, if you didn't like it you wouldn't be here.

5

When she saw me she moved a little closer to the wall, as if trying to make room for me beside her on the bed. The bed itself was standing right next to the big, always closed window, which cut out a random but enviable section of the bright, provocative world of the healthy. There were two or three houses there and a yellowish mountain which was not very high, perhaps it was just a hill, and the bed pushed obstinately against the window looked as if it were growing at its feet, narrow and mean, and inside it Aunt Tirza.

She smiled at me, a grim, even angry smile. She could never stand me. Why did you come? she grumbled, I told your mother I didn't want to see anyone but her.

Mother's busy today, I lied, she asked me to see if you needed anything. She hadn't asked me to do anything, only remarked that she wouldn't have time to visit today, and I got off the bus one stop before the university on my own initiative, I couldn't resist it, drawn once more to the warm and absolute refuge of the narrow corridors, the crowded, ugly rooms, full of coughing and sighs, pain and vain hopes, misery which secretly sprouts stalks of pale, majestic nobility.

Of course I need something, she mimicked me, but I don't think you'll be able to give it to me.

Try me, what could I say.

Your age, she said, your youth.

I didn't look so young to myself either nowadays. I also sometimes wanted to throttle girls in the street because of their youth, but here, next to the faces distorted with disease, I felt quite young and healthy, although this too didn't seem to me a guarantee of happiness. Apparently everybody wants to throttle somebody else out of envy, a kind of pyramid where there's always someone above you who wants to throttle you, nevermind how low you think you are. Even Aunt Tirza, in the hard bed, with the empty bra under her pyjamas, might still arouse envy in someone. Not that this was supposed to console her.

Actually you're looking good, I said.

Am I? she asked seriously and took out a little mirror and scanned herself suspiciously as if it was my credibility she was checking. Her face was thinner than I remembered, but the thinness emphasized her big green eyes, with their cold, hard look, and her high cheekbones. Even now I'd be pleased if people said I looked like you, I said.

Why should they? You're completely different, and we're not blood relations. At the most you could look like your Uncle Alex, which I wouldn't recommend. What about him, she asked with sudden urgency. What does he look like now that he's old?

He hasn't changed much, I said, his hair's completely white, but he's still small and black.

Small and black, she laughed, with white hair, and she went on looking in the mirror as if Uncle Alex himself was looking back at her. I'd like to know how he's aged, she muttered to the mirror, I knew every detail of his face, I'd like to know how his eyes have aged, how his lips have aged. Has he got wrinkles round his mouth?

Yes, I think so. I don't remember very well. I never really noticed.

She tried to stretch, her movements nervous. I don't know why it still hurts, she said.

To stretch or to think about Alex?

Both, she twisted her mouth in a bitter smile, they promised us that the pain would pass and it's a lie. Not in the body and not elsewhere. You have to think very hard before every move you make, because if you fall it never goes away. I've never yet seen a wound that's healed.

Do you regret it? I asked weakly.

Yes, she said, but it makes no difference, because if I'd stayed with him I would have regretted it too. I would have regretted him bringing me coffee in bed, and now I regret it when he's with another woman, bringing her coffee in bed. I assume that the first alternative is easier, in certain senses.

And then I heard the bed next to her groan. An empty bed, or at least that was my impression until it began to groan, until a tiny white woman popped out of the faded sheets. She looked as if she had shrunk in the wash, someone hadn't read the instructions, someone had done the wash in boiling water instead of tepid water, and the elegant evening gown had turned into a rag.

Are you all right, Josephine? asked my aunt with exaggerated concern, almost with enjoyment. Here was the woman from the pyramid who would have been willing to strangle Tirza in her envy. She looked so strong and attractive next to this remnant of a woman with the imperial name.

Yes, I'm all right, wheezed the shrunken rag, a reply which sounded absurd in the light of her groans of pain. She tried to draw a giant wheelchair towards her, but the more she exerted herself the further the wheelchair seemed to recede. I put out my foot and pushed it to her, without even getting up. It was almost insulting, the ease with which I did it, and perhaps it was deliberate too, Tirza apparently thought so anyway, because she gave me a disapproving look as if to say, I could never stand you, and now I know why.

But the little woman smiled at me gratefully, and with surprising agility she jumped into the wheelchair which immediately swallowed her up, just as the bed had done before. In a minute the empty wheelchair disappeared into the narrow corridor.

Where is she in such a hurry to get to? I asked Tirza.

Why are you so surprised? she pounced on me. Did you think the dying had nowhere to hurry to? The dying are busier than anyone, they've got so much to do and so little time to do it in.

What for example? I asked, chastised.

For example her degenerate husband comes to visit her every day at this hour, so she's hurrying to meet him at the entrance to the ward so as not to miss a single minute of his visit. Not even the five and a half steps from there to here.

Why degenerate? I asked, and she shrugged her shoulders. I don't know, maybe I'm wrong. Maybe I've got something against all men, at least the ones who wave their masculinity like a flag.

And then they came in. The creaking of the wheelchair, her agonized face, agonized as if by mistake, as if it had been intended for a different life entirely, a caressing, cradling life, and his beautiful brown hands on the handles, each finger in the right groove, pushing the chair with his fierce walk, restrained by the infinite disability around him, his big body in the black sweater he had worn exactly one week ago when we went to Jaffa, and his chiselled face, with the dead eyes that even his surprise at seeing me there did nothing to kindle into life.

Ya'ara, he said, what are you doing here?

Visiting my aunt, I whispered stunned, apologizing as if I had intruded on his territory.

Her mother sent her, Aunt Tirza volunteered to confirm my explanation, looking at both of us in amusement.

Ah, he relaxed, and examined our faces, you really do look a bit alike.

I told you, I smiled at her, but she was quick to deny the implication, we're not blood relations.

Around us everything turned pink, because the sun of the healthy was stuck in the middle of the window, about to sink right into Tirza's bed, and the woman in the wheelchair turned expectant pink eyes to Aryeh and he said, this is my wife, and pointed to her, as if there were any other possibilities in the room, and his voice didn't tremble, and then he pointed to me and said, this is Korman's daughter, and I wondered if I should shake hands or if a smile was enough, and I smiled and said, pleased to meet you, but I saw that she wasn't satisfied so I held out my hand, and she sighed as if I was imposing a terrible inconvenience on her. I quickly withdrew my hand but then she stuck out her own, pink and wrinkled as the hand of a newborn baby, and when I touched it I felt an electric shock, as if by her touch she had transferred her disease to me.

I got up and asked where the toilets were and I literally ran there, I stood in front of the basin and covered my hand with soap and scrubbed it again and again in almost boiling water. How could she be his wife, the wives of lovers are supposed to give rise to jealousy, not pity, and the lovers aren't supposed to give rise to pity either, but suddenly I felt so sorry for him, that this was what was left of his wife, and somehow it reflected on him too, this fate, to end life childless but in a child-sized body, with a baby's hand and a rabbit's eyes. I remembered all the times he had said to me in the afternoon, you'd better go, my wife will be back from work any minute now, or sent me packing in the morning because he had a date to meet her in a café, he had gone on using her to the last minute in order to guard his privacy, while she lay here groaning. How many times I had imagined her walking into the flat I had just left, tired after work but elegantly dressed and full of the confidence of a woman who has somewhere to return to.

I heard the door opening hesitantly, I never lock a lavatory door for fear of being stuck there the rest of my life, and his face appeared, still bathed in the pink light, and after it his shoulders and the rest of his big body, and he did lock the door behind him, apparently he had more faith in locks than me, and he stood there for a moment leaning against the door, bleakly surveying the little room which contained a wheelchair with a hole in the seat, a pair of crutches, and all kinds of complicated pipes coiled on the floor like artificial intestines, and then he looked at me with an apologetic smile and said, I have to pee.

In the mirror above the basin I saw his back and I heard the jet, and the room filled with a smell of urine so sharp and repellent that I poured more liquid soap on my hand and covered my nose, and I thought that someone should tell him to drink more water, the way his urine smelled was really unhealthy, but who was going to tell him when his wife lay dying, and he flushed the toilet and turned to me with his penis outside his underpants. There was big, dark drop of urine suspended from it, almost black, and I thought, why doesn't he wipe it or shake it off, and I couldn't stop looking at this drop, which refused to fall off but on the contrary, seemed stuck to the tip of his penis like a solid drop of resin to a tree trunk.

My hands were already as red and raw as those of a washer-woman, but I didn't want to turn off the tap because I was afraid of the silence which would suddenly fall, so I added more soap and began to wash my forearms too, perhaps her germs had already climbed up my arms, and in the mirror I saw him slowly advancing and my mouth falling open in confusion because behind me I felt his hands lifting up my skirt.

I thought I'd taught you something, he said in a disappointed voice when he discovered my panties, and I moved aside, letting his big head fill the mirror, darken it with his heavy, threatening eyes, and I asked, why didn't you tell me?

Because it's none of your business, he said, and rudely turned off the tap, without first washing his hands. She'll be all right, he added immediately, to encourage himself or me, and I turned to face him, the dark drop had already fallen onto his trousers and been absorbed into a round, spreading stain, and then he suddenly picked me up and seated me on the basin, as if I were a baby who needed her bottom washed. The basin was cold and the leaking tap dripped onto my clothes, and he stooped and laid his head on my lap as if there was a pillow waiting for him there, and closed his eyes and began to breathe heavily, snoring right into my slit. His head grew heavy, and I looked sorrowfully at his grey hair, and at the skin disintegrating under it, full of dandruff, which was also strewn liberally over the shoulders of his black sweater, and I thought again about his eyebrows, which were buried between my thighs, I tried to remember if they were black or white and failed.

And then someone began knocking at the door, discreetly but firmly, and I heard my aunt asking, Ya'ara, are you there? Are you all right? I mumbled, yes, I'll be out in a minute, and I tried to get off the basin but his head weighed me down, until I gave it a violent shove and he shuddered and straightened up, swaying very unsteadily on his feet. With some difficulty I managed to

lead him to the wheelchair with the hole in the middle of the
seat, I lowered him onto it, his head dropped and he went on
snoring, a rhythmic, sombre snore.

I had the feeling that something terrible had happened while
we were secluded in the toilet like a bride and groom escaping
from their guests in the middle of the wedding, his wife had
probably died and everyone was looking for him to inform him
of her death, and I would have to tell them where he was, asleep
on a wheelchair with his prick hanging out, and I realized that
I had to push it back inside his underpants otherwise whoever
came in after me would realize that something intimate had taken
place here. I went up to him and tried to pull open his underpants
and squash in his penis, which was elusive and slippery as a fish,
as if it wasn't connected to his body at all but moving about
and changing places all the time, the little orifice on the tip too
looked as round and stupid as a fish's mouth, and I saw that
it was hopeless, so I simply pulled his nice black sweater down
until it covered the whole business. I was already bathed in sweat,
from the heat of the hospital, and the fear and embarrassment,
and when the door failed to open I realized that this time I
really was stuck, because my fear of locks made me incapable
of opening them, and my sweaty hands slid over the key until I
heard a faint click and I hurtled out of there, trembling all over,
as if shot by a cannon.

Luckily for me nobody was waiting outside the door. I
advanced slowly and saw Aunt Tirza reading something in bed,
but when I came closer it turned to be her little mirror, not a
book, and her neighbour was dozing with her head slumped in
the wheelchair, just like her husband, and I thought that I could
have pushed him here in his chair and placed it beside hers, they
would have looked like twins, lonely orphan twins, and Tirza
laid the mirror down next to her and said, what happened, I was
worried about you, and immediately added, and what about the
degenerate? And I said I thought that he had gone into the toilet
after me, and Tirza laughed bitterly and said, you know each
other, and I said yes, and in order to change the subject I quickly
asked, how is she, and pointed to his wife, and Tirza said, it's the

end, within a month he'll be an eligible widower, and I asked, does he know? And she said, of course he does, today they tell you everything, and I wondered why he had said to me, she'll be all right.

When he came in a few minutes later I could have sworn he was a demon, the change was so sudden, not a trace remained of the heavy gait and muffled snores. He looked brisk and smiling, his hair combed back and his trousers neatly zippered, with only the faint, round spot testifying to something having happened. He went quickly up to his wife and put his hand on her shoulder, and she woke immediately at his touch and raised her head and smiled at him, a beautiful smile full of love and gratitude, and put her little rabbit's hand on his.

It's better to die in the middle of your life with love than live to a hundred alone, Tirza whispered to me, and I saw that her eyes were full of envy. Are there only two possibilities? I asked, and she said, two's a lot, sometimes there isn't even one.

And then she looked outside, at the big, closed window, and said, I want to sleep now, Ya'ara, and I stood up and said, be well, and she sighed, you too, look after yourself, as if I were the patient here. I turned to the pair of turtledoves and saw his wife with the same loving smile which was beginning to look like a kind of grimace, and I asked him in a whisper if he was leaving soon because I didn't have a car, and he said, wait for me outside for a few minutes, so I sat on the bench outside the room and watched the incessant traffic of nurses and patients which from moment to moment seemed more absurd. They looked like ants just before being crushed by a giant foot, who knew what was in store for them but nevertheless went on rushing to and fro.

He soon came out, looking at his watch, calculating how much time he had lost and how much he had left of the day, and from moment to moment his step grew more and more youthful, more and more vigorous, until I was almost running to keep up with him on the steps, and then through the large parking lot, as if he were trying to wipe out the memory of his moments of weakness in the toilet, and to me too the scene seemed preposterous now, like something I had made up, and I thought that only the spot on his trousers would prove that it had actually happened, but when I sat down next to him in the car and examined his trousers, the spot too had vanished without a trace.

So what were you really doing there? he asked as he drove off, giving me an amused look, and I tried to answer lightly, I told you, I was visiting my aunt.

But your aunt's new there, and I've seen you hanging around the hospital for some time now, he parried, and I said to myself, keep cool, keep cool, and I was sure that I was blushing in shame, because I always had the feeling that he knew something about me I didn't want him to know, and nevertheless when it came it took me by surprise.

So how come I never saw you? I asked to gain time, and he said in his arrogant voice, because I made sure you didn't see me, you know I'm good at things like that, and I said defensively, it isn't a crime to hang around a hospital.

No, it's not a crime, I would say it was a perversion, he grinned, and in the tidal wave of shame which flooded me I was also conscious of the white foam of gratitude, because now I had no option but to confess, and this was apparently what I most wanted, and I said, I know it sounds awful but I like going to hospitals, it's the only place where I feel protected. When I'm upset it reassures me to wander round the corridors, peeping into the rooms as if I'm looking for someone, I like the feeling of constant care, of shelter. I know that all the patients envy me for being healthy but I envy them for being looked after and taken care of all the time, sometimes their lives seem better to me than my own.

What's so bad about your life? he asked, his voice suddenly sad, and I said, I don't know exactly, it isn't anything specific, just that it's mine, that I'm stuck deep inside it.

That's a pity, he said quietly and started to whistle, and his whistling had an instantly calming effect on me, because I remembered the mornings when I would wake up to the sound of my father's whistling, and it was a sign that he was in a good mood, that he wasn't angry with anyone, in other words with me or with her. We had grown so accustomed to relying on these signs that my mother could wake me up and say, good morning, Daddy whistled this morning, and the whole day would look different. And sometimes she would say, he whistled three times, with pride in her voice, and then I would be sure that they had made love in the night.

Sometimes I would lie awake and try to catch their voices amid the noise of the sprinklers, the howling of the cats, the dogs, there were even jackals there, to catch some sound of closeness. Sometimes I would say to myself, what do you care what happens behind their door, you have your own life, but always between me and them, between me and my life, stood some ancient flaw, some deformation begging to be saved.

Do you believe that there were really jackals there? I interrupted his whistling, and he asked, where, and immediately resumed his whistling without waiting for an answer.

Next to my first house, I said, when I was a child, I know there were jackals there but nevertheless I don't believe it. It seems to me a dubious invention, the whole of my former life seems to me a dubious invention, I know it existed but I don't believe it. I don't believe I saw my parents every day, that the three of us sat round the big table and ate, that I asked their permission to do all kinds of things, that we were a family.

A family is when you have to ask permission? he laughed. And I said, yes, mainly. And he said, for me it's almost the opposite, for me it's a heavy responsibility, my parents were poor immigrants, without work, without a language, without dignity, at the age of ten I was already responsible for ten people.

He lit a cigarette and smiled a satisfied smile, proud of his heroic biography, and I looked at him admiringly, he looked so complete, so perfect of his kind, with the grey smoke rising from his grey lips, and his shapely hands on the wheel, and his coordinated clothes, and his hair beginning to curl at the edges, but without forming a single actual curl, and even the signs of old age seemed part of his perfection. I tried to imagine him ten years old, his brown skin peeping from torn clothes, and his curls black and dirty, famished soot in his eyes. So how did he grow up so pampered?

How did you grow up so pampered? I asked him, I was sure you were brought up in a palace, and he laughed in enjoyment, precisely because nobody pampered me for so many years I began to pamper myself, at the end of your life you have to try to strike a balance.

And did she pamper you? I asked.

Who? he asked ingeniously, and I said, Josephine, Josephine, enjoying the gap between the enchanting foreign name and its miserable owner.

He grew serious at once. She did everything she could to make me happy, he said with pathos, as if we were already walking behind her coffin, and I caved in like a kicked dog, deprived of all the pleasure of gossiping with a married lover about his wife, running her down, hearing how boring she was, how she didn't understand him, was unable to meet his passionate sexual needs. Instead I had a man full of guilt turning his wife into a saint. I wonder what Yonny would say about me if I were dying now? After all, I'm somebody's wife too, however strange it sounds. Would he say that I had done everything I could to make him happy?

The moment I thought about Yonny the car turned into the crowded, narrow street and stopped next to our building, ignoring the famous safety limit. In the distance I saw the weak light in the kitchen, I could almost hear the rustle of the vegetables being chopped with weary movements, full of despair and goodwill, and I felt pain throughout my body, as if I myself were a vegetable on his chopping board. Aryeh, I said in a whisper, I can't go home, and he asked gently, why? Because I know exactly what will happen, I whispered, I know what he'll say and what I'll say, I know what we'll have for supper, I know how he'll look at me, it's depressing to know too much, I want to stay with you.

He didn't say anything, but the car grunted and then drove quickly off, leaving the weak light in the kitchen window behind. He whistled again, and I put my hand on his knee and closed my eyes and thought about the dim kitchen with the little window overlooking the bushes, which instead of bringing light to the house stole all the light, and the darkness there always looked much darker than it really was, and I thought about the rubbish bin filling up with vegetable peels and I filled with pity for this rubbish bin filling up with peels in vain and I decided that when I went home I would scrub it and restore its original colour, which I had already forgotten because of the dirt, and I tried to remember where and when I had bought it, and what I had felt at the moment I bought it, if it had made me happy and if it had made Yonny happy, and how long this happiness had lasted, and how it had ended.

And then Aryeh put his hand over mine, only for a minute, because he needed it again for the next cigarette, and he asked, why did you get married? And then I remembered that on the day we decided to get married we went to a shop which had opened that very day and closed a few days later. We passed it on the way home and everything looked so new and tempting, even the rubbish bins, and we bought a white one, that was its colour, white. I wanted a bridal white, and it looked to me like a swan which, however dirty the water it was swimming in, would always remain spotless.

Because he promised to love me forever, I said in the end, and I knew he was the kind of person who keeps his promises.

That's what happens when we let our fears rule our lives, he laughed, you remind me a lot of your mother, and he looked at me appraisingly for a minute, and I said, my mother? How do I remind you of my mother? Do you mean what I said, or the way I look? But he stopped the car abruptly and jumped out in a hurry, as if he was afraid I would go on nagging him with all kinds of questions, and I got out after him and followed him into the building, which looked as if it were being choked with creepers, and I climbed the stairs behind him, and when the door opened I had the feeling that I was entering my real home, at last I had found my real home, in which and only in which my real life would begin.

Slowly and calmly I looked round the flat, examining the furniture and the carpets and the paintings as if seeing them for the first time, because of course up to now I had seen only him, and I was already trying to decide what I liked and what I didn't like, and where my things would go, and then I thought that I would leave them with Yonny, and I remembered that I had to call him and tell him where I was, but I was ashamed to talk to him in front of Aryeh and so I said to myself, I'll find something to tell him when I get home.

The flat was cold, as if nobody lived there, as if it had frozen in mid-life, and also clean with a kind of pronounced, not everyday cleanliness, as if it had been fumigated. Who cleans here? I asked, and he said rather proudly, I do, I don't like people invading my privacy. I passed a finger over the grand piano and it came back clean and I said, congratulations, who taught you to clean, and he said sullenly, I thought we'd agreed that I wasn't exactly pampered, I used to help my mother clean houses when your father was at school, and I heard a note of bitterness in his voice, and I thought to myself that if he was bitter it must be a true story, but it still seemed to me more like a story than real life.

I followed one step behind him in my coat, watching his movements, trying to acquaint myself with his way of life, as if seeing him turn on the heating would teach me something more about him, and I saw him open the fridge and examine it gravely although it was completely empty, and then opening the freezer, which was also almost empty, and taking out a packet of ice-cream and cutting it in half with a knife and putting it on plates. I sat in front of the plate and stared at the ice-cream, I really didn't feel like eating ice-cream in this cold, and it looked as if it had been there since the summer, the cardboard wrapping was stuck fast to it, and I wanted to ask if she had already been sick in the summer, Josephine, but he seemed completely absorbed in his ice-cream, and I said to myself, what difference does it make, and I pushed my plate towards him with its pink frozen lump which had no intention of melting, and he fell on it and ate it greedily, and then he took a bottle of whisky out of the cupboard and drank straight from the bottle, and only after that he took out two glasses and filled them and emptied his immediately.

I was mesmerized by this strange private ritual and I even felt proud that he dared expose himself to me like this, in other words, to ignore my presence. Only after the third glass he looked at me, almost in surprise, and his look was bitter and opaque, and he said, that's all there is, as if he meant the ice-cream, and he lit a cigarette, and I thought how well it would suit me to live with him, because I would always know that he didn't love me and I wouldn't have to torture myself and live in suspense all the time in case he suddenly stopped loving me, and I felt that I had a tremendous advantage over all the women in the world because he really didn't love me.

The flat began warming up and he took off his sweater, under it he was wearing a faded brown undershirt which merged with the color of his skin and looked as if it were a part of him, and I took off my coat and he poured himself another whisky and said go on, and I was glad that I was wearing a lace leotard and not just any old rag under my sweater and I remained in the leotard and panty hose and began stretching a little to stimulate him, but he didn't respond, he went on drinking and smoking until his face grew heavy and his speech grew slurred, and he said, you know I haven't got anything to give you. I responded enthusiastically, as if this was good news, and I moved closer to him and stroked his arms, especially where his skin joined the undershirt, and I kissed his tense neck, which gave off a strong hospital smell, and I thought about the tiny woman who was shrinking from minute to minute, I still couldn't take it in that she was his wife, she looked to me more like a pet animal than a woman, and therefore her expected death too seemed to me less upsetting than a human death, even less than Shira's cat Tulya's death, and I whispered into his neck, take me to the bedroom, because I had never seen their bedroom, and I thought he hadn't heard, because he didn't move, I even thought he had fallen asleep again, but then he stood up and with an unsteady step advanced towards the door which was always closed.

When it opened I understood why he was always careful to keep it closed. It was the most frightening and least sexy bedroom I had ever seen, with two separate narrow beds like hospital beds, a wheelchair in the corner and a smell of medicine enclosed between completely bare walls, but I actually felt a strange excitement, because it was so much less binding, less threatening than a romantic bedroom would have been. So I pulled him to one of the beds, and I felt him becoming aroused, almost against his will, melting reluctantly like the ice-cream he had just devoured, and I thought that the bigger his penis grew the more his wife shrank, until soon she would simply disappear, becoming invisible to the human eye.

I began to pull down his trousers with a new boldness, stemming perhaps from my resignation to his lack of love for me, and I even said to myself that this was true love, that I was learning to love without expecting anything in return, and I looked at his body in underpants and undershirt, surrounded by smooth olive skin, and thought that soon it would be mine, in a minute it would be mine, and I stroked him on top of his underwear, I always preferred to stroke on top of clothing, it seemed safer to me, and I kissed his underpants until I heard him say, I have to be alone now, Ya'ara.

If I hadn't caught him in the hospital he would probably have said, my wife will be back soon, and now he had no alternative but to tell the truth, or perhaps this wasn't the truth either, perhaps he had a date with someone, and although he didn't seem in a fit state to go out I had already seen how quickly he could change.

I raised my head from his underpants and he muttered, I don't feel well, I won't be able to take you home, take money from my pocket for a taxi. I really didn't have enough money for a taxi on me, and I was also glad of the chance to go through his pockets, but I didn't find anything interesting there, a few shekels, a cigarette lighter, some papers from the hospital, and those keys again, what did he open with all those keys?

He had already turned over onto his stomach, breathing heavily and exposing his narrow, muscular buttocks, and I went on rummaging in his pockets, thinking about how I had once assumed that seeing a man's naked backside meant I already had him in my pocket. I thought then that everything was connected, that there was a prick inside the heart, a heart inside the bum, a bum inside the eyes, eyes inside the vagina. I didn't realize that each of these organs can pull in a different direction, and that I could find myself crying with disappointment opposite the backside of someone I couldn't stand, or to be more precise, who couldn't stand me. Because when I left his flat, with stupid tears in my eyes, and waited for a moment in the entrance to the building, it had just started to rain, a small black car stopped next to me and the girl with the cigarette holder, or a girl who looked like her, with short red hair, got out of it and ran into the building, and I fled in spite of the rain in order not to see on which landing the light went on, or which apartment's door opened, and all the time I said to myself, there are other residents, there are other possibilities, why think the worst, but I didn't dare to know the truth. I walked down the almost empty streets, without money for a taxi and without an umbrella, thinking of how he would get up for her, his whole body taut and ready, I had even taken off his pants for him so that she wouldn't have to exert herself, and how her elegant cunt, probably shaved or trimmed, would receive what I wanted, really wanted, perhaps for the first time in my life I felt that I understood what it means to want, and for a moment I felt like going back, but I was afraid of the humiliation, so I simply went on walking, almost blindly, thinking of how I would revenge myself on him, and of how repulsive he was with his inferiority complexes which I had only discovered today, and the smell of his urine, and the old ice-cream melting inside his stomach, and of how the glamorous girl busy riding him now had no idea that only a thin piece of olive colored skin separated her from a dirty puddle of last summer's ice-cream.

6

The next morning I didn't know what hurt more, my head or my throat, or the strip down the middle of my body connecting the heart to the vagina, which felt alive and tingling like stitches after an operation. My cheek stank of aftershave, Yonny had apparently taken the trouble to kiss me before he left, while I was sleeping, and I immediately felt a wave of irritation against him, he always doused himself with such quantities, like a child playing with his father's aftershave and not knowing when to stop, I would never get rid of the smell, but then, when I thought of this kiss I was suddenly moved by the fact that he had stopped next to me, and even stooped down, and pursed his orange lips, and all this effort without expecting anything in return, because I was fast asleep, just like kissing a piece of furniture, or a dead person, when everything is between you and yourself, there's no one to respond to the effort, to appreciate it. I thought that it was a really serious sign that he loved me, maybe the most serious sign I'd had up to now, and I tried to bend down from the bed to the floor and kiss it in order to reconstruct the extent of the effort and evaluate the extent of the love, and when my lips encountered the cold, wintry floor I discovered a book lying under the bed covered with a thick layer of dust, like camouflage, who knows how long it had been quietly hiding there, and I gathered it up in alarm and remembered the ceremoniousness with which the head of the department had lent it to me several months ago, a rare book from his private library.

I returned to bed with the book and began to clean it with the crumpled tissues which had accumulated around me during the night, Yonny was sure I was crying for poor sick Aunt Tirza, and after wiping it clean I began to read it and I couldn't stop, and it suddenly became clear to me that this was what I was going to write my thesis on, the legends about the destruction of the temple, and I thought how lucky it was that there was no temple now, otherwise whenever I did anything wrong I would be convinced that it would be destroyed because of me. The book attributed such small, personal things as being to blame for the destruction, like the carpenter's apprentice who deceived the carpenter and stole his wife, and then incited him to divorce her, and lent him the money to pay her the settlement promised in their marriage contract, and when the carpenter couldn't pay the debt he was obliged to become their servant, and they would eat and drink while he stood and poured the wine, and the tears dripped from his eyes and fell into their glasses. I tried to imagine myself and Aryeh eating salami and drinking cognac while Yonny filled our glasses and cried, and I felt so sad that I began to cry again, and I decided that I would never leave Yonny because now I had discovered that he really loved me, and it was impossible to leave someone who really loved you, but then I thought, just a minute, what about you, where's your love, and I thought that perhaps I was like the woman in the legend, we don't know what she really felt, we can only guess by her actions.

I was so busy thinking about my actions that I didn't do anything until the phone rang and the department secretary said that the head of the department wanted to talk to me, and I could hear the malice and smugness in her voice, I'd always known that she was baffled by the favoritism he showed me, and the truth is that I shared her bafflement, and I kept waiting for it to end, for him to find out that I was less promising than he thought, and to see me as a disappointment rather than a hope. I knew that such reversals could take place overnight, and judging by the smugness in her voice it seemed that the moment of truth had arrived, and my heart began to pound and I gripped the heavy book tightly and in my nervousness I began to dog-ear the pages, until I realized that I was ruining the rare volume from his private library, and at that moment I heard his portentous voice with its American accent saying that there had been a departmental meeting and complaints had been made about my cancelling reception hours and my failure to hand in a proposal for my thesis, and that if things continued like this I could say goodbye to both the grant and the appointment. Not even I will be able to help you, he said, if you don't help yourself. You know how many people want to get their hands on that grant? I waited for him to finish and then I said in an apologetic voice that everything had been held up because I couldn't find a subject for my thesis, but this very morning I had decided. Personal catastrophe in the temple destruction legends, I said, that's what I'm going to write about, and he said that we should meet to discuss it, and added, I have a free hour soon, I'd be happy to devote it to you. Wonderful, I said, I'm on my way, and I started searching through my wardrobe for something suitable for a career woman, that would be my image from now on, a career woman with a promising academic future and a loving husband who even stooped to kiss her, and I thought I would start using a cigarette lighter and cut my hair, and then I would have nobody to envy, I would only envy myself, and if I met him in the street I would smile haughtily and I wouldn't even stop. Who was he anyway? A pump that sucked up all my strength and all my time and all my will and took control of my life, and didn't give me anything in return except the luxury of remaining without strength and time and will, and even this he did indifferently, as if he were doing me a favour by allowing me to waste my life on him.

I put on black leather pants and a blue velvet blouse that suited my eyes, and as soon as I looked in the mirror I was sorry that he wouldn't see me like this, that it would all be wasted on the head of the department, but I kept saying to myself, the destruction of the temple, that's what's important to you now, and nothing else, and again I saw Yonny pouring us cognac and I even dressed him in a frilly apron, like a waitress, and I started to laugh until I realised how sad it was.

I saw that Yonny had taken the car so I walked to the bus stop, feeling a little pressured because the bus went past the hospital and this lengthened the journey, but it drove fast, it was late in the morning and the roads were empty, and I thought of the empty, abandoned house which had waited for me hidden in the heart of the orange grove when I was a child. Shining golden paths led to it, accompanied by gloomy, sceptical cypresses, one of which was always bowed or broken, and glittering gaily at their feet the brightly coloured stars of the lantana flowers, purple and orange and red and yellow and white, which seem to grow bigger the closer I come to the house, until they are almost the size of a ripe tangerine, and when the house looms up in front of me it always takes me by surprise in its beauty despite the neglect, the abandonment, the destruction, and to myself I call it the temple. It is utterly abandoned, apart from me the only people who visit it are hungry, stinking, indigent labourers, and I smell their bitter smell, the smell of weariness and soot and cans of beer and cheap sardines. On the cold nights they light little camp fires, and the floor is already black, and the walls too, but I see it as it should be, gleaming and sparkling, splendid and alluring, and this is the way I want to be seen too, the way I should be, and so I bring people I love there, because it seems to me that only there, in the temple, is it possible to see me correctly. At first I bring my classmates there, and they are a little frightened, uneasy at being alone among the thousands of citrus trees in a deserted house, and then my first boyfriend, and we sit in the wild, neglected courtyard, where huge rare flowers grow secretly, and I imagine that it's our house, and we kiss between the guava trees, and I bite into the fleshy guavas without picking them from the tree, to show him that they are completely red, and my lips are swollen with kissing and I'm afraid to go home, what will I tell my parents, that a bee stung me on my lips, but my boyfriend says it doesn't look swollen, it only feels swollen, and I'm angry with him because it's his fault but I don't show it, so that he won't feel insulted and leave me alone with my parents. And then we mount the big broken steps, and wander round the rooms, reconstructing their magnificence, and we climb a narrow spiralling ladder to the roof, to be confronted by the radiant pride of the infinite orange groves, their absolute dominion, green on green on green. Only when darkness falls do we begin walking home, the cold stings my lips but my boyfriend promises me that you can't see the swelling, and I can't understand how something so palpable can be invisible, and my nipples sting too and I cover the budding breasts under my thin blouse with my hands and he picks a handful of starry lantanas and scatters them over my head, and at home it is these starry flowers which betray me, not my lips, and my mother says, where have you been lying to get those weeds stuck to your head, this is the last time you disappear for a whole day, do you hear, and that night I think I hear my father whisper to her, what do you want of her, you're just jealous because she's in love and you're not. A few months later I lay with him there, with my first boyfriend, on the sooty floor, next to the empty beer cans, the chunks of coal, the scraps of old newspapers, it was our first time, and the last time I went there, because I was suddenly nauseated by the smell of the charred smoke, even the ceiling over my head was sooty, and I could no longer see the house as it should have been but as it really was, a filthy abandoned ruin, and I didn't want to see my boyfriend again either, because he reminded me of the temple, and quite soon after that we split up.

I looked through the window and felt my nipples stinging and tingling like then, and I thought of the pampered young women who went out to pick barley between the piles of horse dung and their breasts grew long and thin as strings with hunger, and of their babies who tried to suck milk from their nipples and died in their laps, and I thought how lucky I was not to have lived then, and to be on the safe side I covered my breasts with the heavy book, and I saw the sky covered with smoke, and I thought, incredible, the smoke from the temple is still rising, and only I can see it, until I realized that it was the hospital chimney, and I said to myself, this time you're going on, you're not getting off, but I sensed danger signals, as if I had to rescue somebody, I was being summoned and I had no right to refuse, and instead of continuing to the university I got off quickly, with the doors of the bus almost closing on me, and found myself at the hospital entrance.

Only for a few minutes, I decided, I'll just see what's happening and take the next bus to the university, I'm not really late yet, I won't even go into the room, I'll just peep in to see if she's still alive. I had no intention of seeing him again, so I had to gather the information I needed myself, even if I had no idea what I needed it for. The familiar hospital smell, medicines and airlessness, food and central heating, enveloped me like an old coat, repellent but reassuring, soporific and consoling, redolent of care which was well-intentioned even if it didn't do any good, and it was pleasant to be surrounded by these good intentions, far more pleasant than the cold corridors of the university, and I thought that if I fainted again as I had in Jaffa, there would be someone to take care of me right away, and they would give me a bed and a locker and I wouldn't have to explain to anyone what I was doing there, and I even thought of pretending to faint and seeing what would happen, but then I remembered the head of the department waiting for me and I began to run. The last time I had run so fast was at gym in school, and now I had the additional impetus of enthusiasm, which I didn't have then, as if something wonderful was waiting for me at the end of the course, and I didn't stop until I reached the door of the room and I stood outside panting and saw to my relief that Aunt Tirza's bed was empty, except for the little mirror glinting on the pillow like a knife, and in the next bed his dying wife lay with her eyes closed, paler than the sheet that covered her.

I went up and examined her carefully, as if she were a part of him and if I discovered the essential principle of her being perhaps I would discover his too. Today she looked frightening but touching, like a monster with a noble soul imprisoned inside it, and all the time you could see the inner struggle taking place between them, sometimes the soul gained the upper hand and sometimes the monster. When she opened her eyes it seemed to me that the soul had won, they were blue and almost luminous, but the longer they remained open the clearer it became that the battle was lost, they were frighteningly big and their look grew increasingly glassy as she realized where she was and what her situation was. Korman's daughter, she murmured in a pronounced French accent when she recognized me, and

I nodded and thought that lately I kept hearing this definition more and more, in the end I would begin to forget my own name, and she said wearily, your aunt is being taken care of now, she'll only be back at lunch-time, and I asked what kind of care, to gain time, and she only sighed and said, you don't want to know, and I said, but care is a good word, you use it about babies, and she said, with the same sigh, yes, but who wants to be a baby in the middle of their life, and I nearly said, I do.

I wanted to stay a few more minutes so I asked her if she needed anything, and she actually met me half-way and said that she would be grateful for a cup of tea, explaining in great detail how to execute this task, and I set out proudly on my mission, maneuvering skillfully between the various sinks and taps, proud of the information I had succeeded in collecting, two spoons of sugar, two teabags and lots of milk, wondering to myself why half a person wanted everything double. When I returned she was already sitting up in bed, a red sweater draped over her shoulders and an exaggeratedly grateful smile on her face, as if I had saved her life, at least. I was already getting restless, because the head of department waiting for me, and also I was afraid Aunt Tirza would come back and be annoyed to see me there, but most of all I was afraid that he himself would suddenly appear in the door and discover that I had turned into his wife's nurse. I was ready to leave, but she became so friendly, almost dependent, asking me to raise her bed, and put a pillow under her swollen feet, and call the nurse because she needed something for the pain, and I felt so useful, with every move I made bringing immense benefit and evoking passionate gratitude, that it was hard for me tear myself away. I wasn't going to do the head of the department any good, I thought, or myself either, so at least I could make myself useful to this strange creature, who was both blighted and radiant at once.

Her feet were heavy and huge, so swollen they seemed about to burst, and a dark yellow colour, and when she raised them to me they filled my eyes. I pushed a pillow under them, which was immediately squashed beneath their weight, and another one behind her back, until it seemed as if she were lying in some

kind of bath, but a completely dry one, and she smiled at me
and took a lipstick from her drawer and smeared it on her lips
with surprising skill, without even looking in a mirror, I've never
been able to find my lips without a mirror in my life, and the red
of the sweater emphasized her beautiful lips, isolating them from
the rest of her distorted face, and I thought that perhaps she too
was a girl who had grown up in the lap of luxury, like Martha
Bat Beythus, suddenly finding herself buried in horse dung, and
then she said in a solemn voice, as if rewarding me for my efforts,
you won't believe it, but I remember the day you were born.

Really? I asked, with an indifference which disappointed her,
it didn't seem so thrilling to me, the day I was born, certainly
not for her, but she said, yes, it happened to be the day I first
met Aryeh, I remember he told me, a friend of mine gave birth
to a baby today, after years of medical treatment.

And I said, are you sure he said a friend of mine, not the wife
of a friend of mine? It seems to me that my father was his friend
then, not my mother, and she shook her head obstinately and
said, I remember every word he said that day, he said a friend
of mine gave birth to a baby today and he was as excited as if
he was the father himself. I remember that we drank to you,
we were sitting in a bar in Paris and Aryeh opened a bottle of
champagne.

She raised the cup of tea I had prepared for her with a flourish,
as if to show me exactly how they had toasted me in champagne
that evening, but she immediately began to cough and the tea
spilled on the sheet and her eyes grew wet and red, until the
horror of the distance between that day and this could not have
been more blatantly demonstrated.

I took the cup away from her and wiped the sheet and brought
her a glass of water and she drank it carefully and in her eyes the
blue mingled with the red until they created purple blots which
looked like a map without names, the ancient nightmare of my
geography lessons, to identify countries and towns in big blots
which looked exactly the same, I never succeeded in identifying
anything, and in her eyes too I didn't see much when she said,
as if to herself, and I didn't even know then that I was already

pregnant, as if remarking on a curiosity, a private curiosity amusing only to those directly concerned, but I couldn't control myself and I repeated, pregnant? I thought you didn't have any children.

We haven't, she said impatiently, I was with someone else then, we were going to get married, but that evening changed everything, the evening you were born. I didn't know yet that I was pregnant, she repeated, I didn't understand why I was throwing up your champagne.

And what about the baby? I asked, sensing an unpleasant shiver running through my body, as if it was me we were talking about, and she said, there was no baby, after one week I packed my bags and moved in to live with Aryeh. He didn't want me pregnant by another man, so I ended it.

You thought you'd have children with him, I tried to soften the fatefulness of the step she had taken, but she said, no, I knew we wouldn't have children.

And nevertheless you terminated your pregnancy, I said, failing to hide the note of rebuke in my voice, and she said firmly, yes, I did, as if she would gladly do it again.

And you're not sorry? I asked almost pleadingly, identifying completely with the terminated foetus.

I'm sorrier that they didn't let me go to ballet lessons, she said with embarrassing anger, the anger of the sick suddenly pouncing on trifles and making mountains out of molehills, you can't imagine how I begged my father, and he said there wasn't any money. Last night I dreamt about it again. Ever since I became sick I've been dreaming about it all the time, how I'm in a ballet class, gliding about in a white tutu with all the other little girls. I'm sure that if I'd studied ballet I wouldn't be sick today. I'll never forgive my father for it.

Is he still alive? I asked, taken aback by her aggression, and she said, no, but what does that matter, I'm not alive any more either.

She closed her eyes, and I thought how fitting it would be if she were to die right now, with those words on her lips, just like a movie, and in the end he would be the one to beg, he would come crawling to me to hear his wife's last words, and I would tease him a little, of course, and pretend to forget, or perhaps I would distort her words deliberately, tell him how sorry she was about that abortion and make him suffer for the rest of his life, but I saw her swollen feet move, and I tried to imagine them in white ballet shoes, and then she opened her eyes and looked at her watch, perhaps she wanted to work out how much time there was to go before he came, and I realized with dismay that this was precisely what I should have done, not now, but half an hour ago, as soon as I arrived. I was in such a panic that for a moment I couldn't move my hand, so I looked at her watch and only afterwards at mine, and I was rather surprised to see that the time was the same on both of them, exactly twelve o'clock. The hour allocated me by the head of the department had just come to an end.

Precisely now that there was nothing left to lose I began to feel pressured, and I told her I was late for a class, and she nodded understandingly, and I asked her not to tell Aunt Tirza about my visit, so she wouldn't be disappointed, and she went on nodding and I saw that the colours in her eyes had separated and again there was blue in the middle and red all around, and she said seriously, I hope you weren't offended, and I asked by what, and she said, because I vomited your champagne on the day you were born, and I didn't know if she was joking so I said, be my guest, *Gesundheit*, and I thought that I couldn't have found anything worse to say if I'd tried. And before I could come up with any more idiocies I took my leave abruptly, despite all my preparations, and next to the door I wanted to ask her again about that day, if she was sure he had said my friend and not my friend's wife, but I felt that I couldn't stay there any longer, that the story of her sacrifice was making me ill, and I began to run down the corridors again, and I didn't stop running until I emerged safely into the cold, grey air.

In the bus I tried to think of an excuse but I couldn't concentrate, I was suddenly so surprised by his involvement in my life, I was even angry, what right did he have to be moved, who gave him the right to be moved while I was lying there in a transparent cage, and why was he so moved when I was born and now he was so indifferent, pity it couldn't be the other way round, and why did he say my friend and not my friend's wife, when the hostility between him and my mother was so obvious, and I was so absorbed in these thoughts that I hardly noticed I was already moving up the university escalator, while sliding down opposite me on the other side was the head of the department, engaged in animated conversation with his assistant, and I wondered if I should hurry down after them but I really didn't have the strength, I had done enough running for one day, so I decided to write him a letter instead, with an apology and a convincing excuse.

I was looking for a quiet place to write my letter, so I went up to the library. Entire fields of bowed heads, like sunflowers after sunset, met my eyes and filled me with anxiety, and I went to sit in a far corner so that nobody would see me. Everyone was busy working, only I was wasting my time on a silly letter of apology, surely I should start work on my thesis too, I could put the letter in his pigeonhole later, so I began wandering round the shelves, looking for material on the destruction of the temple legends, and every time anyone drew near me I jumped, convinced they had something unpleasant to tell me, and I thought of the faithless wife who came to the temple to undergo the test which would prove her guilt or innocence, and when the High Priest went out to give her the bitter water to drink, he saw that she was his mother.

It was exactly here, between these shelves, that I first set eyes on Yonny, I was pushing the creaking trolley full of books and he walked past with Shira, as if by accident, and she signalled me that it was him, and at precisely that moment the sun lit up his face and I saw that contrary to medical advice he had devoted much of his adolescence to squeezing his pimples. The sun illuminated every one of the pits on his face but I was actually relieved that his blemishes were so prominent, there was something confidence-inspiring in a person who walked round freely with a skin like that, instead of wearing a balaclava or a mask, and I immediately gave Shira a thumbs-up sign, to let her know that as far as I was concerned everything was okay.

Afterwards, when we met again, I was disappointed to see that the scars were less prominent than I remembered, apparently the angle of the sun between the shelves then had been absolutely lethal. They stuck faithfully to his cheeks and chin, and I wanted to feel them, to make friends with them, so that they would be mine too.

We sat in a small café, surrounded by a circle of green lawn, with a basket of fresh white bread between us, emanating plaintive smells in my direction, and I remembered how I had sat in exactly the same place with the boy who lived next to the bakery, a few hours before our one and only night together. We had something to settle between us, I don't remember what exactly, something about a girlfriend he had had for a long time, he said he wanted me but was still attached to her, and I said, so let's decide in advance that we'll only be together for one night, and he agreed, he was even glad, we were both glad, as if we had found some trick, some way to have our cake and eat it, and those hours that advanced in a poignant dance towards our one and only night were the sweetest because all the tension vanished when we decided on the end in the beginning, and I stood up and stretched, and my limbs stretched endlessly, and the tables round about saw me expanding, each limb doubling and tripling itself, my hands tickled the café ceiling, and then he stood up and embraced me, preventing me from completing my expansion, and my disappointed limbs fell on him, and I said to him, why did you break my movement, and he laughed, his eyes as green as the lawn surrounding us with a round promise. I thought then that it wouldn't be a problem to stick to our decision, and in the morning we parted, heroic and in love, and I looked at his dear face and I knew that I would never see him again, but I couldn't have guessed that every time I smelled fresh bread I would think of him, and when I sat opposite Yonny I thought that maybe it was a sign, the fact that Yonny had chosen this café to meet me in, a sign that what had begun here would continue with him, how long could I go on dragging round an amputated beginning, and I tried to reconstruct that sweetness, even that stretch, but he didn't get up to break it and it broke of its own accord, and when I resumed my seat I knew that I had to fall in love with Yonny, that it was my only chance of changing that sorrow into joy. Irregularly distributed among his acne scars were a pair of soft brown, almost purple, velvety eyes and orange lips like an overripe peach. There was something missing there, and it took me some time to realize that it was his nose. Not that he didn't have a nose, but it was small and snub like a baby's, a kind of button nose, perfect for a baby but a little absurd on a man, and I asked him how old he was, as if I expected him to say two and solve the problem, but he said twenty-three, which was also my age, and it turned out that we had been born exactly on the same day of the same month, in other words, we were twins. And then I thought that this was another sign, and I couldn't argue with two signs, and I tried to fan my fire. He was in the middle of telling me that his mother had died a few weeks before and that he was still in mourning, and I, like an idiot, said, that's good, because everything seemed to me like a sign, and then I said, let's go to your place and not leave the house for a week, because I had always regretted not having agreed on a week instead of a night with that other boy, and Yonny smiled his gentle smile and said, but I have to go to work, and I said, nevermind, you deserve a vacation, and I went on egging him on and myself too, and we went home hand in hand and kissed in the lift, and I loved him so much all week long and thought only of him, and of how lucky I was that my life had succeeded in joining two parts into one body. He fell in love mainly with my love for him, it was so convincing, and only afterwards with me myself, and when I asked him at the end of the week if he promised to love me forever he said yes and I believed him, and I thought about the morning with that other boy, how we had stood at the window overlooking the bakery, and I asked him what was going to happen to us, and he said, why do you have to know in advance, how can anyone know in advance?

But later on we began to go out into the world and little

by little I started hating Yonny, as if he had done me some injustice, the more he loved me that more I hated him, and I didn't understand why, as if he had deceived me on purpose, and the most frustrating thing was that I couldn't even tell him, it sounded so ridiculous. Sometimes I hated him and sometimes myself, and in my better moments I hated us both. Behind his house there was an enormous park and we would go there in the afternoons and look at the sun and I would ask him the question I always asked every man I had ever been with, the question that had once blazed in my mouth and that now sounded so tepid and dull, will you love me forever? And his yes was so light, so disappointing, as if he had said no. There was always a moment when I would sit on a rock and start swallowing my tears. We were so lost, the pair of us, orphaned twins between the white rocks and the red sun, sheep which had lost their flock, and all the time I would wonder how to get connected to the right life again, and I would say to Yonny, soon I'll make us supper, as if this was the rite which would deliver us from the curse, and he would smile his sad, gentle smile and say nothing. I wanted to yell, why don't you say something, bang on the table, bang on the rock, force me to pull myself together, threaten me, give me an ultimatum, but instead I would bite back my tears between the rocks which had started to turn black.

On our wedding night I persuaded him that fucking would be banal, everyone did it, and we should be original and give the night a different content. Before I had finished talking he was already asleep, and I lay awake and tried to remember the sequence of events, to draw up an interim report on what might almost mockingly be called my love life, to work out why I hadn't left him at the beginning, why I had decided so quickly that it was too late to change my mind, and I thought that he was the only one who had promised to love me forever, and this was apparently why I couldn't let him go, and I thought of the night when the smell of the bread had covered me like a sheet.

And then I heard a soft explosion and a large shadow fell on me and the books suddenly looked like closed, blank, almost identical boxes. The grey afternoon light penetrating the closed windows did not succeed in illuminating the huge library and was pushed back outside, and all the surprised heads suddenly looked up, staring around through slitted eyes as if they had just been born. With a feeling of satisfaction I surveyed the disappointed faces whose light had gone out and whose computers had stopped working in mid-sentence, as if in the interminable competition between us they had been obliged to take time out, to give me a chance to catch up.

I sat down opposite the window and looked at the grey wind, at the shadow of the temple and I was the only one who knew that the shadow would fall to the east as far as Jericho, where the women would shelter in it in the summer, warm and crowded, with their children in their arms, and suddenly I felt muffled longings for my parents, because whenever the electricity failed the three of us would reluctantly unite, sitting obediently round a single candle. I would peep at them in a way which only the darkness permitted, trying to guess what I would have thought of them if they hadn't been my parents. Sometimes I would see them looking at me and I would think in alarm that they too were appraising me in the dark, and what if they decided that I didn't suit them? My mother would stack a pile of books next to the candle as if the power cut was going to last forever, and at the top of the pile she would put the shabby old bible, which always looked wet, and which opened of its own accord at the stories of David, David and Jonathan, David and Bathsheba, David and Absalom, and her voice would caress the verses, soften them for me. I would wait for the saddest parts, where it was possible to cry shamelessly, to join the train of weeping which continued from verse to verse, and my father would sit there impatiently, drumming nervously with his fingers, and say, enough, stop crying already. I would look at us and think that we were what's called a given, the kind of thing that can't be changed, a present which was already a past, the winding verses and the rhythmic drumming of his fingers which even the candle flame obeyed, this was what would decide my fate. Sometimes I would hear jackals howling in the orange groves which surrounded the house, and then my fear would increase and with it the closeness I felt to them, and only when the light suddenly came back on, gladdening but actually saddening, illuminating but actually darkening, and we would all sigh in relief but actually in regret, looking round to see what was left of our day, of our lives, only then our fragile unity would dissolve, their faces would sharpen, and instead of being afraid of the jackals I would be afraid of them, of their unresolved sorrow, howling at night around my bed.

Soon enough the irritating buzz of normality became audible again, suffocating me with its dull stability, and all the satisfied heads returned to their places, but I was already on my way out. I would ask them to light a candle so that we could sit around it, why shouldn't they agree, I had to feel that rare unity again, they couldn't refuse me, why should they refuse? Even in restaurants people sat in candlelight, so why not in their kitchen, when nobody was there to see?

But when she opened the door to me, surprised and happy to see me, the pillow creases of her afternoon nap still lining her thin cheeks, I forgot all about the candle and without meaning to I blurted out, what was there between you and him, Mother? And she, as if she had been waiting for this for years, didn't even ask who.

But then he loomed up behind her back, as if he had been hiding there, for a moment at shoulder height and then his head was sticking up over hers, like a totem pole, his ears pricked and his look stern, and he said, Yonny's just been here, and indeed at that moment I encountered Yonny's aftershave, lurking about like an invisible spy, and I had a bit of a shock, perhaps he had come to tell them that he was leaving me, and I asked, what did he want, with an air of nonchalance, and they stood there in front of me, a parent pole, each of them pondering the question and neither of them answering me.

If he wants to he'll tell you himself, my father's head pronounced at last, he's waiting for you at home, and he examines me as if I'm one of his laboratory rats, as if he's the High Priest and I'm the faithless wife, and I march after them to the kitchen, trying to keep my back straight, filling myself a glass of water from the tap and drinking it to the dregs, like that faithless wife, desperately sucking the rim of the glass, how quickly conspiracies spring up, especially against me, and in order to know what Yonny's up to I have to read my father's face, a task at which I've been failing for years and there's no reason why I should suddenly succeed now, and everything seems to me so hopeless and depressing, all these crooked indirect paths leading from one person to the other, getting to know Aryeh through his wife, my father through Aryeh, Yonny through my father, a kind of endless merry-go-round becoming more and more complicated, and only she stands aside, out of the picture, hiding behind her crumpled cheeks, which don't even hint at some vanished beauty, which look as if she was born with them, standing next to the sink and washing dishes with the innocence of a placid housewife who has nothing to hide, until I suddenly notice that she's washing the same plate over and over again.

I come up behind her and push my glass under the tap to fill it with water again, and she says, it isn't healthy to drink hot water from the tap, but the water is cold, and she asks, aren't you hungry? And I say, I'm thirsty, and she checks to make sure my father isn't there and says, what was that you asked me before, I didn't hear you properly, and I fill another glass and say, I asked about the power cuts, I asked if you remembered how the three of us used to sit round one little candle, and she says, what are you talking about, we had three oil lamps, each of us had an oil lamp, and this too seems to me like part of the conspiracy, or more precisely, like the height of the conspiracy, so I raised the glass and poured the water back into the sink, right onto her hands, which kept clinging to the same plate, and she recoiled and said, have you taken leave of your senses, the water's boiling.

In the main street under their house a policeman was standing with a whistle, and I stood to one side and looked at him and thought about all the things I would whisper discreetly into his ear, come up to flat number three for a minute, I would say, you wouldn't believe the things that are going on there, all hidden from the eye, of course, but you have instruments to deal with

phenomena of that kind, and I, to my regret, haven't, otherwise I
really wouldn't trouble you. You have dark interrogation rooms,
sophisticated truth machines, prisons, and what have I got? Eyes
and ears, a short memory, human wishes, one big limitation,
that's what I've got, and don't think there aren't people who
take advantage of it. You'd be surprised at how much they
take advantage of it. He was young, younger than me, with a
smooth, dark face and a pleasant smile, after blowing his whistle
he smiled almost proudly, and for a moment his eyes rested on
me. He probably had a baby and a young wife at home, too
young, but for the baby he wouldn't have married her, but it
was too late to be sorry now, especially since she was good, good
enough anyway. In twenty years' time he would probably leave
her for some little girl but for the next twenty years he was fixed
up, and so was she, because she didn't know what I knew, and
suddenly I envied her, the policeman's wife, who wasn't going
to be left for twenty years, and I was being left today.

7

On my way I thought about how much I hated the journey there, hated every traffic light and stop sign and grocery shop, all the witnesses to my humiliation, my foolish stubbornness, and above all I hated the house which made my heart clamour and my face blush even before I reached the front door, with the bushes hiding it and the bees hidden in the bushes, a house that had a lot to hide, a house that should be ashamed of itself, a house which only a serious earthquake would suit, the thick heavy door with the bourgeois sign on it saying Even, in other words, Stone, as if there was a quarry inside and not people, and it seemed strange that she had ever lived here, she fitted in so well at the hospital, as if that was her home, it was impossible to imagine her climbing these steps, looking for her keys with masterful movements. I knew that he wouldn't be there but I went anyway, determined to stand humiliated in front of the closed door while he devotedly pushed his wife's wheelchair down the circular corridor which never ended, which always began again, as if by standing in front of it, by sitting on the cold entrance steps, by not going home, I would wipe out the miserable plot waiting for me there inside Yonny's wet orange mouth.

I sat on the steps, staring at the blackening stones of the building opposite, in a boredom which turned into anxiety at the sight of the shadows of the leaves dancing on the walls in a grim, malevolent dance. On the tree it wasn't so bad, but the reflection on the wall was terrifying, and I remembered how I sat just like this, alone on the steps of our house, in the winter, waiting for my mother or father to come home from the hospital and make me supper and tell me what the doctors had said today.

One of them would always stay overnight in the hospital to be with my baby brother, and the other would come home to be with me, and I waited and looked at the dance of the leaves on the walls of the house next door, which grew stormier and stormier, more and more frightening, and I tried to guess by the dance which of them would come. From the neighbours' window the flames of the candles writhed like octopuses, reaching out for me with yellow arms, it was *Hanukkah*, the second or third day of *Hanukkah*, and suddenly I saw both of them in the distance and I panicked, because for a month now I hadn't seen both of them together, ever since my brother fell ill, what had happened that he no longer needed them by his side? I looked pleadingly at the leaves, and again at the road, hoping that it was a trick of the shadow doubling the figure, but slowly they began to separate, the distance between them lengthened, because my mother began running towards me while my father went on walking slowly, as if he was walking backwards, she ran wildly and her beautiful thick plait coiled round her neck like a scarf or a rope and her face was distorted, her mouth open as if she was screaming but no scream was heard, and for a moment I thought that she wasn't my mother, I had never seen her so distraught, and she picked me up as if I was the baby, and went on running madly straight into the citrus grove behind the house and as she ran she opened the buttons of her blouse so that her breasts jumped onto my face, dripping milk, and she cried, you want to suck, right, you have to suck now, and she suddenly sat down under a tree, pushing her nipple into my mouth, and I was infected by her madness and opened my mouth, even though I was already nearly ten years old, and began to suck and suck the sweet airy milk which had been so vital and in a single moment had become superfluous. We saw my father running round looking for us, Rachel, he shouted, he was crying too, where are you, he looked so lonely in the dark among the trees of the grove, where are you, he wept, like a child playing hide-and-seek but taking the game too seriously, and Mother kept cruelly silent, breathing softly, gagging me with her breast until I thought I was going to choke, and I began struggling and in the end I actually bit her in order to free myself and with a mouth full of milk I succeeded in saying, we're here, Daddy. He came running up and bent over us, collapsed onto us would be more accurate, and the three of us sat in the dark under the tree and she went on talking to me as if he wasn't there, saying to me, why did you let on where we were, like a little girl, why did you let on where we were, traitor, he would never have found us, and it looked as if she really meant it, that we could go on sitting here under the tree for the rest of our lives, with him stumbling round us in circles, like a blind man whose dog had run away and whose cane had been broken, and for the rest of our lives it would be dark, and you could say that actually she was right.

Somehow they managed to share happiness between them, but not grief, each of them threw it all onto the other, or grabbed it all for himself, not leaving the other anything, as if it were his own private sorrow, and I tried to escape from her frantic arms, soaked with the splashing milk, and I thought of my baby brother and I didn't succeed in feeling too sorry, I hadn't had time to love him, I had hardly had time to be jealous before he became ill and they took him to the hospital, and I couldn't see him because he was in the isolation ward, and even before he died I had already forgotten what he looked like, we didn't even have time to take a photo of him, his stay in the family was so short. I remember how I tried to comfort my mother by saying to her, it's as if he'd never been born. Were you so unhappy before he was born? So why are you so unhappy now that he's gone? How can you be sorry for something you're used to being without? But she would look at me with hatred, as if I'd killed him myself, even though I was only trying to help. And anyway, I would say to her, you're supposed to be nice to me now, to appreciate the fact that you've still got me, and instead you're behaving as if I'm your step-daughter and he was your real child. The day you became bereaved parents, I would say to her, I became an orphan.

Then I heard footsteps approaching and I thought it was him and I panicked and looked for somewhere to hide, as if it wasn't him I was waiting for, and I went and stood quickly next to

the opposite door like an animal hiding from its hunter, and I
pretended to be waiting for the door to open and all the time
I was thinking, if you're so afraid of seeing him what are you
doing here in the first place, and behind my back I heard voices,
someone was coming precisely to the door where I was standing
and even beginning to rattle their keys, and I stood there without
moving, keeping up my act in front of the wrong audience, and
suddenly I heard the demanding, hopeful sound of a baby crying,
and I began to tremble, because I hadn't heard crying like that
for years, and I couldn't restrain myself any longer and I turned
round and they were standing behind me, a young woman with
a baby in her arms, glowing sweetly and holding a bunch of
keys in her out-thrust hand, as if she was trying to open the
door through my back, and I didn't know what to say and
pointed to the opposite door, the one with the sign saying
Even, and stammered, I'm waiting for them. I said them and
not him deliberately so that it would sound legitimate, a kind of
family visit, and she smiled in relief and opened the door wide
and a wave of warmth burst out and she went inside with the
baby, and a minute before the door shut in my face she said,
you can wait with us, she said 'with us' and not just here, as
if they would actually wait with me, she and her baby, share
the burden, the tension, the frustration with me, and I felt that
she understood how sad my waiting was, because of course it
wasn't him I was waiting for so desperately, but his love, and
that would never come.

   I found myself standing next to the door but on the other side,
not daring to advance in order not to intrude on their lives, and
in the meantime she stripped the baby of all its wrappings, and
when she took off its hat and its face was suddenly revealed I
looked at the tiny face and it looked exactly like Yonny, the
same orange lips and soft brown eyes and brown hair which
in its case hadn't yet begun to curl, a sweet sheep's face, and it
bleated at me like a sheep too, and I thought that instead of all
this nonsense I should really have a baby with Yonny who would
have his face, but then I felt a stab of fear, how did this particular
baby come to have Yonny's particular face, and I looked straight

at the baby's mother, to see if she too looked like a sheep, but
she was completely different. She had a smooth, brisk face, with
light eyes and thick dark lips, and her hair was gathered in a
dancer's bun and she smiled at me warmly and said, what will
you have to drink, and I said water, and leaned against the door
because I felt giddy at the thought that this was Yonny's baby,
and perhaps this was what he was waiting at home to tell me,
and she held out a glass to me and disappeared with the baby
down the passage and after a minute she came back without him.
He's asleep, she announced with a triumphant smile, and I didn't
believe her because just one second ago he was wide awake, in
fact I'd seen the entire expanse of the brown of his eyes, and it
was clear to me that she was hiding him on purpose, and I had
no way now of ascertaining if I had imagined the resemblance or
if it was really there. I wanted to ask her, tell me, is that baby by
any chance my husband's, but I was too shy, so I began to make
small talk, asking her all kinds of questions to get a picture of
her life, and I asked her how old the baby was, and what his
name was, and I immediately forgot everything she said, and
then I said in a kind of forced spontaneity, he doesn't look a
bit like you, and she smiled, yes, he looks like his father, and
I couldn't control myself and I asked, have you got a picture of
them together, and she said, no, I haven't taken a photograph
of them together yet, and I felt that I had to see him again,
and I said, I think I can hear crying, and she listened and said,
no, I can't hear anything, only footsteps outside, and I turned
round quickly and looked through the peep-hole, hoping that it
wasn't him.

Through the peep-hole he looked short and broad, less attractive, less frightening, even a little stooped, because he was carrying a lot of shopping bags, like an old woman returning from the
market he sighed and turned a broad backside to me, looking for
the key in his pockets, all that was missing was a scarf round his
head. What was he doing with all that food, anyone might think
he was planning a party or a festive meal, what did he have to
celebrate, and I already felt insulted for her, for his wife, that
she was lying there shrinking and he was guzzling and getting

fat, and in the meantime I saw him taking his hand out of his pocket and opening the door and quickly disappearing with all his shopping baskets, like an imp in a box full of sweets, and I knew that I had to get out of here leaving another mystery behind me. She looked at me with her clear, sympathetic gaze and said, has he arrived? And I said, yes, but perhaps I can wait here a few minutes longer, to give him time to pee, it came out of it's own accord, God knows why I said it, why to pee of all things, but she smiled at me understandingly, and I was amazed at how everything seemed natural to her, to me everything always seemed unnatural, and I asked her, what do you think, if a baby's born on the ninth of *Av* and dies on *Hanukkah*, should you light candles or not, and I saw the smile disappear from her face and I regretted it immediately and asked her what her baby's name was, as if the second question would erase the first, but she was already suspicious, why do you ask, and I said, because I'd be happy to look after him if you ever need a baby-sitter, I'm crazy about babies, which wasn't true of course, but I had to see that baby again, and she said, okay, I'll call you, but she didn't take my telephone number and I went out and stood in front of the opposite door and rang the bell, first a short ring and then a long one, but the door didn't open.

I didn't hear any footsteps or see any light and everything was so still that if I hadn't seen him going inside with my own eyes I would have been sure that there was nobody at home. I stood there thinking that Josephine would never see this door again, she would never see the round peep-hole and the sign saying Even in thick, smug letters, nor the fine cracks in the wood and the smudged black handle, nor the doormat which had once been orange and was now brown and which had a jolly picture of two cats on it, all these details would be withheld from her forever, and I thought that I should probably be grateful for being here to see it all, and I put my hand on the door handle in order to leave my fingerprints on it and to my surprise the handle bent and the door opened almost of its own accord, with a faint creak which sounded like a snore.

I jumped back immediately to make it clear that I hadn't meant

it, I even turned round to make sure that she wasn't watching me
with her calm pale eyes from the opposite door, and like a tired,
confused army I stood paralysed between the two fronts, until
the light went on in the stairwell and there was a sound of a
door slamming overhead and footsteps descending the stairs,
and I began to feel nervous about standing there opposite a
wide open door, which must have looked pretty weird, so I
quickly went up to close it and get out of there at last, but
instead of leaving I went inside.

The passage was dark but there was a glimmer of light
coming from the far end of the apartment, and a sound of
a motor and the creaking of wheels, as if someone was riding
a motorbike inside the house, and I stood quietly and listened
until I realized that it was a vacuum cleaner rolling heavily over
the big carpets which had looked perfectly clean to me the day
before. The shopping baskets were standing next to the kitchen
door, apparently thrown down there in haste, one lettuce was
lying on the floor with a dark loaf of bread leaning on it, he
had been in such a hurry to clean the floors. In whose honour
was he making such an effort, sucking the secret transparent
grains of dust into the maw of the vacuum cleaner, as if he was
bringing a new woman here to live with him today. After all,
Josephine wouldn't know anything, every day at five o'clock he
would push her round the ward a bit, and then he would come
home to a house innocent of dust but guilty as sin, and she
wouldn't know anything. I heard him press a button and with
a long sigh the vacuum cleaner fell silent and was dragged on its
wheels in the direction of the door. My heart pounded but my
legs were totally paralysed, however much I wanted to get out
of there they refused to move, like once when we were lying on
the lawn in front of the house in the village and I saw the birds
freeze in the air and my father shouted, a snake, go inside at
once, but my bare feet froze and he pushed me hard, hurting my
shoulder as I saw the big brown snake advancing and afterwards
he told me to put on socks, an exciting innovation for me, socks
in the middle of summer, and also that fierce concern of his
for me, but nevertheless I succeeded somehow in getting out

of the apartment, closing the door quietly behind me, although
I couldn't control myself and I turned round and stood in front
of it again, as if I had just arrived, and rang the bell, praying
that the woman opposite wasn't watching my strange dance
around the door, inside and outside. Immediately there was a
sound of wheels, as if the occupants of the flat didn't walk on
their feet, and the door opened with a suddenness which took
me by surprise, almost in a rush, and I said with a silly smile,
hello, it's me, as if we were talking on the phone, and he said, so
I see, and stepped aside adding, come in, and I went in quickly
before he regretted it, and in my haste I tripped over the cord
of the vacuum cleaner and fell flat on the floor, squashing my
face on its hard back, which was still warm with exertion. The
first thought that came into my head was that I had broken his
vacuum cleaner and he would never forgive me for it, and I was
filled with sadness to think that this was how he would remember
me, as the person who had broken his vacuum cleaner, and only
when I raised my head and saw blood on the floor I realized
that it was something belonging to me which was broken, and
I felt my face in alarm and my hands stopped when I came to
my nose. This precious feature, the one I most liked to look at
in the mirror, straight and narrow like my mother's, was now
sore and bleeding. I didn't dare touch it, I didn't dare lift my
face, in case it fell off like a dry leaf dropping from a tree, so
I sat huddled on the floor, covering the crushed organ with my
hands, crying quietly.

For a moment I completely forgot that he was there, so
absorbed was I in my loss, and only when I heard the fridge
opening did I remember that life goes on and he had apparently
decided that this was the right moment to put the lettuce in the
fridge, but I immediately felt something cold on my hands, cold
and hard as ice, and it was in fact ice, three cubes of ice in a
little plastic sandwich bag, which I took without saying thank
you and placed fearfully on my nose, to freeze the pain. I felt
his shadow over me, darkening my knees which were covered
in blood, coming closer to me, and with a sigh of resignation
he knelt down next to me on the floor, and with a white

cloth wiped the blood off the leather trousers I had put on so enthusiastically in the morning. He was evidently good with the sick and wounded, I noted, perhaps that was why his wife had decided to get sick. He evidently liked being the only healthy person around and demonstrating devotion, pity I didn't know it before, it was even worth sacrificing my beautiful nose for the sake of this discovery, and in order to verify it I laid my head on his shoulder, and immediately, in a conditioned reflex, I felt his arm moving and encircling my shoulder, thick and fatherly. It's broken, I whispered sorrowfully, as if speaking of some common loss, and he said in a low voice, show me, and gently and gravely removed the fingers that were hiding my nose, like a groom lifting the veil from the face of his bride. I looked at him fearfully, as if he was my mirror and I would be able to tell the severity of the situation from the expression on his face, but he smiled calmly and said, not too bad. Can you see that it's a nose, I asked, or does it look like mush, and he looked at it solemnly and said, a nose.

We have to go to the Magen David Adom, I said, to have it X-rayed, and he said, don't worry, Ya'ara, your nose is okay, I know what a broken nose looks like, believe me, and I knew that I was supposed to ask him admiringly how he knew and to hear how at the age of ten he had cleaned houses with a broken nose, but there was only one question I wanted to ask him, a question which terrified me and filled me with dread and which had kept me from going home today, but I didn't know how to phrase it and in the end I said, tell me, whose friend were you, my mother's or my father's? And he laughed and took cigarettes and a lighter out of his pocket and lit us each a cigarette and said, that's like asking a child who he loves more, his mommy or his daddy, and I said, but you're not a child, and they're not your parents, and he said, in any case, I'll answer you like that child – both of them, I was friends with both of them. But which of them more, I insisted, and he said, these things change, you know. I thought she couldn't stand you, I said, and he said, yes, things change. But when did it change, I persisted, when did you stop being friends, and he sighed, I don't remember exactly, after you were born, I think, I settled in France, I hardly came to Israel, I got married, the relationship cooled down, that's life, things change, he repeated as if it was some kind of slogan, and I kept on, yes, but to the extent that she pretends to be sick in order not to see you? That she recoils at the mere mention of your name?

I don't know, he shifted his weight uneasily, that's her business, not mine and not yours, and suddenly he stood up and brought another cloth and began cleaning up around me. I picked my feet up like I used to when my mother was washing the floor and I was home-sick, marvelling at the life that usually went on without me, the ordinary routine of the morning that was nevertheless so charged, as if everything she did was actually more than it was, washing the floor was more than it was, making lunch was more than it was, and all these magical, meaningful acts went on every day while I was sent away to school. He wheeled the vacuum cleaner away, dismantled it expertly and pushed it into the cupboard, and then he gave me his hand to help me up and enable him to clean the place under my bum, which really was covered with blood, as if someone had been murdered there underneath me, but he cleaned it all up calmly, and after a minute there were no signs left in the flat, only on my face, where my nose had swelled like a balloon. There was a mirror next to the door and I went and stood in front of it, approaching gradually and cautiously so that I could retreat at the right moment, and I saw a big, ugly wound in the middle of my face, and he suddenly came up and stood beside me with a solemn smile, as if we were facing a wedding photographer, and I examined our common faces, alarmed at their incompatibility, as if we were strangers who had landed up by chance in the same frame, people from two entirely different races, he with his dark face and hair turned fair by age, and I with my fair face and dark hair, he looked black as a shadow by my side, and I was white as a ghost. The mirror underlined something crooked about him, which was usually almost imperceptible, an unpleasant lack of symmetry in his face which he projected onto my face, because there were only the two of us in the mirror, and for a moment it looked as if my face was the crooked one, and I tried to move my lips to straighten it out, because when there are only two people in a frame it's impossible to tell which is straight and which is crooked, but then everything suddenly straightened out, because I was left alone in the mirror. He turned round and went to the kitchen and began putting away his purchases, and I heard him saying impatiently, don't worry, the bone's not broken, as if he had no more interest in the matter. I stood in front of the mirror, seeing my nose swell and the moment of grace vanish, and asked in an accusing tone, are you expecting guests? as if it was a crime to entertain guests in his situation, and he surprised me by saying yes, and even took the trouble to tell me who they were, and it turned out that Josephine's family were arriving this evening from France, her sister and brother-in-law, and she even had an old mother who was coming as well, and soon they would be landing at the airport and he was supposed to be there to meet them, and in the meantime he had to prepare the meal so that it would be ready when they arrived. He stressed the matter of the meal as if they were coming to Israel for the sole purpose of eating his food, and I couldn't resist asking, in pretended innocence, what are they coming for? And in the mirror I saw him standing still for a moment opposite the open fridge, as if it held the answer, and then he said, to say goodbye to Josephine, and it sounded sweet and sad like the name of a movie, to say goodbye to Josephine, or perhaps Josephine says goodbye would be better, or Josephine goes up to heaven, light as a feathery cloud. Instead of a young daughter she had an old mother, and it was all because of him, and I had no idea what it was about him that seemed to her more worthwhile than having children, more worthwhile than anything else, and even now, in her condition, she couldn't bring herself to regret it, and her old mother was probably crying in the plane and saying why can't I die instead of Josephine. I tried to guess if my mother would overtake me on this road or if I would surprise her and succeed in dying before her, which would make their bereavement double, if such a thing is possible. Presumably their sorrow for me would be assimilated into their sorrow for my baby brother, and become an inclusive, comprehensive sorrow for children in general, and they would remain one-time bereaved parents, because if the sorrow at the death of a child is infinite, how can it be doubled? Infinite sorrow plus infinite sorrow equals one infinite sorrow.

Tears of self-pity came to my eyes at the thought that even after I was dead I would still be deprived, and in order to disguise them I said it hurts, referring to my nose, but he was thinking about the visit and he said, yes, her mother is really broken, as if it was obvious that your parents would love you more than your mate, because he certainly didn't look broken and he didn't try to either, and I asked, can I help you with the meal, and to my surprise he said yes.

I went and stood next to him at once, before he could regret it, and we stood side by side in front of the sink as if we were getting married and the sink was the rabbi, and it was full of dishes and Aryeh said, let's start with these, and he took some detergent out of one of the shopping bags and handed it to me and I held the big family-size bottle tightly in my hands, the way that woman had held her baby, and recalling her made me feel uneasy and I asked him, tell me, has your opposite neighbour got a husband? And he said, she's got a baby, that's for sure, I can hear him screaming every night, her husband is apparently quieter.

But are you sure she's got one? I asked, have you ever seen him? What does he look like? And he said, I've seen him so often that I never noticed him. Do you remember if he's tall or short, fat or thin? I nagged, and he said, he's average, I think he's average. Why are you so interested? And I whispered shyly, because her baby looks like Yonny.

Who's Yonny? he asked indifferently and I answered, my husband.

Really? He sounded amused. What does your husband look like?

Like a sheep, I said, and I remembered that I had a photo of him in my bag, and I hurried over to it and began rummaging inside it with one hand, holding the liquid soap in the other, and in the end I found the photo, which was already quite creased and

showed Yonny kissing me on the forehead at our wedding, me
with the veil on my shoulders, like a scarf, and Yonny trying to
make himself taller, we're about the same height, so he could kiss
me, and I'm bending my head a little to make it easier for him, so
much effort for one superfluous kiss, we both look lopsided with
the strain, and I was ashamed to show it to Aryeh but I needed
to know urgently, so I held it out to him apologetically, and he
looked at it indifferently and didn't say anything and I asked in
suspense, is it him? And Aryeh had apparently forgotten what
it was all about and he said, are you asking me if that's your
husband? And I said in an irritated voice, like a teacher trying to
get an answer out of a slow pupil, the neighbour's husband, does
he look like the neighbour's husband? And he looked calmly at
the picture, as if everything didn't depend on his answer, with
his full lips pursed, and in the end he said, I don't think so,
and then he added, I don't know, I hardly remember him.
But why should he look like him in the first place? And I saw
that he didn't want to understand, or perhaps I hadn't made
myself clear, because of course what I really wanted to ask was
whether he was the neighbour's husband, not if he resembled
the neighbour's husband, but why, in fact, should my husband
also be the neighbour's husband? Suddenly it seemed absurd to
me, too, and I put the picture back in my bag with a feeling of
relief which stemmed not from any new information received but
from the confrontation of my anxiety with reality. Embracing the
bottle of liquid soap I returned to the sink, and he said again, you
start on this and I'll take care of the food, and he took the bottle
and poured some liquid soap into a little dish, in which he placed
a new sponge which he had bought today, a blue sponge, and he
stood waiting for me to set to work, and in the end he asked in
a worried voice, you know how to wash dishes, don't you?

I looked at the sink and I couldn't answer him, because I
remembered that when I was here yesterday the sink had been
completely empty, expect for maybe an ice-cream dish and a
glass, and why was it now brimming over, bursting with plates
and glasses and big bowls, as if from last night to now he
had been doing nothing but eating, and not by himself either,

because the dishes came more or less in pairs, two wine glasses, four coffee cups, and the whole thing presented a picture of a rich meal for two, with laughter and sweet words, courtings and touchings, and now I was supposed to clean it all up, as if I was the deceived husband in the legend, serving the food and weeping into the glasses, the husband on account of whose sorrow the Temple had been destroyed, and Aryeh was the wife, and only the third character was missing, the one whose dirty dishes I had volunteered to wash, the one who had sat here with him after I left and enjoyed everything I could only guess at, and I tried to reconstruct the face of the girl with the cigarette holder, the mysterious niece who according to him had returned to France long ago, but I could only remember her clothes, the short pants and the jacket, which she had presumably changed for warm winter clothes long ago, with the result that I now knew nothing about her at all.

I dipped the sponge into the soap and started to scrub the big plates, and looked through the window at the lemon tree growing there, the street lamp was shining directly on it and the lemons shone like little moons, and I thought to myself, what am I doing here, washing the dishes of an old lecher and his mistress instead of washing my and Yonny's dishes at home, standing opposite our window with the dark bush hiding the view, and hearing Yonny's soft voice around me, gentle and conciliatory, instead of that deep cough with all its germs fresh from the hospital. He had suddenly started coughing as if he had tuberculosis, and I kept on washing the dishes energetically, pretending not to hear, but out of the corner of my eye I saw him bearing down on me, tottering slightly, holding a glass in his outstretched hand and whispering, water.

You should stop smoking, I said, ignoring the outstretched glass, enjoying my momentary control over his fate. Water, he repeated, and I took the glass and filled it with lukewarm water, not without soap, and gave it to him, doing everything slowly and deliberately, and by the time the water reached his lips he was coughing so hard he could hardly swallow, and he spat most of it out on the floor, his eyes red with exertion. I stepped quickly aside, so as not to get my leather pants wet, and he fell on the sink like a horse on its trough, thrusting his huge head into the running water, his chin resting on the dirty dishes, heavy and tortured, until the coughing died down.

Then he raised his face to me, grey and dripping, and I thought, maybe he's crying, but his eyes were dry and he took a kitchen towel which was lying on a chair and dried his face. I was always moved by the way he touched himself, with an easy male confidence, and a sweet picture suddenly came into my head, how the summer would come and he would lie on top of me and the sweat would drip off his face like the water was now, warm and salty on my cheeks, and how he would dry it with exactly the same movement. He sat down at the table with his head bowed, and I looked at him sorrowfully, who knows if he would live to see the summer, and I went up to him and sat on his lap and hugged him and he didn't move but he didn't resist either, and my nose hurt but I didn't care, I was so happy on his lap, as if I had found my true place, and I laid my head on his shoulder, and said again, you should stop smoking, and I added, I'm worried about you, and he asked why, and I said, because you're part of my family, and he smiled, why do you have to make everyone part of your family, and I said, you know you're already part of it. I snuggled up against his shoulder, examining his grey profile from close up, the slightly flat, negroid nose and the firm chin under the full lips, I wanted him very much, but not exactly to go to bed with him, I wanted to annex him, to know everything he was thinking every minute of the day, to be part of the things he thought about, I wanted him to want to know what I thought, and for there to be an overlap between his thoughts and mine. I wanted to shake him, so that if he had any love for me, say at the tip of his finger, it would spread throughout his body, but he smiled his secret, self-sufficient smile to himself, a smile neither distant nor close, which was quickly over, and said in despair, how will I manage, I won't manage, but he went on sitting on the chair, and I wanted to console him and I said, I'll help you, there's still time, and he said, looking at the white clock on the wall above the marble counter, there isn't time, I have to leave for the airport in half an hour, I'll take them to eat in a restaurant, there's no time left, and I felt so guilty, because he didn't say it lightly but heavily, as if this change in plan was a catastrophe, which would lead to another catastrophe, and it was all my fault.

He pushed me off his lap and stood up heavily and began returning everything slowly to the fridge with mournful, ritual gestures, the superfluous lettuce and fish and mushrooms, everything he had laid out festively on the marble, displayed like an exhibition of good intentions, and I said, why don't I do it, let me do it all and by the time you get back the meal will be ready, but he shook his head, dismissing my offer without giving it a second thought, and I added, don't worry, I won't be here when you get back, I won't embarrass you, but he went on shaking his head, clearing everything away, and then he stood in front of the sink with an expression of bitter resignation and began to wash the dishes, and I, with my swollen nose, became even more superfluous than the lettuce, because it would come in useful tomorrow and I wouldn't, and the cancellation of the festive meal seemed like a fateful sentence which would completely destroy this already wretched family who were coming to say goodbye in such tragic circumstances, and who would not even have the compensation of a home-cooked meal to sweeten the pill.

Let me finish the dishes at least, I said, but he neither spoke nor moved, entrenching himself in his position in front of the sink, and I knew that I could definitely leave now, but I didn't want to leave like this, and I didn't know what to do to change the atmosphere, so I sat and stared at his back, counting the plates as he washed them to see if they came in pairs, and the tense silence between us reminded me of the days after my brother died, not days, weeks and months, a year at least, when they barely spoke, and they looked at each other with hostility; as if each of them was a murderer. At first my father tried to placate her but he soon despaired, as always, his wick was so short, his despair intensified the hostility, and this may have frightened her but it was too late for her to do anything about it, and so, without a word, they lived together in silence, and only occasionally forgotten things were raked up, all kinds of ancient guilts were spat out in vicious whispers, especially his guilt, again and again, how he had abandoned his medical studies in the middle of the course and been content to work as a laboratory hack, whereas if he had stuck with his studies he could have saved the baby, saved the baby, saved us all, she repeated it again and again and he would run away from the words, saved the baby, close the door and run, running round the orange groves for hours. Even their appearance changed, my father hardly ate, he grew as thin as a skeleton and as frightening, with his eyes dominating his tortured face, while she actually put on weight, eating like a pig, coming home from the supermarket with her baskets and devouring the food, once I even saw her falling on raw minced meat, in the middle of making hamburgers she crammed the soft mixture into her mouth, and I said to her, Mother, it isn't cooked, and she said, it will cook in my stomach, see how hot it is. He would listen and say terrible things to her, usually through me, he would say, she thinks she needs to eat for the milk, nobody needs her milk any more, she thinks that if she gets fat and wears enormous clothes she'll be pregnant, and she would say, me get pregnant by him? Never in a million years, his sperm is rotten. I would protest, but Mother, I'm from his sperm too, and she would suppress a bitter, monstrous smile, and say nothing, running a greasy hand over her short, scarred hair, in the place where the braid had been cut off, as if that was her revenge on him, the cruel amputation of her beauty.

I would run to my room and get into bed, hugging beneath the blanket the only toy I had succeeded in saving, they had put all his clothes and toys into his white crib and taken them away, and I had stolen a soft woolly little lamb from the crib, and for years I would hug it in secret and hide it in all kinds of places where my mother wouldn't find it and throw it away, and every day when I came home from school I would go straight to my room to see if my lamb was still there, and when my friends invited me to their houses I would refuse, because I was afraid to abandon it for too long, and years later, when I went to the army, I took it with me to basic training, and there it disappeared, somebody must have stolen it, and I remember that I was less upset than I thought I would be, perhaps I was even glad.

Do you know about the baby at all? I asked Aryeh, trying to confront his unhappiness with my own unhappiness, and he hesitated for a moment and said, of course I know, I was in the country on a visit then, I wanted to pay your parents a condolence call, but they didn't want to see anyone. I really wanted to come, he added as if I doubted it, I was so sorry, after all those years of trying to have another baby, and he didn't finish the sentence but he finished the dishes, and surveyed the empty sink with satisfaction. Now I'll take a shower, he said, and then we'll go, I'll drop you at home on the way, he spoke gently, as if our tragedy made up for the tragedy of the cancelled meal and he was no longer angry with me, and I followed him into the bedroom and watched him getting undressed, taking off his sweater and trousers and remaining in red underpants and a long burgundy vest, I laughed out loud at the sight, as if he had told me a joke, his underclothes were so youthful in comparison to his outer clothes, which were always neat and serious, and he stood before me exposed and colourful, an old man disguised as a boy, a disguise so successful as to make him unrecognizable, a disguise that had penetrated his skin, and I followed him to the shower, like a tail, and watched as he took off his vest and underpants, even without them he went on looking disguised, with his smooth brown skin, and as he stretched himself under the running water and soaped himself thoroughly, without leaving a single spot on his body unsoaped, as he lathered his pubic hair, just as my mother used to lather hers, I wondered whether she had learned it from him or he from her.

I remembered how I used to watch her in the shower and how disgusted I was by this movement of hers, the crude, efficient handling of the delicate, mysterious organ, the brisk rubbing and lathering of the curls as if it was nothing more personal than baking a cake. Later, when she got fat, she began locking the bathroom door and I never saw the movement again until now, but in him it attracted rather than disgusted me, that white lather inside which the dark, shapely organ lay blackly, and I felt a stabbing all over my body, a stabbing of lust or perhaps of yearning, which I had felt then too, in my first life, and I always thought that I wanted chocolate, but even if I ate chocolate non-stop it didn't go away, just as I knew now that even if I fell on his body the stabs of lust would go on troubling me, because the hunger was something that could not be satisfied.

He turned off the water and stepped out carefully, wrapping himself in a big towel, stood in front of the wardrobe and pulled out a pair of brightly striped underpants and a purple vest, but on top of them he wore a dark blue suit and a grey shirt, as if he was going to a business meeting, and then he took a little comb out of the drawer and combed his hair back, the teeth of the comb etching white lines in his tanned skull, and afterwards he stuck it in the back pocket of his trousers. Of all his actions in this relaxed routine which I observed with the concentration of a spy taking note of every detail so she could pass them on in her report, it was just this last one which annoyed me, it seemed so vain, a middle-aged man with a dying wife sticking a cheap plastic comb into his back pocket. Doesn't it hurt your bum when you sit down? I asked him, and he looked at me in surprise, felt his backside and said, I don't feel anything, and I came closer and felt his buttocks through the elegant cloth of the suit, and in fact I didn't feel the comb, as if it had been completely absorbed into his mysterious body, he seemed so fascinating to me, he and everything connected to him, his dying wife, the old mother coming to say goodbye, the underclothes, but I was sure that somewhere in the world there was a woman, at least one woman, to whom it would seem completely ordinary that he washed himself, lathered his curly pubic hair, that he drove to the airport, it would all seem so ordinary to her that she wouldn't be in the least impressed, and to the same extent there was sure to be another woman in the world, at least one woman, perhaps even the same one, to whom every action performed by Yonny would seem mysterious and compelling, and she would want to follow him to the bathroom to watch him soaping himself, and be moved by his sloppy movements and his white skin, and I had to try to keep this woman at a distance, perhaps she lived at the other end of the world but perhaps she was right behind the wall, and when I looked apprehensively at the wall I remembered the neighbour with the baby, like a forgotten nightmare I suddenly remembered her, and thought that I had to baby-sit for her as soon as possible, in order to examine that baby, not just his sheepish face but also his body, I would undress him and examine the colour of his skin, the structure of his foot, his penis, his ears, that was the only way to learn anything in this life, by yourself, after all I couldn't ask, and there was no chance I would get an answer either, just as I would never know who had eaten from the plates and drunk from the glasses which had filled the sink.

The room filled with the smell of aftershave, and he stood before me, erect between the two narrow separate beds, perfumed and elegant, slightly ridiculous, the hero of a cheap television series setting out proudly and gloomily on a tragic mission, pitiful in his pride, his attempts to appear healthy, to appear whole, as if part of him wasn't shrinking and rotting away. Let's get going, I'm late, he said, scrutinizing my nose, suppressing a snigger, and marching me quickly down the passage, they'll be landing soon, and I thought that when we lived together, suddenly it was clear to me that this would really happen, and so I stopped caring what Yonny was going to tell me in a few minutes' time, how sweet it would be when he hurried me up, come on, we're late, he would say, and that we would include me, and I would dawdle on purpose, I would stand for hours in front of the mirror and look at my nose, just to hear him say to me, come on, we're late.

8

What time exactly did she die, that was what I wanted to know, but this was one detail my mother didn't know. Nor did she understand why it made such a difference to me. She said that Aunt Tirza had phoned from the hospital and told her that Aryeh's wife had died last night. Would you believe that she was lying in the bed right next to her? Yes, but what time, I insisted, phone her up and ask her what time. I have no intention of bothering her now with your nonsense, my mother sounded disappointed. She liked waking me up in the morning with bad news, all kinds of acquaintances of theirs who'd become sick or died, worrying and exciting pains in various members of the family, these were the things that nourished her boredom, the boredom which came after the depression, which came after the years of grief and hatred. There was a degree of gloating in it of course, and perhaps also a hungry hope of widening more and more the circle of the victims of life, which she had entered with the death of the baby, and quickly closed the door to prevent my father pushing in behind her and robbing her of the tragedy. But with others she was more generous, every unfortunate victim of fate was invited to join her there, depending on the dimensions of their tragedy, of course, all kinds of women who had lost their husbands, their children, who had lost parts of their body, who were undergoing painful treatments, all these crowded into her throat and were rapidly passed on to me in our telephone conversations. Did you hear what happened to so-and-so, she would begin, and without waiting for an answer press on with more information. This time it was brief. I didn't even know that she was sick, she said resentfully, like a little girl not invited to a party, only your father knew and he didn't tell me anything.

You remember that Aryeh came to visit him a few months ago? He wanted to consult him about some new treatment, but it was apparently too late. You won't believe it, it turns out that she lay there for a week next to Tirza, and I was there every morning and I didn't even recognize her, it didn't even occur to me that it was Josephine, she'd changed so much. It's true I hadn't seen her for years, but such a change, when she was young she was like a china doll, a delicate china doll, but strong, she added with the generosity she reserved only for the dead. I wonder what he'll do without her now, that big baby, she kept him going, believe me, he wouldn't be able to live for a minute without a woman to keep him going. You'll see, in a week he'll find himself someone new, maybe he won't even wait till the end of the week.

You'd be surprised, maybe it'll be me, I barely restrained myself from saying, but I was a little alarmed by her words. To me he looked so full of strength, so self-sufficient, and suddenly he emerged from her mouth as dependent, infantile, weak. How did she keep him going, I protested, if she was sick all the time?

Tirza says that even when she was dying she worried about him all the time, that he wouldn't be lonely, that he wouldn't get depressed, she saw to it that he had friends to keep him company. She would get rid of all her visitors after a few minutes and send them to Aryeh, as if he was sick and not her, she concluded in a snort of triumph.

So you have no idea what time it happened? I asked again, but she said crossly, Ya'ara, what's the matter with you, instead of asking when the funeral is you ask when she died. You'll come with me, won't you?

I was her funeral escort. She didn't like seeing my father next to an open grave, always accusing of him of pushing, hiding the view from her, but she liked taking me with her. Each time I would vow never to go again, and at the last minute I would give in and go, in a kind of fatuous hope that if I shared in the sorrow, perhaps I would also share in the consolation.

Only if you find out for me what time she died, I said, holding her on a short leash, and she grumbled that I had gone quite mad and that she would be happy to go without me, but a few minutes later she phoned again. Because of you I woke Aunt Tirza up, she grumbled, it happened at about ten last night. Now are you satisfied?

No, I wasn't satisfied. I was as panic-stricken as a hypochondriac who discovers that he's sick, as a paranoid who discovers that he really is being persecuted, because all night long I had the feeling that they would not arrive in time to say goodbye to her, I even said to him when he dropped me outside the house, I hope you make it, and he said, don't worry, I'll get there in time, and he meant the airport, not grasping what I could hardly grasp myself, and I thought of the curious group they made, the perfumed groom in his elegant business suit, the mother trembling with age, her hair no doubt rinsed blue, supported by the sister and her husband, and how they drove with the luggage in the boot straight to the most expensive restaurant in town, something Italian or French, because there was nothing to eat at home, and when they reached the house and trod the dust-free carpets the news was already waiting for them.

I felt dizzy with guilt and remorse, how I had upset his plans with my stupid visit, perhaps if they'd eaten at home as he'd planned they would have arrived in time, and I knew that this fiasco would lead to another, like falling dominoes, because when one little thing goes wrong it always makes something big go wrong after it, and he knew it was my fault and he would never forgive me.

But he actually smiled at me, a warm, friendly smile, over his wife's open grave, standing in the middle of the little group which looked exactly as I had imagined, like a troupe of travelling players from a fringe theatre, each of them playing his part to the hilt. The mother in the role of the mother, wiping away a reserved, European tear, her curls merging with the azure clouds, the sister supporting her with a guilty, excessively healthy face, she had apparently always been less beautiful, less successful, and now she was the one who was left, her husband with his arm around her shoulders, proud to demonstrate devotion in a difficult time, and next to him Aryeh, in the role of the enlightened widower, tall and elegant in yesterday's suit, nobody could possibly guess what funny striped underpants he had on underneath it.

I stood not far from him, my mother always made sure of a good place in the middle, sometimes she even used her fists to push in, and like a good little girl I stood between my mother and my father, who had insisted on coming for once. Judging by their furious faces I could see that it hadn't been easy, and they had probably exchanged remarks which I would have been particularly interested to hear, like which of them had the natural right to be here, him or her, in other words, which of them was more his friend, him or her, and I felt only a modest pride in my heart, for I had outdone them both in this competition, I had honestly won the right to stand here in the intimate inner circle, perhaps honestly wasn't the right word but the intention was clear. Perhaps I was even the last person in the whole crowd to have seen her alive, perhaps it was from my hand that she had sipped the last cup of tea of her life, two spoons of sugar and two bags of tea, if they asked me I could tell them, she must have known it was the end and she wanted to make the most of it. I scanned the sombre faces proudly, trying to locate a girl with red hair cut in a straight line, but she wasn't there, most of the mourners looked quite old, there wasn't even one who aroused my suspicion or jealousy, and when I saw Aunt Tirza advancing slowly between the rocks and the pits, the area looked more like a building site than a cemetery, and the last thing I wanted was for her to say anything about my visit to the hospital, so I hurried towards her, to the surprise of my parents, ostensibly to give her a hand, and she leaned on me with all her weight, so that I couldn't understand how she had managed before, without me.

So he's free now, that vain little man of hers, she said with a spiteful smile, and I wasn't sure if she'd said hers or yours, and I asked, whose? And she said again, hers, and it annoyed me that she'd called him a vain little man, so contemptuously, why not just a man, who did she think she was anyway, what did she know about him, a bitter old woman who hated all men, but nevertheless it bothered me, perhaps she knew more than I did, perhaps he really was a vain little man, who knows what Josephine had told her on the long nights in the hospital, where the light never goes off and the noise never stops, nor the pain.

She was so heavy I almost collapsed, I walked bowed down with my eyes on the ground, and I thought about how the disease had made Josephine so small, whereas it had enlarged Tirza, made her gigantic, authoritative and frightening, so that everybody noticed her and watched our slow progress in suspense, so slow and difficult that I began to suspect she was doing it on purpose, leaning on me powerfully, violently, crushing me beneath her on purpose, and I cursed her and my secrets which made me put myself in ridiculous situations, at best ridiculous, all because I had something to hide.

The moment we arrived at our reserved places the ceremony began, as if they had been waiting only for us, and Aunt Tirza stood with surprising lightness next to my mother, and smiled her sardonic smile, and I stretched in relief, still feeling her weight, and before my eyes the small, delicate, negligently wrapped body slid into the deep pit, she looked just like a twelve-year-old girl, I wouldn't have given her a day over twelve, a twelve-year-old girl sliding down a slide and laughing gaily, but instead of laughter there was the sound of weeping, restrained weeping which grew louder, and Aryeh, with a big black skullcap on his head, said *Kaddish*, without faltering, as if he had been practising it all his life, pronouncing the words clearly and fluently. I looked at him in fascination, I had never admired him as much as I did during those moments, the black skullcap covered the grey and reconstructed the dark hair he once had, and his face looked boyish with emotion, and suddenly I hoped that he would say *Kaddish* for me too, that he and nobody else would do it, and I decided to talk it over with him when I had a chance, it wasn't a big thing to ask. And when he was finished his face fell, and at the sight of the earth flying from the pit I saw his shoulders shaking, and someone came up quickly and gave him a hug, he had a big black skullcap covering grey hair too, and

I saw to my horror that it was the judge from Jaffa, who looked a lot more alert and in control of the situation confronting the fresh grave than he did confronting his double bed. Aryeh returned his hug warmly, and I felt a shameful prickling all over my body as I remembered his soft white body, and then I noticed a strange commotion around me, I heard stifled laughter and I saw my father deserting our family unit and advancing towards them in spite of the whispered protests, and the two of them received him warmly into their embrace, and the three of them stood there, reunited at last, hugging and crying. I was quite taken aback to see that my father was crying too, I didn't think she was so dear to his heart, and my mother standing behind me was taken aback too and I heard her whispering something venomous to Tirza, and Tirza saying, let him, let him, why shouldn't he enjoy himself a little.

And he really was enjoying himself, to judge by the volume of his crying, I don't think he cried as much for my brother as he cried for that woman who was almost a stranger to him, hugging Aryeh on one side and Shaul on the other, putting himself at the centre without any problem, as if he was the widower, and thus they stood there, on the brink of the pit, three men, neither young, handsome nor happy, crying their hearts out as if they had all been in love with this woman, and I looked at my father, clasped like a baby in the arms of the two men I had slept with, exactly as I myself had been clasped in their arms only a short time ago. His fair slender presence stressed Aryeh's dark strength, and I thought of my mother looking at them from behind me, how could she have failed to fall in love with him then, when she saw the two of them together, with that dark mysterious opaqueness, he looked so strong and gave you a feeling of such security, security but not trust. Even here he looked elusive, suspect, next to the two of them, who looked so human and mortal, full of blemishes and weaknesses. My thin, short, balding father, Shaul fat and slightly stooped, while he was tall and erect, his blemishes were not displayed but hidden, and therefore he was the most dangerous. I heard my mother and Aunt Tirza whispering mockingly behind me,

the three musketeers, they sneered, each of them crazier than
the other, the fatty looks quite normal, protested Tirza, but my
mother snorted contemptuously, where from normal, I heard
that he fancies little boys, and I was horrified and I couldn't
control myself and I turned round to face her and said, why
do you have to sling mud at everybody, he's a judge after all,
suddenly it was so important to me to clear his name, all of
a sudden he had become dear to my heart, and my mother
immediately pounced, what's he to you? Where do you know
him from? And then she began to hum like a hornet, who will
judge the judge, and I felt like pushing her into the pit, to lie there
with Josephine and tell her lies to the worms, and I shouted in
a whisper, my throat hoarse, because of you, it all happened
because of you, and she whispered back, what happened, and I
whispered, because of you the Temple was destroyed. I saw the
fire leaping from her bitter mouth, yellow and radiant, writhing
between the fresh graves, leaving a boiling black strip behind it,
and advancing rapidly all the way to the Temple Mount, and
there it multiplied into countless strips slithering up the Temple
walls, turning them yellow and then black. I looked up at the sky,
in a minute a hand would emerge from the clouds to receive the
keys of the Temple thrown up to the sky by the High Priest, and
so intent was I on finding the hand that I lost his bold face, so
many people suddenly surrounded him, my father could hardly
extricate himself and return to his place, caught between the
pride of the ceremonious male fraternity and the shame of the
encounter with the customary female venom, and I lost sight of
Aryeh. Here and there his black skullcap bobbed up among the
heads, but the bold, beloved face, abandoned to such despair,
was hidden from me, and I was afraid I would never see it again,
as if it was him they had buried there and not her, and I felt a
profound grief descending on me, a bitter, absolute grief, and
stunned by its intensity I let myself be dragged along with the
crowd to the cars, trapped between my parents, who had united
against me, like two warring gangs sporadically united by their
mutual fear of the police. I looked at the rows of pale graves and
I thought of my brother Absalom, such a long name for a baby,

and how my father had lamented him, O my son Absalom, my son, my son Absalom! Would God I had died for thee, and only the ancient lament justified the name they had chosen for him after the event, and how frightened I had been that it would really happen, that the baby would suddenly emerge from the earth and my father would enter it instead, and how betrayed I felt by this lament of his, and how I had taken my revenge by thinking how crowded he would be in the tiny grave, how he would have to lie curled up in a ball and how all his muscles would hurt.

In the car I squeezed into the back seat next to Aunt Tirza, who sat with her broad hips spreading and her legs opened wide and looked indifferently out of the window. I'm sorry to be such a nuisance, she said to my parents, but in a month or two you'll all have to come back here again, and when they protested politely she said, no hypocrisy please, I've got exactly the same thing as she had, there's no reason why it should end differently in my case, and I couldn't resist asking her, how did she die exactly, what did she say before she died, and Tirza laughed bitterly, you've seen too many movies my dear, real death is usually less eloquent than staged death, she didn't say anything. How long didn't she say anything? I asked, and Tirza shrugged her shoulders, I really don't remember, when I came back from my treatments at noon she was sleeping, and she went on sleeping till evening. Aryeh came at five and she was still asleep. He said he would come back later with her family, but when they came she was no longer breathing.

So she didn't say anything all afternoon and evening? I nagged, and Tirza said crossly, I told you she was sleeping, maybe she muttered something in her sleep, I really didn't pay any attention, what's the matter with you today, tell me, what's the matter with you in general? But I didn't answer her and I looked out of the window at the ugly buildings and thought how frightening and incredible it was that in the end I really was the last person to speak to her, to see her alive. I tried to reconstruct every word she said to me, it was clear to me now that I hadn't left the bus for nothing, that I hadn't missed my appointment with the

Head of the Department for nothing, but I couldn't remember anything, except that she had vomited on the day I was born, and the more I tried to remember the harder it became, and my head began to ache, in the corner of my eye the sharp winter sun shimmered and I could hardly see a thing, and as in a dream I heard my father ask, have you spoken to Yonny yet? And I said, no, he was sleeping when I got home yesterday, and I was sleeping in the morning when he left, and Tirza laughed, that's one way to get through married life, how come I didn't think of it before, and I asked fearfully, why, Daddy? What do I have to talk to him about? And he was silent, and all of a sudden yesterday's muffled fear returned, that Yonny had told them he was leaving me, leaving me for good, and I felt that in a minute I was going to vomit, she had vomited on the day I was born and I would vomit on the day she was buried, but just then the car stopped and my father said, we've arrived, and I was surprised that he knew where I lived, a man so strange to me, and I got out without a word and vomited in the middle of the street, in the place where the car had stopped a moment before.

I went straight into the bathroom and stood in the shower until the hot water ran out, I shampooed my hair and put on a conditioner, and I even tried to lather my pubic hair like them, but from close up it didn't look out of the ordinary or noteworthy, just something people did every day, and when I came out of the shower I cut my nails, my toe-nails too, all the time I kept trying to reassure myself that everything was all right, and now I was pure, lucky I couldn't be put to the test of the wayward wife. I could cut my nails and feel pure, and even if Yonny suspected something I could deny it, just as he could always deny it, and it was quite easy to believe what you wanted to believe, to forget the facts, just as I had forgotten Josephine's last words, and I made a deal with him in my heart and I said, I'll forgive you for having a baby with Aryeh's neighbour, and you'll forgive me for everything I've done, and for a moment I hoped that it really was his child, otherwise I wouldn't have anything to forgive him for and the whole deal would collapse, and I decided not to even try to find out in case I was wrong, and to keep it all in my heart, between me and him, but only between my heart and his heart, without saying a word. I put on a tight mini skirt and a striped sweater, combed my hair and looked in the mirror, the swelling in my nose was hardly noticeable, even my mother hadn't noticed anything, and it seemed to me that everything would be all right now, I would manage, and only occasionally I felt stabbings of longing for the face which had been hidden from me, and I was sorry that I had missed all the expressions crossing it today, but I tried to console myself with the thought that this was nothing compared to what I was going to miss in the future, because my mother was no doubt right, and his girlfriend with the red hair and the cigarette holder would be there before you could say Jack Robinson, and if I didn't take the trouble to remind him, he would forget me before the month was out.

Then I began to make up my face, enthusiastically and with a feeling of furtive excitement, like a little girl baby-sitting and trying on her employer's lipstick. All the time I felt I was stealing from someone, even though everything belonged to me, the make-up that darkened my skin and hid my wrinkles, and the eye-liner that accentuated the shape of my eyes, and the mascara that thickened and blackened my eye lashes, and the blue eye-shadow that deepened the color of my eyes, the blusher that emphasized my cheek bones, and the shiny crimson lipstick, secretly and with deep enjoyment I made up my face, for years I hadn't made it up so perfectly, and in the end I emerged as beautiful and glamorous as if I was somebody else, and I laughed at myself for painting my face now, when I came home instead of when I was going out, the opposite of the normal order of events. I decided that since I was so beautiful it was a pity to waste it on the yellow walls, and I should take myself out, perhaps I should go to Yonny's office and find out what he had said to my parents yesterday, but I hesitated about this, because if he was suspicious any unusual behavior would only deepen his suspicions, and getting all dolled up to go and see him at his office would definitely be unusual, so I decided to go to the university, to make the secretary's eyes pop out and to suck up to the Head of the Department, but after a minute this too seemed silly, I didn't want to spoil my make-up with false smiles, and in the meantime I lay down to think about what to do, nothing seemed festive enough, and in the end I fell asleep before I succeeded in deciding which was more foolish, to put on make-up in honour of going to bed or like the ancient Egyptians in honour of going to their graves.

I woke up the sound of the door slamming, and jumped out of bed in a panic, my heart beating so hard it shook my whole body, for fear that he had really left me. This was how I would wake up as a child, to the sound of the door slamming behind my father after one of their fights, always with my heart pounding, with the fear that he would never come back, that I had missed my last chance to see him, to beg him to stay with us, and in this state I burst out of the bedroom, in my mini skirt and with the heavy make-up smeared on my face. I saw all the signs of Yonny's presence, the smell of his aftershave, the jacket on the chair, the briefcase on the floor, but he himself wasn't there, and I cursed myself for letting him get away, what was I going to do now until he came back, if he ever did, and I ran to see if his shaving gear and toothbrush were there, and I saw that everything was in its place, and I calmed down a little, even though it was possible to buy everything in duplicate, if you really wanted to deceive someone. I roamed round the house, checking to see if anything was missing apart from Yonny, and in the end, when I reached the kitchen, I discovered that the trash can was missing, and like an idiot I repeated to myself, Yonny and the trash can are missing, what does that mean? And then they appeared in the doorway like a particularly heavy hint, Yonny and the empty bin, which I had actually intended to empty this morning, but I forgot, and he looked at me in surprise and said, where were you? And I said, in bed, I was sleeping, and he said doubtfully, with all that make-up on? Precisely when I'm telling the truth he doesn't believe me. I quickly tried to invent a little lie that would sound more credible than the truth, but nothing occurred to me, so I turned my back to him and went to look in the mirror, and there, to my horror, I saw the smudged mascara surrounding my eyes in big black rings, right down to the red blusher, and the lipstick wiped off half my mouth and shining boldly on the other half, and I looked as if I'd just come back from a wild fuck, and I muttered miserably, I put on make-up to go out, but then I fell asleep, and he asked suspiciously, to go out where?

I went to wash my face, trying to wash off his suspicion in the hot water, how had something so beautiful become so ugly, because I really had made myself up in his honour, so as to be beautiful and disguised when he returned, to wait behind a painted mask for his announcement, but this too sounded as if I had sucked it out of my thumb. I wiped a piece of wet cotton over all the places which had all of sudden become ugly, worn out with rubbing and smearing, I could actually see my face aging in front of me, and the cotton was covered with all the colours that had previously covered me, black and brown and red and blue, and all the time Yonny was looking at me expectantly, scratching his snub nose, waiting for me to finish, but I was afraid to finish, and I kept on scrubbing my face, which now looked pale and faded, and in the end he said impatiently, stop that ritual, it's enough, and I shut the tap and said, so what will we do, as if there was nothing to do except stand in front of the mirror, putting on make-up and taking it off again, and he said, we'll go on a honeymoon, we haven't had a honeymoon.

We really hadn't had one, but its absence didn't particularly bother me, I even encouraged it so as to strengthen my feeling that it wasn't a real wedding, at least not my real wedding, in fact, we never had a honeymoon, and I thought I'd keep it for my real wedding, and I said carefully, where will we go, to see if he was serious, or if this was a strange way of hinting at something, and he said, to Istanbul, tomorrow morning, I've already made all the arrangements, your parents helped with the money, all you have to do is pack. He spoke with the pride of an outstanding boy scout who has performed all the tasks set him and is now waiting for the appreciation due to his success, and I really did appreciate it, I was so happy that this was their secret and nothing else, I felt the relief pouring through my body, it showed you should always expect the worst and you might get a pleasant surprise, and I kissed him and said, I don't believe it, how did you think of it, I

didn't have the faintest idea, and for a moment I really loved my
father, and even her, it seemed to me a kind of family project, a
late honeymoon, five years after the wedding, I almost suggested
that they should come with us and look after us there, because
all of a sudden I began to be frightened of Istanbul. I imagined
it as one great noisy colourful bazaar, easy to enter but hard
to get out of, full of unfortunate couples who had come there
on their honeymoon and had failed to find their way back, and
they were hungry and exhausted, all the oriental delicacies of the
market were laid out before them but they didn't have a penny
left, after spending days and weeks in the vast, endless labyrinth
where nobody understood their language, one pointed east and
one west, one south and one north, and it all looked the same,
there were no landmarks, the stalls were the same, the sky was
the same, crowded with the spears of mosques which turned to
churches and vice versa, and the couples who had set out excited
and in love, wept on each other's necks with hatred, because each
in the secret of their hearts blamed the other. She says to herself,
if I had a better husband he would have taken me out of here
long ago, and he says to himself, she probably knows the way
but she's keeping it to herself on purpose, she's testing me to
see if I can do it, and home seems further and further away,
and I looked at Yonny in dismay and said, why Istanbul? Why
not somewhere else? But then I thought that from this point of
view all places were the same, they were all equally frightening,
and anyone who couldn't cope should stay at home. Let's have
a honeymoon at home, I said in my most seductive voice, we
won't go out of the house for a week, like in the beginning,
we'll walk round the rooms, we'll be together all the time, but he
laughed disappointedly, why, what's the problem, and I said in a
pampered voice, I'm afraid we'll get lost in the Istanbul bazaars,
and he hugged me as if I was a backward child, my fear filled him
with strength, and he said, don't worry, I've been studying the
city for a month, and he took a brightly coloured guide-book
out of his briefcase and waved it at me. But I wasn't about to
give in so quickly, and I said, but how do we know that we can
trust that guide-book? Maybe it's all part of a plot? Have you

ever heard of anyone who went to Istanbul with that guide-book and came back? And Yonny went on waving it at me as if he were chasing a fly, convinced as always that I was only joking, and he said, everybody goes and comes back all the time, nobody ever gets stuck anywhere. So I calmed down somewhat, even though his information sounded too general and not really precise, and I decided that if I felt uneasy, I would simply persuade him to stay in the hotel, I could always invent a migraine.

He climbed up to the storage space under the ceiling and threw down a suitcase we received as a wedding gift, and it fell on my feet and it hurt but I didn't say anything so as not to spoil things so I shook off the dust, and then I started rummaging in the wardrobe and I asked, is it hot or cold there, and he said more or less the same as here, a bit colder, and I came across the sexy flesh-coloured nightgown I had once bought and some transparent panties and garters, a kind of special uniform which had been lying neglected in the closet, and I pushed them into the big suitcase, perhaps the Byzantine nights would arouse desire, would break the spell which prevented us from growing together, from maturing, and when I took out a few sweaters I discovered another forgotten treasure trove of stimulating accessories behind them, without even realizing what I was doing I had accumulated them and put them to sleep in the closet until the time was right. There were black bodysuits, and fishnet pantyhose, and transparent black silk knee stockings, and daring bras, and I stuffed them into the suitcase too, as if I were going to work there as a high-class whore, and I laughed and looked at Yonny, seriously folding his cheerfully checked flannel shirts and cramming them into the big shoulder bag, and I thought about how I would surprise him in the hotel with all my outfits and how happy he would be, and how happy I would be to make him happy, in a room which wouldn't remind me of anything, surrounded by faces I didn't know and which didn't know me, and perhaps he would forget all about the bazaar, my dear Yonny, who instead of leaving me was inviting me on a honeymoon. What stopped us from being happy? For a moment I could see us from the side, as if someone was making a movie of us, and it was almost enviable, this sweet packing for our honeymoon, our youth, how young he looked compared to Aryeh, without a single streak of grey in his hair, and you could say that we were at the beginning of our lives, and that we would grow up together, like everybody else, or most of them at least, and we would have a baby and then another baby, and two careers, and two salaries, and we would overcome difficulties like everybody else, and come to terms with what we lacked like everybody else, and the main thing was that I could always rely on him, lean a little without breaking him, feel safe.

I was so happy that I sat down inside the suitcase, snuggling into my daring clothes, and stretched my arms as if I had just woken up, and said to him, come here, I want you. I didn't really want him but I wasn't really lying, because I very much wanted to want him, and I thought that if I persuaded him I would persuade myself as well, and when I saw that he wasn't responding I held my arms out to him from the suitcase and he leaned over towards me in surprise and said, perhaps we should eat first, I'm dying of hunger. From below his stomach looked big and flabby, even though it was empty, and it put me off a bit, but I decided to try again anyway, and I covered my face with a stocking or pair of panties, it was hard to tell, and I said in a seductive voice, the food isn't going to run away, but I am, and he laughed as if it was a joke, not hearing the threat, and said, but the shop's closing in a minute and there isn't even any bread, I'll just pop down for a minute, you can wait in the suitcase. Before I had a chance to protest he was gone, and I immediately jumped out, why on earth should I wait for him in the suitcase, what did he think I was, some seedy conjurer's assistant, and not only did I jump out myself but I began taking out everything I had packed so enthusiastically, it suddenly seemed so hopeless, and everything lay scattered round the room, patches of exotic lace on our plain second-hand furniture, and then I saw him behind me, coming in quietly, empty-handed, and I asked him, what, was the shop shut, and he said, I didn't go to the shop, I realized I may have hurt your feelings, so I came back, and his voice was miserable, lifeless, joyless. I tried to remember if he was like that before we met, or if it was my fault, but how could I possibly know, before we met I'd never met him, and the first time I saw him, for instance, he had a sad voice, and I thought that it was because his mother had died, but then he was sad and now he was miserable, and the misery was worse than the sadness, and I thought, what should we do now, what should we ever do, put everything back in the suitcase? And get into it ourselves? And never come out again?

I tried to sound light-hearted and I said, nevermind, maybe we really should have something to eat first, and he was surprised that I wasn't making a fuss and ran happily to the shop, but quite soon he returned even more miserable than before and said, he's just closed, he shut the shop the minute I arrived, and I felt like hitting him, spanking him on the bottom like a little boy, but I decided to maintain my light-hearted tone, and I said, nevermind, there's bread in the freezer, and he said with exaggerated enthusiasm, great, I'll make an omelette, and in the meantime I put everything back in the suitcase, which looked dark and gaping like an exposed vagina, and then I closed the lid and zipped it up, who needed an exposed vagina in the middle of the house. When we sat down to eat I began to ask him all kinds of questions, why Istanbul of all places and so on, and how long had he been planning this surprise, like a professional interviewer who has to pretend that everything interests her, and he answered willingly and at length, talking with his mouth full, and I tried to cheer up and said to myself, this is your life and it could be a lot worse, but I felt as if I was sinking, and he launched into a description of his vacillations between Istanbul and Prague, and how the minute he decided on Istanbul he knew it was the right place, even though up to then he'd inclined towards Prague, but he thought I would be enthusiastic about the bazaars, the leather garments, and the more he talked the more irritated I became, because I would actually have preferred Prague, why didn't anybody ask me? I'd always envied women whose husbands surprised them with gifts like this, but now I realized how domineering it was, how inconsiderate, because I for instance would have preferred beautiful, noble Prague, and I would have preferred to go some other time, not precisely when I had to console the bereft, and I felt the wave of nausea rising in me again, and I ran to the bathroom and washed my face in cold water opposite the little mirror, how many more times was it possible to begin life again from the beginning, how many more times was it possible to try?

I went out to him and he was alarmed, because of my wet face he thought I'd been crying, and he asked, did I say something to offend you? I'm sorry, Moley, I try so hard and nothing comes out right, and I wanted to say, so try less and think more, but I didn't know myself if this was right. Presumably it wasn't right, what good would it do if he thought more, none as far as I could see, what he needed to do was not to think more but to be different, and perhaps that wouldn't be enough either, because actually it was me who needed to be different, but how was it to be done? Perhaps in Istanbul it would work out, perhaps when I finally emerged from the Istanbul bazaar I would be different and he would be different and life would be different, and suddenly the trip seemed to me a kind of mission, not a pleasure trip but a punishment trip which would strengthen and purify, and I felt like I did before enlisting in the army, afraid and proud, and with my head held high I cleared the table, stepping briskly, left right left right. He looked at me in suspense, attentive as ever to every nuance, and said that he was going to take a shower, and his voice was festive and charged with significance, as if it was in my honour, you can come and sit next to me, like you did once, and I remembered that once, when we still had hope, I liked to sit on the lavatory seat while he was taking a shower and we would talk, chat of this and that, and those were the days of our love, if he died that was what I would miss, only that, not actually him but that easy intimacy of sitting on the closed lavatory seat, and I tried to recall his voice then, rising from the running water, if it was lifeless and joyless, and it seemed to me that it wasn't, that then he had a sweet, lively voice, a voice full of expectation, but how long can expectation last?

The bathroom was full of fragrant steam, and I smiled to

myself at the thought that lately I'd been spending most of my
time watching men in the shower, a kind of call-girl to keep
men company in the shower, that was what I'd become, and
he opened the curtain and smiled back at me, his curls grown
straight and long in the water, and he said, I think the phone's
ringing, you'd better answer it, and I said, it doesn't matter, let
it ring, but he insisted, it must be my father, to say goodbye,
and I went out into the dry, cold rooms and the telephone
rang insistently, and I didn't feel like picking it up but in the
end I did, and I heard the husky smoker's voice, the beloved,
hated voice, the charred, burning, provocative voice, and he
said, Ya'ara. I said nothing on purpose, because I wanted to
hear him say my name again, I was even a little surprised and
proud that he remembered it at all, Ya'ara, and I said, yes,
Aryeh, and he said, I thought you'd be here now, and I heard
my blood stop flowing in the force of my joy and my sorrow,
and I asked, are you alone, even though I could hear a lot of
voices in the background, and he said in a sense I'm alone, and
I asked, when are they all leaving, and he said, soon, at night,
and he hesitated for a moment and asked, will you come to me
tonight? And I said slowly, my whole mouth hurting with the
words, do you really want me to come? And he said, yes, and
I said, all right, I'll try, and put the phone down.

I stood trembling next to the phone, and I thought, how dare
he, how dare he ruin my honeymoon because of his mourning,
and then I thought, it's not his fault, he simply wants me, which
is exactly what I've been waiting for, from the minute I first set
eyes on him at my parents' door, but I immediately remembered
what my mother had said, or maybe it was Tirza, that within a
week he would bring some girl into his house, and perhaps it
was only an accident that it was me, and perhaps nobody else
wanted to, and if I went to him tonight, what would become
of Yonny and our honeymoon, and if I didn't go, what would
become of me?

I went back to the bathroom, tense and exhausted, hiding
behind the dense vapour, and fell onto the lavatory seat, and as
in a dream I heard his voice in the distance, rising from a well

deep in the ground, who was it, he asked, and I said, nothing, it doesn't matter, I didn't have the strength to make anything up, and I thought that the Day of Judgement was at hand, the great and terrible day of the Lord, the day when I would have to decide. Is anything wrong, he asked, his voice wet and clear, and I said, no, nothing's wrong, and I thought of this lousy life, lousy wasn't the word, that if it already offered you two gifts, they had to be one at the expense of the other. And what if I wanted both to be with Aryeh in his grief and to go to Istanbul, why did I have to choose, I didn't think it would come so quickly, I didn't believe it would come at all, and now I wasn't ready, I wasn't able to decide. But in this case not deciding was a decision too, because if I missed the first moment that he needed me, I might lose him forever, I would never hear his murky voice saying Ya'ara so gently, Ya'ara, come to me tonight. I thought of all the days that had passed since I had seen him at my parents' place, how I had searched for him in the streets, how I had wanted him, how I had wanted him to want me, and now it had happened, what did I care how or why, the only thing that mattered was that he wanted me now, and Yonny said, towel, and I went out and stood opposite the wardrobe and tried to remember what I was looking for, and I couldn't, I passed over all the shelves in order to remember, shelf after shelf, as if I were saying goodbye to them, and I remembered how we had assembled it ourselves, which was why it was crooked, and Yonny kept saying that we had to take it apart and put it together again, and I would mock him, tell me, is that what's bothering you now, and he would say, you should be taken apart and put together again too, you're crooked too, and then he came up behind me, naked and dripping, and said crossly, what's the matter with you, where's my towel, and I mumbled, sorry, I'm looking for the shelf with the towels, and he pushed me aside almost violently, and said, it's right in front of your eyes, what's the matter with you, and took a towel, but he too apparently forgot what he had intended doing with it, and stood there dripping water with the towel in his hands.

I looked at his body, shelf after shelf, he looked to me like a wardrobe, I loaded each limb with something else, I began at the bottom, with his big flat feet, and above them his surprisingly slender ankles, only now did I sorrowfully note their fragility, and rising from them white legs growing thicker, with dark hairs, with rough, pink knees, soft thighs, broad hips, and between the thighs sparse black pubic hair, flabby testicles, and a pink, slightly lopsided penis, and then the high waist, with a drooping little paunch, pale chest and slightly sagging shoulders, leading to broad, tanned arms, as if they had been stuck onto the white body in an expert collage, looking like particularly successful prostheses, an imitation which was superior to the original, and I always liked to imagine them holding our baby.

Only when I reached his sloping neck did he begin to dry himself, with slow movements, as if he wanted to give me time to part from his nakedness, I might see him again but not his nakedness, and he took white underpants and a white T-shirt from the cupboard and got dressed quickly and got into bed, and I stood in the little puddle of water he had left behind him and I didn't know what to say, everything had suddenly come apart and I didn't know how to put it together again.

He took the alarm clock out of the drawer and said, you'd better finish packing, we have to be at the airport at seven, and I took all kinds of things out of the wardrobe, without paying any attention, and stuffed them into the suitcase, and I took my face creams and cosmetics, and the book next to my bed, and shoes, and sandals, and he laughed, you should take boots instead, so I crammed in my boots without taking out the sandals, and then I heard the phone ring again and I thought maybe Aryeh's changed his mind, and for a moment I even hoped it was him, if he was going to regret it then let him do it now, when something could still be saved, but it was my parents, and my mother cried jubilantly over the phone, well, what do you think of our surprise? And I said, thank you very much, Mother, it's nothing compared to the surprise I've got in store for you, and she laughed, and then asked suspiciously, what do you mean? And I said, nothing, I hope I'll be able to pay you back some day, and she said, nonsense, we're happy we can help, Daddy sends you best wishes for your trip and kisses too. I returned to the bedroom on tiptoe, hoping that he had fallen asleep, but he was lying on his side, surrounded by a halo of pale light, reading his guide-book, his wet curls shining on his head, and he looked at me with honeyed eyes and said, I'm sorry if I hurt your feelings before, it was really stupid of me, and I said, nonsense, Yonny, I've already forgotten it, and I got into bed and turned to the other side. I felt his hands on my back, half stroking, half massaging, to be on the safe side, and this annoyed me even more, it was my back after all, not his, so where did he get off touching it, and I said in a childish voice, my back belongs to me, and he pressed up to me from behind and asked, what did you say, in the masculine gender, at moments like these we both talked as if I was a man, and I said I'm tired, Ratty, and he said, so go to sleep, Moley, tomorrow you're sailing across the river.

I introduced him to all this nonsense with the animals from *The Wind in the Willows*, I used to talk like that with my girl-friends in the army, and I infected him with it quite quickly, and I said, what's going to happen, Ratty, I'm afraid, and he said, it'll be all right, Moley, don't worry, from tomorrow everything will be all right, but his fingers went on roaming obstinately round my body, and this was so incompatible with out babyish prattle, as if someone had attached the soundtrack of *Pinocchio* to a blue movie, and my entire body shut down, but he didn't stop, sending one hand to my breast and the other between my legs, trying to insert his fingers with uncharacteristic aggressiveness, intrusive and annoying, apparently he thought that my previous invitation was still valid even though it definitely wasn't. I almost shook him off rudely but then I said to myself, what do you care, it's the last time, and I turned to him and opened my legs wide and pulled him into me, and his touch was smooth and slippery, like rubber, even though he didn't have anything on, it always felt as if he was wearing a condom, and I held his bum hard, and all the time I repeated to myself, half in prayer and half in threat, this is the last time, this is the last time, and he asked, is it nice, do you want more? And I didn't say anything, and then he asked again, but in the masculine gender, and it sounded so jarring in the middle of a fuck, Moley, answer me, and tears welled into my eyes, and I shouted, yes, yes, pinching him angrily on his broad bum, and then, with a sudden groan, he came, with the sad wail of a jackal, and put his head on my breasts and his whole body clung to me, soft and grateful.

I began to stroke his curls and waited for him to fall asleep, this was usually the procedure, but he was in a talkative mood and he whispered, I love to feel you so close, and I said, me too, what could I say, and he whispered, I'm too excited to go to sleep, I feel as if tomorrow's our real wedding, and I said, me too, and he waited a minute and asked, in the years we've been together, have you ever been with anyone else like this? And I felt a wave of tears engulfing me and I thought this is your chance, to tell him everything, and begin again, why protect him all the time, him and yourself, but I couldn't do it, and I only whispered, no, why do you ask, and he said, I have a feeling that you keep a lot to yourself, and he stroked my hair, it's all right, Ya'ari, I don't think you're my property or anything like that, I only want to know, that's all, and I said, there's nothing to know, let's go to sleep, Ratty, and he turned round and switched off the light and said, goodnight, Moley.

I knew that I would never hear that voice say those words again, and I lay quietly in the dark and tried to calm down, promising myself that it still wasn't too late, I could stay here in the warm bed, drive to the airport in the morning, have a baby with a sheep's face, and I tried to calculate for and against, profit and loss, until my head was bursting with tables. Then I decided that if I succeeded in falling asleep, it was a sign that I should stay, and if I didn't fall asleep, it was a sign that I should leave, and I tried to think of nice things to put myself to sleep, but I felt a hard kicking inside me, as if I had a wild horse in my stomach, and it began to hurt, it grew stronger and stronger, as if I had a whole stable of wild horses inside me, every minute another one was born, like the horses surrounding the celestial palaces, horses of darkness, horses of the shadow of death, horses of blood, horses of iron, horses of mist, standing over troughs of fire and eating. I couldn't remain lying down, so I got up quietly and went to the bathroom, washed myself quickly in cold water, and went back to the bedroom to make sure that he was sleeping, his breathing was quiet and even, and I stood there and looked at him with pity and terror, as if looking at a sick baby in its sleep, and then I dragged the suitcase quietly into the living room and got dressed in the dark, taking clothes out of the suitcase at random, and at the door I stopped to look for a pencil and paper, I wish I could go with you on a honeymoon, I wrote to him.

9

The night was different from what I had imagined, from what it had looked like in bed, less dark, less bitter, the end of winter was already in the air and I thought, where will I be in the spring, where will I be in the summer, dragging the suitcase swollen with bras and garters, stockings and panties down the hated road. A number of taxis stopped next to me but I preferred to walk, sweating in spite of the cold, I didn't want to get into any conversations now, only to advance slowly, to pass the shops and traffic lights in a kind of private victory procession, to nod gravely at the parade saluting me, but I kept looking behind my back to see if I was being pursued, and it seemed to me that I could hear him whisper, Moley, come back to me, come back. Why was he whispering if he wanted me to hear him, why didn't he shout, a whisper that grew weaker and weaker, until I had to stop and bend down in order to hear it rising from the depths of the earth, like the whispers of the survivors of an avalanche who, by the time the rescue teams reach them, are already dead.

I sat down on the narrow pavement, a fist of sorrow doubling me up, and I thought that it wasn't too late, I could still go back, he was probably asleep, I could go back quickly and get undressed and get into bed as if I had never gone out, Aryeh had probably forgotten that he'd ever invited me, and I looked round, searching for a sign, and I remembered the star resembling a sword which shone over Jerusalem for a whole year before the destruction of the Temple, never moving from its place in winter or summer and even in daylight it could be seen shining in the sky, but I stood up immediately, kicked violently forward, I couldn't forgo this chance, and I stopped in front of his door, panting for breath and listening to the sounds around me. From

the opposite apartment rose the loud, demanding cry of the baby
I had volunteered to mind, but the Even apartment was quiet,
and I knocked gently, almost caressing the door which was so
familiar to me, more so than his face which appeared in the
doorway, heavy and serious, and he quickly locked the door
behind me and led me into the bedroom, which had changed
beyond recognition. All the medical equipment had disappeared,
and the beds had been pushed together and covered with a
floral bedspread and big, soft cushions, with bedside cupboards
holding round reading lamps on either side, and on his side I
saw an ashtray full of dead cigarettes and a glass full of liquor,
while the cupboard on the other side had nothing on it, as if it
was waiting for my face creams. How had he managed, only
yesterday the room had looked like a clinic, and now it was
as polished and anonymous as a hotel room, exactly how I
had imagined the room in Istanbul, and for a moment I felt
angry with him, how quickly he had obliterated her traces, how
quickly he would obliterate mine, and I tried to work it out, if it
had taken him a day to get rid of her, after she had lived with him
for nearly thirty years, how long would it take him to get rid of
me, if I lived with him for let's say a year? How did you manage,
I asked him, and he said in an apologetic tone, it's not as if I had
to create something from nothing, all I did was put everything
back where it was before, and I looked round suspiciously, I
had actually felt more at ease in the previous decor, and I put
my suitcase down on the floor and sat on it as if I was in an
airport, and he looked at me and said, what have you brought
us, and I said with a crooked smile, all kinds of surprises, because
suddenly I was ashamed of bringing it, I'm invited for the night
and I turn up with an enormous suitcase like Mary Poppins.

Let's have a look, he said and picked me up and opened the
suitcase and immediately pulled out the sexy black underwear,
and studied it curiously, item by item, and finally said, not bad,
and began to laugh, and it was so humiliating that I nearly
cried, I sat down on the bed with my head between my knees
and hoped that he would have a coughing fit which would
wipe out his laughter, and then he sat down next to me and

put his arm around my shoulders and said, don't be insulted, I'm not laughing at you, I'm delighted by your suitcase, and I can promise you that you won't leave here until we've made use of every one of these articles, and he raised my head and looked at me and said, it's good that you make me laugh, consoling the grieving is a virtuous deed.

You don't look so grief-stricken to me, I said, and he retorted sharply, I hate being told what to feel, I'll grieve in my own way in my own time, I left the Yeshiva High School at the age of fourteen precisely because I refused to be dictated to, and I'm not about to surrender now, you hear? Nobody's going to tell me when to be sad and when to be happy, I'm glad to see your garters, I'm glad she's not suffering any more, he said in one breath, I'm sorry for the price she paid, I'm sorry for the price you're paying, there used to be a saying that love was free, I've never heard such nonsense in my life. Love free? Love extracts the highest price there is. And when he had finished his speech, which sounded plausible but well-worn, as if he had already delivered it on all kinds of occasions, he stood up and removed his elegant funeral trousers and lay down on his side of the bed, in his underpants, and began to laugh his unpleasant laugh again and said, you look disappointed, Ya'ara, you came for a fuck and instead you get a lecture, and I lay down next to him and cuddled up to him and said, not at all, I love listening to you. It really was nice, to hear him talking to me, really talking to me, warm and reassuring as I always felt he could be, and I said triumphantly to myself, it's worth it, it's worth it, it wasn't an illusion, it wasn't his alienated silences I was attracted to, but what I heard behind them, his virile, provocative words, every word he said sounded provocative to me, the movement of his tongue in his mouth looked provocative to me, the way his dark lips met, the way they held his cigarette, and he offered it to me and said, it's not an ordinary cigarette, there's a little consolation prize inside it.

It has no effect on me, I said, because I'd smoked before, and I'd always been disappointed because it didn't do anything for me, but this time perhaps it was different stuff, or I was different, because all of a sudden I was filled with strength, I felt I had the strength to lick his dark, fragrant skin from top to toe and this is what I did, and it seemed to me that in this way I was sticking his broken parts together, that he was some rare archaeological find and I had collected all the pieces and now I was sticking them together with my spit, and only when I was finished would I know what it was, and I was curious to see what would emerge, but I wasn't allowed to open my eyes while I was doing it, only at the end. He lay like a statue smoking in silence, from time to time I heard him laughing, but it didn't bother me, I was even happy for him, that he had found something to laugh about, and thus little by little I stuck his long slender legs together, and between his thighs his beautiful penis that stretched as if after a long sleep, and I went on moving upwards and I nearly ran out of spit but I kept trying, because I didn't want to leave him without his head or shoulders. When I had finished I looked at him proudly, it had come out so well, a human being constructed from scratch with everything in the right place, and I wondered if God had felt like this after creating Adam, it excited me to think that we had an experience in common, God and I, and all the time I felt something burning between my legs, so I took his hand and said, see how hot it is, like an oven, and he began to undress me and said in pretended concern, we have to bring down the temperature, it's dangerous, and he took a cube of ice from his drink and sucked it and laid it at the door and slowly pushed it in, and I shivered with pleasure and felt it melting inside me, and I thought, I've melted you at last, my love, I've melted you at last. In the meantime he rummaged in the suitcase until he selected a brief lace bodysuit and dressed me in it as if he were dressing a baby, on my naked body, and took a black silk stocking and gathered my hair up into a topknot and secured it with the stocking, and kissed the exposed nape of my neck, and my breasts which almost tore the delicate web of the lace, and all the time I went on hearing the low, vulpine laughter, or perhaps I was imagining it, or perhaps it was me laughing, hearing the foxes prowling round the Holy of Holies among the ruins.

The delicate web lay on me as heavily as iron bars, and the

bed rocked to and fro as if I was lying on a ship at sea, I
rocked so hard, a ship transporting convicts. It was strange
to be imprisoned in the heart of the sea, in the heart of the
greatest freedom, but I wasn't being transported to a prison but
to Istanbul, where I would be sold into the Sultan's harem, and
I would never be able to escape, he would have his way with
me forever, and then I saw him lighting a cigarette in the corner
of the bed, at a great distance from me, and in a hoarse voice
he asked, you want a little more consolation? And I said, yes,
and he looked at me with gentle eyes and asked, do you have
sorrow, in a matter-of-fact voice, as if he were asking, do you
have change, and I moved over to him and laid my head on his
knees and said, yes, I'm in mourning too.

He asked no more and handed me the red-tipped reefer and
said, I've put a lot of consolation in it, and he stroked my
hair, and went on apologetically, I don't know if this bed can
contain any more sorrow, and suddenly he stood up, and I said
in alarm, where are you going, and he said in a whisper, to pee,
and suddenly I noticed that we were both whispering, careful
not to wake someone up, and I asked, why are we whispering,
and he said, we're not whispering, you're definitely not, you let
out a few screams there that must have amazed the neighbours,
and I was ashamed and asked, is that awful, and instead of an
answer I heard the jet of his pee, fizzy and monotonous, and then
he said, don't worry, they must be sure that it's me screaming
and tearing out my hair. And then he came back and lay down
next to me and suddenly pulled me to him and seated me on top
of him, raising and lowering me as if I was a rag doll, taking me
down and raising me up, widening and shortening, straightening
and twisting, gripping and thrusting away, and it hurt like it did
the first time, between the beer cans and the coals, but this time
I didn't care, I was so turned on by the renunciation of will,
of control, I didn't even have to decide whether to move my
bum to the right or to the left, up or down. I heard him say,
scream now, honey, so everyone can hear how grief-stricken
you are, and I screamed, because he said so, and I wanted to
do whatever he said, it wasn't even a question of wanting to,

but a kind of knowledge that whatever he said I did, and it didn't even bother me that he called me honey, and underneath my scream of grief, from the total renunciation, suddenly rushed a torrent of sweetness, as if I was being drowned in a bed full of honey, and his movements inside me became soft and cradling too, as if I had a little baby being put to sleep between my legs, and so I simply fell asleep, like the women I had always envied, who could fall asleep next to all kinds of men who had never promised them that they would love them forever, and nevertheless they slept soundly, and I had a vague feeling that I had discovered something tonight which I had to write down so I wouldn't forget, but I didn't have the strength to open my eyes and when I woke up I didn't remember anything.

I was alone in the big room, and my head ached, and suddenly I looked at the clock in a panic and it was nine o'clock, the very moment when the plane was taking off to fly happy couples to Istanbul, and I thought, what have you done, what have you done, what have you done, and I rang home quickly just to hear his voice, to know that he was all right and to hang up, but there was no reply, he must have gone alone on our honeymoon, and it made me laugh a little to think that we were spending our honeymoon apart, until I remembered that it wasn't a joke, that it was for real, but there was nothing I could do now, I couldn't phone the plane and ask the pilot to come and pick me up, there was nothing I could do any more, nothing at all. I got out of bed and saw that my lace garment was torn, and there were marks from his hands on my body, and all my muscles hurt as if after a pitiless gym class, and I limped to the bathroom and showered in boiling water until I could hardly breathe, and afterwards I rubbed myself all over with body lotion and put on my cream-coloured nightgown, and that was as much as I could do. The blinds were drawn, and I didn't dare open them in case anybody saw me, from the interior of the flat muffled voices reached me, here and there I recognized his voice, hoarse and restrained, among the others, most of them female. I advanced to the door so that I would be better able to hear, tried carefully to open it a crack, and discovered that I was locked in.

I leaned against the door, boiling with rage and insult, who did he think he was, a Turkish sultan? Locking me into his bedroom as if I was his chattel, and who knows what was happening in the other rooms? Maybe there was a different girl locked up in every room in the apartment, celebrating his new widowerhood with him, dripping lustful sweat while the mourners gathered in the living room wiped away their tears. For me of all people, who never even locked the bathroom door, to find myself locked up in his bedroom, utterly at his mercy, and what if he forgot about me? I could die of thirst and hunger in here until the middle of the night, and I wasn't even allowed to open my mouth, so that nobody would know that I was here, desecrating the memory of the dead woman and her bed.

In my despair I returned to the bathroom and drank more and more water from the tap and washed my face to calm myself and then I went back to bed and tried to see everything differently, what other option did he have, he couldn't have locked the door from the inside unless he woke me up, and he apparently wanted to let me go on sleeping, and he couldn't have left the door open, if her mother or sister came in to put a coat on the bed or lie down for a moment they would discover me at once, and he was probably waiting for an opportunity to slip into the room and smuggle in something for me to eat and drink, just as I once took to Aunt Tirza the leftovers of her ex-husband and his new wife. I tried to hear what was going on, and had the distinct impression that the commotion was increasing, the door kept opening and closing almost without a pause, and I realized that there was little chance of his coming to my rescue soon, but suddenly I heard footsteps approaching the door and to my horror the handle moved up and down a couple of times until whoever it was gave up, and I went red all over in fear and shame of being discovered, how lucky I was locked in, anyone who wanted to pee when the guests' toilet was occupied would try to come into the bedroom, but nevertheless I wished I, not Aryeh, had the key that way I would have been able to slip out and mingle with the guests as one of the condolence callers, after all, I had been the last person to speak to her, even if nobody knew that had happened, even if it shouldn't have happened, it did. I wouldn't have minded acting as hostess, handing out refreshments, making coffee, for myself first of all, what wouldn't I give now for a cup of coffee, and I tried to think of ways to escape, just like a real prisoner, we were only on the first floor, I could easily jump out of the window and walk in officially through the door, and I opened the shutter a little to check whether there were bars on the window, and to my disappointment there were, rather close set, and grotesquely enough they were heart-shaped, and I stared at them blankly and said to myself, honey, you're fucked, instead of eating breakfast in the Istanbul Hilton and looking out at the Golden Bridge joining Europe to Asia, you're staring at heart-shaped window bars and eating your heart out while your stomach growls with hunger. I remembered how he had called me honey last night and I felt a little disgusted, what did he think I was, I said to myself, he doesn't think, he sees what you show him, the way you sell yourself is the way you'll be bought, and you insist on paying such a high price for selling yourself so cheap, nevermind cheap, for nothing, you're even prepared to pay whoever's prepared to buy, and I tried again to phone Yonny and again there was no answer, but nevertheless I found it hard to believe that he had gone without me, dear Yonny, my sad, pathetic, orphaned Yonny, now we all shared the same fate, Yonny who had lost his mother, I who had lost my brother, and Aryeh who had lost his wife, we were all one big unhappy family.

I tried to determine who was the unhappiest member of our family, and at first I decided on Yonny, who had gone off alone on his honeymoon. While the widower enjoyed a passionate sex life the groom was lonely as a dog on his honeymoon, but setting out alone didn't necessarily mean coming home alone, and our late honeymoon might easily turn into an early honeymoon for Yonny and someone he would meet over there, which actually seemed to me almost inevitable, according to all the unwritten laws of love life, and according to these laws I would be the unhappiest, because anyone who wanted to take even one slice of bread more than he already had would end up with nothing.

I looked around me in a panic, trapped inside these laws like one of my father's rats in a dark laboratory, and I wondered how I was going to evade them, how I was going to hide from my fate, as if this fate was a ball in a children's game, a game where you were out if the ball touched you, and I looked at my watch to see how far Yonny was from me now, and it still said nine, which seemed improbable, because even if time passed slowly it still passed, even if you didn't do anything it still passed, which was a comforting thought in the last analysis, and I realized that it had stopped, my watch, which was always too sensitive to every passing mood, it had probably been screwed up by last night's violent screwing. Now I felt even more lost, without any idea of what the time was, and whether I should dream of breakfast or lunch, and how long it would be before everyone went home, it seemed to me that it was customary to allow the condolers to rest between two and four, but even if everybody else went home the grieving family might prefer to stay here to rest instead of shlepping back to the hotel, out of consideration for the bereft mother with her blue curls. I wondered if she went to the hairdresser to have her hair done or if she did it herself with her thin hands, and I remembered Josephine's emaciated body, how easily she had slid into the pit, almost waving her arms in glee, and I wondered what she had been like as a child, her mother was probably sitting in the living room and telling everyone who was willing to listen what she had been like as a child, gifted and accomplished, playing the piano and reciting Baudelaire, or Molière, whoever, from her flowery lips everything sounded sweet to the same extent, and she had died like a flower too, shrunk, wilted, shed her petals, and into the rubbish bin with her. I've always been depressed by flowers when they wilt, drooping their dry heads towards the jar with its foul-smelling water, giving off an air of neglect, better to look at an empty jar than one with a wilted bunch of flowers. I always told Yonny to spare me this when he occasionally brought me flowers, the beauty isn't worth the ugliness, I would say to him, they'll wilt within a week at most, and before I remember to throw them out another week will pass, and in the meantime I won't understand where the stink is coming from, and why the house seems neglected and depressing, and on the way to the rubbish bin the dry leaves will crumble in my hands and scatter all over the house and invade my life, and it will take me such a long time to get over it, the trauma of having a bunch of flowers in the house.

I thought that perhaps I would pass the time by trying to hear what they were saying in there, not necessarily about her, to tell the truth she herself interested me a lot less now, I was from the side of the groom, not the side of the bride, why try to hide it, something in her dying had excited me, but when the dying was over she seemed to me actually rather a dull woman, who had lived for a few years and died, and left an anonymous bedroom with windowbars shaped like hearts joined closely together, and it seemed to me that her dying was more impressive than her life, it was apparently her opportunity to demonstrate nobility of soul, and she knew that it was her last chance and decided to take advantage of it, with a certain justice, but God knows what it had to do with me, and why I had to be more virtuous than the Pope, in other words, the husband. I took a chair that was standing in the corner and pressed myself against the door, and at first I heard muffled voices which gradually grew clearer, a woman came in and was greeted enthusiastically, with a very loud voice, not young, to my relief, I heard her quite clearly saying that she had just come from the vet, and don't ask what had happened there. Someone asked anxiously if the dog was sick, and she said, don't ask, I went to castrate the dog, because he started making trouble and I didn't have the strength to deal with it, and everybody told me, castrate him, it's for his own good, and then when he was already lying anaesthetized on the operating table, the vet said to me, what are you, blind or something, this dog's a bitch, and I was as shocked as if he'd said it about my husband, I was so sure it was a male, and I said what should we do, and he said, for all practical purposes it makes no difference, in fact it's even more important to sterilize a female, because their heat is even more of a nuisance, so I said to him, go on, do it, and I sat in the waiting room and after a few minutes he came out and showed me her womb, and it turned out that she already had four puppy fetuses in there, small and round as nuts, so I began yelling at him and I said to him, put it back in her stomach, murderer, and he said, what do you want, we agreed on sterilization, he never thought of checking, and now it was all in his rubbish bin, the womb and the puppies, and the dog will recover, he said, she won't know anything, but I know, and it's driving me crazy.

I heard her begin to sob, and to tell the truth I almost scratched the door myself in my shock, and everybody started to console her as if she was the mourner here, and nobody even remembered Josephine, and someone said to her, maybe it was even Aryeh, try to forget everything that happened, pretend it's still a male and not a female, which is almost true now she hasn't got a womb, and it's perfectly natural for a male dog not to have puppies, so what's the tragedy? And she said in her loud voice, great, do you console yourself by those methods too? And I didn't hear his reply, and some other woman with a young voice asked, can I give you coffee, Tammy, and I immediately felt pressured, because who else could be serving coffee there so naturally if not his niece with the cigarette holder, or some other woman friend of his, wandering round freely in his life? I heard the tinkle of teaspoons turning round in cups, and Tammy apparently calmed down because I didn't hear her any more, but after a few minutes her voice rose again and said, imagine the shock, as if they suddenly told me my husband was a woman. All of a sudden I saw black, the big empty room spun round and I tried to get back to the bed and on the way I bumped into my suitcase and almost tripped, and I fell on it emotionally as if it was Yonny, a memento from my previous life, when I was a free woman, free to come and go, and I delved into it lovingly, smelling the smell of home which now seemed to me like the sweet smell of freedom, and among all the erotic accessories I came across something hard which I had thrown in without thinking, the rare book which the Head of the Department had lent me from his private library, the legends of the destruction of the Temple.

I hugged it to me warmly and began to page through it, joyfully meeting all my friends, as if coming across an old class photograph in a strange house, the wayward wife who took the bitter cup from her son the High Priest's hands, and drunk it to the dregs while he stood opposite her shouting and weeping, not because she was sure of her innocence but because she was sure of her guilt, and I met the priest's daughter whose father was slain before her eyes, and when she screamed they slayed her too and mingled her blood with his, and so an entire family perished before my eyes, and I met Martha Bat Beythus, and the rest of the delicate daughters of Zion who had never gone to the market in their lives, scavenging in vain for food among the piles of horse manure and hugging the pillars and dying everywhere as they stood, while their babies crawled between them, each of them recognizing his mother and trying to climb up and suck milk from her breasts, and failing in his efforts until he too died deranged in his mother's lap, and I imagined her in the image of the neighbour with the baby, lying dead at her door while her baby crawled next to her, his sheep's face thin and white. And above them all the shadow of Jeremiah going up from Anathoth to Jerusalem, weeping as he walks between the dismembered bodies, and seeing on his way a woman dressed in black with dishevelled hair crying out who will console me, just as we ourselves had done last night, crying who will console us, he in my ears and I in his. And the person I was happiest to meet there was the carpenter's wife who had married the apprentice, again and again I read the legend, trying to discern from the few words what she had really felt when her husband waited on them and his tears flowed into her cup and it was for that hour sentence was passed. I hugged the book tightly and opened it wide so that it would hug me back with its paper arms, and I covered us both with the blanket and tried to go to sleep in order to pass the time, like on the Day of Atonement, and I must have dropped off for a while, until I heard the key turning in the lock and I sat up quickly in bed, so he wouldn't think I was asleep and go away again, and he stood over me and put his finger on his lips and sat down on the edge of the bed with a savage look in

his eyes. I looked round to see if he had brought me something
to eat but his hands were empty and cold on my breasts and
his face, contorted into an expression of intent concentration,
came closer and closer to mine until I could hardly see it, and he
quickly peeled off my nightgown, digging his hands roughly into
my body, and he put my hand on the fly of his black mourning
trousers and whispered, how much do you want him, honey,
and I whispered, a lot, and he said, show me how much, and
I didn't really understand what he meant, or how such a thing
could be shown at all, but I wanted to please him and I kneaded
his trousers with rhythmic movements and he stood up and said,
you haven't convinced me. What do you want me to do, I almost
wept, and he said, I don't want anything, what do you want, and
like an exemplary pupil I said, you, and he said, so think about
how to convince me, you'll have another opportunity tonight,
and he began walking to the door, and I ran after him naked
and said, you can't leave me like this, let me out, and he said,
but the whole family's in the other room. Bring me something
to eat at least, I begged, and he said, first show me how much
you want him, and I, in a fit of rage, knelt on the floor and
fell on him like a famished animal, biting and scratching and
swallowing everything in sight, until I could hardly tell where
he ended and I began, or distinguish his front from his back,
and I pulled him down to the floor and said, come on, I can't
wait any more, but he bent over me, pulled up his trousers and
laughed his vulpine laugh and said, a little starvation is good for
you, it makes you fight, and I turned over on the floor, I couldn't
stand the sight of his face any more, and he laughed, you'll get
him tonight, honey, exactly like this on the floor you'll get him,
you've succeeded in convincing me that you really want him.

I heard him leaving the room and locking the door, I didn't
have the strength to get up from the floor, my whole body hurt
with hunger for him, apparently I had succeeded in convincing
myself too, and I felt his absence inside me even more intensely
than his presence, and at the same time I began to be afraid of
him, of his weird games, what did he need them for, perhaps I
was mixed up here with someone it wasn't such good idea to

be so dependent on, the kind of person who locked women up in his bedroom, what did I really know about him after all, and nevertheless I knew that even if I had a key to the door I wouldn't leave now, not yet, not before tonight.

I walked slowly to the bed, heavy and overcome with excitement in expectation of the night, a whole night with him, and then I heard him coming back, holding a round tray with the tips of his fingers like a professional waiter. The tray held a big mug of coffee, a glass of juice, and two sandwiches, a plate of cut vegetables, and a bowl of fruit, and I wondered how he had managed to prepare it all in two minutes, he must have prepared it in advance and he was only having a bit of fun at my expense, who did he think these games of his worked on, and I had to admit, apparently on you, honey. He put the tray down on the bed and said, room service, and his face was completely different, quiet and calm, suddenly he looked like a kind, friendly uncle. I fell on the coffee and the food, I felt as if my happiness was brimming over at the mere sight of this tray, a work of art, no less, and he took a piece of carrot and chewed it with a bored expression on his face, and I asked him, are we alone, and he said, not really, her mother's sleeping in the other room. What's the time, I asked, and he said, three o'clock, and I remembered that this was always the worst hour on *Yom Kippur*, the hour you most wanted to eat, but once you were past it you felt as if you could go on fasting forever, and I asked for more coffee, and he came back immediately with a shining red thermos flask, and put it on the tray and said, at the beginning I used to bring Josephine coffee from home in this thermos, but later on it made her feel sick. I looked at the thermos flask and thought how superfluous his remark was, in really bad taste, what did I care about the history of this thermos flask, and he too fell silent, as if he was flooded with the appropriate melancholy thoughts, and after a moment he said, then I still thought it would end well, and I asked with my mouth full, how can something like that end well? And he said, they didn't find anything, we all thought it was psychological, her hair hurt, you know, have you ever heard of a disease where your hair hurts? And I said,

never, and I even stopped eating in honour of the gravity of
the moment, and he laughed bitterly, she had beautiful blonde
hair, even when she aged her hair remained young, without a
drop of grey, everyone was sure she dyed it, and in the end
it was her hair of all things that hurt her, she was in agony.
She would brush her hair and cry, just imagine, I was sure it
was something psychological, something that could be cured by
love, you know how difficult it is to realize that some pains can't
be cured by love? All those years she thought I didn't love her
enough, and we both had the illusion that if I gave her all the
love she needed, everything would be all right, and suddenly it
turned out that it was nothing, this love, zero, an aspirin was
worth more. He spoke as if he felt personally slighted, as if he
was Cain, angry at the rejection of his offering, and so we both
sat there, gazing profoundly at the thermos flask, as if it was a
reincarnation of Josephine, and he whispered, now I realize that
it was the pain of separation from her hair, it knew before we
did that its role was done, that it would no longer be allowed
to adorn her dear face. I felt my hair fearfully, these stories are
so infectious, and he sighed and looked at me sternly, as if there
was a lesson to the story which I was supposed to grasp, before
it was too late, and I smiled at him apologetically and said, can
I have something sweet? Not that I needed it so much, but I
wanted to change the subject, and he said, yes, we cleared out
her locker in the hospital, you have no idea how much chocolate
had accumulated there. He went out quietly, without locking the
door, and returned with a few boxes of chocolates, and said,
I have to tidy up a bit, the attack will soon be renewed.
Can I help you, I asked, and he said, I don't think that's a
good idea, and I said, why shouldn't I sit there with you as if
I'm just a friend, you're allowed to have female friends aren't
you, and he said, better not, I have a feeling your parents will
come today. I almost jumped out of bed in alarm, why hadn't I
thought of it myself, my mother wouldn't miss an occasion like
this, it was even surprising that she hadn't shown up first thing
in the morning, unless she had decided not to seem too keen,
and the idea that I could have been caught there stunned me

to such an extent that I immediately covered myself with the blanket, and pushed the tray away, and he said, why don't you sleep a bit, you might have a stormy night ahead of you. Why only might? I protested, and he laughed, it all depends on you, and I was fed up with his chauvinist arrogance, and I said, fuck off, I don't need your favours. To my astonishment he turned round savagely, and pulled the blanket off me, and hissed in an aggressive whisper, don't say anything to me that you don't mean, you hear, the last thing you want is for me to fuck off, and for the time being you certainly do need my favours, so don't say things you don't mean if you don't want me to leave you high and dry, and I tried to pull the blanket back, and I mumbled, what's the matter with you, why are you so sensitive all of a sudden, and he let go of the blanket and said, I hate it when people say things they don't mean.

Don't you ever say things you don't mean? I asked him, and he said, try me and see, and he gave me a disappointed look, like a butcher who had received a mediocre joint, and I pulled the blanket over my head and hoped that he would stay and mollify me a little, but I heard him go out and lock the door, and the fear of him came back to me, his sharp, unpredictable mood swings, his suppressed violence, his games of honour which, however childish, were also threatening, and I had the feeling that I wouldn't escape from this room unscathed, if I ever escaped from it at all. I was too tense to sleep and I lay awake, looking at the pile of chocolate boxes, and tried to listen to the voices, I decided that if I heard my parents I would begin to scream, and they would come and rescue me, but it was quiet in there, except for the noise of dishes clattering in the sink, running water and heavy, old man's coughing. I tried once more to call Yonny, hearing the sound of the ringing filtering through the rooms of the little yellow flat, leaving the living room to pass through the kitchen to the little bedroom with the crooked wardrobe, it must be dark there now, with the heavy trees hiding the last rays of the sun, and the faithful radiators warming up slowly and steadily, and perhaps there was a letter waiting for me on the hall table, the saddest letter you could possibly imagine, and there was really no point in trying, because what would I do with it, what would I do at all, what could be done with this life, from which there was no chance of escaping unscathed, like a disease, where you take medication to get rid of one problem, and the medication causes another problem. You take medication for a headache, so the headache goes away but you get an ulcer, you take medication for the ulcer so you get heartburn, you take medication for the heartburn, you get nauseous, you take medication for the nausea, you get a headache, and in the end the last disease comes creeping up and finds the door wide open, like the Golden Gate in distant Istanbul, and all that remains is tying up all the loose ends and finishing the story. You were bored with Yonny, so you went to Aryeh, and with Aryeh it isn't boring, that's true, but you can't breathe next to him, so now go look for someone who isn't boring and who you can breathe next to, and even if you succeed in finding him, it'll turn out that he prefers men, or little girls, and that's only if you succeed in getting out of here in the first place.

I wondered how other people succeeded, not all of them but a large number, it seemed so impossible from the depths of this bed, contrary to the laws of nature, succeeded in staying together and having children, and apropos children I suddenly heard loud crying, and I understood that the neighbour's baby had woken from his afternoon nap, and suddenly I thought, maybe Yonny's not in Istanbul at all, maybe he's right here, on the other side of the wall, with the sheepish baby and its mother, and we're spending our honeymoon in almost the same place, and if the walls were transparent we would be able to see one another, each of us in a second life, and even wave to each other, a friendly wave full of good wishes. What a pity it was impossible, what I would like most of all was to live a number of parallel lives, without one thing being at the expense of the other, surely this was the solution to all our problems, to take medication for a headache without it giving us ulcers, and to take medication for ulcers without it giving us heartburn, and I thrilled to the notion of this great new gospel, this message of redemption, and thought about how I would spread it when I got out of here, and thus instead of passing from incarnation to incarnation after we died it would be possible to live all our lives in the course of this one, and I was so delighted at my solution to life's problems that I fell asleep immediately.

I woke up to the nagging sound of crying buzzing in my ears, and I thought, oof, that damn baby again, but the crying was really close, and I looked for Aryeh next to me and he wasn't there, and only then I realized that it was me, that my face was wet, and my mouth was open and drooling, and my nose was dripping, in short, that all my body was weeping. The room was completely dark, there were no cracks of light shining through the shutters, only a pale, thin ray coming from under the door. I heard the bell ring, someone had apparently forgotten that you weren't supposed to ring the doorbell during the *shiva*, and I heard the enthusiastic cries of people happy to meet, and I filled with envy of all the people who were sitting there, those children of light who, even if they had a bit of trouble and frustration here and there, weren't ruining their lives, and I said to myself, the problem with you is that you don't distinguish between your life and your love life, even though there's actually a wall dividing them. It seems to you that it's all the same, but love life is only a part of life, and not the most important part, it's only a little pocket in the suit of life, and this is something all the people sitting there know. That's why they're sitting there drinking coffee and eating cake and you're lying here in the dark locked up like a prisoner in jail, like a patient in a lunatic asylum, and they've even put you in isolation as if your disease is dangerous, and they only let one person look after you, because he is apparently so sick himself that you can't harm him, but don't be sure that he can't harm you, honey. And from the warm, friendly hullabaloo there suddenly rose my father's voice, and to put an end to any doubts I even heard someone say, Korman and his dreams again, affectionately and not with the contempt of my mother, whose voice I didn't hear at all, and I immediately pricked up my ears and went to sit next to the door, thirstily drinking in the pure, pleasant voice, he had a pure voice, for years I'd been looking for the right word and now I'd found it. Like a river I heard it flow, a river with tiny wooden boats, a toy river, if such a thing exists. For years I'd wondered if I could trust this voice, how was it possible to tell, if someone looked old but sounded young, what could you trust, the appearance or the voice, and if he looked ill but sounded healthy, and if he looked sad but sounded happy, looked full of hate but sounded loving, how was it possible to know? For years I'd asked myself if this sad old man with the happy young voice was happy or sad, young or old, and if I should pity him or envy him, and the upshot of all these doubts was that I never managed to love him, and now, in this darkness, I felt a great love for him, and I wanted him to come and sit next to my bed, like he did when I was sick, worried and embarrassed, and to read me a story, some legend, even one that I already knew by heart, the story of a man, a carpenter's apprentice, who coveted his master's wife. One day his master needed a loan. He said to him: Send your wife to me and I'll lend you the money. He sent him his wife, and she stayed there for three days. The carpenter went to him and said: My wife, whom I sent to you, where is she? He said: I sent her off immediately, and I heard that the youths abused her on the way. The carpenter said: What shall I do? And the apprentice said: If you want my advice, divorce her. The carpenter said: The divorce settlement specified in the marriage contract is large. The apprentice said: I'll lend you the money, and give her her settlement. He divorced her, and the apprentice married her. When the time came to pay the debt and he could not pay it, the apprentice said to him: Come to me and work off your debt. And they sat eating and drinking – and he stood and waited on them. And his tears dripped from his eyes and fell into their cups – and for this hour sentence was passed. And perhaps by virtue of his pure voice the story of the legend would change, and when he came to the words 'sentence was passed', they would be changed to words of consolation and reconciliation.

Besides his voice, I recognized the loud voice of the lady from this morning, with the dog, or more accurately, the bitch, apparently a close friend of the family if she took the trouble

to come twice a day, or maybe she was simply bored now with
the dog recovering from her operation, and I heard her exclaim
enthusiastically, Istanbul! How lovely! At first I thought that
maybe she was taking her pet to convalesce in Istanbul, but
suddenly I grasped that my father was telling her proudly about
his daughter, his only, successful daughter, who had gone on a
trip with her husband to Istanbul, and I felt so ashamed that I
wanted to bang my head against the door, but I was afraid to
make a noise, and I just prayed that he wouldn't say it was a late
honeymoon, and that Aryeh wasn't listening, perhaps he was in
the kitchen, but no, I heard him talking loudly, as if on purpose
for me to hear, about Istanbul. I've been almost round the world,
he said, and if there's one city I'd go back to it's Istanbul, and
my father mentioned Prague, and Aryeh said, no, Prague's too
perfect, so perfect that in the end it's boring, Istanbul is full of
sin, full of contradictions, there's something very attractive and
at the same time repulsive about it, it's a hot, cruel place, I don't
know if it's suitable for a young couple on their honeymoon,
he laughed, but for someone who's passed the halfway mark
in his life, who knows what he wants, it's the place. And I
thought that this was exactly the way I would describe him,
full of sin, full of contradictions, and he was apparently my
Istanbul, whereas Yonny was Prague, and perhaps in a certain
sense I had travelled there, and I cheered up a bit because my
being here seemed less absurd, and also less frightening, after
all he was a friend of my father's, he wouldn't really hurt me,
but I immediately said to myself, honey, without parents, you
can't take your parents everywhere, and I remembered their
first visit to me in basic training camp, how they had swept
through the gates of the army base with the rest of the crowd,
carrying baskets like everybody else, with pots in the baskets
like everybody else, but nevertheless they looked different, lost,
at odds with each other. I had looked forward to seeing them
so much, I sat next to the gate with my new friends, in my new
uniform, and waited eagerly, until I saw them, groping blindly,
pale, timid, fish flapping on the shore, and immediately I wanted
to run away, to hide from them. I didn't have the strength to

bear the gloom in their baskets, the poison in their pots, and mockingly I said to myself, these are the people you thought would save you, these are the people you thought would rescue you from this depressing place, and I began to walk backwards, staring at them hypnotized, afraid to turn my back on them, as if they might shoot me, they advanced and I retreated, until I saw their eyes focus and they began to wave to me, and I walked forwards slowly, defeated, into their dry embrace. We proceeded with the baskets until we found some space, and we sat down on the ground, my mother spread a tablecloth on the new grass, it was the beginning of winter, the cloth looked like a plastic sheet for bed-wetters, and she set out disposable plates and glasses, and then she discovered that she had forgotten to bring paper napkins, and her face blackened with sorrow, and she said, Shlomo, why didn't you remind me, and he said, I did remind you, I went over the whole list with you, and he began to rummage in his pockets and brought out a crumpled list, and showed her, and she said, but before we left the house you didn't remind me, and they began to quarrel.

You can't do anything properly, he grumbled, and she yelled that she had been getting ready for this visit for two weeks, making sure that everything was tiptop, and she had only asked one thing of him, to check the list, and I snatched the list from his hand, which for some reason was written in long lines, and I read it sorrowfully, like a love letter that comes too late, when the heart is already broken or indifferent, and it said, avocado sandwiches, strawberries and cream, apple juice, salty biscuits, chocolate milk, egg salad and tuna salad, cheesecake, paper napkins, disposable plates and cups, disposable cutlery, and I read it again and again as they bickered, and my friends walked past arm in arm with their boyfriends, and I thought that if I had a boyfriend everything would be different, and I said to myself, I'll marry the first one that promises to love me forever, just to escape their clutches, and I didn't notice that they had fallen silent and were looking at me, until my mother said, why are you crying, and I said, you only brought cold food, and I wanted hot food. I only said it because it was the first thing that came into my head, because the family sitting next to us were eating *cholent* from deep bowls, and the smell of the stew soothed me, and my mother said, I can't do anything right, I can't do anything right, and I waited for the visit to be over, and I repeated to myself, let this teach you a lesson, never to be homesick for them, they'll never be able to help you in real life, but when I said goodbye to them at the gate of the base I filled with piercing pity, where would they go now, what was waiting for them at home?

Then I heard my father's voice again, I pressed my ear against the door to be certain, and he said, apparently to Tammy, but it seemed to me that he was speaking to me, that he knew I was there and he was answering my question, I know you think I'm unhappy, he said, that my life is a failure, but let me tell you that I'm a happy man, definitely a happy man. Yes, yes, he added, apparently Tammy was unconvinced, I'm completely at peace with myself, and when I heard this for a moment I rejoiced in the good news that had reached me through the back door, but the next moment I was boiling with rage at him, and I felt cheated, as if I had wasted my whole life feeling sorry for someone who was just pretending to be miserable, or even worse, that he wasn't even pretending but I in my stupidity had misunderstood him, and then I heard Tammy answering him gently, as if she was talking to a retard, yes, Korman, we know, everyone knows how happy you are, whenever I think of happiness I see you before my eyes.

I knew that she was laughing at him, but I didn't know what it meant, was it really so ridiculous, his declaration, was he really a symbol of unhappiness, even more so than I suspected? There was an oppressive silence, I could feel the uneasiness in the living room, until a vulpine laugh broke the silence, and Aryeh said something about Istanbul, about a cemetery, and Tammy asked, a café next to a cemetery? And Aryeh said, yes, on top of the hill overlooking the Golden Horn, that's where they would meet, in the most beautiful place in Istanbul. I remember that story, my father said enthusiastically, the French writer and the Turkish woman, she was a married woman, and when they were caught he was deported to France and she was executed, and Tammy asked fearfully, how did they execute her? And my father said, presumably they stoned her to death, like we did to adulteresses, and Tammy shrieked, oh my God, I don't believe it, and Aryeh said, there are pictures of them there, in the café, she was a beautiful woman.

I told Yonny they had to go there, my father said, it's the most beautiful place in Istanbul, and Aryeh asked, who's Yonny, and I wrung the cold handle of the door, Daddy, Daddy, do you know the story of the man who had an only son and he arranged a marriage for him and he died under the wedding canopy? That's how God felt after the destruction of the Temple, and that's not the only story I want to tell you, to project on you, rather, in exchange for the story you just projected on me. And then a deputation from the bride's side apparently arrived, because the house filled with murmurs in French, and I returned to the dark bed and I kept mumbling Daddy, don't go, stay here with me, watch over me, but quite soon I heard him saying goodbye, and Tammy, with her jarring voice, called after him, wish Rachel a full recovery, and I was surprised, only yesterday she was as healthy as an ox, what had happened to her, and I felt as abandoned as a little girl left in the kindergarten with a new teacher she didn't really know yet, and again I wondered why she missed the condolence call, maybe she really is sick, or else she has some other reason, but it must be a good one, because she never misses occasions like this. I decided to phone her and hang up, just to hear her voice, to make sure she was still capable of speaking, and I picked up the receiver, and to my surprise I heard voices coming from it, a soft murmuring as from an ancient shell which had absorbed the sound of the sea, and I pressed it wonderingly to my ear, until I realized that I was listening to a conversation, a woman's soft voice, deep and magical, gently melodious, I couldn't tell if she was speaking or singing and I couldn't understand a word, at first I didn't even try to understand, it was such a pleasure to listen to it, like music, and only when I heard his voice rising from the earphone, warm and soft and sweet, but nevertheless his voice, only then I tried to decipher their rapid French, mainly to check if the only words I knew, *je t'aime, voulez vous couchez avec moi*, passed between them, but I can't say I succeeded, they spoke so fast, and all their words sounded the same. I listened angrily, cursing the day I decided to learn Arabic in high school instead of French, what did I think, that he would have an Arabic mistress, what else could a mistress be but French, it was so obvious, and I realized that a little lovers' tiff was developing between them, nothing serious, the kind of argument after which it was a pleasure to make up. She spoke in a choked voice, breathing fast, the words tumbling out of her mouth, and he was slower, measured, trying to calm her, what was he promising her there, and in the end she did calm down, like a spoilt little girl sniffling and hugging her doll when the storm subsided, and she said in an ingratiating voice, *alors*, but not *mon amour*, just *alors*. He also said *alors*, and I almost said *alors* too, to fit in, and she said, *je t'embrace*, which is to do with kissing, I think, and she hung up, and I remained with the receiver in my hand, surprised by her haste, this girl did everything so quickly, and he was apparently surprised too, because I heard him breathing hard into the receiver, and so we remained, each of us communing with our own surprise, as if the conversation had taken place between us, and I felt a sudden comradeship with him, her disappearance from our lives had been so abrupt, I could still hear her rabbity breathing, quick, provocative, childish, and I heard him sigh and cough, and suddenly I was afraid that he was holding the receiver because of me, to hear if I was really there as he suspected, and I wanted to hang up but I couldn't, I had to be coordinated with him, then after a wave of coughing I heard him put the receiver down and I immediately followed suit.

I covered my head with the blanket and lay without moving, almost without breathing, in case he came to check up on me, and I tried to invent signs, if he came immediately that meant his conscience was very black, if he delayed it was a sign that his conscience was middling, and so on and so forth, but he didn't come at all and that was apparently a sign that he simply didn't care about me, and I completely forgot why I had picked up the receiver in the first place and all I could think about was how nothing had changed, absolutely nothing, ever since the day I had seen him in the shop with the cigarette lighter, it was just a stupid illusion on my part that he really wanted me, whereas I was still playing the role of a stop-gap, a substitute mistress who, like her sister the substitute teacher, was the lowest of her kind. But instead of feeling sorry I felt relief, that I didn't have to keep the flame of his love burning any more, that I didn't have to keep anything because I didn't have anything, I didn't have to do the splits at night in order not to disappoint him, I didn't have to fuck standing on my hands or perform similar acrobatic stunts, and I realized how much the idea that he wanted me at last had really oppressed me, how it had filled me with joy and also with dread, dread which had covered the joy, which had strangled it, as if I had to guard a sack full of gold, and I was surrounded by robbers, and there was no way I could succeed, so while it was true that if I succeeded it would be mine, it was so hard to succeed that it was better to give up in advance, simply to leave it where it was and run away, maybe put a coin or two in my pocket as a sweet souvenir, and that was in fact what I was doing here now, stealing a little coin, which would remain in my pocket as a memento when I returned home, if I had a home to return to. Again I felt fear and oppression, and again I imagined the dark, square rooms, perhaps they had gone to Turkey too, and there they would float on the Tigris and Euphrates all the way to Babylon, with all the used furniture and the tableware we had received as wedding gifts, and the white rubbish bin, and the Kings of Babylon would loot them and take the dishes for their banquets, right before our eyes, just as they had murdered the High Priest before the eyes of his daughter, and it was quite clear to me that the house was no longer standing, how could it go on standing when we had been scattered to the winds, and I decided to phone again, but I had forgotten the number, it had gone clean out of my mind, as if I had never known it, and that was how he found me when he came into the room, lying in bed with the phone in my hand, as if I had just finished listening to him talking to his lover.

All of a sudden, without warning me in advance, he switched on the bright light, and I blinked at him foolishly like a mole, and whispered, switch it off, they'll find out there's someone here, but he only grinned, I'm here aren't I? I'm not supposed to sit in the dark, even if I'm in mourning, and then he looked at the phone and asked with ostentatious politeness, am I disturbing you in the middle of a conversation? And I said, no, the conversation hasn't begun, and he asked, is it urgent, and I said, no, no, and with a masterful movement he took the receiver from my hand and replaced it and lay down next to me, spreading out his entire body, which would not be mine, his smooth dark body, with its ripening buds of old age, with its virile, aggressive maturity, which I would never understand no matter how much I rubbed against it, that exact and painful combination of dominance and delicacy, callousness and depth, crudeness and sensitivity, authority and licentiousness, as if a master chef had prepared him from a unique recipe, rare measures impossible to repeat, especially since the chef or the recipe had already been destroyed, and he turned his face to me and looked at me sorrowfully, an almost paternal sorrow, and said, Istanbul, eh?

I shrugged my shoulders, embarrassed and proud, as if I had received a medal for bravery or sacrifice, and I knew I deserved it but wasn't sure it was worth it, and a bit ashamed too, because he had found out what I had sacrificed for the sake of lying like this next to his magnificent body, which would not be mine, and I didn't even know if he was mocking me or sympathizing with me, and he said, a great city, Istanbul, a magnificent city, intoxicating to all the senses, and he lit a cigarette with a sigh, actually I've been thinking a lot about Istanbul lately, because that's where Josephine got sick, we wanted to go there together for years and it never worked out, and when we finally made it we had to come back in the middle, she lost consciousness, and all of a sudden her health deteriorated, and you know what the level of the medicine there is like, it wasn't worth the risk, so we returned immediately, and she felt so guilty for spoiling the trip for me. And were you angry with her, I asked, and he said, I don't like admitting it, but yes, I was a little, I thought why couldn't she have waited a week, and she kept on saying, when I get better we'll go to Istanbul, and in the end she said, when I die you must go to Istanbul, and I hugged him and said, so let's go there together, take me with you and I'll console you there, and he laughed and said, maybe, maybe, and I knew that with him I wouldn't be afraid at all, even in the middle of the bazaar I wouldn't be afraid, because my fear of him completely wiped out my fear of the world, and I pressed up against him, and he stroked me absent-mindedly, thinking of something else, and said, I'm tired, so many faces. Then why don't you stay here with me, I said, don't go out again, and he said, I can't leave them there alone, and he looked at his watch, it's already almost nine, I think we'll shut up shop soon, and his eyes closed, and his lips parted slackly, his hand on the bottom of my stomach, in the place where babies grow.

I held his hand and thought about my mother's pregnancy, which had seemed to me so long then, absolutely endless, and it really was three times longer than the life of the baby who had grown in there, but of course I didn't know that then, when I looked at the tremendous, aggressive stomach, trying to imagine that it was me inside there, that I had a chance to peep at her before I was born, and it was a little embarrassing, to see myself inside her, and I thought soon I'll be born all over again, and my first life will be over, and something different will begin, and I would say to my mother, if it's a girl call her Ya'ara. I was so used to being an only child that I really believed that children weren't added on, but only changed places, like in a royal dynasty, after all, people didn't say, here comes another king and now we have two or three kings, they said, the king is dead, long live the new king, and in fact I was quite surprised that I went on living after the baby was born, and they gave him a name of his own, and he wasn't me, because he was a boy, and my mother's stomach disappeared and he grew big and fat, as if there was room for both of us in the world, until it turned out that there wasn't. I knew that if they had to choose between us they would choose him, and I wasn't even surprised, I even justified the choice, after all, I couldn't save them any more, I was an option which had been totally exhausted, but the baby was brand new, he threw the gates wide open, all their hopes could be loaded on his plump, fragrant shoulders, and I think that on the whole I shared in their sorrow at the lack of consideration shown by fate, in the hidden rage which developed against me, in the shrinking and dwindling of their love.

His hand drowsed on the bottom of my stomach, dark and beautiful, and if there was a baby there I would have said to him, feel the movement, and held it tight, but in the circumstances what did I actually have to say to him, falling asleep next to me as if I was the wife he had been married to for years, the familiar wife of his bosom by whose side he could relax after passionate telephone calls, and I thought to myself how few roles there were to play on this stage, how few possibilities. Once Josephine had lain here, today it was me, tomorrow the rabbit, yesterday Yonny had lain by my side, today it was Aryeh, tomorrow it would be somebody else, so much effort in order to obtain more or less the same thing, and I filled with a wonder that was beyond sorrow, a sour, indifferent wonder at all the metamorphoses that still awaited me, I felt them in my stomach like the kicking of a baby, so many metamorphoses in order to find myself at the end in more or less the same place as before.

10

I heard a knock, so soft that it seemed to be coming from inside me, and a faint voice whispering, Ya'ari, and I almost answered, I almost said I'm here, and ruined everything, and then the voice said, Ari, and again there was a knock and he leaped up as if the bed was burning, without saying a word to me, and next to the door he switched off the light and left the room, quietly locking the door behind him, ignoring me completely, and I thought that I had never been so non-existent in my life. I wasn't angry with him, in the light of the circumstances, but nevertheless I had to admit that he behaved as if it came quite naturally, and actually so did I, I wasn't terribly surprised at the fact that I was locked up here for hours on end, trying to pick up information through the walls, without anybody knowing where I was, and the only one who did know keeping me hidden as if I was a backward child, or a demented wife, and I thought, *alors*, who calls him Ari, his mother-in-law with her blue curls or his sister-in-law, or perhaps his lover who had come to mollify him after their lovers' tiff, and she would probably want to sleep over, and how would he explain to her that the bedroom was occupied, and that he couldn't be hers tonight, but the fact that the bedroom was occupied didn't necessarily have to spoil their plans, there were other rooms in the house, and after everybody went home he could fuck her right behind the bedroom wall, with me locked up inside it, and perhaps even lock her up there, and navigate between us, he was the one with the keys, and suddenly I realized the full horror of my new status as a non-existent woman who couldn't change her situation or even know it, and who clung to all kinds of clues, and had no idea if her fears were groundless or rather her hopes were groundless, and who was dependent on a man who chopped and changed, one minute she was a desirable woman and the next she was a nuisance, and I said to myself, if you're dependent on him you won't go far, or the opposite, you'll go too far, so far that you'll never be able to return to your former life.

I tried to think about it, my former life, of Yonny and all of them, as if they were stones tied to my feet so that I wouldn't disappear, be utterly effaced, and I thought of a stone in the shape of Yonny, which was actually a statue of Yonny, heavy and hard, and I dressed it in Yonny's checked shirts and sent it to walk round the bazaars of Istanbul as if it was a real person, until I completely forgot that it was a statue, and I was fascinated to see him with his own face, completely detached from me, walking round there with all he had, his babyish snub nose, and his flabby testicles, what was he thinking about, this person, apart from his soft bed in the hotel, apart from the café overlooking the cemetery, what was going through his head, what was he living for, what did he have in his life, what did anyone have in their lives, it seemed more and more of a mystery to me. Take my mother, for example, she had her thirst for disasters, and that was what kept her going, to see what would happen tomorrow, and how terrible it would be, and I had this obsession with winning Aryeh, to see if I could make him love me, but what kept me going before I met Aryeh, suddenly I had no idea, and those days seemed to me empty and desolate, like blank pages, each the same as the other, even more frightening than my days now, and perhaps it wasn't really winning him but understanding him, and through him myself, and all of us, not that I knew who all of us were, but I had begun to think in the plural, as if there was a multitude standing behind me, and I wasn't alone on a pointless mission, but the authorized representative of a large and growing group which was risking its life in the suspect's bed in order to obtain information capable of shedding light, on what exactly wasn't quite clear, but if we called it the secret of life we wouldn't be far wrong.

He had the secret of life, and I was supposed to get it out of him, that was the mission imposed on me, and I would explain this to Yonny when he returned with his snub nose and his flabby testicles, strange how they accompanied him everywhere, this was what I would explain to him, and he would have to forgive me and take me back, and it seemed to me that I had already felt something similar once before, an urgent and insistent need to solve something, and I remembered the guard who lived with his dog in one of the huts next to our house in the village. I didn't understand exactly what he was guarding, and it preoccupied me more and more, I never saw him patrolling round the neighbourhood or doing the kind of things that guards were supposed to do, most of the time he would hang around outside his hut, with a piece of raw meat for the dog in one hand, and in the other a knife which he sharpened in a daily ritual, in order to cut the meat with it. He would put a large stone on the log of wood standing outside the door to his hut, and place his big foot on the log next to the stone, and begin to sharpen, making sawing noises, and then he would pull out the meat, as if cutting it out of his thick foot, and slice it up, while the dog danced round him excitedly, catching the scraps of meat thrown at him one after the other, in an almost sadistic abundance, before he had finished one scrap the next arrived, and the next, and instead of concentrating on eating he had to keep on catching the new scraps, in growing desperation. I would stand there and watch, and once I couldn't stop myself from asking, why don't you give it to him at his own pace, and he looked at me with an unpleasant expression, and said, it's my dog, he spoke rudely, but he went on looking at me curiously, and he slowed down the pace a little. His face was young, but his breathing was heavy and wheezing, and between the too short shirt and the dropped trousers there was a thick strip of flesh, pink and throbbing, as if it had a heart of its own, which looked exactly like the strips of meat he was throwing to the dog.

He wasn't the first guard who lived in that hut, people even called it the guards' hut, and most of them were sickly old men who wandered round the village at night, but he was the first to make me ask the question, and from the minute it arose it never stopped bothering me, what exactly was he guarding? He was almost always to be found sharpening his knife on the log of wood, his trousers dropped and the division between his buttocks exposed, his eyes blue and impudent in his round face, unshaven, the stubble of a ginger beard covering his cheeks, and I got into the habit of walking past every morning on my way to school to look at him, and in the afternoon on my way back, and at night I would go out for a walk, circling the little neighbourhood and advancing cautiously to the last hut, right next to the orange grove, where the road ended, and I would find him there in the light of a lamp, sharpening the knife, and I would shiver with a frisson of sweet fear, that in a minute he was going to hold it to my throat, but it didn't seem to occur to him at all, he was so absorbed in what he was doing. Gradually I began to believe that he was hiding something, what I didn't know, except that it was vital, he was hiding something vital, and if I discovered it I would bring salvation to us all, to me and my mother and my father, and perhaps even to broader circles, and I would circle round him, the dog already knew me and didn't bark at me, but he never said anything and only sent me an occasional blue-eyed look, bold and mocking.

Once I went past and he wasn't there, the door of his hut was open, and I couldn't control myself and I went inside, stunned by the absolute emptiness, there wasn't even a chair, a cupboard or a table, only a huge, wine-coloured waterbed covering the floor, quivering like a huge fish, and when I turned to leave I saw him standing behind me, his breath heavy and stinking, and he asked, what are you looking for here, and I noticed that he had a foreign accent, and I said, you, and he asked, why, what do you want of me, and I said, I want to know what you're guarding, and he smiled, his face grew even rounder, I'm not guarding anything, I live here. But you're living in the guards' hut, I persisted, and he said, so what, I'm not interested in what was here before me, if a man lives in a kennel does that make him a dog? If he lives in a pen does that make him a goat? And I asked, why haven't you got any furniture, and he said, sniggering at me with yellow teeth, I have what I need, I do everything in bed. But what do you do, I asked, and he said, get use of life, and I didn't know if

he got it wrong because Hebrew wasn't his language, or if that
was what he meant, if it was a message, and I saw him wiping
the knife on his trousers, passing it right across his groin, and a
pink stain spread there, and it was clear to me that he was hiding
something, something disgusting, and the more disgusting it was
the more redeeming it was, and I couldn't drag myself away,
and from the corner of my eye I saw a thin, fair figure rapidly
approaching, and my father yelled, Ya'ara, come home at once,
and he pushed me because I was walking so slowly. When we
got home I saw that his face was red with rage, and there was a
reek of insecticide in the rooms, my mother was spraying them
against the cockroaches, she was moving in a crouch along the
walls and spraying, and he yelled, if I ever see you hanging round
that guard again I'll lock you up, and I said, he isn't a guard, the
fact that he lives in the guards' hut doesn't make him a guard,
just like if someone lives in a pen it doesn't make him a goat,
and he yelled at my mother, did you hear her, she's acting like
Tirza, just like Tirza, and my mother went on spraying silently
until it was impossible to breathe in the house, and he said, if
you want to kill us do it at once and not little by little, I didn't
know if he was talking to me or to her, and I shut myself up
in my room, hugging the soft woolly lamb, and I thought, if he
isn't a guard why does it seem to me that he's guarding me all
the time.

When he went away a few days later, in the wake of my
father's complaint, I felt far less protected, I was too frightened
to sleep at night, and now, when I remembered him, I thought
that I would tell Aryeh about him when he came tonight and
lay down next to me, I would tell him even if there was no
moral to my story. This was apparently the root of love, to
want to tell someone about every trifle that happened to you,
in the hope that on the tortuous path from your mouth to his
ear, the story would achieve its meaning, its justification, as if
it had all happened simply so that I could tell it to Aryeh when
he came to me at night, and not only it but every little thing that
had ever happened, that was happening, that would happen in
the future, this was their whole point, to tell them to Aryeh,

even if Aryeh wasn't in the least interested. In the meantime I heard sounds of parting, people saying good night in a number of languages, and the door closed and was firmly locked, and I sat up and waited for him to come and free me, but he didn't seem to be in a hurry, and I heard his voice, all by itself, arguing heatedly with himself, until I realized that he was talking on the telephone, and I fetched the telephone and put it down next to me, I didn't dare pick up the receiver but simply put it under my head, as if it were a pillow, perhaps something would get through to me, and I heard his voice raised in anger, and then the slam of the receiver and the sound of a curse, and dishes clattering against each other, and only then, I didn't even know how long I waited, because my watch still said nine, only then the door opened, the light went on, and life came in.

I tried to smile at him, but it came out crooked, like the twisted smile of a woman trying without much success to maintain her self-respect when her husband comes home late, and he said hello, and I saw that he was still preoccupied by his telephone call, and I was touched to see that he was trying, but the curse was still in his eyes, and when he looked at me it was aimed at me, and I felt his gloom, his bad mood, in all my body I felt it, as if I was to blame for the mishap behind the curse, and I didn't know what to do, how to dispel his anger. I tried to be quiet and self-effacing, but in my ears I heard the whistle of anxiety, like the whistle of the locomotive when the train comes closer and it turns out that the barrier isn't working and the accident is inevitable, and the only question is how great the disaster will be.

Come out for a bit, he said, you must be feeling claustrophobic by now, and I cautiously crossed the threshold, as if I was crossing a dangerous border, and advanced timidly, glancing from side to side, perhaps some visitor had been forgotten in one of the rooms, and in the living room I sat down immediately on the sofa, staking out my claim, freezing with cold in my thin nightgown, and he said, hungry, and I said yes, with exaggerated gratitude, and he took a few things out of the fridge and heated them up and called me to the kitchen. I sat down obediently at the round table opposite a large plate containing a schnitzel and potatoes and salad, a standard meal of the kind my mother used to give me after school, and I tried to eat politely, without making a noise when I chewed, because all of a sudden I had become unwanted, I felt it in his every movement, and when you're not wanted you shouldn't be heard breathing, because you haven't really got the right to exist.

He cleared the dishes out of the living room and emptied the ashtrays, making a lot of angry, ostentatious noise, and I thought how strange it was that nothing depended on me, how hard it was to get used to, after all there's usually some kind of connection between what you do and how you're treated, but in this house the rules were different, I became wanted or unwanted because of things that didn't depend on me, I was a kind of pale moon here, which had no light of its own and was at the mercy of the sun. Who knows what lovers' quarrel had brought me here, and what reconciliation would send me away, or the opposite, the way the rules worked wasn't clear to me at all, and I must have been so absorbed in my sorrow that I started to cry into my plate, and he stood opposite me surprised, what's wrong, and I said, nothing, and then I wailed, you don't want me here, and he said, why do you say that, without hurrying to deny it, and I wailed, because that's how I feel, and he said, sometimes I forget that you're here, and then when I remember I'm glad. He said it with difficulty, as if squeezing the last drop of juice out of himself, and I understood that this was the maximum I could expect from him at the moment, and I felt a little better, because at least I believed him, and then he added, I'm not holding you here by force, you know, you can leave whenever you wish, and I replied, great, but where to, I've already missed Istanbul because of you, and I started to hate him for returning my freedom to me so generously, because what was I going to do with it now? He took out two cans of beer, and two big glasses, and poured the beer into them, and sat down beside me, his mood appeared to improve, and I watched his supple movements, as if his joints had been treated with olive oil, and I tried to strengthen myself, you mustn't give up now, you mustn't despair, the end is near, even though it wasn't clear what this end was, and I sipped the beer and began to cheer up, and I thought of the suitcase with all the provocative clothes, and the long nights, and the shortness of life, every night seemed to me more or less as long as half my life, and worth as much. I put my hand on his and asked, so how are you doing, and he was a little taken aback and he said, all right, and immediately caught himself and added, in the circumstances, and I said, of course, and I asked, so who's been coming, from the other side of the wall it sounds like a carnival, and he smiled, yes, people are happy to get together, you know what it's like, and my fingers looked so white on his hand, they almost gleamed. Look, I said, and he looked and said, Josephine was white too, we were like day and night, and he stood up and began looking for something in the drawers, and came back with an old shoe box secured with rubber bands, and started rummaging in it, laughing to himself in enjoyment, and then he pulled out a photograph and showed it to me, displaying the proof of his words, and there they were, entwined with each other like creepers, or more precisely, he was the tree trunk and she was the creeper twining round him, and they were both naked, even though they almost succeeded in hiding each other's nakedness, and the difference in the colour of their skin was truly startling, almost like the squares on a chess or domino board, and they smiled at the camera, proud in their nakedness, young and beautiful, his chest hiding her breasts, their genitals pressed together and covering each other.

I was so excited that I wanted to go on looking at it for hours, there was so much material for me there, an abundant windfall enabling me to examine all his body, all his youth, all her body, all their love. I didn't know where to begin, with the dark hair covering his big head, with the open smile, the white teeth, the happy laughter in his eyes. He looked young, younger than I was now, handsome but far less attractive, a bit foolish with his happy smile, and I thought that if I had met him then I wouldn't have fallen in love with him, but she, she looked so desirable that it alarmed me, with flowing golden hair and shining eyes, and a small straight nose, and blooming lips, and her nakedness too, emerging discreetly from his body, looked exquisite, painful, how brief her flowering was. I sensed him examining the picture behind me, and I asked quietly, was she really so beautiful, hoping to hear him say no, that the picture was misleading, because her beauty burdened me, and he said, even more beautiful, she was gorgeous, and he tried to take the picture away from me, but I hung onto it, and neither of us let go, until we almost tore it in half, until I said, wait, let me look a little longer, and I examined their intertwined legs, their erect but tender stance, and I asked, how could you be unfaithful to her, she looks so lovely, and before the sentence was out of my mouth I realized I'd made a mistake.

Abruptly he snatched the picture from me and returned it to the box and began tying the box up with all the rubber bands and pieces of string. His movements were violent, and then he roughly removed my plate from the table and the glass of beer which I hadn't finished drinking, and said in a hoarse voice, I wasn't unfaithful to her, I was never unfaithful to her, you hear, and I was alarmed but I couldn't shut up, and I said, you can't fool me, you were unfaithful to her with me, or have you forgotten? And he went red and waved the beer mug at me threateningly, and yelled, what are you talking about, what do you know about anything, I was never unfaithful to her, I was faithful to her to the last minute, and she knew it! How dare you accuse me, who the hell are you to sling mud at me? And he banged the glass mug down on the marble counter next to the sink, and it smashed into tiny pieces, how could such a big mug break into such small pieces, a huge beer-cellar tankard, proof against the wildest drinkers, so easily destroyed. I saw him looking in surprise at his hands, turning them over like the pages of a book, behind my back I saw it, because I wasn't there any more, like a panic-stricken refugee I fled back to the bedroom, and there I shut the door, trembling with fear, with despair, with disappointment, and I began rummaging in the suitcase, and I was so tense that I couldn't find anything, I hardly knew what I was looking for, presumably something to wear, but all I could find was underwear, and how could I go out into the street in that, and I saw black, and I began to swear, what did you think, that you would never get out of bed again, only garters and boots, that's all you could think of, and then I remembered that I was wearing something when I arrived here yesterday, incredible that it was only yesterday, it seemed like a month at least, I didn't arrive here in garters and boots did I, so where the hell were my clothes, and I began rummaging between the blankets, and under the bed, trying to remember where I had taken off my clothes. Look in your head, my mother used to always say, first of all look in your head, but my head was at least as paralysed as my hands, paralysed and depressed and afraid, in a minute he would burst into the room and kill me, and I tried to remember what people did in the movies, it seemed to me that I had seen someone barring a door with a chair in some movie, so I took a chair and dragged it to the door and there I discovered my clothes lying quietly folded on the seat, and when I was dressed I quickly closed the suitcase and without lingering next to the kitchen I opened the front door and went outside.

It was a fine spring night, as if in the one day I was locked up the seasons had changed, and I started to sweat in my warm clothes, and I felt heavy and lost, and I quite soon stopped running and started walking slowly, almost standing still, because I realized that there was nobody chasing me, and I wasn't actually in a hurry, there wasn't actually anybody waiting for me anywhere, and I put the suitcase down on the pavement and sat on it, like a superfluous tourist in this new night world, in which frightening, unexpected things happened. I felt that I was sinking and I kept repeating to myself, hang in there, don't sink, go home, repair your life, so the glass smashed, so what, you have something to hold onto, go home, and tomorrow go to the university and sit in the library among the books and let that man go insane without you.

I tried to imagine myself in a room full of books, relieved and happy, dancing among them like a butterfly among flowers, drinking once from this one and once from that, and then to my horror I suddenly remembered the rare book from the Head of the Department's private collection, the legends about the destruction of the Temple, and I opened the suitcase and conducted a feverish search and it wasn't there, because of course I hadn't put it in, I had left it lying abandoned on the big bed like a wounded soldier on the battlefield, and who knows what would become of it there, perhaps it would be the next victim of his wrath, perhaps he would tear it to pieces like he had smashed the beer mug to smithereens, and all its heroes who had known so much suffering, like the High Priest and his daughter, and the aristocratic daughters of Zion and the carpenter robbed of his wife, all of them would be destroyed again in a new catastrophe, and I knew that I had to rescue them from his claws, and even if it was an excuse it wasn't just an excuse, and I decided that I would walk in without saying anything and go straight to the bedroom, take the book and leave, without even looking at him, but when I stood in the dark stairwell I felt my eyes hurting with the desire to see him, and when he opened the door my body hurt with love for him, love and pity and sorrow and longing, but I didn't say anything and I hurried to the bedroom and extricated the book from the blankets and hugged it, cradling it in my arms. He followed me, slow and sombre, and stood in the bedroom door, and the air was sharp, and when I tried to pass he put out his hand, so slowly that I could see the movement advancing towards me, and stroked my face, and I saw that his hand was bandaged, and I said, I love you, I know it's not right, but I love you, and he began to undress me gently and said, it's all right, it's all right, and this time he didn't even ask me why, and I said, I didn't mean to hurt you, and he said, it's all right, I know, and in a second I felt him enveloping me, inside and out, warm and full, and I felt joy, the word is joy, as if on meeting someone I thought I would never see again, someone I thought was dead, it was the joy of being able to repair the past, of curing a person mortally ill, of bringing separated parents together, it was so joyful and so impossible, and I knew it wasn't real but at the same time I couldn't resist this sweetness, and all the time I said to myself, the world is dead and I'm full of joy, the world is dead and I'm full of joy, and sometimes the words turned over in my mouth and I said, I'm dead and the world is full of joy, I'm dead and the world is full of joy, and it seemed to me that it was actually the same thing, and I turned over in his arms and all the time I thought, what luck, I could have gone through my whole life without feeling this, without getting use of this, this is my true honeymoon, and I'll never have another one, and even if it only lasts a few hours it will be worth it to me. And then I heard him breathe a sigh of pleasure which turned immediately to a sob, and I held him tight and whispered, don't cry, I love you, and he wailed like a little boy, I wasn't unfaithful to her, I was never unfaithful to her, she knew it, she told me herself, before she died she told me. What did she tell you, I asked, and he whispered, that she knew I was faithful to her, that she didn't doubt it, and I said, yes, I know, and I felt his body growing cold, shrinking, even his shoulders, his waist, his knees, like a risen cake coming out of the oven and beginning to sink, and he turned onto his other side and his sobs turned into snores, and I, who had been waiting all day for this night, lay next to him disappointed, and I counted the loud snores, and I stroked his back, hoping that it was only a short nap, from which he would wake to love me till morning, because I wasn't in the least tired, I had spent most of the day sleeping, but it didn't look as if he was going to wake up soon, so I got out of bed and went to the living room. I found my faithful suitcase next to the door and I took out my nightgown and put it on and sat down in the kitchen, opposite the old shoe box which had remained on the table, wrapped up in rubber bands, and almost indifferently I began rummaging through it, an indifference which turned into growing excitement, until it seemed to me that all the emotions I had looked forward to experiencing tonight were welling out of this old box, in an abundance which almost overwhelmed me.

I felt like the guard's dog, being thrown piece after piece of the meat of his dreams, until he became frantic and his dream turned to a nightmare, as the limbs leaped at me from the pictures, living limbs, naked or draped more seductively than nakedness in all kinds of sophisticated accessories which made the articles in my suitcase look like the work clothes of a pioneer woman from the beginning of the century. There were so many eyes there, in so many colours and shapes, green and blue and black, round and slanting, and so many breasts, and nipples, and vaginas, and bums, and hair, a human butcher shop crammed full to overflowing, and how painful it was not to belong to this butcher shop, and how painful not to belong to him, because he had never photographed me, and it seemed to me that I was the only one in the world not to be photographed, not to be worth a photograph. I tried to find a familiar face but it all seemed strange and distant, as if the photographs had been taken in another country or another time, and again I saw the picture of him and her, almost the most innocent picture in the box, and next to it more pictures of them taken in the same period, if not on the same day, in one of them she was sitting on his lap, both of them completely naked, his dark hands covering her white breasts, and in another she was lying with her legs open, her vagina like a delicate pink bud, and her face radiant with excitement, and before that there were a few more presentable pictures of them, in a few Parisian cafés, perhaps at the beginning of their acquaintance, gradually I realized that the pictures were arranged more or less chronologically, and in this order too I tried to arrange them on the kitchen table, blurred childhood snapshots, groups of skinny children next to dark women with headkerchiefs and bearded men in black suits, and gradually more light entered, brighter clothes, opening smiles, and one picture which I pounced on at once, of two young boys with their arms around each other, and I was almost certain that they were Aryeh and my father, that this was exactly the picture my father had been searching for so desperately, pulling out drawers and dropping them on his feet. I identified Aryeh easily, tall and black-haired, with a broad smile exposing white teeth, a smile I didn't like, too confident, too arrogant, a little stupid in its arrogance, and next to him a short fair boy, with a pale, almost spiritual, not to say tortured face, and this, without a doubt, was my father, at the gates of his life, with a hesitant, suspicious smile, so different from that of his friend, and nevertheless there was expectation in his face, the expectation of happiness, the readiness for happiness, and the more I looked at him the more

difficult it was to part from him, and I wondered which of them
I would have chosen if I was alive then, if I was my mother,
the confident smile or the timid one, how difficult it was to
chose a mate, even a smile, for there are moments when the
confident one is preferable and moments when the timid one
is, how was it possible to fix on one smile for the rest of
your life. It was so hard for me to part from the photograph
that I pushed it quickly into my suitcase, and then I turned to
the pursuit of my research, and I arranged them in order,
gradually I saw Josephine retiring from the picture, occasionally
she still appeared, fully dressed, even a little aunt-like, at all kinds
of functions, but it was clear that an army of bold-limbed young
women had pushed her aside, and the light in her eyes died
down, I could actually see it happen, the moment when the
light went out, and I looked with hatred at the new women,
who presumably were no longer young today themselves, and
perhaps not healthy either, and perhaps their limbs too were
already buried under the ground. There was one of them who
looked like a gypsy, swarthy and enchanting, wearing one black
scarf on her breasts and another round her waist, very loosely
tied scarves, and indeed in the next picture they were already
undone and she was completely naked, covered only in long
black curls, lying on a red carpet, and he was crouching over her,
it was definitely him, I recognized his narrow shapely buttocks,
and it wasn't clear if they were before or after, and immediately
I saw them in the middle of doing it, her riding him and him
inside her, as the concentrated pleasure on her face showed,
and the fourth photograph in the series shed a little light on
its predecessors, on the identity of the photographer at least,
for next to the bed I saw Josephine, small and pale, in a light
petticoat, her beauty already faded, and the gypsy sending a
broad hand right between her thighs, and I couldn't see how
this hand was received, willingly or unwillingly, I could only
guess. In the next picture she was already with someone else,
tall and slender, with cropped hair and small breasts, and from
picture to picture I could see him aging, his black hair turning
grey, his smooth skin wrinkling, his teeth yellowing, his eyes

growing duller, narrower, and above all the smile, his healthy
smile, growing reserved, ambivalent. With the pictures arranged
in front of me on the table I could cast a rapid glance over them
and view them like a short, comprehensive two- or three-minute
animated movie on the love life of a certain Aryeh Even, a very
crowded life without a doubt, who knows how he had managed
to do anything else, and who knows how he had any strength
left, and in fact it seemed that he hadn't, something I myself
could testify to, as I tried to knock on the last coach of this
crowded train. What was the wonder that it was so hard to
enthuse him, apparently he had already exhausted his entire
stock of enthusiasm a long time ago, and apart from committing
suicide in the middle of a fuck he had tried everything, and maybe
he had tried that too, who knows, and I should probably pack
up my hunger and get out of here, because he wasn't going
to satisfy it, hunger and repletion couldn't go out to dinner
together, and suddenly I felt disgusted by the photographs, I
couldn't bear to look at them any longer, and I began stuffing
them back into the shoe box, from the end to the beginning,
burying his old age first and only then his youth, and when I
was almost ready to close the lid I saw another picture which
I hadn't noticed before, of an attractive young woman, fully
clothed for a change, sitting opposite an almost empty plate
with knife and fork in her hands, her hair in a braid, her
face delicate, a narrow wedding ring on her finger, smiling a
reserved smile at her plate. Rivetted, I stared at the picture, even
though I knew it very well, I had seen it dozens of times, but I
had never been so interested in her as I was now, in my young,
pretty mother, with a serious expression on her face, as if an
important thought had just crossed her mind, important and
interesting but not fateful, perhaps even something connected
to the empty plate, and I quickly threw it too into my suitcase,
like a leaf it dropped into the black clothes, even though I had a
copy of it at home in my album, it was the picture of her I liked
best, and I didn't want to leave it there, in his revolting box,
among all his whores, what did she have in common with them,
how would I ever know, the past was so obscure, cut off by

a heavy screen, perhaps even she herself didn't know, so how could I know? I thought of my daughter, the daughter I would once have, what would she know about me, and it was clear to me that she too would rummage in this box one day looking for pictures of me, for he would go on haunting us for ever, seductive and damned, drawing hungry hearts to himself like a magnet, and I wanted to leave her a little note there in his box, my dear daughter, I wanted to write to her, even after you load your weight onto mine we'll still be frozen air, sharp as a spear, but instead I carefully wrapped the box in all its rubber bands and ribbons and switched off the light. I walked round the dark house, from room to room, occasionally opening a drawer, but nothing there interested me any more, neither the letters from the bank, nor the condolence telegrams, nor the French diplomas, everything seemed insipid compared to what I had already seen, and I sat down again on the suitcase, which I found more comfortable than all the armchairs, and I thought that the time had come for me to leave, this man was too rotten for me, just as it wasn't a good idea to sleep in a rubbish bin it wasn't a good idea to sleep in his bed, and I went to the bedroom and looked at the big bed but he wasn't there, it was as empty as my mother's plate in the picture.

At first I thought I wasn't seeing properly, because he was almost the same colour as the darkness, but when I went up and felt the soft blankets I couldn't feel a body, and I thought that maybe he had evaporated, shrunk to nothing, like his erection his whole body had vanished, leaving behind it a box of pictures instead of children, and all the women in the photographs, those of them that were still alive, would say *Kaddish* for him round his open grave, and I thought this in relief, even hope, because it seemed the simplest way of getting rid of him, without conflict, without the pang of lost opportunity, I had done my bit and all the rest didn't depend on me, and I was really disappointed when I heard a muffled fart, and the tap opening and closing, careful to wash his hands even in the middle of the night, but what did it help him when he was so filthy inside, and heavy steps approached and his body fell onto the bed, and in the flame of his cigarette lighter I saw his face concentrated on the lit cigarette, and I heard him say, you're still here, in a mixture of mockery and surprise, apparently he too was hoping that I had disappeared, vanished from his life without scenes, without farewells, without accusations, and now we had a disappointment in common, and this was perhaps what brought us together for a moment, the disappointment of each of us that the other had not yet disappeared from his life.

Do you want me to go, I asked, and he sighed, I haven't got the strength for this, why concern yourself with my wishes, concern yourself with yours, do what you want, and I said, but I'm not alone here, there are two of us, and he said, haven't you learned yet, two is two people alone, and let me tell you a secret, three is three people alone, and so on and so forth, and even in the dark I could guess at the expression of satisfaction on his face at this insight, and I tried to make up my mind if what he had said was clever or stupid, original or banal, and I couldn't decide, and I said resentfully, it seems that you specialize in threesomes, and he bristled and demanded aggressively, what do you mean? Nothing, I stammered, and he sniggered, you've been prying, have you, and I kept quiet, ready to absorb another attack of rage, this time perhaps more justified, but instead he went on sniggering, as if he was determined to be unpredictable at any cost, and he said, I hope you enjoyed yourself. Less than you enjoyed yourself when you had those photographs taken, I said, and he laughed, yes, on the whole I really enjoyed myself, why deny it now that most of the pleasures of life are behind me, and I said, insulted, you don't leave me a chance. Don't take it personally, he said, I'm talking to you about that big basket of pleasures, surprises, presents, I've opened nearly all of them, the basket is almost empty, and for you it's still full, Ya'ara, don't worry so much. I was born with an empty basket, I said, it's got nothing to do with age, I've never felt as if I had a basket like that.

You don't feel it all the time, only when you look back, when you've passed the middle of your life, the picture becomes clear, he said, and in order to make our picture clear too he switched on the reading lamp and began rummaging for his weed and and preparing a little more consolation for himself, and I was rivetted to his movements, to his dark naked body, and since I was still sunk in the pictures in the shoe box it seemed to me that his whole body was full of fingerprints, he looked like a leopard, supple and covered with the round marks of the fingerprints and lips of all the women who had made love to him all those years, and at the same time he didn't look used, just as leopards don't look used, and he stretched in enjoyment and took a drag on the joint and offered it to me, continuing where he had left off, yes, I enjoyed it but I wasn't dependent on it, he said this almost threateningly, as a stern warning, and I understood that it wouldn't be a good idea to argue, and I only said, where did you find the time to do anything else, and he laughed, you forget how old I am, everything is spread over so many years. But the body is the same body, I said, and it's the only one you've got, and it's covered with spots, and he examined his smooth dark skin anxiously, turning his arm from side to side, and then he heaved a sigh of relief, as if he had really been afraid of what he might find, and said, it's your jealousy talking, child, and I didn't even try to deny it, and he said, your life is open, Ya'ara, why are you in such a hurry to close everything, even when you've already opened up you're in a hurry to close down at the first frustration, and this was the first time he had ever related to me, to my world, and it embarrassed me a little, who did he think he was intruding on my privacy, and I asked resentfully, what do you mean? I don't know myself, he said, it's not the details, it's the picture in general, instead of attacking life like a winner you hide, waiting for a blow, emerging every now and then only to return immediately to your cave. It's your right, of course, everyone is entitled to choose his own path, but you're frustrated, that's obvious, hiding in your cave isn't enough for you, you want more, but for that you have to take risks, and you don't dare do it.

I do take risks, I'm here aren't I, I tried to defend myself, and he dismissed me patronizingly and said, you're descending to details again, the question isn't where you spend a night or two

of your life but how you conduct your life in general, if you rule
it or are ruled by it, and I shrunk in shame, I wanted so much to
be that masterful woman he described, who didn't need a man,
who didn't calculate profit and loss, who didn't pay a price for
security, who went her own way, and I imagined a strong, sturdy
future, without Yonny who weakened me by being so protective,
without Aryeh, in a small roof apartment, because our flat was
really that cave he spoke of, dark and gloomy, and I had to get
out of it into a flat with a view from the top, which showed the
whole picture, not the little details which always dragged me
after them, and I would sleep with whoever I fancied, and not
with someone who promised me that he would never leave me,
and from time to time with Aryeh too, and this body of mine,
I still hadn't really decided what to do with it, or discovered
what relation it bore to me, this body would lead a life of its
own, a wild, secret life, it would be my horse and I would ride it
fearlessly. For a moment I was stunned by the power of the image
I had conjured up, but I immediately sank, like once when I tried
to draw, and the picture in my head was perfect and magical but
on the way to the paper it all vanished and what came out was
totally pathetic, I now saw the gap between the glorious vision
and its realization. I saw myself alone in a cold top-storey flat,
at best practising jumping off the roof, with a phone that never
rang, except when my mother called, and occasionally Yonny
and his new wife would drop in, and bring me the leftovers of
their *cholent*, and I would eat it without even heating it up, and
my tears would fall onto the plate, and I was flooded by a wave
of self-pity, and afterwards by anger against him, who was he to
tell me what to do, and I said carefully, you were married all
those years too, you were shut up too, and he said in the same
patronizing tone, you didn't understand me, it's got nothing to
do with marriage, it's got to do with how you perceive yourself,
marriage is secondary here, you can be single and closed up too,
and you can be married and open, the question is what need led
you to get married, how you make choices, how you lead your
life, the question is if you live forever like a schoolgirl afraid
of her teacher, skipping classes now and then but keeping up

an innocent façade, so they won't tell your parents, or if your highest authority is you yourself, for better or worse, with all the implications. It seems to me that you're still trying to toe some imaginary line all the time, in order not to stand out too much, not to pay too high a price, maybe that's okay in high school, but it would be a pity if you lived your whole life that way. Believe me, he added, I'm not an interested party here, I'm not trying to persuade you to skip this or that class, I can simply see you, even though you think I see only myself, and I'm sorry for what I see.

Mortified and deflated I sat next to him, with my back hurting, a cold hand gripping all my muscles, unable to move, because I knew that he was right, absolutely right, but what could I do about it, I was standing opposite a big mess without knowing how to even begin to tidy it up, and if it would take me the rest of my life and if I should even try, and I hated him for intruding so rudely into my privacy, as if he had taken a photograph of me without my knowledge while I was sitting on the lavatory and picking my nose. Now he was waving the photograph in front of me and saying, this is you, you tell me if it's possible to love you or not. Who did he think he was, where did he get the nerve, what did he expect to gain, and he said, you know, I looked at your father today, when he was telling everybody how you were in Istanbul on your honeymoon, and I felt like taking him by the hand and leading him to the bedroom and opening the door and saying, Shlomo, she's here and it's none of your business, and then leading him back to the living room and continuing the conversation as if nothing had happened, and I'm sure he would have swallowed it, believe me, it wouldn't be the first toad he's swallowed, you'd be amazed at what people are prepared to swallow.

But then he wouldn't have been able to sit here and declare that he was a happy man, I said, and Aryeh waved his hand dismissively, nonsense, he would have made that declaration even if you were dead, don't you understand? He's happy because he's decided to be happy, not because life has given him any special privileges, you know it hasn't. His happiness isn't connected to you, it doesn't stem from the fact that you've got a good husband and you're having a good time in Istanbul, it isn't connected to you at all, and you don't have to hide things from him in order to make him happy, or from your mother either, or even from your husband. Truth is a toad that people usually succeed in digesting with relative ease, you don't have to keep it from them, and I said, it isn't only that I feel responsible for their happiness, I'm also afraid to suffer the consequences, and he said, yes, that's a familiar dilemma, but only on the face of it, because if anyone doesn't accept you as you are he'll fade out of your life, one way or another, nobody can go on pretending for ever.

But I myself don't know what I am yet, I said, in the morning I'm bold and in the evening I'm afraid, in the morning I'm ready to set the world on fire and in the evening I want a man to look after me, and he said, so find a man who'll be prepared to look after you in the evening and free you in the morning, just remember that everything's possible, the world is far more open than you think, it's all one big gateway, believe me, and his style began to get on my nerves, he talked like a home renovator, confident and crude, tear down the wall here, move the bathroom there, as if it was bricks he was talking about and not the quivering, pathetic, problematic stuff of the soul. How could he talk that way, be so mistaken, unless I was the one who was wrong, and we should really live as if we were stones, renovate our lives according to our changing needs, and not let our souls get in the way, and I remembered how the other kids had laughed at me in grade two or three when the teacher asked what inner organs there were in the human body and I said, the soul.

I looked at his broad face, illuminated by the little lamp, his eyes half closed, his lips avidly sucking in the burning consolation, and everything seemed to me impossible and unbearable to the same extent, and I was filled with sorrow, drinking and drinking sorrow from a big cup, drinking and drinking, because it was quite clear to me that he didn't see himself as part of my life, just as a contractor coming to renovate a flat doesn't see it as his home, and doesn't intend living in it, and presumably Yonny in distant Istanbul didn't see himself anymore as part of my life either, and it appeared that nobody was part of my life, and with a certain justice, I myself would have been glad to abandon it, but I had nowhere to go, and this life was mine alone, even before a room of your own you get a life of your own. The more he tried to open it up for me the more I felt it closing in on me, with all the weight of the things I had lost, and it was hard for me to breathe, and he said, you should sleep, Ya'ara, it's almost morning, and indeed a dull, purple blue light penetrated the room through the cracks in the blinds, cool and arrogant, and I lay next to him, my shoulder in his armpit, rubbing against his sticky, gummy sweat, and he surprised me with a comforting hug, and his whole body was soft and sweet, like hot porridge on a winter morning.

Soon it will be summer, I said, and he said, right, and I said, I hate the summer, and he said, yes, so do I. I hate the winter too, I said, when you think of the future in terms of the seasons of the year, it seems hopeless, and he sighed, yes, and in a few other terms too, and the slices of light coming through the blinds grew brighter and brighter, and I thought that we should stay here forever, in the bed opposite the closed blind, helpless refugees from the changing weather, and I tried to fall asleep but I couldn't, and his breathing got on my nerves, even when he was awake he snored, and I was annoyed with him for hating summer like me and hating winter like me, this new solidarity between us oppressed me, as if the misery had now been doubled, and we were both besieged, outside sweltering heatwaves and vicious rains raged, and only slender heart-shaped windowbars separated us from them.

I saw him lean over to my side of the bed and bend over in the direction of the telephone, and I pretended to be asleep, hoping to catch him red-handed in an intimate conversation, but instead he took one of the chocolate boxes and I heard him peeling off the plastic and opening the lid, and then grotesque, maddening sounds of sucking rose from his side of the bed, he sets himself up as my mentor and in the end he takes out his frustrations on old chocolates his wife didn't manage to polish

off before she died, and then I began to feel sorry for him because
he couldn't fall asleep, he was really grieving, it seemed, only you
saw it more at night than during the day, and again I felt as if
I were drinking sorrow, holding the big shattered beer mug and
drinking, and then I heard a faint but sharp explosion, and I
heard him swearing, and then running to the basin and spitting,
and I immediately ran after him and we both stood opposite
the brown mess in the basin, and he picked at it with nervous
fingers and went on spitting and swearing, fuck those bastards,
they can't even be bothered take the pits out of the cherries, I'm
going to sue them today, I'll show them, until he fished out a
little yellow fragment of tooth covered with nicotine stains, and
then he opened his mouth wide in front of the mirror and in
the pale morning light the dark, embarrassing grimace of his
lips, with the front tooth broken, looked like a tragic reversal
of the confident youthful smile which had gleamed at me from
the photographs.

He washed his face and rinsed his mouth savagely, splashing
water all around him, swearing all the time, his thick dark
tongue probing the gap which had suddenly appeared in his
mouth, trying to stop it up, and because of this all the curses
and threats coming out of his mouth sounded ridiculous, like
a seven-year-old with his milk teeth missing, and he threatened
law suits and damages, you'll see, at eight o'clock this morning
I'm phoning my lawyer, I'm nobody's mug, I'm telling you, he
repeated as if I had expressed doubts, but then he hurried into
the bedroom and looked at the box, and he switched on the light
in order to ascertain that there was indeed a warning written on
it, to the effect that the fillings of these chocolates contained
cherries with pits, and he flung the box away in disgust, and
the round little chocolates scattered over the bed and the floor,
and one of them rolled under my arm, seeking shelter under my
wing. I held it as if it was a newborn puppy, and I warmed it in
my hands, and when it began to soften I put it on my stomach,
and I began to smear it like chocolate spread on bread, and this
calmed me a little, because I didn't know what to do with his
rage, and again I felt that it was really my fault, because I was the

reason all these chocolate boxes had reached the bedroom, and I thought how quickly everything got spoilt, we were supposed to be making passionate love, not nibbling like mice in the middle of the night, and if we had made love his teeth wouldn't have been broken, and I thought about my mother, who would always say in despair, I can't do anything right, and it would only make me angrier with her, and so I didn't say I can't do anything right to him, but went on smearing the chocolate on my stomach, until I felt the hard pit in my hand, and I hid it in my navel, and I said to him, look how sweet my stomach is, and he interrupted his stream of curses at the point when he was saying, who was the idiot who brought these chocolates to the hospital, what did he want, to break her teeth? I'll ask everyone who comes in at the door, until I find out who was responsible, I'm telling you, he waved his hand in the air and I took it and placed it on my sticky stomach, and he recoiled for a moment but then gave way to his curiosity and lowered his face and sniffed, and in the end he stuck out his fleshy tongue and licked and gathered up a few more soft chocolate puppies and smeared them over the inside of my thighs. I was surprised by this enthusiastic cooperation and I responded gladly, in spite of everything he was ready for adventure, even when his wife was dead and his tooth was broken, and I tried to wriggle and writhe the way I was supposed to, but nevertheless I was keenly aware of the discrepancy between what I imagined that I was supposed to feel and what I actually did feel, because in the end I just felt like a person who for some reason was having her stomach licked, and not like a woman having a passionate erotic experience, and I didn't know who was to blame for this mishap, him or me. I was surprised that he himself wasn't aware of the mishap, licking and licking until it itched, as if he didn't have anything better to do with his time, at his age, and I heard him say, do you like it, do you want to be licked like a cat, and I grunted yes, because I didn't want to hurt his feelings, and then he said, you're dying to be fucked like a cat, and again I grunted yes, to tell the truth I'd never really thought about it, but what were we doing here after all, and quite soon I found myself on all fours, with him stuck inside me, and I wondered to myself if this was harassment or pleasure. I felt him pulling my hair hard, as if calling my head to order, and then I really started getting into it, just when it was all over and he let out a coarse yell that sounded like a continuation of his repertoire of curses, and pulled out of me drained and dripping, like one of the wrung out socks my mother would collect in a basin and send me to hang out in the yard, on the wire lines stretched between two poles, opposite the mountains, and I would stare suspiciously at the wires, I was always afraid that they were electricity wires, and my contact with them via the wet washing would electrocute me, that it was a well planned trap, and that she was sending me parting looks through the window, and in the end I would say what the hell, here goes, and I would begin to hang up sock after sock, and I would look at the mountains, they weren't particularly high or magnificent, but they were dreamy, especially in the morning when the sun came up behind them, and in the evenings when they were merged into the purple sky, and between them and me lay citrus groves and fields of carrots, and sometimes even strawberries, I was always discovering new surprises there, and then he suddenly jumped up and yelled, where is it, and I said, where's what, and he said, the tooth, the piece of the tooth, where did I put it, I have to take it to the dentist for him to reconstruct it, and we switched on the light and started searching feverishly, turning over the pillows and the blankets, and I got up to check the basin, and he suddenly shouted, don't move, and advanced towards me stealthily like a tiger about to pounce on a rabbit, and stretched out his hand to the fold in my buttocks and pulled out the lost piece of tooth. Like Benjamin when the precious silver cup was found in his sack I stood before him, innocent but accused, and nothing I could say would help, the finger was pointed at me, and I turned my back to him, and since I was already on my way to the basin I went into the bathroom and took a shower, washing off the stupid chocolate, but under the hot jet of water I began to be angry with myself, why did I have to spoil everything, just when he was turned on I remained cold, and when I thought of his thorough licking I suddenly felt excited, the reconstruction excited me far more than the event in real time, and perhaps it was actually always so, perhaps it was more thrilling to imagine things or reconstruct them than to experience them, because that way you have full control, and I basked in the memory until the hot water was finished and then I stepped out of the shower and dried myself with his towel, and when I returned to the room I saw him fast asleep, with his mouth wide open, his tongue covering his front teeth and the piece of broken tooth lying in his open hand.

Without thinking, in the sudden glee which is only possible in the wake of a great disappointment, with trembling fingers I plucked the rare, precious, irreplaceable fragment from his hand and threw it quickly into the lavatory bowl, where it was immediately encircled by tiny, almost invisible ripples before it vanished from view when I flushed the bowl, never to be seen by either of us again, and you could say that this, too, constituted one more small and secret thing we had in common.

11

When did I know that all was lost? The moment when I felt the rain wetting me as if I didn't have a roof over my head, I knew that this wasn't my place, that I had no place. I tried to run away, to escape from the bed which had turned into a water trap, with the heavy, waterlogged pillows, with the blankets which were wet and squelchy as mud, and I couldn't move my hand, or my foot, or my neck, I lay there like a bag of bones, and the water fell onto me, and I heard voices around me, people asking, is this the first rain of winter or the last rain of spring? And a mother saying to her child, go and see if the squill is blooming, and if the wagtail can be seen, and if the fields are full of blue lupins, and after a few years the child returns, Mother, he says, it must have been the last rain of spring, because the fields were as blue as the sea, with waves made by the wind, and the mother says, I'm glad you remembered to come back, I've acquired a new family in the meantime, and he cries, so make room for me in your new family, and she says, but you have brown eyes, and we all have blue eyes, how can you prove that you belong to us, and he cries, I'll put out my eyes and plant blue lupins there instead, and I tried to scream, Udi, don't put out your beautiful brown eyes, I love them, but I couldn't move my mouth, I'm your real mother, Udi, don't you remember me, how I lay for hours on the veranda without moving, and he looked at me with the shining eyes of Udi Sheinfeld, the brother of Orit my class-mate, and said, you're not my mother, you're only becoming more like her from minute to minute, and I saw before my eyes Mazal Sheinfeld, his and Orit's mother, who lay dying on the open veranda of their house.

I was always surprised by her name, the incongruous com-bination of Spanish and Ashkenazi, I always thought that it was this combination which had sealed her fate, that if she had married a man with another name she wouldn't have lain dying like that on the veranda in broad daylight, at such a young age, on a deckchair which had turned into a bed. From a distance she looked like a carefree holiday-maker, and only when we came closer, Orit Sheinfeld and I, did the still white of the sheets proclaim the gravity of the situation. No limb moved under those sheets, and her face too, with the Yemenite brown which had turned to pale grey, was still, only a weak wheezing from the sunken mouth testified to the remnants of life. We would walk past her with our heavy satchels, reeking of spilt lemonade, sticky with bubble gum, our coloured pencils clattering with the swaying of our young backs, open the rural screen door and go straight into the kitchen.

Orit would take out fresh bread, they always sent the six-year-old Udi to the grocery shop for bread in the morning, and he would run past his mother who slept on the veranda at night as well, his mother whom he couldn't even remember walking, because the disease had broken out immediately after he was born, and run back again with his brown eyes shining, and Orit would make sandwiches for herself and her brother, and for me too when I slept over there, moving from place to place with a slight limp, a graceful limp whose cause I can't remember, but she had a big scar on her leg which justified it. We would have sandwiches for lunch too, and afterwards we would play with little Udi, and when Gidon Sheinfeld, their father, came home from work and sat with us, leaning against the wall, his long narrow testicles would peep out of his wide khaki shorts, and we would explode with laughter.

During the *shiva* I sat there everyday with Orit and Udi, looking at the pictures of the beautiful young Mazal Sheinfeld, and at the balls bouncing between his legs as he rushed about, offering refreshments to the condolence callers, and I would try to find a connection between these two sights, trying to imagine the swarthy beauty cupping the pale testicles in her dark hand, but the movement looked more like one of weighing than one of desire. What had attracted her to him? He had narrow lips,

almost cruel, and thin hair, and only his bitter fate gave him
a certain halo, and I thought that when I grew a little older,
when I was fifteen or sixteen, he would fall in love with me
and I would move in to live with them, but I would sleep with
him in his room and not with Orit, and after a few years my
movements would grow heavy, and I would hardly be able to
touch his testicles, and they would shift me onto the veranda
even though I would be barely twenty years old. But in the
end it didn't happen, because after the mourning period was
over I stopped being friends with Orit Sheinfeld, suddenly the
house seemed far less interesting to me without the bed on the
veranda, and Orit began to bore me with her fresh bread, how
many sandwiches could be eaten, so I stopped going there, and
I felt terrible about it, in fact I still feel terrible about it, and
whenever I see a young woman walking down the street with a
graceful limp I hang my head in shame, even though I heard years
ago that she had undergone an operation which had removed
her limp completely, and I always knew that I was going to
be punished for my behaviour, how could I have ignored the
looks she sent me, and especially Udi, he would come up to me
in the playground at break and nestle against me like a cat and
say, why don't you come over to our house, and we'll play that
you're my mother and Orit's my father, we always killed off both
his parents in our games, and I would invent excuses and say
that I was too busy and I wouldn't even stroke his cropped hair,
afraid of being infected. All the time the illness had been in their
house I wasn't in the least afraid, and precisely when it departed
I began to feel frightened, Mazal Sheinfeld might be dead but the
disease was alive and looking for a new body to paralyse, and
now it had finally found one. I hadn't thought about them for
years, and just this morning, imprisoned in this room in a house
of mourning, I had seen Udi, his brown eyes, and because of that
my hands and feet refused to move, and I wept although there
was nobody to hear, sobbing with regret for Udi and Orit, my
dearest friends, my family, and I know that the punishment has
caught up with me and I'll never walk again. I'll be taken home
to my mother and father on a stretcher, and they'll have to guess

my wishes, even when I could talk they barely succeeded, so how will they manage now that I'm dumb, and they'll sit next to my bed and read me stories, just like the story I can hear right now, a familiar story, in a familiar voice, and I hear my mother's calm voice reciting the terrible rebuke, thou hast shamed this day the faces of all thy servants, which this day have saved thy life, and the lives of thy sons and of thy daughters, and the lives of thy wives, and the lives of thy concubines, in that thou lovest thine enemies and hatest thy friends. For thou hast declared this day, that thou regardest neither princes nor servants, for this day I perceive that if Absalom had lived, and all we had died this day, then it had pleased thee well. Now therefore arise, go forth, and speak comfortably unto thy servants, for I swear by the Lord, if thou goest not forth, there will not tarry one with thee this night, and that will be worse unto thee than all the evil that befell thee from thy youth until now, and I know that this rebuke is intended for me, how had I hated my friends Orit and Udi, and Yonny, flesh of my flesh and bone of my bone, but soon the king will come out to me and sit at the gate and the light of conciliation will be shed on the strife-ridden land, and then I hear Aryeh's voice, choked and moved, and he says, you were my radio, and then to someone else, she was my radio, in the war, for ten days she sat by my bed, after I was wounded, and read to me from the Bible, it was the only book there, in the hospital.

My mother said Aryeh didn't speak at all, at first I didn't know if he could hear me, the doctor told me to change his tourniquet every half hour and sit next to him. How did I know that he was taking anything in? Sometimes I would skip a word or two and he would twist his lips, and laugh and say, well, I came straight from the *Yeshiva*, I changed the fire of the *Torah* for the fire of the Syrians, and one day later I'm lying half-dead and hearing verse after verse, I said to myself, the *Torah* is pursuing you, there's nowhere for you to run to.

After ten days I left out the last words of every verse and he filled them in, my mother said, it was the first time I heard him speak, and a few years later I thought I saw him at the university, in Terra Santa, and I went up to him and said, and that will be worse unto thee than all the evil that befell thee, and he replied, from thy youth until now, and then I knew that it was him. We had both changed so much, he was a child when he came to us in the war, and so was I, I was barely sixteen, and already my class-mates were dying like flies, and after a week it was all over, and they told us, go and start building your lives, study, get married, have children, and how was it possible, life was dense with sorrow, it was impossible to breathe, suddenly you had a past, all at once you had a past, and it was heavy, it dragged you back.

The minute I was well I fled from the Emek, he said. It was a brief and lethal visit, I never knew it in times of peace, I came, I was wounded, and two months later I was back in Jerusalem, a semi-invalid, sometimes I was sure that the whole war was a figment of my imagination. I sat up in bed and rubbed my eyes, perhaps this entire conversation was a figment of my imagination, I had heard them so clearly, clear and close, not the way I had grown accustomed here to hearing through the walls and doors, the muffled echoes reaching me from the direction of the living room, and I couldn't understand what was happening, and it was only when I heard my mother saying, it's so pleasant sitting out here on the balcony, and him answering, yes, Josephine lay here a long time before she was hospitalized, and someone adding, it's such a lovely day, the first day of spring, I realized that their clear voices were coming from the balcony joining the bedroom to the living room, a balcony whose existence I had not been aware of up to now. Through the closed blind I could even make out their figures, sitting at their ease around a wicker table, apparently having allowed themselves to leave the French hullabaloo emanating from the living room and to create a proud local enclave which even boasted tales of heroism. I felt as if I were watching a play, only instead of a scene with one actor there was an audience of one watching a number of actors, I thought I could recognize the third actress through the blind, and I asked myself if all this was meant for my ears, if it was in my honour that they had seated themselves on the balcony, so that I would hear more clearly, or if it was in spite of my hidden presence, and at first what I had heard hardly made an impression on me, the clear voices dulled the significance of the news. The fact that I didn't have to strain my ears in order to decipher murmurs through the wall, and that everything was being dished up to me in bed like room service, made it seem like a dream which is ostensibly surprising but actually presents things which are known and self-evident, and only gradually I began to understand that the mystery of my life was being unravelled here, but I didn't want to hear anything, I couldn't hear anything, because everything in me was paralysed, even my ears, and Tirza asked, what about Shlomo, and my mother said, he was here yesterday, wasn't he, Ari, calling him by this intimate pet name.

No, what about Shlomo then, Tirza said, when you met again, and Aryeh said, we stood there in Terra Santa, Shlomo and I, and suddenly this pretty girl with a braid comes up and says to me, and that will be worse unto thee than all the evil that befell thee, and I say, without understanding what I'm saying, like a robot, from thy youth until now, and Shlomo asks me who she is and at first I say, I don't know, I swear I don't know, and only then I realize that she's the voice from the Emek, and Shlomo fell in love with her on the spot, I saw it in his eyes, and Tirza laughed disagreeably, and said to my mother, you remember the day of Elik's funeral? Your whole kibbutz was empty, and when we came back from the funeral a husband found his wife with somebody else. Everybody treated her like a whore, they shunned her completely, and two weeks later she walked into the sea and went on walking straight ahead until she drowned, and my mother said, yes, she was a wonderful woman, I think everyone was so angry with her not because she cheated on her husband, who was just an ox, but because she did it on the day they buried Elik, the day the whole kibbutz was in mourning, that she took advantage of the occasion, and she couldn't forgive herself either. I pulled the blanket over my ears, which were beginning to hurt, like a husband who doesn't want to catch his wife red-handed, because then he will have to lose her, and I didn't want to hear the end of the story in order not to lose my mother, who suddenly seemed to me beloved almost beyond bearing, and I remembered how she used to read to me from the Bible before I fell asleep, and my father would say, explain the hard words to her at least, she doesn't understand anything, and she would say, there's no need to understand, only to listen, and I simply listened to the sound of her soft voice reading expressively, and we would weep together at the sad passages. I would hear her begin to cry and join in immediately to cover up for her, even if I didn't understand what was so sad about it, I believed that she had a good enough reason, and most of all we would cry over David and Absalom, because that was a story that couldn't end well, the only way it could end well was if it had never begun, but since it was doomed to begin it was impossible to escape the sorrow, because the victor is the biggest loser.

Whenever she read David's lament we would weep without restraint, and then, when the baby was born, it was clear to me that we would call him Absalom, but my father objected, and I remember them quarrelling about it all week until the *Brith*, and then, when the *mohel*, the man who was to perform the circumcision, asked what his name was, my father was silent and my mother said Absalom with a little question mark, as if she were seeking confirmation from the *mohel*, but in all his short life we never had time to call him by that long name, and only beside his grave, when my father read the terrible lament out loud, I knew that he was taking revenge on her for her choice, accusing her, and ever since then I never saw her open the Bible. Sometimes I would ask her to read it to me before I went to sleep, especially when I was sick, but she would say rudely, I'm not a radio, and her voice stopped being soft too, and grew hoarse from quarrelling and cigarettes, and now for a moment the old softness came back as she said pensively, it's unbelievable how some little thing you do without even thinking can accompany you all your life. That story I read to Aryeh at the age of sixteen haunted me all my life with both my children, but in my case it was split into two, with Ya'ara I fought and Absalom I lost, and Tirza said, what do you mean you fought, she fought you, and my mother said, it makes no difference who started, the question is if you go to war or not, David didn't start either but neither did he avoid the war, he could have given in to Absalom and let him have the kingdom without a fight, and he didn't do it. That's how it is, she sighed, when you fight your own child you can't win, even if you win you lose.

I listened to her in astonishment, not understanding what she was talking about but knowing that it was some sort of elegy, for me or her or the relations between us, and more than the contents I was surprised by the tone, they spoke like such close friends, all three of them, after the way they had slandered him so viciously in the cemetery only two days ago, and I didn't understand what was going on here, how was it possible, she always spoke of him with such hatred, almost loathing, and I thought of how mysteries are never solved but only grow more complicated, you imagine that you're there and in the end it turns out that you were had for a fool. And nevertheless I had to admit that I liked their tone, I liked the friendship between them, the frankness, I had never heard her talking to my father so frankly, she was always careful not to give him a chance to use any scrap of information or regret or soul-searching against her, the insane competition between them never let up for a minute, and then I heard Tirza ask, so Shlomo and Aryeh were rivals for your hand? And my mother sighed, no, not really, it was all settled in advance, it seems to me, and Aryeh said, it was all too long ago for us to start reconstructing exactly what happened then.

What a pleasure it is to grow old, my mother laughed, everyone who feels desperate should be reminded that in thirty years' time it will give him a good laugh, everything should be seen from a distance of thirty years at least, and it seemed to me that she was almost shouting, and suddenly I began to suspect that it was all being staged, perhaps she knew that I was there and she was putting on a show for my benefit, and only the goal was unclear, to give me an improved version of events, to teach me a concentrated lesson, pass me a secret message. I sat up and arranged the pillows behind my back to make myself comfortable, the numbness began to go away and I thought, perhaps my paralysis will be postponed for a few years, and so I sat and watched them as if in a theatre, a bed theatre, something super-innovative, where the actors are seen through the screen of a blind and the audience is supposed to guess who they are, to fill in the details himself. I recognized my mother's dress easily, a brown dress which always looked good on her, and her profile looked handsome through the blind, the screen flattered her, but not Aunt Tirza, who looked thick and stiff on her chair, and he, the giant cat, the king of the cats, looked completely tame one minute and like a savage wild cat the next, even through the blind I could feel his magnetic power, and the back of the chair he was sitting on looked like a long, erect tail. I enjoyed listening to them talking without tension or bitterness, like a little girl whose parents have made up and she can go to sleep secure in the knowledge that when she wakes up in the morning she will find both of them at home, in a good mood, and indeed, without intending to, I fell asleep, even though what I wanted most in the world was to go on watching the play being enacted on the balcony for my benefit, and I woke up furious at having missed the end, and now I would never know what I had missed, there was nobody to ask, there was nobody else in the audience but me, and the balcony was empty, the sun was gone too, and I couldn't even see the round wicker table, and I began to doubt the reality of everything I had seen and heard, and the only evidence that I had been trying to watch something was the pile of pillows behind my back, and I couldn't forgive myself for falling asleep a moment before the truth came out in front of my closed eyes.

Next to the bed, on the little bedside cupboard, I saw the round tray with the red thermos flask, a glass of orange juice, and a fresh roll, and I wanted to pour myself a cup of coffee but there was nothing to pour it into, he had forgotten to bring me a cup, there's always something missing, something whose absence makes it the most important thing. I tried to drink straight from the thermos flask, but its round rim tasted of some chilly perfume, or of lipstick, and I remembered how she had painted her lips bright pink on the last day of her

life, and how her lips had shone in her twisted face, as if
they didn't belong to it, as if they were trying to escape the
fate of that distorted face, and perhaps they succeeded in the
end, and they had escaped here, to this polished little thermos
flask, a delicate pair of lips, so delicate they lacked almost all
sensuousness, cyclamen lips, floating now in a sea of coffee like
dumplings in soup, and in a minute, when I tilted the flask,
they would meet my lips, get into my mouth and stay there
forever. I looked into the thermos flask in dismay, the hot steam
burning my face, hiding the narrow opening, until I ran into the
bathroom and tried to pour the coffee slowly into the basin, to
see if there was anything there or not, and the aromatic brown
coffee spilled regretfully into the white basin, disappearing into
its thirsty maw, until the stream turned into a thin trickle, and
it too stopped. I bent over and examined the upturned thermos
flask, trying to look into its shiny darkness, but I couldn't see
a thing, and I filled it with water and emptied that out too,
watching it grow clearer as the muddy dregs of the coffee were
washed out, and in the end I went back to bed and drank the
orange juice in despair, thinking how close I had been to the
coffee, and how far from it I was now, just as I had been so
close to the truth before it slipped away, close to their youth,
their past, the past that was a tame cat one minute and savage
and frightening the next, just like him, the past that howled at
me at night and cried out for change, and I of all people had to
change it, I who could barely move anything in the present, never
mind the future, I of all people had to repair the past, because
since it was spoilt I was spoilt too, and my only hope of coming
right lay in putting it right, if it could not be put right neither
could I. The relaxed sentences reaching me from the balcony
showed me how right everything could have been, because I had
never heard such relaxed sentences in my parents' house, and
here, behind the blind, I had been given glad tidings of broken
parts being joined, like the two fragments of the biblical verse
uniting, and that will be worse unto thee than all the evil that
befell thee from thy youth until now. But how could you mend
the past without knowing it, it was hard enough to reconcile

yourself to the fact that the future was unknown, so how was it possible to reconcile yourself to an unknown past, and I picked up the comb and stood in front of the mirror, as if the solution lay there, and began to comb my hair, for the first time since coming here, I went on combing until my hair shone, and then I plaited it into a long, thick braid, like my mother's braid hidden in the wardrobe, contemptuously wrapped in newspaper, like a fish from the marketplace, a braid which had been removed in an instant, with the wave of a hand, from its rightful place on her head to a drawer in the wardrobe.

The night when the shadows danced on the walls, and the candles flickered in the windows, and my parents came home from the hospital without my little brother, was the last time I saw the braid on the back of her neck, and in the morning she got up without it, looking naked and exposed, all of sudden masculine and ugly, and I asked her, Mother, what have you done, and she said, I cut it off in mourning, and nothing beautiful will ever come near me again, and I asked her where it was, and she said, in the garbage, but a few months later when I was looking for something in her wardrobe I came across the newspaper out of which, smooth and gleaming, slid her thick braid, thicker than mine, longer, but nevertheless similar, and I would try to stick it to my hair, tying it on with a scarf or an elastic band, and it always slid off my neck as if it had a will of its own, but now it lay there snugly, making me walk more erectly, bearing my love for him as if it were my mother's love, and I thought of the young woman in the narrow corridors of the university, I saw it in black and white, a white face and black hair, meeting the two young men, one black and one white, and then, like the two fragments of the verse joining into one, her memory joined his memory and united into a single event, lasting a few days, in the war which had broken their youth. I actually knew the story of the boy soldier, she had told it to me a number of times without mentioning his name, a boy soldier who had been severely wounded and by whose bedside she had sat for ten days, but if it was really him, why didn't he have a single scar, if he'd been so severely wounded, all the kisses he'd been given hadn't left a mark on him, that was true, but how was it that his severe wounds hadn't left a mark either, and then I thought that perhaps it was his sterility, perhaps this was the disablement he had hinted at. In fear and pity I saw before me his big, beautiful body, hollow of sperm and eternally sad, and I was overcome with dread like a prophet whose mission had become clear to him, I had been chosen to fill the void in his body, to penetrate the smooth, dark, beloved skin and be swallowed up in the dark void as in an ancient cave, never to see the sunlight again.

I rummaged frantically in the suitcase and pulled out the picture of her I had hidden there, and I looked at it and in the mirror, and we were quite alike with our braids and serious faces, and I said to her, why didn't you do it yourself, Mother, why didn't you console him yourself, you loved him after all, and all at once her love became clear to me through the braid on my head, and I felt no grievance against her for loving another man all her life instead of my father, on the contrary, it was better for her to have loved someone else rather than not loving anyone, not knowing what it meant to love, and I wondered how you got through life when you loved another man, and you knew it was hopeless, not like me, who ran after him and ambushed him, but like her, without doing anything, how you went from day to day without islands of hope to climb onto, and I saw the terrible emptiness of her life, because there comes a moment when you know that nothing will change, I could already feel that moment approaching myself, when it's no longer possible to say, one day I'll have a man I'll love, or one day I'll have a life I'll love, a moment when you know that in this incarnation at least nothing will change for the better and that's it, this is life, more or less, and then everything pales, fades, all of sudden the radiance that gives everything a point is gone, and life remains naked, ashamed of its nakedness, and when it happens first you want to die, and then you want to cry, and then you say, as long as it doesn't get any worse. Through the heavy braid I could feel her dejection and I sat on the bed and stroked it like a cat, and I heard the door open and he was standing there, basking in the light of her love, holding a big blue mug in his hands, blue as the shirt he was wearing, a short-sleeved summer shirt, the buttons open to reveal his broad brown chest, with a few grey hairs peeping out to emphasize his deep tan. Like on the first day I met him, only then it was the end of summer and now it was the beginning, smiling with his mouth closed to hide his broken tooth, holding out the mug and saying, I forgot, and putting it down next to the empty thermos and trying to pour out the coffee, and when nothing comes out he chuckles, did you finish it all? As if I've played a particularly entertaining trick, and I say, yes, and then I say, no, because of course I still want coffee, and then he asks what have you done to yourself, examining me sternly, and suddenly I have nowhere to hide, the curtain of my hair is drawn back and my face is revealed, with all the little lines and sunspots, and his face becomes unpleasant, and he grabs my braid, pulls off the rubber band violently, together with a few of my hairs, and roughly parts the three strands of hair and mixes them up, wiping out every trace of my magnificent braid, and all this only takes a second but to me it seems like hours, slow and frightening as a mythological rite of exorcism, and I felt myself beginning to tremble, and then I saw that it was him who was trembling, or the whole world that was trembling, I could no longer tell, and he sat down on the chair opposite me and began to shout, get out of here, I'm sick of your provocations, and I felt that I had no air to breathe, that I couldn't move, paralysed like poor Mazal Sheinfeld, and he stood up and kicked my suitcase, kicked it towards me and yelled, enough, this time you've gone too far.

I got up with difficulty and got dressed and began collecting my things, this time I remembered the book, and I threw everything into the suitcase and closed it. I did everything in slow motion, I tried to speed up my movements and failed, as if I was struggling against the force of gravity, and when I stood in the doorway he sat down on the bed opposite me and covered his face and said in gentler voice, why do you provoke me, what are you trying to achieve, and I said, nothing, I don't know anything, I don't understand anything, and he said, that

braid, I hate it, and I asked him why, and he said, like you'd
hate a snake that tried to bite you, and I said, why, I don't
understand anything, and he looked up at me from the bed,
suddenly he looked like a little boy, and said, you really don't
know? And I said, I swear on the Bible, and he said, that's
how she went round, that mother of yours, the princess from
the Emek, tossing her magnificent braid and twisting us round
her little finger with her limitless pride. I was astonished by this
description and I said, how can that be, she loved you so much,
and he laughed bitterly, she loved me? The only person she
loved was herself, as far as she was concerned I was a slice
of nostalgia, memories of the war, a shared verse, but it never
occurred to her to take me seriously. I was a black kid from a
slum, with a dubious past and an uncertain future, not like your
father, with his European doctor parents from Talbiyeh, with
his good education, and what does she say to me, he sounded
as if it had all happened yesterday, she loves me, but she wants
children, children she wants, that's what's important to her, and
she knew about my wound, she knew more than I did, she was
the only one who sat at my bedside then, and the doctors told
her everything. You understand what she said to me, I didn't
fit in with the future that was growing in her head, under that
braid, she wanted to marry a healthy, well-off man, and have lots
of children, a normal family is what she wanted, and I would say
to her, I would beg her, Rachel, you must never turn your back
on love, you'll pay for it all your life, but she knew better than
anyone, and without even telling me she went and married my
best friend, and I dropped out of university and left the country
leaving a curse behind me, I cursed them that their marriage
would be childless. From time to time I heard news about them,
I heard that your father had been ill and stopped everything in
the middle, and the truth is that I was sorry for him, but I said
to myself, it serves her right, it serves her right, she thinks she's
got life in her pocket, that everything can be planned. I always
asked friends from Israel if they'd had any children, and I saw
that the curse was working, but on the day you were born she
beat me, she received her justification, and I heard your father

on the telephone, the first thing she did was get him to phone me in Paris and tell me the news, and he was so naïve he didn't understand a thing, he was sure I was happy for them.

That was the day you met Josephine, I said, and he said, right, how did you know? But he didn't wait for an answer. Josephine wanted me on any condition, that was her greatness, she knew how to love, without expecting anything in return, she was ready to give up a lot in order to be with me, she gave up a baby that was already in her womb for me, do you understand what I'm saying? And that's why I stayed with her to the end. You think your mother didn't try to get me back? You can bet your life she did. Your father had already given her a child, she didn't need him so much any more, and she suddenly discovered that she couldn't live without me, that I was the real love of her life, you were sleeping in your pram when she came and suggested that I move in with the two of you, that we bring you up together, as if you were mine, but I couldn't forgive for that old rejection, and I was glad that her life was ruined, and later, when Absalom died, I knew she was being punished, and she knew it too, and for years afterwards she refused to see me, and I know I shouldn't be telling you this, but when I see you with that braid it comes up in me like vomit and I can't control it. I was stunned, his story was so different from the story I had in my head, that I couldn't understand it at all, I couldn't take in the details, only his cruel, resentful, vindictive tone, unforgiving, unforgetting, unpitying, and all the time I thought, there must be some mistake here, that can't be the way it was, even Josephine had a different version, she said he was happy when I was born, suddenly this was the only thing I cared about, if it was a happy day for him or an unhappy one, I couldn't bear the thought that he was sorry when I was born, and only afterwards I thought about her.

He lay down on the bed, smoking with his eyes closed, his face twisted, and my mother came back to me in all her hatred, because when two people meant for each other refuse to accept their vocation, they sentence themselves to a life full of hatred and blame, and everyone is to blame for the missed opportunity, she's to blame for turning her back on love, and I'm to blame because for my sake she renounced the love of her life and in exchange I gave her nothing, and he himself is to blame for refusing to go back to her when she wanted him, and Josephine was to blame for proving to him that there were women capable of true love, an ever widening circle of blame, encompassing almost the entire world, and how could I even imagine that it was possible for me to escape this circle, I had no more chance than a baby fighting nuclear weapons. I went up and lay down on the bed next to him, with my back to him, because I didn't want to see him, suddenly I felt revolted by him, by all the juicy bits of information I'd been awaiting for so long, and now they seemed poisoned, unfit for consumption, and he stood up and said, forgive me, I shouldn't have done that, you keep making me lose control, I think we shouldn't be together any more, everything between us is too charged, this evening when everybody leaves I'll take you home.

He undressed slowly, with heavy movements, and went into the bathroom to take a shower, and I heard the water running and thought about the snowman in the story my mother used to read me, the beloved snowman who was dirtied with mud, and when the children tried to wash off the mud the water melted him and nothing was left. I always protested against the iron logic of the story, I would say, why do they have to wash him, and my mother would answer, because he got dirty with mud, and I would shout, trying to change the harsh sentence, it's better for him to be dirty than not to be there at all, and she would say, they want him clean. But that's impossible, I would shout, they want something impossible, anyone who wants the impossible loses everything.

I looked at the bedside cupboard with the dangerous chocolate boxes on it, and I thought about her life which had been open for a minute and then had closed, and I saw her knocking on the gate, begging it to open, but it was too late, one mistake leads to another and in the end you get a mistaken life. She gave him up to give birth to me, and Absalom, and she hated us so much for it that Absalom died and I can't get a grip on life, whereas if she'd chosen him I wouldn't have been born at all, a sweet and enchanted possibility, I would have remained like a closed box, a perfect, untested promise, and no doubt whenever I woke her up at night, and whenever I disappointed her, she thought of the price she had paid, and whenever I didn't do my homework and whenever I was cheeky, and all because of the broken pieces of the verse that never united but remained like amputated limbs, and that's why Josephine got sick too, because the gratitude he gave her wasn't enough, it was love she wanted, only love, and in him love had rotted, like stagnant water which never sees sunlight and air, so what did he have to give her, and what did he have to give me, the leftovers of an ancient rage, a sense of victory gone sour, the victory of the weak which is the closet thing to defeat. There was nothing left for me here, and tonight I would leave and go wherever my suitcase took me, like a seeing-eye dog I would let it lead me, because the wider my eyes were opened the less I saw.

I heard him singing in the running water, he sang in a voice full of feeling, by the rivers of Bablyon, there we sat down, yea, we wept when we remembered Zion, a sad voice but youthful and uninhibited, and I thought how to spite her he had remained young while she grew old, to remind her always of the past, so that her dream never died but only became more and more impossible, and I heard his voice calling me, Ya'ara, it said without waiting for an answer, sure that I had not gone yet, bring me a towel, and I opened the wardrobe and began looking for towels, and everything there was so neat and tidy, the towels folded stiff as planks, and I took the first one, which was black, and without meaning to I pulled out the one underneath it too, and I tried to fold it and failed, so I took him both of them, and he smiled mockingly and said, who's the second one for? Have you got another man here waiting for his towel? He was trying to remind me of that day in Jaffa, but I said, yes I have, and I thought of dear Yonny, waiting for his towel, standing there still, in the little bathroom, shivering with cold, because when I left him it was winter, and he was still standing there wet and waiting for me to come and dry him. I wrapped myself in the big towel although I was dressed, and went back to bed and he hurried after me, and stood naked opposite the wardrobe, and I tried to find a secret scar on his body and I couldn't find one, and I asked, did you go to bed with her? And he didn't answer but I saw that he had heard the question, his body moved as if a wind had passed through it, and he turned to face me aggressively and said, why are you so preoccupied with the past, Ya'ara, why don't you ask for instance if I'm going to go to bed with you, and he came closer and closer to me, or perhaps it was only his penis that swelled and came closer while he stayed far away, and he said, you can't have everything, when you're busy with the past you neglect the present, what's more important for you to know now, if I went to bed with her thirty years ago or if I'm going to go to bed with you now? I laughed in embarrassment and asked, what should I say, and he said, the truth, and I said, if you went to bed with her, and he turned back to the wardrobe and began getting dressed resentfully, and I protested, but you told me to tell the truth, and he said, yes, but you pay a price for the truth, didn't you know? The more he got dressed the more I wanted him, I wanted him up to my forehead, as if I'd been lying for hours in the sun and my skin was burning, and I thought about how I always did the wrong thing, it was too late to save her life now, and in the meantime I was losing my own, and I said, come, I want you, and he looked down at me arrogantly from above, and said, but now I don't want to, I couldn't even if I wanted to, and he pointed at his groin, you see, it's all dead for you there, there's nothing there, if I had a slit I'd think I was a woman, and indeed a strange silence rose from there, the emptiness of an inanimate object. Does everything die so quickly, I said, insulted, and he said yes, that's the way it is, and I was suddenly furious with him and I yelled, only a minute ago you were so keen so how come you're not any more, you're simply offended by what I said, why do you ask questions if you can't face the facts? And he immediately lost his temper, I can't face the facts? It's you who can't face the fact that I don't want to fuck you, and I yelled, you're a liar, my mother was right not to marry you, and he laughed a loud, nasty laugh, and I held my throat, which had begun to hurt from my yelling, and I looked at the orange afternoon light filtering through the blinds and I said to myself, in a few hours' time this will also be the past, and I won't be here any more, I have no idea where I will be but I won't be here, that's for sure, everything here is sick, sick, and I couldn't believe what I was hearing, because suddenly I heard my own thoughts exactly being hurled at me in his accusing voice. Everything here is sick because of you, he yelled, you spread sickness around you, Josephine was the picture of health compared to you, you make me act in a way that makes me hate myself, I refuse to put up with it any longer, and I was almost sorry that there wasn't anybody else present, even one of my parents, for example, someone who could judge between us, but what difference did it make who was right, it was clear that this room couldn't hold the two of us, and I had to get out before more condolence callers arrived and I was stuck here till the middle of the night, but I couldn't let him have the last word and I yelled, liar, you're a dirty liar, that's what you are, and in the middle of the laughter which had overcome him I heard him say, I don't understand what you're doing here at all, if I'm so bad what do you need me for, and I yelled, I don't need you, I wish I'd never met you, and he said, so stop meeting me, nobody needs you here. So why did you phone and ask me to come to you, I shrieked, you ruined my whole life with that phone-call, and he said, I phoned you? You phoned me and asked me if you could come, you think I would phone you, and on the day I buried my wife? And I fell on him, in my rage I didn't know what I was doing, I fell on the lips that had spoken those shocking, lying words, and tried to rip them off his face, and he pushed me onto the bed and held me pinned down there, repeating the unbearable words over and over again, I phoned you? I've never phoned you in my life, I don't even know your phone number, I've never phoned you in my life, and then the doorbell rang and the second half of the third day in the seven days of mourning for Josephine Even began.

12

If anyone had asked me which was easier, coming to blows or making love, I would have said the second, of course. But now, lying in his bed and panting with hatred, I felt how much more physical my hate was than my love, less vacillating, less defeatist. All my strength was mobilized on its behalf as I got under his down quilt, angrily crushing the soft pillows as if they were his lips spewing out those words, and I closed my eyes tight because everything I saw disgusted me, every piece of furniture, every corner of the room, even the white walls, the picture hanging on them, a huge picture of a threatening black crane, and the open wardrobe, even the blinds which had not been raised for two days soaked up the disgust, for they had heard the words, everything which had heard the words, seen the deranged smile surrounding them like a picture frame, a smile so broad that it split his lips until a drop of blood appeared in their corner, everyone who was present, human or object, was contaminated, contaminated for ever. I tried to propel myself to move, the fact that you haven't got anywhere to go doesn't mean you have to stay, and the fact that you made a mistake doesn't mean you have to perpetuate it, but the knowledge was so appalling that I couldn't move, the absolute, certain knowledge that I, Ya'ara Korman, born on such and such a date, in such and such a place, whose eyes were such and such a colour, and all the other data which there was no way of changing, which simply had to be lived with, the knowledge that to all of these facts a new one had been added today, and they had to crowd together to make room for it, to make friends with it, the fact that in such and such a month, in such and such a year, I had made a mistake, a grave mistake,

which had changed my life for ever, turned the past into a realm
of eternal longing and the present into a nightmare and the future
into a beast of prey, and now I had to learn to live with it, like you
learn to live with a disability, but it wasn't simply a disability, it
was one I had caused myself, like someone shooting himself in
the foot, and after that he has to go on living with himself as well
as his wounded foot, or someone who gets into a car and runs
himself over, both driver and victim lying under the wheels, both
accuser and accused, and I thought of dear Yonny, who was lost
to me forever, and his love which would be taken from me like a
cloth abruptly taken off a table, and how pitiful the table looks
in its exposure, how dreary and stained. I could see his face, how
a new toughness would be added to his soft features, and how
surprisingly well it would suit him, as if it had always been there,
just waiting for an opportunity to come out, and a new firmness
would be added to his soft voice, and how he would explain to
me politely that something in him had snapped and we would
never be able to return to our previous life together, because as
far as he was concerned that honeymoon in Istanbul had meant
the end of our marriage, and then he would add, did you know
that the Turks once ruled almost the whole world? And I would
say, maybe we could try again, it's always possible to part, and
he would go on, the remnants of glory, mouldy pride, that's
all that remains to them, and I would plead, I'll make it up to
you, Yonny, I'll fix everything, but he would say, their rule was
cruel, and now all that's left in Istanbul is the cruelty without the
power, and this would conclude our conversation and I would
pack up my mouldy pride, and my clothes and my books, and he
would pack up his, because neither of us would want to stay in
the flat, and half the crates would have his name on them and half
would have mine, and at the door he would shake hands with
me as if we had just concluded a business deal, a firm, serious
handshake, and there would be a spark of happiness in his
eyes, not provocative, not defiant, but the modest, considerate
happiness of someone released earlier than he expected, and
I would never see him again. Nothing would remain of the
years we had spent together, not even a small child to be torn

between us, no property to quarrel over, but absolutely nothing, each of us would end up almost as empty-handed as we had started off, and maybe one day I would bump into him in the street, and we would sit in some little café, and only then he would dare to tell me how terrible it had been to wake up in the morning wrapped in the sweet excitement of setting out on a journey, to quickly run through a list of things that still had to be done, little last-minute things, and only then to realize that the bed was empty, the bathroom was empty, the kitchen was empty, and nevertheless to take his suitcase and go, because that was Yonny, not one to change his plans, not one to lie in bed and cry, but to cry in the plane, to cry in the hotel, to cry on the move, not like me, who cried standing still, and anyone who cries on the move succeeds in the end in saving himself, while someone who cries standing still, like me, is lost, like me, and I was horrified by this picture of the future which loomed before me even clearer and more certain than the past, and I knew that I wouldn't be able to stand it, I had to stop it, to find some way of stopping the great stone from rolling down and crushing me. First of all, I had to get out of bed, even sitting on the lavatory was better than lying in bed, and best of all was standing by the window, and in the end I succeed in reaching the window and opening it, and the air falls on me in excitement, the sharp, perfumed air of spring, and the orange trees in the garden are blossoming, sending me regards from the citrus groves that surrounded our house in the village, blooming like brides and grooms, stirring in me thoughts of love, which are always more delightful than love itself, and I would wander among the trees, happy in my thoughts, climbing onto a little hill and looking down on a world which was one great, endless citrus grove, and I would think about how I would bring the man I loved here and show him this wonder, and it would answer the great question which had not been asked, which would never be asked. Perhaps I would take Yonny there when he came back, I would wait for him at the airport and take him straight there, from the mosques of Istanbul to the citrus groves of the Sharon, and there, on the little hill, I would succeed in winning his heart again, and again

I went to the suitcase and rummaged inside it, checking to see
that everything was there, and I looked around me and began to
plan my escape, which turned out to be relatively simple, because
in his haste he had forgotten to lock the door, or perhaps he had
left it open on purpose, and I could slip out through the corridor,
stealing past the living room, or even go inside for a moment and
shake his hand solemnly, as if I had just arrived and gone straight
from the front door to the lavatory, but what was I going to do
with my enormous suitcase, I couldn't let myself be trapped here
by a suitcase. I decided to slowly raise the blind giving onto the
balcony which I had just discovered today, and then I saw that
the key to the balcony door was hanging on the handle, swaying
gaily to and fro, just waiting for me to notice it, and I opened
the door and pushed my suitcase onto the balcony with a few
kicks, and closed the blind behind it, and then, before I could
change my mind, I walked out into the corridor.

From the living room rose a rhythmic murmur, a kind of
quiet, restrained singing of many voices in unison. Most high
God, they sang, bountifully dispensing benefits, the Creator of
all things, who remembering the piety of the fathers will send
a Redeemer to their posterity, and I advanced cautiously until
I reached the lavatory, and went in quickly, and sat down on
the lid of the toilet bowl to calm down. Like a little island
in the middle of a dangerous ocean the narrow little cubicle
seemed to me, and I looked around me and noted the lack of
a woman's hand, who knows what the man of the house was
up to when he didn't even notice the lack of toilet paper and the
stench like that of a public lavatory rising from the toilet bowl.
I heard footsteps approaching and quickly thrust out my foot
to stop the door from opening, because there was no key, but
even my relatively long leg failed to reach the door, and even
though the footsteps receded I went on trying, stretching my
legs as far as they would go, and I wondered what people did
who were caught here in the middle of their business, with their
pants down, they had two possibilities, either to jump up and
hold the door, dripping into their pants, or go on sitting on the
lavatory and risk an embarrassing exposure, and I was surprised

at the owners of the apartment for confronting their guests with
such a difficult dilemma, I was especially surprised at Josephine,
I would have expected more consideration for her guests from
her, and I even thought, who knows, maybe that's why she got
sick and died, after all the Temple was destroyed for less. And
then I remembered my precious book, abandoned to the mercies
of the passers-by at the bottom of the suitcase left standing on
the balcony, and I flushed the water and stepped out of the
lavatory, and hurried to the front door trying to look as grave
and troubled as I could, stopping for a moment at the living room
door in order to see him there, surrounded by men, swaying to
and fro in prayer, and a woman came out of the kitchen where
a number of women, including the mother-in-law with the blue
hair rinse, were sitting at the round table, and signalled me to
wait, saying, they'll be finished praying in a minute, you can
wait in here, and I followed her into the kitchen and sat down
on the only vacant chair. Will you have something to drink? she
asked, and I said gladly, coffee, suddenly it was so simple to get
a cup of coffee, outside that room, and she deftly poured some
coffee into a mug and pushed the sugar and milk towards me,
and she smiled and said, I'm Ayala, Aryeh's sister.

Your parents must have loved animals, I remarked, calling
you after a deer and your brother after a lion, and immediately
regretted it, fearing I had hurt her feelings, but she laughed
warmly and said, yes, they did, I always told them it was a pity
they didn't worry about their children as much as they worried
about every stray cat in the street. I smiled at her gratefully,
and she inquired, cake? And without waiting for an answer she
handed me a pale, fragrant slice of cheesecake on a fancy plate,
and in fluent French pressed the bereaved mother to take another
slice, moving gracefully and gently about the crowded kitchen.
She was short and plump, her big, soft breasts prominent in the
tight knit she was wearing, with a tanned face and shining blue
eyes. She didn't look in the least like him, perhaps only in the
pouting lips, but his were grey and hers were red, and when she
smiled, which was most of the time, wrinkles spread from her
shining eyes to her lips, but they were as captivating as dimples.

She charmed me to such an extent that I simply drank my coffee in silence and looked at her in admiration and wonder, the way she moved about the kitchen, the way she attended to everyone's needs, smiling, joking, where had she suddenly sprung from, this delightful woman, how come I never knew she existed, as if, had I known, I would have acted any differently, I would have changed my attitude to the world. I was so busy staring at her that I didn't notice she was talking to me, you're Korman's daughter aren't you, she asked, and I was mesmerized by her lips and said nothing, which was apparently interpreted as an admission, and she said, you look so much like your mother that it's astonishing, I remember her when she was about your age, it's incredible how much you resemble each other, all that's missing is the braid, and I smiled a crooked smile, and said, yes, the question is if it's such a good idea to look like my mother out of all the people in the world, and I couldn't resist adding, I'd prefer to look like you. She looked at me compassionately and said, it all depends on you, you know, I too only began to look like myself after a great many vicissitudes, and I thought, if anybody else tells me today that it all depends on me I'll scream, but from her I was prepared to take it, because it was said kindly and sympathetically, and I wanted to ask her where she had been all this time, why she hadn't been to visit me in my prison, behind the wall, but all of a sudden a shadow fell over the kitchen, and it filled with men. I recognized the French brother-in-law, and Shaul, who gave me a denying look, afraid that my presence would betray his secret, and immediately removed himself from the kitchen, and all the others were unknown to me, and Aryeh came in last, I saw his sister examining him in concern before she said, Ari, Korman's daughter is here, and he gave me a quick look, I expected him to be angry at me for breaking out and crossing the border, but he seemed amused, and said mockingly, with deliberate exaggeration, Korman's daughter, what a surprise, and smiled, I love surprises, and his sister embraced him and I saw how much they actually resembled each other, she looked like his brighter side, but next to her he too looked bright, calm and quiet, and he said, why aren't you in Istanbul? I heard that you were on holiday in Istanbul, and I felt myself blushing and I said, we came back, I used the plural deliberately, as if I was still part of a couple. What was it like, he asked, and I said, disappointing, Istanbul is disappointing, I expected much more, and he said, you should always lower your expectations, otherwise everything is disappointing, and Ayala said, right, the picture you had in your head is always more perfect than what you see with your eyes, that's true of everything, and I said, so perhaps it's better to stay inside your head, not to see places, not to meet people. But then you never grow up, he said, that gap between what you see in your mind's eye and what you see with the eyes of the flesh is growing up.

Why do you have to grow up at all, I said, seeing Ayala examining us curiously, her sensitive nostrils quivering like those of an animal scenting something suspicious, and he said wearily, because that's life, Korman's daughter, giving up on growing up means giving up on life, and she began to clap her hands, and laughed, and said, I don't know why but suddenly I feel as if I'm in the theatre, and then Shaul came back into the kitchen, stooping a little, dragging something behind him, and to my horror I saw that it was my suitcase, and he cried, see what we found on the balcony, how could you leave a full suitcase out on the balcony, and Aryeh looked at the suitcase indifferently and said, it's not my suitcase, I have no idea what it's doing on my balcony, and Shaul immediately recoiled and moved away from the suitcase, and so did everybody else, and I too moved aside, and everybody looked apprehensively at the suitcase as if it was about to explode. We have to call the police, said Shaul, and someone explained in French to the old mother what was going on and she let out a little shriek and immediately covered her withered mouth, and so we all stood around the suitcase, just as we had stood around Josephine's freshly dug grave only three days before, and I felt as if was going to faint, I felt so ill I couldn't breathe, and I didn't know how I was going to get out of this mess, and all the time I sensed his amused eyes on my face, as if to say, you gave me a surprise and I'm paying you back with a surprise of my own, and then I saw another

pair of eyes fixed on me, the shining eyes of Aryeh's sister going
back and forth between us, and she put her hand on Shaul's arm
as he was on his way to the telephone and called out in forced
animation, how could I have forgotten, it's my suitcase, and she
immediately made for the centre of the circle and snatched the
suitcase and stood it next to the wall, and Aryeh said, I don't
know why, now I feel as if I'm in the theatre, and he clapped
his hands with his lazy, arrogant movements, and the circle
slowly broke up, most of the people wandered into the living
room, and I was left alone in the kitchen with Aryeh's sister and
the blue-haired lady, who looked broken-hearted and perfectly
groomed, even though this sounds like a contradiction, in her
both things went together. Again I was sorry that I didn't know
French, because there were a few things I would have liked to
ask her, such as if it consoled her to know that she was at the
end of her life, because presumably getting a blow like this in the
middle of your life would be much harder to bear, knowing that
you still had quite a long term of suffering to serve, I for example
despair at the very thought of the years ahead of me, waiting
for me like monsters, each uglier than the one before, and I'm
supposed to ride them one after the other, along their private
routes, to gallop enthusiastically and display *joie de vivre*, to
embrace the thick hairy necks which fill me with disgust, closing
my eyes for fear of seeing their faces plainly. I closed my eyes,
my face still burning with shame, and I felt a cool hand on my
arm, and I heard her say, Korman's daughter, go home now, and
don't come back here, you hear, even if he calls you don't come
back, and I opened my eyes and said sorrowfully, he won't call
me, because when I saw him among all the other people I felt
once more the heavy and depressing weight of my attraction to
him, and she took my suitcase and walked out of the apartment
with it and I trailed behind her, and at the door I said to her,
Ayala, life disgusts me, and she whispered, don't talk like that, if
you talk like that you'll disgust life, and she gave me a motherly
hug. Have you got children, I asked her, and she said, I have
children but my children haven't got a mother, and it sounded
strange because she looked lucky, like someone with everything

going her way, and I wondered what kind of trouble lay behind her words, but she had no intention of going into details, and graceful and erect she turned her back to me and went back into the house of mourning.

It was the most frightening hour of the day, the hour when the light is more dangerous than the darkness, because it becomes very precious, very rare, an hour when I'd always been afraid of wandering round outside. When I was small I would hold on tight to my mother's hand, not believing that we would succeed in getting home safely, and even when we got there, I couldn't believe that it was really home, and not some sophisticated trap that looked exactly like home. I would inspect my room, look under the bed and inside the wardrobe, and when she tried to reassure me I would inspect her too, in case she was also a sophisticated trap which looked like my mother, and now, when I looked outside from the darkening stairwell, I thought that my whole life had become a sophisticated trap that looked like my life, and I had to free myself of it even though the springs were already round my neck, I could feel them there like artificial hands, as if someone with hooks was trying to strangle me, and I couldn't breathe and I couldn't walk and I sat down on the steps, trying to stroke my neck, but the springs tightened from inside, and I tried to put my hand inside my throat and release them, but I couldn't get deep enough, and my hand still reeked of his cigarettes, and it tasted of his mouth, sharp and bitter.

In the windows of the building opposite cosy yellow lights went on, and in my house it had been absolutely dark for three days, and how could I go back there now, how could I switch on the lights, with Yonny's sorrow lying on the floor tiles like a gigantic unburied corpse, making the closed apartment stink, and the neighbours were already beginning to sniff the air, conferring with each other about whether to break down the door, and I would say, it isn't him, it's his sorrow which is greater than him, and that's what's left for me, because he himself isn't coming back. I can hear the sounds of the evening begin, like the routine of some great project which I would give anything to be part of, children being called home, omelettes flipping over

in frying pans, baths filling, and suddenly all these sounds are
drowned by screams, I can hear them right next to my ear, as if
they're directed at me, get out of here already, I can't stand it any
longer, and I stood up in a panic, looking at his door, and then
I saw the door opposite opening and a big parcel being thrown
out, a parcel with arms, and even legs, but without the will or
capacity to move, and she collapsed immediately onto the stairs,
breathing heavily, and I went up to her and put my hand on her
shoulder, and she raised her head and when she recognized me
she dropped it again onto her knees in a gesture of confirmation
and despair, and I asked, what happened, and she wept, I can't
go on, I can't go on any longer, and then she suddenly sat up
straight and screamed, my baby's in there, now he's going to
take my baby away from me, and she jumped up and ran to
the door and began banging on it and screaming, give me Nuri,
give me Nuri, but the door stayed shut and she trembled all over
and her face was contorted with weeping. I stood up and put my
arms around her and whispered, don't worry, I'll get your baby
out of there, I don't know why I said this to her but the moment
it was said it became a fact, and she looked at me gratefully and
sobbed, I want my little cub, I can't live without him and he can't
live without me, and I said, tell me what happened, I'll help you,
and she said, I took the baby to the orthopaedist, because he's
got a problem with his legs, and when I came home I found my
husband going berserk, he's made up his mind that I'm in love
with the orthopaedist, he says there's nothing wrong with the
baby's legs and I made it all up so I could meet my lover, and
that I fuck him in front of the baby. Just imagine, he's hardly
six months old and my husband's trying to teach him to talk so
that he can spy on me, and then a window opened in her flat
and somebody shrieked, take your rags out of here, you fucking
whore, and balled up clothes flew into the little garden, blouses
and bras and panties hung from the blossoming citrus trees, and
I asked, and are you really in love with the orthopaedist, and I
hoped that she would say yes but she said, of course not, he's
nothing to me. This convinced me and I couldn't understand
why it didn't convince her husband, and she told me that once,

a few years ago, she'd left him for another man, and ever since he'd been prone to attacks of insane jealousy, and sometimes he was sure that the baby wasn't his, and when she said the word baby her body convulsed again, and she looked at me imploringly and held out her hands and sobbed, my hands are empty without my baby, bring him to me. But then you said that the baby looked like him, I reminded her, and she said, yes, but he claims that if I was thinking about another man when I was with him in bed it's enough to make the baby somebody else's, and how can I prove to him that I wasn't thinking of anybody else, and her weeping grew louder, and the sound of the baby crying rose from inside, echoing her own weeping, and I said, don't worry, we'll get him out of there and you'll both come home with me, my house is empty now and you can stay there for a few days until everything settles down, but I had no idea of how to get the baby out of there, and I said to her, now keep quiet and go and hide in the corner, so he'll think you've gone away, and I'll try to do something.

After she had hidden herself so well that it really seemed as if she had gone away, I got up and rang the doorbell and I saw someone peeping through the peephole and I rang again, more insistently, and he opened the door a crack and asked me what I wanted. I smiled heartily, people have always told me that I have a confidence-inspiring smile, and said, I'm from the flat opposite, you know that we're in mourning, sitting *shiva*, and he said, yes, I saw the death notice, and he opened the door, a small man with a strained, almost familiar face, and pointed to the notice pasted to Aryeh's door, and I looked at it in surprise because it hadn't been there when I arrived the night before last, and now it hit me in the eye like conclusive proof of everything that had happened. We haven't got a quorum for the evening prayer, I said in a serious voice, the mourners sent me to ask you to join them, it's really important, and he pointed to the back room, which was now silent, and said, the baby's just fallen asleep, and I said, I'll stay here with him for a few minutes, as long as it takes, and he looked at me dubiously and said, I don't know where my skullcap is, and I felt like saying, maybe it's hanging on the tree outside, but I smiled and said, don't worry, they'll give you one, there are enough there for everybody, and he looked around hesitantly and in the end he sighed, okay, I won't deprive them of their prayers, and crossed the landing, leaving the door open behind him, and I hurried to the baby's room, and the minute the Evens' door closed behind him I picked the baby up and ran out of the flat, leaving the door open, and she jumped out of her hiding place and snatched him from me and we both ran, her with the baby and me with the suitcase, and kept running till we reached the main road.

There was a crowded café on the corner and I pushed her inside, it looked like a good place to hide, and I wanted to put off going home for a while too, because I was suddenly afraid that once she settled in she would never leave again, and we sat down panting among hordes of hedonists, everyone there looked happy and carefree and only her life and mine were coming apart at the seams, but she too had looked carefree to me only a few days before, like the queen of the neighbourhood she had looked to me then, with her key in one hand and her baby in the other, and in the blink of an eye everything had changed utterly. She unwrapped the baby's blanket, and I looked at him tensely, and this time he looked completely different, like another baby, his eyes were lighter, almost blue, and his hair was fair and not brown like Yonny's, no, he didn't resemble Yonny at all, but neither did he resemble his father at all, and for a moment I could understand the anxious man who had opened the door to me, because how could you ever really know, and once you began to suspect it was hard to stop, after all, even I was surprised. They say babies change, but such a big change in such a short time, perhaps she was actually a baby trader and now she had me in her trap, and I would go to jail for aiding and abetting in the kidnap of a baby, and who knows what had happened to the previous baby, with the sweet sheep's face, if only I had one like him as a memento of Yonny.

You have no idea how grateful I am to you, she said, and I smiled bitterly because I didn't know what to say, and then a young waitress with long legs in a mini-skirt appeared before us, and I thought sadly that I had never been really young, there were always girls younger than me, and now it was becoming more and more serious, it seemed there were more and more girls younger than me in the world and less and less women older than me, certainly in the café, and I felt nauseous and I ordered tea with lemon, and so did she, and it annoyed me that she didn't have a will of her own, and I thought of how she lost all her glory the minute she was deprived of her safe house and devoted husband, just like a painting which loses it glory when it's removed from its frame, and the same went for me, with my pathetic suitcase, which had suddenly grown old and worn, and I had to go home and squeeze myself back into the frame of the picture of my life. The baby started to cry and I tried to make him laugh and I held his hand and remembered the story my mother used to tell my brother, he couldn't understand a word of course but he would calm down immediately, and so I started telling him this story, which I didn't know I remembered, about little Absalom and his big black cat which was called Aryeh, and everybody asked him why his cat was called after a lion, it was like calling a snake Rabbit or a dog Fox, but Absalom didn't want to tell them. He knew that Aryeh was king of the cats and he deserved the name of a king, but he knew that everybody would laugh at him if he told them this. Prove that he's king of the cats, they would say, and he couldn't prove it, he could only sense it. He felt that more than Aryeh was his cat, he himself was Aryeh's child, and Absalom was very glad to be a cat's child. The baby smiled at me, amazing how that story works, and kicked his little legs, and I saw that one leg was longer than the other one, and I said to her, he seems to have a problem with one of his legs, and she said, yes, he has, that's why I've just been to the orthopaedist. So what did the orthopaedist say, I asked, and she said, that it would be all right, but it was hard for me to believe her, because how could something like that be all right, and I said to her, it seems to me that this orthopaedist is a charlatan, and she said, you sound exactly like my husband, and I felt sick when I thought of the little man who had gone to do a good deed and in the meantime his baby vanished. What will you do, I asked her, and she apparently felt my hostility, and she said, don't worry about me, I'll sit here a bit until I've calmed down and then I'll go home, he'll have calmed down too in the meantime, and things will settle down until the next time, and I breathed a sigh of relief and I was able to feel sympathy for her again, and I asked, isn't there anything to be done? And she said, no, I should never have left him then, it screwed him up completely. Or else you shouldn't have gone back, once you'd already left, I said, why did you go back to him? And she said, I've forgotten, and buried her face in the baby's tiny shoulder, exactly like my mother used to bury her face in Absalom's shoulder, and I looked away, it seemed too revolting to me, not to say cruel, to think that this tiny shoulder could wipe out your mistakes.

Through the window I suddenly saw her husband running round like a beetle and I remembered who he reminded me of, of little Uncle Alex, who had enjoyed an Indian summer late in life, and I didn't want to be present at their inevitable meeting, and I said to her, he's on his way here, and as he approached I saw that he had a skullcap on his head, apparently he had managed to pray a bit before he caught on to what was happening, a white skullcap glittering like a little sun, and she clung tightly to the baby but there was pride in her eyes, somebody was looking for her, not like me, for whom nobody was looking, and I stood up and walked out of the other entrance at precisely the moment he walked in, his eyes darting round in expectation and rage and the skullcap shining on his head.

I beat a hasty retreat from the main road and turned into a little street, afraid of meeting familiar faces, monstrous routine questions, and the hated route looked completely different, longer and darker, in the quiet side streets, rising and falling like waves, and all the time I tried to comfort myself with the thought that this was the last time, I would never see this quiet, irritatingly affluent street again, I would never have reason to tread it again, it would not lead me to him or from him and it would cease to exist as far as I was concerned, even if it was wiped off the face of the earth I would not miss it. This whole section of the city suddenly became superfluous, even infuriating, the refined, happy houses, with their cultivated gardens and big windows open to the street, as if they had nothing to hide and anyone could look inside the rooms, and I stood opposite one of these windows and saw shelves of books, books as far as the eye could see, and I could even smell them through the window, a smell of aromatic dust, long years, old paper. This must be the season of the year when books blossom, together with the citrus trees, and their blossoming is perhaps less blatant but more soothing, and I breathe in the familiar smell, which is precisely the smell of the rare book lent me by the Head of the Department, and suddenly I know that this book-filled house is the home of the Head of the Department, here he leads his quiet life, strolls from book to book, and I feel like climbing through the big window and sitting among the books, piling books on the table and laying my sick, tired head on it, and then the light went out in the window, as if the show was over and the curtain had come down, and it was time to wake up and go home, and I walk away slowly, trying to draw out the magic and make it last, like after the movies I used to see in the village. Once a week they would show a movie, and more than I remember them I remember the somnambulistic walk home, my feet bumping into stones and not feeling them, because the sweetness of the movie envelops me, accompanies me like a regal train, painting the road in soft colours, every movie is a proposal for the future, and all I have to do is choose, enter the wide gate, and now the gate is closing, perhaps a narrow crack remains, with no light coming from it but only a smell growing fainter all the time, and if I don't hurry it too will close, like these streets which are gradually narrowing, growing more crowded, and the windows are growing smaller, and here's the dark downhill slope I know so well, but suddenly everything seems strange, as if I've just returned from abroad and my eyes are accustomed to other dimensions, everything seems smaller, tiny, and I rush down the slope to our ground-floor flat, my legs trembling with tension, for what will I do if he's there and what will I do if he's not there.

The flat is closed and dark, and the old door opens obediently. For a moment I forget where to switch on the light and I stand

there in the dark, listening to the sounds of the house, and the
walls painted yellow by mistake give off a pale, subdued glow,
and I stroke the wall like a blind person, if only I could read by
its bumps and hollows everything it had seen, I would know what
Yonny had done that morning, if he called my name out loud, if
he looked for me first in the bathroom or the kitchen, and which
floor tile he was standing on when he saw my note, and what he
did after he read it. My hand encounters the switch and I press
it down and see before my eyes a white note and I snatch it up in
suspense and read, I wish I could go on a honeymoon with you,
and I recoil from the note which is now directed from him to me,
it's no accident that he left it here, that he didn't take it with him
or throw it in the rubbish bin, but left it where it was and gave it
a new role, and I angrily crumple up the cruel words which have
been readdressed to me with redoubled cruelty, and go into the
bedroom, seeking evidence of his sorrow, signs of his despair,
traces of his insult. Our covers are heaped on the bed, full and
swollen, as if our lifeless bodies are still lying beneath them, and
I even check to make sure, but no, we're not there, only warm,
fleshy air, with faded body odors, and the wardrobe is open,
his shelf is half empty, and his shoulder bag is missing, there's
no doubt about it, he went without me on our honeymoon to
Istanbul, and however ridiculous it may sound, I feel a little
insulted, how come he didn't stay here to grieve for me, how
did he dare to go without me, he didn't even try to look for
me, like the husband of Aryeh's neighbour, he made no effort
at all, I wasn't so far away, after all, hardly fifteen minutes'
walk. In the kitchen I see the coffee cup he drank from before
he left, he drank it to the dregs, he didn't leave a single sip, as a
memorial for the generations to come, and the fridge is almost
bare, and there's no bread, of course, and no sign of regret, or
any particular agitation of spirit, simply a flat left empty for a few
days, where life has stopped and will never be resumed again.

It all seems so temporary to me that I don't even feel like
putting my clothes back in the wardrobe, and I spill the contents
of the suitcase onto the bed, to fill the empty space on Yonny's
side, and cover my seductive clothes with the thick blanket,

afraid to even sit down, as if I mustn't be caught here, this isn't my house, I only came to peep at my former life, to nag it a bit, and soon the civilities will be over and I'll be thrown out. I feel as if I have to request permission for everything, only it's not clear from whom, permission to use the lavatory, the telephone, and I smile obsequiously at the yellow walls and pick up the phone, but I don't have his number, and I look it up in the telephone directory, surprised that I remember the alphabet at all, and for a minute I really do get mixed up, which comes first, R or S, his name is Rose, Professor Rose, and I hear his voice, with its heavy Anglo-Saxon accent, authoritative but very human, and I apologize for disturbing him, and then I apologize for not keeping our appointment, my mother died, I suddenly say and I begin to cry, to my own surprise, and I had to go to the funeral, and he immediately expresses his sympathy, and I don't know how to get out of it, and I say, she's not my real mother, she's my step-mother, my father's wife, I mean. He is silent for a moment, and then he says that he understands, but immediately adds, I don't want to burden you at such a difficult time, and of course we'll try to take the circumstances into consideration, but you really have to hand in your proposal soon, otherwise your appointment won't be confirmed, and I say, I want to meet you, I don't want to wait until the end of the *shiva*, and he says, God forbid, it isn't so urgent, and I insist, it's all right, she's only half a mother so half a *shiva* is enough, and I arrange to meet him tomorrow at half past ten in his office, and only then, when I have something to do tomorrow, am I able to start thinking about Aryeh.

Little by little I approach this thought, cautiously, like passing a place where there's been an accident and you're afraid to find out what happened, and full of dread you open the door of the burnt or crumpled car, because who knows what you'll find inside, perhaps a charred corpse will suddenly fall out, and I think of him with sorrow, without the hatred I felt before, like thinking about somebody sick, and I say, he's lost, he's lost, he's lost, how could I have known that he's lost, wandering round the rooms and muttering everything's lost, how could

I have known that everything's lost, that all new things are worse than the old ones, that it's always better not to know than to know, and then I thought of my mother and her double sorrow, and how I had succeeded in twice separating her from her love, once before I was born and once after, because with a baby in a pram he no longer wanted her, that was obvious even though he didn't dare say it to me, and to her dying day she would never forgive me, and I couldn't even be angry with her, because she was right, quite right, and I decide to phone her too and apologize, like I had apologized to the Head of the Department, and I dial and speak in a soft voice and she shouts to my father, Shlomo, it's Ya'ara, and to me she shouts, so how are you, how's the honeymoon, and I whisper, wonderful, fantastic. How's Istanbul, she asks, and I say, wonderful, and she asks, how's the hotel, does it really have a view of the Golden Gate? Take a lot of snaps because I have to see it, take a photo of the view from the window, and I say, okay, and ask, how's everything over there, what are you doing? Nothing special, she says, everything's okay, and I ask, how's Aunt Tirza? Hanging on, my mother says, and I whisper, Mother, do you remember Joab's words to David, after the death of Absalom, and she answers quickly, yes, why? And I answer, I dreamt about it today, I dreamt I was lying in a big bed and listening to you read it from the Bible, in that thou lovest thine enemies and hatest thy friends. I heard her taking deep breaths and my father's voice asking in the background, apparently he had noticed that she was listening intently, what, what do they say, and I said, tell him that I'm not they, I'm she, and then I asked, why did you stop reading to me from the Bible, and she said, stop it, Ya'ara, you know why, there's no point in discussing it now in a long-distance call, and I whispered, don't tell Daddy, it's not long-distance, and she asked in alarm, what are you talking about, and I said, I feel close to you now, I wanted to ask you to forgive me if I ruined your life. This is a waste of money, she said quickly, and I said, it's a waste of life, and she said, have fun, thanks for phoning, and I hung up and straight afterwards the phone rang and I didn't pick it up, I was sure it was her, suddenly realizing what I'd said and trying to check up on me, full of dread and despair. I counted ten rings and disconnected the phone, and in the silence that fell I lay down on the sofa in the living room, and wondered who else I owed an apology to, maybe to Shira, whose cat I had killed, leading it to its death, and thus I had emptied her little life, which was empty anyway. What have I done, I thought in horror, emptied an empty life, humiliated a humiliated man, burnt down a burnt temple.

I fetched a blanket because it was chilly, they'd stopped heating the building in honour of the spring, and covered myself on top of my clothes, I didn't even take off my shoes, I felt so transient, and surveyed the familiar sights like a sick person who knows his days are numbered, that everything will go on without him. A new family would come to live here soon, a young couple at the beginning of their lives, like we had been, but the woman wouldn't run from window to window like me, to make sure that no smell of bread was threatening to break in, and the estate agent wouldn't say, there's no bakery round here, a grocery shop at most, and she wouldn't blink apologetically at her husband, I'm allergic to the smell of bread, it makes me depressed, and then I heard a faint knocking at the door, not my mother's loud, nervous knock, and nevertheless I didn't dare move, for fear of being caught here, I covered my head with the blanket, and blocked my ears, and through all the barriers I heard a voice thick with cigarette smoke calling me, and I jumped up quickly and opened the door a crack, and I saw him standing and smoking in the dark stairwell, a little distance from my door, beginning to retreat, wearing a boyish sailor shirt, narrow blue and white stripes, the stubble of his new beard lightening his dark face, and when he saw me he threw his cigarette onto the floor and stepped on it, and then he quickly kicked the butt outside, into the neglected yard of the building, and I stood leaning against the door, keeping it open a crack, so that he couldn't squeeze in without the bulge hidden in the depths of his trousers rubbing up against my hips.

I had imagined it so often, how joyful it would be, how full of grace and consolation, to see him standing in my doorway, knocking on my door, calling me to him with all his broad, full presence, all his yellowing teeth, all his shapely fingers, all his outer- and under-garments, with all his narrow eyes, which moved further apart when he smiled and closer together when he was serious, and now they come closer together as his smile vanishes, his visitor's smile, and he says, I just wanted to check if you were all right, that you arrived safely, and I don't answer, clinging tightly to my cup of victory, and it's beautiful but heavy, hard to hold, and I say, I arrived, I'm here, as if he couldn't see for himself, and retreat slowly into the apartment, without turning my back to him, and he advances after me, he's never been here, it's strange to see him here, completely out of place. How can I receive him here when I'm a guest here myself, this apartment belongs to my former life, but I have no new life yet, so I have nowhere to take him, I have no life at the moment, and already I feel angry at him for intruding, and then, oh sweet happiness, he wants me, wants me, but in an hour from now he'll deny that he was ever here, and I remember what his sister said to me, don't go back even if he calls you, and these words peck at the sack of sweet happiness and it spills, trickles out of the tiny holes, sticky and coagulated, the way the ants like it, and he says, my sister sent me here, like a child he says it. What is it about this flat that makes everyone who crosses its threshold talk like a child, soon he'll start calling me Moley and I'll call him Ratty, and I ask, why, and he says, she thought there was something wrong, that you weren't feeling well, and I can't understand it, why on earth did she send him, after warning me not to go back, maybe it was some kind of trap and she was listening behind the door, testing me, and I had to answer coldly, send him away politely, but his presence here is so new to me that I can't bring myself to give it up, like a toy just taken out of its box, standing in front of me erect, fragrant, unused, with its funny striped shirt and its broken tooth, and the stubble on its cheeks, how come I didn't notice it before, and I'm dying to touch the new toy, see how it works, I've waited so long, and we stand at the entrance, I don't want to let him into the living room, and he isn't eager either, he just stands next to the door erect and smiling, almost the same

smile he had in his boyhood photographs, a little foolish, and as
on a blind date we appraise each other, keeping our impressions
to ourselves, and then he says, I bet you'd like something to eat,
after I've starved you for three days, and I say, but how can you?
You're sitting *shiva* for your wife. You think they check such
things in restaurants, he sneers, and I say, but if people come
to console you, what will they think? He licks the broken tooth
with his tongue and says, they'll think I went to the dentist, in
any case Ayala's there, and my mother-in-law, and all the rest
of them. And what about the dentist, I ask, and he says, don't
worry, I've already been there, he'll be able to reconstruct it, as
if I were his wife he told me not to worry, never imagining that
I flushed the precious fragment down the toilet with my own
hands, and then he looked me over with a critical eye and said,
are you coming?

I took the hint and said, just a minute, I'll go and change, and
in the bedroom I pounced happily on the wardrobe, and pulled
out the wine-coloured velvet dress, which was finally appropriate
for the season, and I made up my face and put on perfume, but a
moment before stepping out of the room I felt disgusted by all
this effort, and I thought, what are you so happy about, what's
there to celebrate, the fact that he suddenly smiled at you, and
I took off the dress and put on a pair of old denim overalls, and
quickly left the room before I could change my mind. I saw him
standing next to the window, softly humming the song he sung
in the shower, when we remembered, when we remembered,
when we remembered Zion, and for a moment I thought it was
Yonny, because Yonny liked standing next to this window, and
I felt something turning over gently inside me to see Yonny there,
only yesterday he had been one of the stones of the house and
suddenly he was making my heart tremble next to the window,
the dismal window overlooking the garbage bins, we could see
everyone who came down to throw out his garbage from it, and
we had a kind of game, reporting to each other on the garbage
traffic in the building, who was in charge in each apartment, and
if the traffic was particularly brisk we would try to guess why, it
was our folklore, the kind of thing which always sounds idiotic

and even disgusting to anyone outside, just like the pet names couples invent for each other, but nobody would understand, definitely not the person now standing at the deserted post and looking down at the bins, nobody would understand how sweet it was, how reassuring, to hear Yonny say, you won't believe it, today the husband's throwing out the garbage, and I would laugh gleefully, she must have let him fuck her last night and now he's happy, and Yonny would pull a pious virgin's face and giggle, it was disgusting conversations like these that gave us a feeling of intimacy.

So what would you like to eat, he asks, turning politely to face me, and I say, your song makes me sad, and he looks surprised, what song? The one you've been singing all day, I say, when we remembered Zion, and he shrugs his shoulders, I don't even know that song, I was just whistling something. Do you want to eat French, Italian, Thai, Chinese, Oriental? And what I want most is Yonny's salad, and I say Chinese just for the sake of saying something, and he says, there's an excellent new Chinese place in town, I even took Josephine there from the hospital last week, and it makes me sick to think of her eating, and I say, what, could she eat anything? And he says, hardly, she couldn't really taste anything, but she drank tea, she loved tea. Are you telling me, I think proudly, after all, she drank her last cup of tea from my hands, even if nobody knew about it, it happened, even if it wasn't supposed to happen, it happened, and I recoil slightly and say, perhaps we shouldn't go there, and he, gallantly, reassures me, why, you needn't worry about me, I feel comfortable with it. I didn't have the faintest desire to sit in the place where she had sat, to drink the tea she had drunk, even though lying in her bed didn't bother me, but he had already made up his mind, he opened the door for me, and after a minute the car door, and with an aggressive screech joined the movement of headlamps puncturing the night with pairs of small, round, yellow holes.

How did she manage to climb these stairs, I asked him as we climbed the narrow winding stairs leading to the restaurant, in an old building in the city centre. It was hard but I helped her, he bragged, shoving me in the small of the back to demonstrate how he had pushed her, and I felt sorry for the sick woman, gritting her teeth and climbing the cruel steps in order to please her husband. She had a will of iron, he said, when she wanted something she wouldn't allow herself to give in, and I said, but why did you let her exert herself like that, there are Chinese restaurants that are easier to get into, and I waited fearfully for his reaction, but to my surprise he said, you're right, I never thought about it, I wanted to take her to the best restaurant in town.

But she couldn't taste anything, I said, and he began to laugh, a frightening, unpleasant laugh, exactly as we emerged into the restaurant, as if we had risen straight from Hell, and a tiny waiter came up to us with an obsequious smile, and seated us at a little table next to the window, and said in stilted English, you were here before a few days, not so, sir, and Aryeh said yes, the remnants of his laughter still hovering round his lips, and he asked him, do you remember the woman who was with me? The waiter nodded eagerly, she had apparently left a powerful impression on him, and Aryeh said, she's dead, and the waiter looked at me as if I had murdered her myself, and retreated, walking backwards and making a series of little bows, and was immediately replaced by a waitress with two huge menus, and I hid behind my menu and thought, this place killed her, the effort to climb those steps, to look healthy, to please him, she only did it for him, and I was sure that she had suffered through every single minute, it must have been a nightmare for her, a terminally ill woman, to drag herself out of bed to go to a fancy restaurant, it was too much of an effort even for me, it could kill even me, to sit opposite him and eat politely and make civilized conversation as if nothing had happened, as if I hadn't ruined his life even before I was born, as if he hadn't ruined my life in exchange. He too was hidden behind his menu, only his beautiful fingers were visible, tapping it nervously, and I couldn't stand the tension and escaped to the toilets, where I rested on the lavatory seat, trying to pass the time, repeating to myself that now he was waiting for me, he wanted me, but I could barely persuade myself to go out to him, because his sudden courtship alarmed me no less than his sudden rage.

I ordered for you, he said when I rejoined him, I discovered their specialty, you can rely on me, and I said, wonderful, thank you, because I was relieved to have the decision taken out of my hands, but at the same time I was annoyed, where did he get off deciding for me, who did he think he was, and suddenly he asked, when's your husband coming back, this was the first time he had shown any interest in him, acknowledged his existence at all, and I said, the day after tomorrow, I think, and he said, you're separating, without even a question mark, and I was horrified to hear it said explicitly, and again I was angry, who does he think he is, deciding for me, but at the same time I wanted to signal that I was available, and I said, it looks like it. It's not a good idea to drag such things out, he said, and I asked what he meant by such things, and he shrugged his shoulders and said, bad relationships. But we have a good relationship, I tried to protest, and he said, that makes it even worse, and passed his long fingers over the short stubble of his mourning, and I thought that he was actually right, the good relations between us were worse than bad relations, because you grew addicted to them, you couldn't do without them, and he said, Ayala, my younger sister, dragged out a good relationship with a man who didn't suit her for ten years, and when she left him they already had four children, and her husband, a wonderful guy, agreed to let her go only on condition that the children stayed with him, and now he's in America, married to some woman who's bringing up Ayala's children, and she's here alone.

I began to tremble when I heard this, as if the story was about me, and I asked in a faint voice, does she regret it, and he said, that's not relevant, you can't judge by results, the step she took was right in itself, but now her life is a lot more difficult. So she changed a difficulty she could live with for a difficulty she can't live with, I said, and he said thoughtfully, I don't know, you can live with any difficulty, if you have hope, and I said, hope for what, and he said, at my age you don't look at things through a magnifying glass so much, you know that things change, circumstances change, the children will grow up eventually, they'll come back to her, everything's still open, and I, in order to be rid of this fate that was threatening me like a rapidly advancing hurricane, said, and what if my husband does suit me?

If he suited you you wouldn't be here, he sneered, and I thought, he's right, I'm like the woman in the legend, only my actions can bear witness, because all the rest is unclear, hidden, and nevertheless I tried again, maybe he suits me and I don't know it, and he exposed his broken tooth and said, maybe. I want him so much to suit me, I said, and he cut me short coldly, yes, I understand, letting me know that I had exaggerated my display of emotion, and I immediately wanted to take it back, and I put my hand on his, why was it never possible to talk to him about us, to ask what was going to happen to us, he always talked about my life as if it had nothing to do with his life, and he held my hand and said, don't be afraid, and for a moment I really wasn't afraid, I fawned on his hand, and I drank wine, and I tried not to think about the future, and just to enjoy the dishes he had ordered for me, rice with all kinds of nuts, and sweet crisp noodles, and I thought, what luck that I haven't lost my sense of taste, that's what life's all about, being able to taste things. He scarcely touched his food, only drank and smoked, carried away by a confused story about all kinds of wild bohemian parties he had gone to in Paris many years ago, there too I was an outsider, he said, but in this country being an outsider is a curse and there it's a blessing, it didn't take long before I was right in the swim of things, and it seemed to me that he was telling this to her and not to me, to my arrogant mother who didn't want him, and he began to slur his words, apparently he had begun drinking at home, and now he was ordering another bottle, and the waitress brought the wine and made eyes at him, they were green, her eyes, and beautiful, and I wondered if there was any difference between us as far as he was concerned, everything was always so impersonal with him, nothing ever had anything to do with him. The minute after I thought that he was hinting I should leave Yonny for him, he grew distant again, and now he was reaching out to stroke my hair, right before the waitress's eyes, and I sent her a triumphant look, you see, he wants me, me, and then I saw that he was looking at her too, not triumphantly, however, but provocatively, and the food stuck in my throat and I began to cough, just as Josephine had coughed on the last day of her life, spilling the tea I had brought her on the hospital sheets. The waitress ran to bring me a glass of water without my asking, and I drink it in despair, he doesn't want me, he doesn't want me, but suddenly it occurs to me that I'm so busy trying to work out if he wants me or not that I've forgotten to clarify if I want him, it's become axiomatic, something self-evident which needs no proof, and perhaps the time has come for me to try to examine myself, but how to do it is the question, it seems that it's easier to examine the other person. On the face of it the other is a closed book to you while you yourself are open, but in fact almost the opposite is true, because one minute I'm full of love for him, full as the plate in front of him, and thinking about how we'll go to bed together soon, and how we'll wake up in the morning, and everything seems thrilling to me, and when the *shiva*'s over we'll go to Istanbul, and I'll begin a new life, and my mother and father will never speak to me again, and he'll be my family, and his sister will adopt me, and I'll leave everything behind me, Yonny and the little apartment, I won't even go back to take my things, I'll buy everything new, so as not to mix the old with the new, maybe we'll even live in Istanbul, in order not to meet any familiar faces in the street, and I see how difficult it is to fit him into my life, much more simple to begin a new life in his honour than to fit him into the existing one. And then I feel sorry for my parents, especially for my mother who will lose me and him at once, and for Yonny who will remain alone with the crooked wardrobe full of clothes, what will he do with them, and I begin to have reservations about Aryeh, I see all his flaws, his thinning hair, and his deep lines, and his yellow teeth, all the signs of his advancing old age, his shortening life, and under all this lies his unstable, aggressive personality, and I think, what have I to do with him, I want to go home, to my little life, and perhaps this is why it's easier to worry about what he wants, because how can I trust myself, but how can I trust him, one minute he's smiling at me and the next at the waitress, and I notice that her hair is cut in a fashionable bob and I'm suddenly sure that she's the famous cigarette holder herself, his true love who accompanied him to the clothes shop. Perhaps he brought me here on purpose to provoke her, or to see her, perhaps the whole thing is a sick trick they're playing on me, and the food sticks in my throat and I ask him in a trembling voice, why did we come here of all places, and he says, you wanted Chinese food, didn't you, and I calm down a bit because of course it really was my choice, but perhaps he led me to it, I don't remember any more. He studies the menu again and recommends the fried banana with ice cream, but I can't stay there any longer, the suspicion is choking me, and I say, I don't feel well, let's go, and I stand up quickly, and almost fall down the stairs, why did I ever go to the bloody restaurant with him, I should have taken him home, to my first home, to show him the endless world of the citrus groves, and my beloved ruin in its heart, and there we would have been saved, but why is he hanging back, and why is his face so hard when he finally joins me, I wanted to pamper you, he says angrily, but apparently you can't take it.

I was sure you were in love with the waitress, I wail, and he says, that's exactly what I mean, you can't stand being pampered, you can't be happy, you immediately try to punish yourself, and punishments aren't hard to find, but it's a pity you have to find fault with others. So swear there isn't anything between you and the waitress, I say childishly, and he says sullenly, the facts are meaningless, nothing I say will reassure you, you know it yourself. That's not true, I weep, anything you say will reassure me, I can't stop crying, and he, instead of trying, whistles an irritated whistle all the way back, ignoring me, and next to his building he says, I wanted to drop you at your place, but you're in no fit state to be alone now, in a patronizing tone, as if he's doing me a big favour, and I say, you don't have to, only if you want to, feeling the familiar dependence clutching me again. It was only a few hours ago that I left his house, and here I am again, back in his trap, at his mercy again, grateful to him again, a miserable prisoner of love again, and I can't understand how it happened, he was the one who came to me, after all, he was the one who called me.

When we go inside, stepping down the passage in single file, I know that I'll never leave this place again, that I'll never win him and never be free of him, only a few hours ago I escaped almost by a miracle, but miracles don't happen twice, and in bitter resignation I go straight to the bedroom, like a horse to the stable, and there I take off my clothes and get into bed. He lingers, I hear the phone ring, the fridge open and close, the familiar sounds of my prison, and then he comes in with a beer can in his hand, relaxed as a tiger already sure of his prey, peels off his striped shirt with a sigh of relief, and his blue trousers, and lies down next to me naturally, and it seems to me that I have to please him, because this time it was me who spoilt things, and I begin stroking his back and he purrs with pleasure like a big cat, and then I feel a little bump that from close looks like a wart on an apple, swollen and elongated, and he says, yes, scratch me there, and I feel a little disgusted but I remember that in true love nothing is disgusting, so I go on scratching round the wart, until I feel a wetness on my fingers, which turn red at the tips, and I say, your wart is bleeding, and he says, ahh, and I say, you should see a doctor, you should take care of it, and he says, the only doctor I'm prepared to go to is the dentist, the others will manage without me.

But it's dangerous to leave it like this, I say, and he sniggers, it's more dangerous to leave the house. You know how hard it is to reach the doctor safely? And what for? I don't trust any of them, all diseases come from one source, which no doctor knows how to treat yet, everything comes from the mind. So go and get treatment for your mind, I say, and he says, entrust my mind to the hands of strangers? I don't trust anyone, and I won't be dependent on anyone, he speaks with such hatred, as if everyone is his enemy, and I say, so how can they help you, and he says, I don't need help from anybody, and the wart moves on his back like a beetle, and he says, stroke it, maybe that will help. I recoiled a little but I began to stroke it, and gradually the whole world shrunk to the size of his wart, and it was a clear and simple world, without tensions or contradictions, only one task which could keep me occupied for the rest of my life, to stroke his wart, because when you come right down to it, it's no more degrading than anything else, than stroking his prick or his ego, even less so, because it may really be of some use. Little by little his breathing grew heavier, and I thought that he'd fallen asleep, and I stopped for a moment and I heard him snigger, occupying yourself with somebody else's warts is relaxing, isn't it? Again that patronizing attitude, as if he was doing me a favour to let me touch him, and I sat up angrily in bed, how had I fallen into his trap again, how had he succeeded in twisting things again to make it seem as if I was the one who needed him, and I heard him say, I know what you need now, and he thrust me roughly backwards and sat me on top of him, with my back to him, facing his smooth, dark, motionless legs, completely detached from the rest of him, innocent, boyish legs, the toes arranged in a nice, sloping line, from big to small, without any deviations, and when he jiggled me on top of him I thought that whenever I saw an apple I would remember him, because of the warts, which meant that I would never stop remembering him because you see apples everywhere, like you smell bread everywhere, and so my world was closing in, and I would have to walk around with my nose stopped and my eyes closed, and I tried to remember the taste of apples, if they were sweet like the sweetness he was spreading through my body now, as if there was a funnel dripping honey at the end of his penis, and precisely because he was bitter his honey was sweet, because you felt the contrast, and that was what made it so thrilling, covering me with honey like Herod covered the Hasmonean child who refused to marry him, he killed her entire family and he wanted to marry her but she fell from the roof and died, and he buried her in honey for seven years so that people would say, he married a princess.

To and fro I row, with rhythmic movements, trying to free

myself, bumping into his body, and underneath me I feel his movements, up and down, and we collide with each other more and more violently. Like two coaches abandoned on old railway tracks, and the force of the collision pushes me forward until I almost fall off the bed and I can no longer see his legs, and it seems to me that I am there alone now, and all the sweetness gushes up from inside me, and this is the sweetness I love best, the kind that wells up inside me, like when I pressed up against the shelves in the library in the old neighbourhood, with honeysuckle and lantana branches in a flame of colour and scent at the windows, and soothing whispers coming from the reading room, and I'm alone among the shelves of thick novels, and I've read them all at least once but I come to visit them anyway, because they guard my future, they're my watch dogs, and I would stroke the dusty shelves, and take down a thick book, and immediately find what I was looking for, and from the old pages it would well up, this beloved sweetness. I would turn to face the window, put the book between my hot thighs, look at the citrus groves and the couples disappearing into them, and once I saw Absalom there, tall and handsome I saw him rising from the earth, as if all those years in the grave he had grown and developed, and now he was coming back to life, emerging into the world at a time that suited him, an age that suited him, the earth had nourished him as if he were a tree. I was so happy to see him, and I thought of how glad my parents would be, how I would bring him to them like a present, how I would leave him at their door and run away, and never return, and then he thrust his face towards me from the other end of the bed, and turned me round to face him, and I was almost surprised to see him, and I said, I forgot you were here, I thought I was alone, and he said, I know, it's all right, and I believed that he really did know and it was worth it, all of a sudden it was all worth it, because it was sign that he knew me from within, if I could forget him. I kissed his mouth, which was dry and muscular, and I pressed up against him and said, I want to be here with you always, and he said, are you sure, and I said, yes, and he said, why, and I said, because I love you, and then he asked me

the most off-putting question, what do you love about me, and
I said, that your footsteps among the bookshelves don't make
a sound, and he asked, and what else, and I said, all the rest I
hate but apparently that's what counts.

13

According to my watch the time was nine but according to Aryeh's, peering at me dark and threatening from his left wrist, it was already almost ten, and I jumped out of bed and got dressed quickly. He lay in the middle of the bed, his eyes closed, his left arm, with the watch, over his forehead and his body covered up to the shoulders by a floral sheet which gave him the look of a harmless old Indian woman wrapped in a sari. When I opened the door, carefully reconnoitering the long passage, I heard him ask, where are you going?

His eyes were still closed but his mouth was open, with his broken tooth peeping out, and I said, to a meeting at the university, and I couldn't understand why my voice was apologetic, as if I had something to hide, and he opened his eyes and asked, so important that you have steal out while I'm sleeping? And his voice grew aggressive, and mine even more apologetic as I said, I'm not stealing out, I didn't want to wake you, and he kicked off the sheet and said, so why didn't you wait for me to get up?

Because my meeting's at half past ten, I said, I mustn't be late, and he said, everybody is late at the university, you think I don't know the university? And I lost my temper and said, why are you talking nonsense, and he sat up suddenly and said quietly, don't you dare talk to me like that, you hear? I don't know what you want of me, I stammered, and he said, the question is if you know what you want of yourself, only yesterday you said that you wanted to stay here forever. I do, I said, but that doesn't mean that I can't go out for a few hours, I was going to come back, and he yelled, don't come back, you hear, if you go now then don't come back, and I looked despairingly at my watch and it still said nine and I didn't dare go up to him to see what the time was now, but I knew it was late, and I felt so tense that I almost wept, what do you want, what do you want of me, and he said, I don't want anything of you, just for you to be consistent, if you say that you want to stay here forever, and that you love me, how can you say that a meeting at the university is more important to you than I am, and I yelled, you're twisted, look how you twist everything, where's the contradiction, why do I have to choose, isn't it enough that in the important things I have to choose, do I have to choose in nonsense like this too? Why does it mean that I don't love you if I have to hurry to a meeting, and he said, because that's the way I see it, and you're supposed to consider my feelings, and immediately, in a patronizing tone, not that I need you here particularly, I just wanted to put your declarations to the test, and I see that as I always knew you can't be relied on in anything, you just talk, you've got no idea of what it means to love, of how a real woman behaves when she's in love.

I don't believe it, I screamed, I don't believe I'm really hearing this, and he went on, I can't believe that I let you sleep in Josephine's bed, she was a real woman, she knew how to love, not like you, and I shrieked, I've never shrieked like that in my life, but she's dead, you pervert, that's why she's dead, you killed her with the insane tests you gave her all the time, and he shrieked right back, how dare you blame me, get out of this house.

That's exactly what I'm trying to do, I yelled, and he announced with a snort of triumph, there, you see, you admit it yourself, your meeting is just an excuse, and I walked out of the room and slammed the door as hard as I could, and I heard the dark voice behind me, I'm warning you, Ya'ara, if you go there's nowhere for you to come back to, and I said, I know there's nowhere for me to go back to, but I forgot to shout, and nobody heard the words but me. I hurried outside, and as I descended the steps I saw a taxi drawing up next to the building and the grieving family stepping ceremoniously out of it, the mother and the sister and her husband, and the mother nodded to me, she apparently remembered me from yesterday, and I said *bonjour*, careful to get the accent right, but my voice shook because of my crying, which grew louder as I walked away from there, and all the way to the bus stop I cursed him, and then myself, how could I have been so mistaken, how could I not have seen him as he really was, how could I have failed to realize that he was completely dependent on my dependence on him, that this was the only thing he wanted from me.

In the empty bus I sat next to a window, weeping at the lively streets and the white smoke rising from the hospital chimney, and I thought about Tirza lying there, reading in the little mirror, opposite the desert landscape, with a new patient in the narrow bed next to her, with or without a husband, with or without children, what difference does it make at this stage, and perhaps it doesn't make any difference at the stage I'm at either, and I got off into the cool corridors of the university, its stifling modern basements, here and there a giant window through which the world looks far more tempting than it really is, a world in a display window, up for sale, and I feel like stopping the rapid footsteps around me and saying, what are you running for, believe me, there's nowhere to hurry to, I've just come from there, from that real, glittering, expensive world, and nothing there is what it seems, everything's rotten, believe me, there aren't as many worms in the cemetery as there are in the most beautiful streets in that world, but I held my tongue and went into the toilets to wash my face, and when I saw myself in the mirror I cried even harder because I looked so sad, even sadder than I felt, with red eyes and swollen eyelids and bitter lips, and I thought, how am I going to get out of this mess, how am I going to get out of this mess.

Just then someone came out of one of the cubicles and stood next to me to wash her hands, and she looked so right, not beautiful but all right, everything about her was all right, she didn't have an open wound in the middle of her face like I did, she looked like I did before it all began, and opposite the mirror I mumbled, Oh that I could go back to the beginning again, Oh that I could go back to the beginning again, until I stumbled out of the toilets and climbed the stairs to the Head of the Department's office, looking in the other direction as I passed

the Teaching Assistants' room, but unable to avoid hearing the
cheerful chatter coming from inside it, and I felt like someone
from another world, like a refugee, the survivor of a distant war
coming face to face with her previous existence and fleeing from
it, appalled, as if it were the enemy.

His door was open, and I knocked on it and went inside
without waiting for an invitation, and I saw an open book in
front of an empty chair, and I sat down in the chair opposite,
and laid my head on the cool wood of the desk and tried to
hold back my tears, but they raged in my eyes, the more I tried
to suppress them the less they obeyed me, wetting my knees like
when I washed the dishes opposite the little window and the
water would slide down my apron onto my knees, and Yonny
would potter about next to me and tell me all kinds of things. I
would play little games to make it more interesting, listen to only
every third word, for instance, and then he would ask, what do
you think, and I would begin to stammer, I didn't hear so well,
tell me again, and then I would listen only to every second word,
the effort would make my head ache, and the third time round
his voice would be low and lifeless, and I would say crossly,
speak up, I can't hear you, why are you whispering if you want
me to hear you, splashing water angrily out of the sink, and the
wet would spread to my stockings, and now too I could feel the
wetness making my skin prickle, as if some insect was crawling
over me, and a sudden warmth on my shoulder, and a pleasant
voice with a heavy Anglo-Saxon accent saying, may you know
no more sorrow.

I raise my red, swollen face, and he looks at me gently and
asks, did it come as a surprise? And I ask in alarm, what,
because everything that happened to me this morning surprises
me, horrifies me, but he could hardly be referring to that, and
he says, Mother's death, Mother he says, as if she's his mother
too, and I think, I really shouldn't lie, how am I going to get
out of this now, and I mumble, she was only my step-mother,
and he nods politely, so I assume your biological mother is no
longer alive, and I want to shut him up already, and I say with
my head bowed, no, she died in childbirth, like in the Bible. Your

birth? he asks, and I say, no, my brother's, and he asks, how old is your brother? And I whisper, he died too, a few months after my mother, and he recoils slightly, sits down on his chair, appalled by my morbid family history, and heaves a sigh that sounds like a grunt of astonishment, and suddenly he looks to me like a little pig, pink and soft, and I begin to laugh in despair, because this meeting which I had anticipated as if it was my salvation, now seems as hopeless as everything that had preceded it, no more but also no less.

In order to hide my laughter I bow my head again, so he'll think it's an understandable outburst of weeping, and it apparently works, because he presses a tissue into my hand, and I mop up my wild tears with it, and my head begins to ache when I raise it to the pale eyes of the Head of the Department, and I say to him, almost imploringly, you won't believe, Professor Rose, what's been troubling me for the last few days, the fate of that carpenter whose wife was stolen from him by a trick, and as if that wasn't enough he had to wait on her and her new husband too, and his tears of sorrow flowed into their cups. For several days now I haven't been able to get him out of my mind, sympathizing with him in his plight and cursing the apprentice who stole his wife and the wife herself who conspired with him, but this morning, on my way here, I understood something.

What did you understand? He peers at me doubtfully, the astonished grunt still hovering over his full lips, ready to leap out again, and I try to stop it with a question, what was he crying for, in your opinion, what exactly was he crying for when he stood and waited on them?

What do you mean, surely it's obvious, the Head of the Department sat up, he was crying for himself, for his wife who had become somebody else's, for the terrible injustice which had been done him! And I look at his lips confidently meeting and parting, and I say, yes, that's what I thought too until this morning, but now I realize that it wasn't for the injustice done him that he was crying but for the injustice he did his wife, he's the villain of the story, even more than the apprentice and certainly more than his wife.

What do you base your argument on, he asks coldly, almost contemptuously, and I'm afraid that the vestiges of his faith in me are crumbling, and now he too will be against me, but I can't stop, I whip the book out of my bag and open it wide. I base it on what's written here, why did he agree to send her to the apprentice to obtain the loan in the first place? He was clearly endangering her, simply in order to get hold of the money, and why didn't he take the trouble to look for her for three whole days? For three nights he went to sleep without her, got up in the morning without her, and only on the third day he went to the apprentice to ask what had happened to her, and then, when he heard that the youths had abused her on her way, instead of taking her home, looking after her and comforting her, he agrees so easily to divorce her, as soon as the apprentice offers him the money for the contract. Why doesn't he try to get to the bottom of it, why doesn't he ask her, after all, he was the one who sent her on this adventure in the first place. Don't you see? There's a sequence of crimes and omissions concealed here, right under our eyes, a whole sequence of crimes which seal the fate of the Temple!

The Head of the Department looked at me in embarrassment, blinked rapidly, for a moment I thought he was winking at me, until he said in a serious voice, but the wife doesn't seem like such a saint to me either, Ya'ara, I haven't actually studied this legend myself but it's my impression that she collaborated with the carpenter's apprentice.

How can you tell? I pounced on him, it's impossible to judge her by her feelings or her words because they aren't described in the text, but we can't judge her by her actions either, because she's completely passive. She was sent to the apprentice by her husband, we don't know if she stayed with him for three days of her own free will or if he locked her up, perhaps he himself was guilty of the abuse for which he blamed the youths, and then her husband divorces her and the apprentice marries her. What's the wonder that she agreed to marry him after she was abandoned so shamefully, don't you see that the legend doesn't blame her?

He takes the open book from me and reads, his eyes accompanying the words with a worried expression. Yes, he admits, her actions do not appear to bear witness against her and therefore it's impossible to convict her, even if she's guilty it's impossible to blame her.

Right, I say, encouraged, but you know who else the legend blames, apart from the carpenter and his apprentice?

Who, he asks with interest, and I say, you, me, all the listeners and readers in all the generations who swallowed the simplistic, tear-jerking message and ignored the true course of events. Nothing is easier than feeling sorry for the weeping, betrayed, humiliated carpenter, but how can you ignore the cruel fatefulness of the details? The legend misleads the readers on purpose, tests them, and even we failed to pass the test.

You're right, he sighs, spreading his arms out apologetically, the beloved book buried deep in his lap, and I know that he won't part with it again, but why do you think that the legend misleads us?

Why do you think life misleads us? I say, and he raises his eyes to me and I see the struggle between them, one of them for me and the other against me.

You remember what God said to Moses, I coax the favorable eye, Moses was writing down the *Torah* and he complained about a verse that gave an opening to heresy, and God said to him, Son of Amram, write, and if anyone wants to err – let him err!

You think it's possible to prevent error? If anyone wants to err he'll do so anyway, and we both apparently wanted to err in our reading of this legend, each of us for his own reasons, and it's not so terrible, because all three of them are already dead and sentence has already been passed, but if we err in our reading of life we pay a real price. That's what I'll try to examine in my thesis, I'll try to find other legends of the destruction which purposely mislead the reader, which help him to fail the test, because the error is above all spiritual, and therefore its correction must be spiritual, don't you see? Heaven is full of pending sentences which haven't yet been passed!

He looked up in surprise at the narrow strip of sky painting his window, as if to see the sentences hanging there, and smiled faintly. I doubt if you'll find any more material, he said, I can't think of even one more legend which will fit in with your thesis, but go ahead and try, if you succeed it could be extremely interesting, and if not, you'll have wasted your time.

You could say that about anything in life, I said, if you don't succeed it's a waste of time. It's a waste to be born if you don't succeed, it's a waste to get married if you don't succeed. And he said, yes, but here it's easier to judge, the criteria are clearer, and I said, in every field they're quite clear, it's just hard to admit.

You may be right, he said, but we won't go into it now, I want an outline of your thesis in a week's time, or else we won't be able to keep you on here next year, and I said in alarm, only a week? I had to try to save my entire life this week, so how was I going to manage? But he was tough, this is your last chance, Ya'ara, there was pressure on me not to give you even that, but because of your loss I'm prepared to give you one more chance, if you don't prove that you're making progress now the university won't be able to offer you anything.

And if I don't manage to get it done in a week, I tried to argue, and he said firmly, then your appointment will go to somebody else, I'm sorry, and I said, okay, I'll try, and rose heavily to my feet, and he smiled, it's not enough to try, you must succeed, and I whispered, Professor Rose, if you only knew what I'd sacrificed to come to this meeting, and he said, excuse me? What did you say?

Nothing, I mumbled, there comes a moment from which nothing will ever be simple again, and he said in an official tone, yes, the moment when we're born is that moment, you apparently came late to that realization, and I laughed, or else I've only just been born, I was simply born late, and I turned to the door with my eyes lowered, and then I remembered, you know, once somebody said to me that everyone who errs knows in advance that he's going to err, he simply can't stop himself. The surprise is perhaps in the size of the error and not in the fact that it takes place, and the Head of the Department snickered and said as if to himself, anyone who doesn't want to err won't err, and I saw his big feet in shabby sandals and socks, stretched out in front of him with the irritating ease of someone who has every aspect of his life under control, and I couldn't resist it and stepped on them as if by accident, with both my feet, and he pulled them back and hid them under the desk, and I said, sorry, I didn't see, and I was so ashamed that I went up and hugged him and asked, does it hurt? And he said, no, it's all right, and I felt his glasses trembling on his eyes in the intensity of his surprise.

In the Teaching Assistants' room the door was open, and there was nobody there, and I went in quickly and shut the door behind me. There was a long narrow table standing against the wall, and at one end a small window opened onto a vast view, a narrow corner window with the whole of the Temple Mount squeezed into it, the golden dome of the mosque surrounded by stately trees, and the sinking City of David, and all around narrow roads with cars gliding slowly past, like a funeral procession, and the new city swallowing the gold with long sharp wolf's teeth, towers and high-rise buildings, and peeping out between them here and there faded red roofs, like poppies in a field on the last day of spring, and I opened the window and stuck my head out, to come closer to the brilliant sight, to breathe in the soft air of the brief spring, perfumed air, with a faint smell of fire, and I saw the flames slithering up the mount, advancing implacably on their bellies, surrounding the Temple which was narrow at the back and wide in the front and resembled a lion, I saw how the radiance turned to coal, and how the tears of the carpenter flowed into the empty cups when the great famine began, and afterwards into his hands falling to pieces in sorrow, and when they stood facing each other, two lifeless skeletons, as the great fire painted their lean bones pink, weakly bowing their heads like a pair of cyclamens, did he ask her to forgive him then, and did she say, I've forgiven you but heaven hasn't?

The door opened behind me and I turned round to see Netta, who came into the room with her springy walk, holding a cup of coffee, the black curls crawling over her head like insects, and in her other hand a pile of papers, and she said, what a visitor, mockingly and not joyfully, I've been doing your work for two months now, and I said, you're not doing it for me, you want to show them that they can do without me, and Netta smiled triumphantly and said, right, and it's even easier than I thought, and I laughed, because I actually liked her honesty, and I said, but I'm not a threat to you, you'll get where you want to, don't worry, you would never get yourself into trouble for the sake of love.

Love? she said in alarm, God forbid, this is my love, and she pointed to the pile of papers and divided it in two and said, I'm prepared to share my love with you, let's mark the exercises together, like we did at the beginning of the year, and I remembered how we would sit in this room, with the little window peeping at us from the corner, pencilling comments in the margins of the exercises handed in by the Introductory Course students, and in the evening Yonny would arrive, sit down on the narrow table, crumpling a few pages underneath him, and I would collect my belongings and leave with him, and there was that halo of home and safety guarding me, and now it's gone, and Netta gives me a penetrating look and says, you've changed, and I say, how, and she says, I don't know, and pushes the papers towards me and I recoil, not yet, I have a million things to do, I'll come back later.

She shrugs her shoulders, falls avidly on the pile, and I leave, floating like a ghost down the corridors of my former life, sliding down the escalator into the bus, which has already started driving slowly off, I don't know why I'm in such a hurry, there's nothing waiting for me at home, apart from a little note I find on the door, hastily folded, which says in my mother's elegant handwriting: Yonny's landing at three-thirty in the afternoon, be there to meet him! with an assertive exclamation mark, and I go into the dark apartment and read the note again. How much anxiety and dread there are in the few words, in the little exclamation mark, and I say, poor Mother, poor Mother, I say it perhaps a hundred times, and afterwards, poor Daddy, and

afterwards, poor, poor, poor Yonny. I look at the big clock
on the wall and it's already almost twelve o'clock, and I call
the airport and there really is a flight arriving from Istanbul, at
fifteen-thirty, how does she know he's on this flight, what did
she do to find out, to save my life, the effort invested in the few
words breaks my heart, and I quickly reserve a place in a taxi
to the airport, and only then I look around me, not knowing
where to begin, and I run to the grocer and buy bread and wine
and cheese, and vegetables and fruit, especially his favorite green
apples, and in the shop next door I buy flowers, a bunch of white
flowers, as befitting someone coming home from a honeymoon,
and with mounting excitement I run home, and put everything in
the fridge, and throw out all the old food, and open the shutters,
and the windows, as if to let the shy spring in, and it hesitates but
in the end it enters, wandering about the rooms with delicate,
dancing steps.

All of a sudden I become efficient and energetic, something
akin to happiness, clear and unequivocal, even more agreeable
than happiness because you're less afraid of losing it, and I
decide to bake a cake in his honour, his favourite chocolate
cake, and without the cookery book I succeed in remembering
everything even though it's years since I made it, and when it's
in the oven I begin to clean the house, enthusiastically wiping
away the sorrow and neglect, and I make up my mind that it
has to succeed, when he sees how hard I've tried he'll forgive
me, the cake will break him, if nothing else will, and I change
the sheets, preparing the bed for our late love, and I hardly think
about Aryeh, even when I think about him I don't really think
about him, because I'm in too much of a hurry, my hands are
in too much of a hurry, my feet are in too much of a hurry,
even my heart's beating fast, like preparations for a wedding,
because this will be our day, mine and my dear Yonny's, who
will have to forgive me. Sometimes you have to descend in order
to ascend, I'll tell him, sometimes you have to part in order to
meet, and today we're meeting for the first time, a real meeting,
and I won't let him turn me down, I'll fill him with love like you
fill up an empty container, and he'll fill and fill until he won't be

able to move with the weight of my love, and in the evening we'll go to my parents, hand in hand, maybe with our arms around each other, and my mother will see that everything's all right, that she doesn't have to worry because I have somebody to look after me.

I bathe quickly and then make my face up discreetly, the way he likes it, not too much, and I put on a white dress, even though it's a little ridiculous to wear such a festive dress on an ordinary day, but it's my wedding day, in the arrivals hall at the airport my real wedding will take place, and all that great crowd of arriving passengers and their families will be our wedding guests, they'll sit on their luggage and watch the emotional meeting of the bride and groom, and all of them together will be the witnesses and the sanctifiers of our union, and all of them together will sing in a great voice around us, they'll carry us shoulder-high and sing, once more will the voice of mirth and the voice of gladness, the voice of the bridegroom and the voice of the bride be heard in the cities of Judah and the streets of Jerusalem, and like pilgrims on the three pilgrimage festivals we will all go up together in a great procession to the Holy City.

Enthusiastically I spread out the carpet on the clean floor, and take the dark cake out of the oven and put it next to the flowers, and the combination of the white and the brown reminds me of him, of the moment when my hand was on his, and I arrange the apples in a bowl, and on almost every one of them I find a brown wart, and I think angrily that I'll never be able to forget him, and I turn the apples round so that each of them will hide the brown wart on the other, and suddenly I realize why things never worked out between us, because instead of hiding his warts I only emphasized them, that's why it didn't work out, but I won't regret it, because today is my wedding day, and tonight, on this bed, I'll get pregnant, and all my sorrow and all my joy, all my fears and all my memories, all my disappointments and doubts, all my anxieties and wishes, all of them together will be transformed into a living creature, soft and exquisite, tender and tempestuous, a baby who in twenty years time will rummage through old photographs, and from now on I'll live only for her, because my love life is coming to an end today, in this taxi journey, in this care not to dirty my white wedding dress.

I press up against the window in the crowded taxi, and out of the corner of my eye I see the flame, a tree blooming red behind one of the buildings, an unextinguished brand, and I see that I wasn't dreaming then, on the way to Jaffa, it really happened, and this flaming tree reminds me of a great danger, and I think that it's forbidden to look at it too closely, just as it's forbidden to look at the sun, and I turn to look at the woman next to me, a young woman with a floral scarf on her head, and she tells the woman sitting next to her, an older woman, perhaps her mother, about a baby who was born in her building and died two days later, and he couldn't be buried because he wasn't circumcised, so they performed the circumcision after his death, and I'm appalled, what about the foreskin, did they bury him with the foreskin, or did the bereaved mother wrap it up in newspaper and hide it in the wardrobe, like my mother hid her beautiful braid, which even lying in the drawer was more full of life than she was.

The taxi stops at the entrance and I enter my wedding hall with festive steps, surveying the assembled crowd, and it seems a little strange to me that I don't know anyone, they're my guests after all, and nobody comes up to congratulate me, I suppose it must be difficult to recognize a bride without a bridegroom, soon, when Yonny arrives, everything will become clear, when he walks down the slippery lane, serious until he sees me, and then his face will blaze with joy, blaze like the crest of that tree, and I'll run up to him and we'll advance slowly together to the sound of the congratulations of the crowd, who will finally understand what's happening here. I stand there, hiding behind the broad back of a young man, to be on the safe side, because suddenly I have a terrible fear that perhaps he won't come walking into the hall alone, perhaps there'll be a woman leaning on his broad, bronzed arm, which looks like a prosthesis against the background of his naked body, and perhaps he won't be hurrying to our sparkling flat, but to hers, some solitary traveller unable to believe her luck, and I am more and more convinced that this is what will happen, and nevertheless I decide that even then I won't give up, the wedding will take place even if the groom has reservations, in fact despite his objections it will take place, despite the objections of his new lover. The arriving passengers stream down the marked lane, a milling, swarming herd without a shepherd, looking round in expectation of a happy surprise, and all kinds of hands wave around me, loving hands, longing to embrace, and then I see him, advancing slowly, alone, so slowly that he seems to be walking backwards, so alone that everybody seems to be withdrawing from him, as if he's sick, and he is not part of the cheerful bustle and excitement, sunk into himself he advances, the familiar bag on his shoulder, his face pale and worried.

For a moment I see his downcast eyes searching, furtively he's searching for me, shamefully he's searching for me, and I want to break out of the crowd and embrace him, but something stops me, something paralyses me, like the beautiful Mazal Sheinfeld, as his eyes come closer, childish and helpless, facing slightly downward at a doglike angle, perplexed but hopeful in spite of everything, and the soft, heavy body advances towards me with its sloppy walk, and for a moment I see him in his own right, Yonny apart from me, Yonny entitled to a life of his own, and I say, leave him be, let him go, don't stand in his way, for at his side I suddenly see a transparent figure walking next to him, tenuously attached to him, I see the happy Yonny, his eyes shining and his stride rapid, and the gap between them is sharp and piercing, and the happy Yonny looks at me indifferently, independent of me, and the unhappy Yonny is looking round in despair, and I know that even if I pounce on him warmly, it will be more like the warmth with which an animal pounces on its prey, and I see an attractive young woman in a purple trouser suit coming up rapidly behind him, and a young man with fair curly hair breaks out of the crowd and rushes up to her, and they embrace fervently, and Yonny's eyes linger on the couple, enviously watching their embrace, and I understand that this is the only thing connecting us to each other now, the only

thing we have in common, envy of the attractive young couple
in love.

He is already walking past me with his babyish nose, and I see
his vulnerable back, and his surprisingly slender neck turns from
side to side, searching for me, in spite of everything searching
for me, and I am angry at this search which has become so
pathetic, I'll never forgive you, I say, for searching for me after
you let me go, and I am swallowed up in the crowd, watching
him from a distance, his back in the green checked shirt, with
the shoulders stooping slightly forwards, and now he leaves the
hall, advances slowly towards the taxi rank, and the green of
his back turns grey, suddenly it clouds over, and I see the sky
opening, the thin skin of the world cracks, and behind it a great,
electrifying radiance is revealed, and I think, if this is lightning,
where's the thunder, how can they be separated from each other,
lightning without thunder is like a bride without a groom, and
again the skin splits and the lightning seems to cut the world in
two, half the world for me and half for him. He has already
almost vanished into his half, standing obediently in line for a
taxi, and I in my half peep at him from behind a parked car,
my dress stained by dirty rain, rain mixed with sand, hard to
believe it was once white, just as it's hard to believe that I was
full of expectation, even hope, that I thought we would go home
holding each other, and sit opposite the flowers and the cake, but
I forgot to think about what would happen afterwards, about the
moment when one human being has to truly face another, and
face life, fragile, broken life, which is vengeful and vindictive
and which no illusion can appease.

I sit down on the wet pavement, watching the rapid advance
of the long queue, only a minute ago he was last and now he's
among the first, all you need to get ahead is perseverance, it
seems, all you need to do is stand in one place, whereas I rush
about from place to place and always remain behind, so that I
can get away at the right moment, and I see him looking round
in one last, exhaustive attempt, and I wonder if he'll give up his
place at the head of the queue for my sake, if he'll leave the taxi
rank now and start searching again, but it doesn't happen and

an empty taxi draws up, and he squeezes in with his grey back, his pale, pitted face, his sheep's curls, his snub nose, and now he's inside, settling with a sigh onto the bench of his new life, and I know that this sight of Yonny setting out on his way, this painful sight, will remain in my eyes forever, like a cataract, and never go away, and everything that happens in my life, sad or happy, will stand abashed beside it, a kind of criterion by which everything else will be judged.

As soon as the taxi disappears I go to the end of the queue, treading in his big footsteps, the wild spring rain jumping around me, hot and dark, with a taste of sand, and I get into a taxi, which fills up quickly and will probably catch up with his quite soon, and so we will go up to the city in a strange convoy, leaning on each other for the last time, and I shiver with damp and fear, because the cars whistle past us one after the other, like arrows shot from a taut bow they whistle in my ears. If I were sitting with him in the taxi now, held in his arms, I wouldn't even notice it, but when I'm alone all the sounds are intensified, there's no one to absorb the blast, and I feel all the pot-holes in the road, the sharp swerves, and I think, how will I cope, how will I get through this day, this evening, where will I go?

Again I press against the window but with my eyes closed, there's nothing to see outside, there's nothing to see inside, all I see now is Aryeh prowling round his house among the condolence callers like a caged lion, and I wonder at what moment he'll find a pretext to leave the house and come to me, it's absolutely clear to me that this will happen, he won't give up my dependence on him, our sick games, so easily, but this evening there'll be a surprise in store for him, because the door will be opened by Yonny, disappointed that it's not me, and Aryeh will stand before him disappointed that it's not me, and they'll stand there facing each other, the two men in my life, who succeeded in cancelling each other out, and then in cancelling themselves out, left me utterly alone, abandoned to the whistling of the cars.

When we reach the city the taxi begins to empty, each of the passengers takes his luggage and gets out, and only I am left, and the driver turns to me and asks me where I want to go, and I open my mouth like a fish, because that's the one thing I haven't thought about, and he laughs, honey, if you haven't got anywhere to go you can come home with me, and I almost decide to get off at my parents' place, but I can't stand the thought of their questions, and I say, the university, and the driver says in surprise, so late? You're so dedicated? Because it's already getting dark, and I don't reply, I haven't got the strength to talk, and again I see the smoke rising from the hospital chimney, the smoke of the destruction disguised as the smoke of repentance, enveloping Tirza's heavy body as she stands at the dark window, waiting only for me.

At the entrance to the university the taxi stops, and I get out heavily. The driver asks, what about your luggage, and I say, I haven't got any luggage, and he marvels, what, you went abroad without any luggage? And I say, I didn't go abroad, I just went to meet somebody coming back. So where is he? Why are you alone? he asks in surprise, and I say, that's a good question, a whole book could be written about that question, and I ride up the escalator, against the stream, because everybody's going down now, surging down the steps in a raging torrent, and only I go up, running quickly before it's too late, as if my life depends on it, and I go into the library, the subtle smell of books envelops me, and I ask the librarian for the book, and she says, but it's a reserved copy, you can't take it out, and I say, I'm not taking it out, I'm going to read it here. We're closing in fifteen minutes, she warns me, and I say, okay, fifteen minutes is enough, and with the book in my hands I sit down at a table in the corner, and page though it with trembling hands, without even knowing what I'm looking for, but when I find it I'll know.

Everybody around me is packing up, I see Netta in the distance putting the pile of papers into a big bag, and only I am still intent on the book as a mother on her baby, examining its perfect limbs, I keep turning and turning the pages, and I know that no cruel rule will separate us, and when the loudspeaker calls on everyone to leave the library I go to a remote corner and lie down between the shelves, on the hard carpet, listening to the soft footsteps rising from it, and I hear the chief librarian pressing the staff to hurry, I have a wedding this evening, she says, I have to lock up, and after a few minutes the glaring lights go out, only the pale emergency light remains on, and I know that until tomorrow morning I'm a prisoner here, without anything to eat or drink and without anyone to keep me company, alone with my book.

For the first time since it all began I breathe a sigh of relief, crawl over to the pale light and sit down under it, only the whisper of the pages is audible in the great halls, and I go on searching until I find the legend, and I know that I've found exactly what I need, the legend about the daughter of the priest who abandoned her faith on the eve of the destruction of the Temple, and her father mourned her as if she was dead, and on the third day she came and stood before him and said to him, my father, I only did it to save your life, but he refused to rise from his mourning and his eyes streamed with tears until she died, and then he rose and changed his clothes and asked for bread to eat, and I know that I've already heard this legend before, many years ago, that my mother read it to me one night when there was a power cut and the three of us were sitting round a single candle, and my father said, why are you telling her that story, can't you see that it's too sad?